OMISSIONS

THE WILLIAMS LEGACY BOOK 3

TRACY BROEMMER

Omissions

by

Tracy Broemmer

Women's Fiction

Published by Tracy Broemmer

Edited by Lexie Broemmer

Cover Photo by Can Stock Photo

Cover Artist: Trisha FitzGerald-Jung

CHAPTER 1

*E*zra swung his denim-clad ass in a lazy circle and grinded his middle against his wife. Liv wasn't sure if the music was to blame for the half-assed dance move (old country made Wade sloppy like that, so maybe classic rock did it to Ezra) or maybe it was the longneck bottle that dangled from his right hand. Shay, talking to Amber, reached back and patted Ezra's ass with the same half-assed enthusiasm. Maybe it wasn't the music or the beer but something a little more personal.

That possibility stabbed Liv high in the stomach, and guilt soured her hunger. She dragged her eyes from her brother and his wife and whatever was or was not going on there and looked to where her husband manned the grill. Removed from the action, alone in the kitchen, she crossed her arms over her chest and cocked her head to watch him. He, too, held a longneck bottle, though his grip on it was tighter, more certain. Kind of the way he used to hold her.

When he shifted and reached with the tongs in his other hand to turn the skewers of meat and veggies on the grill, her eyes were drawn to the silver wedding band she'd put on his finger so many years ago. She wondered if he'd ever taken it off. Slipped it in his pocket as he scouted a bar or a room full of women. Then again, cheating was just as easy with the ring right there in plain sight.

"So, I ran into Stacie Adamson the other day."

Liv blinked, but she didn't move. Didn't draw her eyes away from Wade or turn to look at her sister when she heard her in the kitchen behind her. Wade wore loose-fitting jeans and a maroon t-shirt. The t-shirts used to be okay. They fit tight across his broad shoulders, his chest, and his thick arms. In fact, when they were much younger, the t-shirts and the way they defined Wade's body had been a turn-on. But that was before. When Wade's body turned her on. She wasn't sure it did anymore. He still looked great. The washboard abs might not be quite as defined as they had once been; maybe she couldn't bounce a quarter off them now. But he didn't carry the spare tire a lot of middle-aged men did. His arms were still thick and hard. Still had a nice ass, though she had to look with her imagination to see it in his baggy jeans. No need for Viagra yet, but then again, somewhere in the past twenty-four years, he'd decided that the TV and MLB and cars were more interesting than sex, and Liv had finally stopped asking for it.

From him.

She hated the damned t-shirt. The Girard Drywall logo—two-inch square on the front, left chest and over his shoulders on the back. Jesus, he had a closet full of nice clothes; didn't she buy him nice things? Why the hell did he always have to slide back to the damned t-shirts?

"Liv?"

"What?" she snapped as she turned away from the window. Ingrid, the purple streak in her choppy black hair fresh and edgy, stared at her silently.

"Fuck." The word tumbled out on a sigh. Ingrid's heavy stare lingered when she ducked her head and rubbed her fingertips over the bridge of her nose. "I'm sorry."

With a deep, cleansing breath—she hated her yoga class and honestly found that deep breathing did nothing for her except make her dizzy—she picked up the big plastic pasta fork and dipped it in the boiling pot of macaroni.

"She said you haven't called."

She'd just bought Wade a goddamned Tommy Bahama shirt, for God's sake. Not the flashy kind with the big-ass beachy picture on the back. She'd been with him over half her life; she knew what he liked and more importantly, what he didn't like. The Tommy Bahama shirt was solid sky blue. He hated royal blue, and navy would make him look too washed out this early in the year, and besides, she'd thought when she picked it out that it would set off his eyes. Who the hell knew if she was right? The damned shirt was still hanging in the closet with the tags on it.

"Do you buy Luke's clothes?"

With a glance at the timer on the microwave, she set the pasta fork down and leaned over to grab the strainer from the cabinet to the right. Frankly, she was sick of macaroni and cheese, but the kids would eat it. Her kids would live on it. Well, not Grace. She'd suddenly declared that she'd given up carbs because she'd gained two pounds the past year. Liv suspected all the piercings and metal in Grace's ears made up those two pounds, as Grace still appeared as tiny today as she had on her first day of high school and in less than two weeks, she would graduate.

She and Wade had a baby old enough to graduate from high school. Where in the hell had time gone?

Ingrid cleared her throat. "I'm sorry?"

Liv set the strainer in the stainless steel sink and reached for the oven mitts.

"Why?" She cut a quick look at Ingrid. Was an apology in order? What the hell had Ingrid said that she'd apparently missed?

"Do I buy Luke's clothes?" Ingrid's eyebrows, so black

and thick Liv assumed she had them dyed to match her hair, drew down in confusion. "Is that what you asked me?"

Liv nodded. She turned the burner off and lifted the big pot of noodles. Ingrid joined her at the sink as she hefted it over the strainer and poured the water and noodles out.

"You okay?"

"I'm fine." Liv shook her head. She was. Fine. No open, bleeding wounds. No severe chest pains. Just the damned headache that had taken up space behind her eyes six or eight months ago and had yet to move on. Just the fact that Gracie was going to graduate and move out, which meant Charlie was going to be a junior and in two years, he would graduate and move out. The fact that she looked at her husband a hundred times a day and wasn't sure if she liked him anymore, let alone loved him, and she wasn't sure what would happen when both kids were gone and life would shrink down to just her and Wade.

Shared memories and old love and kids together didn't automatically mean she was still in love with him, did it?

"I wish Mom were here," she mumbled.

Ingrid reached a hand through the steam and rested her fingertips on Liv's arm. Ingrid's hands did big things. Ingrid wrote bestselling thriller novels that people all over the world read and loved. Liv was a small-ish town high school English teacher. She'd dabbled in poetry when she was in high school like every other girl in the world. Nothing special about her.

Nope. Ingrid, Amber, and even Ezra had gotten all the creative genes.

There were days Liv hated Ingrid's hands. Ingrid herself. Oh, she loved her. She loved the absolute hell out of all of her siblings, but there were days. She was usually more careful about what days she chose to spend with them.

"Me, too."

Chin still tucked, Liv lifted only her eyes from Ingrid's hand. Up over her red blouse, the perfect breasts she'd once been jealous of and now worried about since her sister had confessed to having a lump removed when she'd lived in Chicago, and up further to meet her gaze.

"Some."

"You miss Mom some?" Liv snapped her head up now to look at Ingrid head on.

"I buy some of his clothes." Ingrid spoke calmly.

Liv shifted at the sink when Ingrid picked up the strainer to dump the macaroni back into the pot, set it back on the stovetop, and pulled open a drawer to find the kitchen scissors.

"I thought you did this homemade." Ingrid perched on the end barstool. Liv watched her grab a radish from the vegetable tray on the counter. The crisp snip when Ingrid bit into it grated on her nerves.

"What?"

"The mac and cheese." Ingrid popped the rest of the radish in her mouth and nodded at the cheese packet in her hands. "Homemade."

Liv shook her head to dismiss the thought. Who the hell had time to make homemade stuff? She fed her family from boxes most nights. Okay, *sometimes* she did things from scratch. She used to, anyway.

"Sometimes." She spoke so quietly she wasn't sure Ingrid had heard her.

"You said you were going to call her."

The scissors clattered to the counter, and Liv squeezed the liquid cheese—Charlie called it gold—into the pot of noodles. Stacie Adamson was the realtor she'd promised Ingrid she would call. She hadn't yet. The end of the school year was busy. Liv wasn't much of a phone person anyway, especially not if she had stuff to do.

Calling Stacie would take five minutes, ten tops, from her day. She knew that. All she needed to do was set up a meeting so they could to talk to Stacie. Like that would be easy. They all had their own damned schedules. Why the hell had she been given the task of calling and setting up the meeting? She knew damned well that she'd pick a date and time and at least one, if not all three of them, would balk and say it wouldn't work.

She didn't care.

No one had handed her the task. She'd claimed it as hers, because she didn't want to sell the house. If Ingrid offered to do it, the house would be on the market tomorrow.

Ingrid had talked to Stacie. What if—?

"Where'd you see her?" she asked as Ingrid attacked another radish.

"Java." Ingrid licked her lips and leaned her elbows on the counter. Liv knew Ingrid had taken to spending a day or two a week at Java Infusion, a local café, working on the new book. Seemed like a crappy place to work, as according to Ingrid she did a lot more catching up with people in and out of the place than she did writing, but Ingrid claimed the people watching was good for the creative mind.

"Did you tell her—?"

"Did I tell her that you're dragging your feet on the phone call because you don't want to sell Mom and Dad's house?"

Liv tried it again. The deep, calming breath. Because she really needed it, she hung her head and pulled in another one. Looked back at Ingrid and still wanted to ask her why she had to be such a bitch about everything, so she decided the breathing technique just wasn't working.

Eyes on Ingrid, she moved to the fridge to grab a beer. She pushed the door closed, twisted the top off her bottle, and took a long drink. Ingrid's perfectly thick brows shot up in a sweet little arch, and Liv swallowed a mouthful of bitterness with the beer.

"You want one?" she asked as she lowered it.

"No."

Well, that was new. Ingrid never turned down alcohol. She

made her way back to the counter, to the pot on the stove, and snatched the pasta fork up again. Ingrid crunched a raw carrot now.

"Are you pregnant?"

The back door opened—no banging noise as it hit the wall like it would at her parents' house, because Wade kept this fucking house perfect and tight and well-oiled and dreamy—but she saw it from the corner of her eye. Saw the look of horror on her youngest sibling's face, too. Amber carried two dead soldiers with her. She narrowed her eyes at Liv as she set the bottles down and moved around the counter to stand by Ingrid.

Also new. This bond between Ingrid and Amber. Liv had no doubt one of them would piss the other off before the night was over, but lately, when they were good, they were shiny good. So shiny, in fact, it made Liv's head hurt.

"Why would you ask me that?"

Liv stirred the mac and cheese once more and decided it was ready. She wiped her hands on the apron she wore and then dropped them on the counter.

"You're not drinking." Liv shrugged. "And you've eaten half of the veggies on the tray."

Amber leaned into Ingrid. Liv watched Ingrid slide her hand over to brush Amber's elbow and then move it back near the tray.

"Jesus, Liv." Amber sighed. "That's kind of insensitive, isn't it?"

"Asking my sister, who happens to be having regular sex now, if she's pregnant is insensitive?"

Before Amber could speak again, Ingrid gave a tiny shake of her head. Liv eyed them suspiciously.

"I'm on the pill—"

"Should you be? I quit—"

"And I have a glass of wine outside." Ingrid tilted her head to the side. "And I'm hungry. I missed lunch today."

"Why?"

Ingrid lifted her hand and combed her fingers through her hair.

"Has it always been purple?" Amber asked her.

"What?" Ingrid shot her a quick glance and then turned back to Liv. "I was writing. Got caught up."

Liv nodded. Ingrid had recently shared an unpublished manuscript with her. Not the typical I.G. Arenson thriller, Ingrid had buried it once finished. Liv had found the manuscript pages in a box at Luke's house when Ingrid moved in with him, asked her about it, and found with a few pokes that her sister wasn't terribly sure of herself when it came to her writing. Bestseller list and all.

"Yeah?" Liv chewed on her lip. "The new thing? That you told me about?"

"What new thing?" Amber asked quickly.

"Um." Ingrid looked toward the door when it opened again. Wade hollered at Liv to tell her the meat was ready. Liv nodded absently and again when he asked if the inside stuff was done. Nathan, Amber's fiancé, and her daughter, Hadley, exploded into the kitchen, both of them nearly shrieking with laughter. Ingrid tore her eyes from them and looked at Liv again. "Just. Not...I don't know yet, Amber."

Liv felt a little prick of shame when Ingrid rolled her eyes. How was she supposed to know if Ingrid had talked to Amber about the new book idea? Wasn't like she'd thrown it out there hoping to tag Amber. Was it? Ingrid still watching her, eyes cool and her mouth drawn in a flatline, Liv groaned. Yep. She'd done it on purpose. She'd missed something earlier between Amber and Ingrid, and rather than ask them, she'd lobbed her own bullet out there and hit Amber. On purpose.

Amber moved away from Ingrid. Liv could pretend like she hadn't seen that mix of hope and defeat cross her little sister's face, that she was simply abandoning their conversation to join Nathan and Hadley, but she knew better.

"Why do you do that?" Ingrid rubbed her forehead with her fingertips.

"I don't do that," Liv answered.

"You did."

"I did, but I don't." Liv shrugged. "I don't make a habit of it."

"So why start now?"

Liv turned her back to Ingrid. Let her eyes roam over the plates stacked and ready for use on the back counter. The pile of forks and steak knives. Napkins. They were ready. No more avoiding Wade, now, either. She'd have to suck it up and sit down by him and play the happy wife role.

Ingrid was still watching her, and Liv considered telling Ingrid she didn't know why she'd stirred the pot with Amber. She did, though. She knew. And judging from the way Ingrid was looking at her, Ingrid did, too.

Misery loved company. She'd picked the wrong night to hang out with her family, and rather than let her siblings round out the hard edges of her day, she'd lash out and make sure they left her house tonight as unhappy as she was.

CHAPTER 2

"I'm just saying, my doctor suggested that I consider alternative methods of birth control." Liv shrugged. She stretched her legs out in front of her and scooched her butt lower in the lawn chair on the deck. "Because of my age."

When Ingrid didn't flinch, Liv rolled her head on the chair to look at her. Eyes closed, she might have been asleep, except for the little tilt of her lips.

"You're older than me," Ingrid reminded her.

"Yeah, a couple of years." Liv rolled her eyes. "Seriously, Ingrid. Shouldn't you be more careful? Now?"

Ingrid squirmed in her chair and dropped her feet from where they'd rested on the deck rail. Liv watched her lean forward and prop her elbows on her knees and rub her hands back over her head and her neck.

"My doctor said there's no absolute proof that oral contraceptives cause breast cancer."

"Yeah, but you have family history."

"So do you." Ingrid turned to her and speared her with an angry glare.

"But I've been off the pill for a couple of years."

Ingrid's eyes grew big and round, but she only wagged her eyebrows and looked away.

"What?" Liv asked.

A shaft of warm golden light fell through the kitchen window to the deck. It dusted Ingrid's right elbow and her knee, and when she turned again to look at Liv, the light hit the purple streak in her hair.

"You're brave."

"What does that mean?" Liv snapped. She heard the back door open and looked up to see Amber cross the deck toward them. A few short weeks ago, Amber walked like she had a metal rod stuck up her ass, always stiff and all business. Liv had cried happy tears for her the morning after Nathan had proposed. Well, the morning after Nathan proposed the second time and Amber had said yes. Amber didn't complain about the life she lived, but she'd never seemed entirely happy in that life, either. She'd grabbed at moments here and there, but often times, she'd been so busy working or raising her daughter, Liv thought a lot of the happiness passed her by.

Liv had heard it said that a woman in love glowed from within. She'd seen it happen when Ingrid had come back earlier this year, after their dad had died. She'd watched the color and the joy come back to Ingrid's face, but she'd been slow to piece together what was going on. In fact, she wasn't sure she'd have figured it out if she hadn't dropped in at Dad's house one day and heard what sounded like something rutting around upstairs. She'd followed her ears, mystified even as the rutting around sounded more like a headboard banging a wall and the squeak of mattress springs, and she heard the unmistakable moans of someone enjoying themselves. She should have been mortified to find her sister in bed with the guy she'd hired to fix up the house before they sold it. But the first thing that struck her was the beauty in the act. Nevermind that she was looking at her sister, they'd made an erotic picture, and who wouldn't claim five seconds of Luke Ashley's bare ass as he pumped his hips in that age-old rhythm?

She wasn't sure, even now, if or when Ingrid would have told her, if she hadn't seen it herself. Then again, they'd have all found out what was happening when Ingrid moved in with Luke.

Amber glowed these days, too.

Liv was truly happy for both of her sisters. They'd both taken a longer, harder road to get where they were, where they wanted to be. But Liv envied them, too. She envied them the new, exciting stage of a relationship and the promise of a long life together.

Twenty-four years into her long life with Wade, she was disillusioned with marriage and disappointed in Wade. In herself. She had a new understanding for her mother, but she'd been gone six years, and the missing her, the hole in her heart where her mom should have been, grew bigger every day.

"Private party?" Amber curled her fingers around the back of a chair, but she hesitated before dragging it next to Ingrid. Liv wondered if they'd ever bridge the gaps the years and the miles had put between them. Liv was old enough to be Amber's mother. Ingrid had mothered their baby sister for a while, but she'd turned eighteen, married her best friend, and run off to Chicago faster than most of her graduating class had their caps and gowns off. Amber had been five when Ingrid left, and Liv had *sort of* picked up the slack her sister left in her wake.

Amber shied away from both of them now like an abused animal. Liv got it. She was wary with Ingrid after she'd dropped them all and walked away. But Liv resented the way Amber had pulled away from her the second Ingrid had come back home.

"Sit down." Liv shook her head.

"Where's Shay?" Ingrid asked Amber.

"They left."

"Why?" Liv leaned around Ingrid to look at Amber. Amber half stood, tugged the chair around so they were sitting in a circle, and then dropped her butt back to sit down.

"She wasn't feeling well."

"When is she ever?" Liv mumbled.

"Did he use protection?" Ingrid asked, and Liv's heartbeat was like a hammer throwing an explosive blow at the rest of her body. She hated this. She'd been weak, and the second Ingrid was home, she'd caved and shared a secret that had the power to ruin her life.

It was over. Hadn't taken her but a few times to realize that whatever she was looking for, she wasn't going to find it in the backseat of a car or a room in a squat, nondescript motel down by the river.

She closed her eyes now as a wave of nausea rolled over her. For a second, she smelled the sickly sweet Cherry soda someone had spilled right outside of his car mixed with his sweet, heady cologne applied with a heavy hand.

He had called her baby, and her stomach had roiled because it felt sleazy, and it had taken every ounce of self-control she had to keep her mouth shut. Wade used to call her baby when they'd first started seeing each other, and the reminder of those first sweet days of love and attraction with him had no place with what she had been doing that night. He'd been rough, and he'd shoved her knit shirt and her bra up out of his way to fasten his lips over her nipple, and Liv had been desperate for some sort of connection and for release, and she'd tugged at his belt and his zipper with eager hands. Freed his penis and then he was inside her before she even really saw it.

Aware that both of her sisters were watching her now, Liv stood up and wandered away from them. She swallowed the sour taste of regret and avoided looking in the direction of the garage. Odds were, Wade was entertaining Luke and Nathan there, all three of them nursing yet another beer, eyeing, admiring Wade's latest diamond in the rough. Liv didn't care about the girlie posters he'd tacked up through the years; she'd stopped noticing them, to be honest, but God, how she hated every goddamned car he dragged home to work on. She'd spent many nights propped in the doorframe of the garage, watching her husband's hands caress hunks of metal that might look beautiful when he was finished with them but would never respond to him the way she used to.

"When was the last—?" Ingrid cleared her throat. "I mean, there's no chance—"

"I had a hysterectomy a few years ago. Got tired of dealing with all of it after thirty years."

"You were thirteen?" Amber asked quietly. Liv paced to the end of the deck and then turned. She liked the distance, needed it if they were going to ask more about the things she'd done in that car. But she hated standing so far apart and seeing Amber and Ingrid so close together.

Amber lifted her hand to fluff her hair, and Liv imagined the diamond on her finger sparkled. In the near dark, she couldn't see it.

"Yep."

"I was fourteen," Amber mumbled. "So I have that to look forward to?"

"Was that a veiled insult to my age?"

"It's not." Ingrid sighed impatiently. "It's not what I was asking—"

"How old were you?" Amber asked her.

"What?"

"When did you start your period?"

"I was seventeen."

"Wow."

"Is it over?" Ingrid turned her head back to Liv. "The thing you're doing?"

"Ingrid." Liv held her hand up to stop her. Her chest was tight, and the air was too thick to breathe. "Don't."

"Because you have a family history," Ingrid reminded her. "Mom was older when she had Amber and Ezra."

Liv rolled her eyes.

"I just told you I had a hysterectomy. And yes, he used condoms."

"He could have stealthed you."

"Are you kidding me?" Liv snapped at Amber. "First of all, I just told you that I can't get pregnant. I haven't been pregnant since after Charlie. And second, why would he do that? He's married, too, and he has kids—"

"Wait." Amber cocked her head sideways. "What?"

"After Charlie?"

Liv felt her shoulders fall as she deflated.

"I don't wanna talk about this. Not now."

"When?" Ingrid asked with a quick shrug. "The guys are in the garage. If memory serves, we normally have to drag their asses out. No one's gonna sneak up on us."

"You were pregnant? After Charlie?"

Liv bit her lip.

"Liv."

"Hmm?"

"Get your ass over here and sit down." Ingrid nudged her chair with the toe of her booted foot. "I mean, what? You told us you had an affair. Aren't we over that?"

"The details are dirty, Ingrid." Liv rubbed her fingers under her eyes, but she retraced her steps and dropped back into the chair.

"Do you love him?"

Liv pressed her lips together and turned to look at Amber. Uncertain who she was asking about and not sure what she'd say anyway, she blinked and then brushed at the tears in her eyelashes.

"Why didn't you tell us?"

"I miscarried." Liv licked her lips. "Very common. Not a big deal."

"Yeah, except it was to you."

Liv dismissed Ingrid's concern. "Wade was…" Liv drew in a sharp breath. "My rock. He knew what I needed before I did."

"And still, you have two sisters who didn't know about it until fifteen years later?" Amber shrugged and tossed her hands up in frustration.

"Listen to yourself, Liv," Ingrid whispered. "*Wade* was your rock."

Liv ducked her head and covered her face with her hands.

"And now you want to leave him? Because you're bored?"

Amber made a sound that was half laugh and half cry.

"You told me you would stay with him. Remember that?"

Liv pushed back when she felt Amber tap her foot on her leg.

"It's not that simple."

"That's it? That's all you've got for me?"

"Amber, honey, grow up. Why am I your poster child for a happy marriage?"

"Yours is the only I thought I knew of."

"There's no true black and white," Liv mumbled.

"So if you're still thinking about divorce, does that mean you're still seeing the other guy? Are you in love with him?" Ingrid asked her.

"No." Frustration boiled inside her. She tucked her hair behind her ear and shook her head. "Not seeing him. I don't love him. It's not like that."

"But you don't love Wade?" Amber asked her. "Do the kids know?"

"God, no! Stop!" Liv lifted her head and looked around wildly. The confirmation that she and her sisters were the only people outside was little relief.

"I wanna understand." Amber twisted her lips in a pout.

"I do, too, Liv. I really do."

"How did this become about me?" Liv sniffled. She swiped at her eyes again. "You need to find an ob-gyn, Ingrid. You need—"

"Wait." Amber sat forward in her chair. She rested her hand on Ingrid's arm. "Did you find another lump?"

"No—"

"She's on the pill." Liv swept her hand out to indicate Ingrid, the sister who was risking her health while taking an oral contraceptive. "She needs to get off of it."

"Why?" Amber frowned and shook her head.

"Because it can increase the risk of breast cancer."

"I talked to my doctor," Amber announced.

"The one who sculpted your boobs?"

"They're real, thank you," Amber rolled her eyes at Liv, "um…anyway. I told her about Mom, obviously. But I told her Ingrid had a lump removed."

"And?" Liv asked her.

"I scheduled a mammogram. Just a baseline. She wants to watch closer."

"Good." Liv nodded.

"Does it hurt?"

"You'll be fine," Liv assured her.

"Yeah? I've heard it's like slamming them in a freezer door."

"More like laying down on the floor and closing the garage door on them," Ingrid said with a frown. "Nice slow squish."

"Great." Amber groaned.

"Relax. Hurts smaller boobs more."

"The best part is peeling the tape off your nipples when it's done."

Amber looked from Ingrid to Liv and back to Ingrid.

"What?"

"You'll be fine," Liv said again.

"Why tape?"

"Ingrid, you need to find a doctor."

"I will."

"And get off the pill."

"I'm not going to ask Luke to use a condom, Liv. Good God, I'm almost fifty years old."

"Bullshit. I'm not even almost fifty, and I'm the oldest."

"Whatever. I'm not gonna ask him to use condoms. I like…" Ingrid shrugged.

"Well, me too, but there are other ways."

Ingrid turned wide eyes to Liv. "What? No. No. I'm not gonna ask him to do that."

"Why not? You're in a committed relationship with him—"

"What if she wants to get pregnant?" Amber stared at Liv with a frown.

CHAPTER 3

*L*iv squeezed her eyes closed in denial. Gray dawn crept into the bedroom around her, poked at her to make sure she was awake. She stretched and ducked her head in her pillow when her sweaty nightgown clung to her chest. With a kick of her legs, the heavy comforter moved just a bit from her shoulders and down her side. Still hot, she opened her eyes to a squint and lifted her head to look at the ceiling fan. The blades turned in a lazy circle; Liv made a mental note to turn it up a notch. She'd forget, as always. Maybe one of these days, once the full-fledged Midwest summer humidity settled over them like a wet wool blanket, she'd think to change the fan setting. Until then, she'd sweat through the nights.

Not that it would make a difference.

With a sigh, she rolled over and stared at the ceiling, the white seemingly glowing in the washed gray daylight. Beside her, sprawled on his back with an arm tossed up over his head, Wade snored softly.

Her sisters had stayed late last night; she and Wade had walked both couples to their cars just after eleven. Amber had told them she planned to go to her shop early this morning to work in her darkroom. Liv lifted her head from her pillow to look at the alarm clock on her side of the bed. Just after five. Wow. That was a record for her. She doubted Amber was awake yet. Hoped not anyway. The insomnia hadn't hit Liv until forty. Maybe Amber had a few years of solid sleep left. Maybe she wouldn't deal with insomnia.

Ingrid did, though.

Family history.

She heard those words now in Ingrid's voice. Felt her shoulders tense up even as she rolled back to her side.

She didn't think about it often.

Liv squeezed her eyes closed again, but this time she wanted to ward off the bad thoughts, not the morning. She *did* think about it. *Often.* Not the sex part. And God knows, there wasn't any romance or love to it.

But she couldn't get away from the guilt. The shame he'd left her with. Well, he hadn't forced her; she'd made her choices. And that was it. The fact that she'd actively chosen to betray her marriage vows to her husband. She'd conveniently pocketed Wade, not her ring—she had worn her ring every time she'd fucked him—and she had taken a casual acquaintance inside her body. She'd ridden him so hard and desperately, and still, in the end, she'd walked away with a bigger emptiness than when she had gone searching for something…more.

Since she had ended it, the emptiness had eaten away at her, and only shame filled that spot now. Shame and self-hatred.

She had tossed and turned most of the night, and as always, she'd finally slept after three. But she was awake now, so she moved quietly, cautiously, so as not to wake Wade. Their mattress was firm, and it barely shifted when she climbed out of bed. At the door, she turned to look back at him. The sheet covered his legs, his hips. His chest and arms and shoulders were bare, and Liv wondered when she'd last kissed him there. When had she last lingered over his body for his pleasure? Her sisters had suggested she do just that, but she didn't want to.

They'd had sex since she had cheated. Fast and distracted and unsatisfying, true, but they'd had sex. But she didn't miss *sex*. She missed a time, a stretch of time in their marriage when everything was sweet and intimate, even their fights.

She had wanted to be with him last night after their company had left. They'd walked side by side up the driveway, and Liv had slipped her fingers through his at the kitchen door. She didn't ask, not with words. But she had clung to his hand and pulled him back to her when he'd taken a step toward the car—it was an El Camino, but she couldn't remember what year it was. He had come to her. No words. He'd come to stand before her, and he'd leaned in to nuzzle her neck.

And Charlie had opened the door to ask her if they had any frozen pizzas. Rather than bite her son's head off, Liv had pulled away from Wade and rested her head on his chin, and when she couldn't talk around the knife in her throat, she only shook her head.

"I don't know," she had finally croaked out. What she had wanted to do was suggest to Charlie that he go and look in the freezer. That if that didn't turn up a frozen pizza, it was probably safe to say they didn't have any. He'd have belly-ached then, griped about being hungry and that there was nothing in the house to eat, and Liv's head already hurt. She'd bit down on any smartass comments, waited for Charlie to go back inside and close the door, and then looked up to meet Wade's eyes.

"I'll be up soon."

The verbal equivalent of a cold shower. She had stood for a moment and watched him approach the car, whistling a George Strait song as he went.

She could try now. Get back into bed with him and slide

her fingers down over his belly and cup him in her hand. She could pleasure him and let it go at that this time. Ingrid and Amber had both reminded her it wouldn't hurt to be more giving.

Her heart raced at the thought. Her sleeveless nightgown skimmed her thighs, and now she was cold. Wade's skin would be warm with sleep. If she kissed him now, he would kiss her back. Maybe without opening his eyes. Her fingers twitched at her sides as she considered touching him. Pushing his briefs down enough to free him, taking him in her fingers. It had been so, so long since she'd taken the time to touch him, but she remembered his scent and the feel of his body in her hand. She clenched her fists at the memory of his cock waking up in her fingers, stretching long and thick at her touch.

With a loud snort, Wade turned his head on his pillow and lowered the arm he'd had over his head. Liv watched him scratch his belly in his sleep and then slide his hand on down to scratch his balls. Spell broken, she sighed with disappointment and headed to the kitchen to her other man. She'd been married to Mr. Coffee as long as she'd been with Wade, though she'd had to replace Mr. Coffee twice through the years.

Sobering thought.

She had replaced the coffee machine. She'd replaced her washer and dryer set once. She'd had a couple of new cars. Was she simply ready to trade Wade in for a newer model? Was she being stupid and flighty? Or was the itch she felt deep under her skin about something more significant than needing a newer model?

Liv flipped the can lights over the counter on and stood for a moment at the window. The chairs she and her sisters had sat in last night were still gathered in that sad little circle; one lone bottle still perched on the corner of the table. She'd missed it when they'd come in last night.

She'd always hated parties, even little ones. Not because of the mess left behind, but the way any mess left behind— one beer bottle or twenty beer bottles and overflowing ashtrays and a stack of used paper plates and crumpled napkins—painted any room in the house or even the deck a lonely shade of empty.

Did Ingrid want a baby?

God, that had rattled her last night. She would have laughed it off, but Amber had sat there all sincere and important like Ingrid had actually confided that to her. Liv had opened her mouth to question Amber, question Ingrid since it was her plumbing and life and future they were talking about. Who in the hell would want a baby at this age? Seriously? Liv loved her kids to the moon and back, even on the days when she'd sell them to the highest bidder. They were great kids, and Liv was close to both of them. She'd never change a thing about motherhood, except that yes, some days, her mothering capabilities felt as stellar as a drunken game of Whac-A-Mole, swinging blindly to smack them down before they got out of hand.

But a baby? Being up with a newborn every night? Nursing a baby? Would that hurt Ingrid now? After she'd had her breast cut into? Would it hurt for a baby to nurse?

Liv moved from the window with purpose. Shivering, she rubbed her hands up and down her bare arms as she crossed the kitchen to the pantry to get the coffee. Maybe it wouldn't hurt Ingrid; after all, Luke had definitely had his hands and his mouth there a million times over by now. Still, she had a scar, and it seemed like she'd feel something when anyone touched it.

She carried the coffee and a filter back to the coffee machine and laughed softly at the direction her thoughts had taken. Wouldn't Ingrid be thrilled to know Liv worried about what if felt like when Luke licked or sucked on her scar?

The baby thing, though. Liv seriously couldn't imagine

wanting to do that again. She froze, the lid of the coffee in her hand, and decided it was different. Sure, sure, Ingrid had insisted she had no desire to get pregnant now. She'd given the question as much weight as she might have if Liv had asked her if she'd done a naked rain dance lately and assured Liv and Amber she had no intentions of trying to get pregnant.

Liv still worried.

For one thing, if Ingrid and Luke were in a committed relationship—hello, living together?—then Ingrid should feel comfortable talking to him about birth control options.

And even though Ingrid had blown the topic off—the whole baby bombshell Amber had dropped—she'd said she had no desire to get pregnant now.

Now.

As in, maybe she *had* wanted to at one time in her life. Maybe she'd actively tried to conceive at one time. Maybe she regretted not having children; Liv had always assumed Ingrid didn't want to be bothered with kids. She'd always pictured Ingrid living a glamorous life with no time for any family, let alone people who were completely dependent on her.

Maybe Liv was wrong to make the assumption.

But why hadn't Ingrid ever told her otherwise? No, they'd never been the sisters who swapped emails or even phone calls on a regular basis. They'd didn't share stories or secrets, and until recently, they'd never shared dinner ideas or recipes.

Ingrid hadn't even told Liv about the cancer scare until after the fact. She'd relied on a friend instead. Said a lot for how they'd grown up and away, that was certain. Amber blamed Ingrid, always had. But Liv was the oldest. Maybe she should have forced some family togetherness.

She laughed now. The four of them were stubborn as mules, they had all made some jackass mistakes, and forcing family togetherness might end up in an all out brawl.

The coffee machine lumbered and hissed its way through its cycle. Liv tidied up what she'd left behind last night when she'd escaped to bed and left Wade to his stupid car. She didn't even know what time he had come up to bed.

Maybe she would fix him breakfast. She could take it to him in bed, but honestly, the thought of the quiet early morning on the deck was more tempting. She took a moment to fantasize about it. Biscuits, maybe, and coffee. She and Wade alone on the deck with no one around. No kids asleep in the house, no kids poised and ready to explode out the door and interrupt conversation between them. No talk of the car. No worries about her family. Just her and her husband.

"Down girls," she mumbled when her nipples grew hard under her nightgown. Sure, who wouldn't want to straddle her guy on the semi-private deck and tug her nightgown off and feel his lips and tongue, warm and wet from his coffee, on her skin?

She could almost picture it, back at the window with her eyes on the deck. Ingrid had told her several times about making love on the deck or in the hot tub. But Luke and Ingrid's house was much more secluded. Not that something sexy like that would fix anything in her marriage.

Didn't mean she couldn't want it, though.

Her thoughts turned darker, and rather than something tender and intimate there, Liv saw herself in the hotel room. Spread-eagle on the bed, Asher Crowe's open mouth fastened on her neck, his fingers pinching her nipples painfully hard. She ducked her head now and covered her eyes, ashamed of the memories but stuck with them now.

Indelible. She'd gone looking for something temporary and interesting and fun, and instead, she'd created sickening, shameful memories that she would never be able to let go of.

Asher wasn't big like Wade. Anywhere. But he was sexy, and he was okay with his hands and his hips and his dick. But mostly, he'd been a stingy lover, and though there had been a few orgasms—one that he'd milked for her, ridden her slow and hard to wring every last bit of satisfaction from her body—Liv decided he was simply average in bed.

Wade used to do that. Push and push until he had wrung every last ounce of pleasure from her body. Only when she'd sobbed and quivered under him would he throw his head back and call out her name and God's name and let go.

She missed that.

Asher Crowe had left the door wide open. If she wanted sex, all she had to do was text. She hadn't sent a single text. Liv wasn't naïve. As sexy as he was, as prominent as he was in the community, odds were she wasn't the only woman he serviced outside of his marriage vows.

She didn't miss bone-melting orgasms.

She missed her husband's ravenous need and his possessive hands and the way he felt inside her body as he lost control.

"What're you doing up?"

His voice, still low and thick with sleep, chased a chill over her bare arms. He was in the doorway across the room, but he was too close to her now. Head full of bad thoughts, of herself and Asher together, she hunched her shoulders and ducked her head.

She heard him cross the room, the soft sounds of his bare feet on the tile floor, and she braced herself for his touch. He'd never hit her. Wade Girard would never hit a woman. But the feather soft touch of his fingertips over her shoulders burned; the guilt in her stomach stretched and poked its way into the base of her throat.

"Couldn't sleep," she mumbled. Back to him, Liv bit her lip and closed her eyes.

"Why didn't you wake me?" He moved in behind her. If his hands sliding low around her hips didn't tell the story, the press of his erection against her lower back said it all. Liv coughed, gagged on the memory of Asher Crowe pinning her down on the bed, his hands roaming freely over her ass and her thighs.

"It's five o'clock, Wade."

"And?" He pressed into her, nuzzled the back of her neck with his lips. "We used to be good at morning sex."

Liv sighed and relaxed against him. *Used to be* were little words that packed a big punch.

"You were sleeping when I came to bed," he told her.

He gathered the hem of her gown in his hands and inched it up. Liv focused on the feel of his callused fingers on her stomach. Asher's hands were smooth, his nails buffed to perfection. Wade flattened his palm over her stomach. She imagined her belly sixteen years ago, stretched tight with their son inside her. Had a flash of Asher taking her hand and making her stroke herself.

Wade cupped her breast in his left hand and teased her nipple with his thumb. Liv sucked in a quick breath at the punch of electric need that ripped through her. She turned her head to take his kiss. Imagined Asher slamming her against the wall of the motel room, spreading her legs and driving into her. Wade's lips were soft and warm on hers, his fingers gentle on her breast.

She felt his other hand move lower, his fingers searching for her center. Liv swallowed hard, Asher between them still, as Wade flicked his tongue over her chin. He pinched her nipple with his thumb and finger. A flash of need ignited inside her. His fingers slid lower into her panties. Lightning shot through her when his fingers slid over her core, and she moaned out loud.

"Wade." She shook her head and turned her face away when he moved his mouth back to hers to kiss her.

"Liv—"

"I can't." She dropped her head forward and reached to cup the back of her neck. When he moved his hand over her breast again, Liv shoved it away. She took a deep breath when he stepped back from her.

"Why not?"

Yeah, Liv, why not? She pressed her lips together and breathed through her nostrils for a second, reaching for the calm her yoga instructor promised her was somewhere inside her.

"We're in the kitchen," she reminded him as she turned to face him. "Both kids are home."

His eyes, dark with suspicion, took her in from head to toe. Liv painted innocence on her face, she hoped, and waited him out. Her eyes dipped to his white briefs, to his obvious arousal, and then climbed back to his face. She could touch him. When they were younger, he'd tell her that waiting all day to get home to her to make love made his balls blue and his dick hurt.

She considered it now. Taking him in her hand to jack him off. Going to her knees in front of him.

"It's five in the morning," he reminded her. "Neither of them will set foot down here until at least ten."

The image of Asher Crowe, back bowed, head thrown back as he pumped his hips over hers filled her mind. Liv gave herself a mental shake and turned back to the cabinet.

"Coffee's ready," she announced even though the machine had just beeped, and Wade hadn't asked for any to begin with.

"So am I, Liv," he muttered.

Okay. So she'd bite the bullet. Give him what he wanted, as long as it didn't get sappy and personal.

"Okay." She turned, hands at the hem of her gown, only to find herself alone. She heard him on the steps then. Turned back to the coffee with tears in her eyes.

CHAPTER 4

*T*he hair on the back of her neck stood on end, but Liv managed to hold the shiver down. Kristen Richards, propped in her doorway, didn't seem to notice Liv's internal battle, so apparently she wasn't a terrible liar. She'd worked with Kristen for the past ten years, and they'd been close friends for eight of those ten years. If Kristen wasn't noticing her twitchiness, maybe Wade wouldn't figure it out, either. Maybe she was being paranoid. She was more uptight about getting caught now that the affair, the thing, was over than she'd been when she was sneaking around.

"Another day down," Kristen reminded her.

Liv nodded. "Sure, but it's only fifth hour, so it's not down for the count."

Kristen laughed and then drew her head back to look down the hallway. Liv took advantage of the moment to rub her hands up and down her arms, trying to chase the chill away. Wasn't going to work. Not as long as she could hear that voice.

Dylan Crowe sounded just like his father. Worse, he looked just like him, too. The first day she'd faced him in her classroom after she'd mounted his father in his car, she'd almost thrown up. Same as the night it happened, when she had come home and looked at herself in the mirror in the bathroom she and Wade shared.

As a teacher, she didn't like to dislike any students. But she was human, and she did dislike some of them, and Dylan Crowe had always been at the top of that list. She had never cared much for his father, either. Still didn't, to be honest.

Kristen stepped into her room, and Liv pushed her chair back in a moment of panic. Her chest squeezed so tight it hurt to breathe, and her hands felt weightless with fear. Kristen rested a hip on her desk as Liv moved slowly, casually across the room to the wall of windows.

She'd been afraid that Dylan Crowe would take one look at her—he had those same dark, bedroom eyes, and Liv had no doubt that he could charm a girl out of her pants in zero point two seconds—and know instinctually what she'd done with his father. She hadn't backed down that morning; she'd met his eyes and offered him the same smile she offered all of her students every day and returned his good morning the same as always.

No one knew. Well, okay, her sisters knew, and as stormy as her relationship with her sisters was, she trusted them. She'd never told another soul, not even Kristen, and other than this huge thing, she told Kristen everything.

Wade didn't know. He'd been acting a little off now and then, sure, but maybe that was because he noticed something was different. Just because something was off between them didn't mean he would jump to the conclusion that she'd cheated on him. Even if they split up, she didn't want to hurt him with this.

Did she?

Did she want to leave him? Did she want to hurt him?

The fact that she was on the fence about loving him, leaving him, hurting him was a knife in her heart. She'd never thought of herself as a cruel person, but damned if there weren't times lately when she was cruel and spiteful.

Liv crossed one arm over her chest and rubbed at the ache in her throat with her other hand. Kristen was talking to a group of her students now. Something *she* usually did, joking around before class started. Liv loved most of her kids. But this had been a bad year, and she was more than ready to call it over and slink back home to hide.

Of course, then she would have to dodge Gracie and Charlie. Neither of them had any idea what she'd done, but they both believed Wade walked on water. If Liv left him, she'd lose her children. Wade wouldn't take them; after all, they were grown up now. But they would side with him, and neither of them would ever forgive her.

It had taken her and Ingrid a long time to forgive their mother when she'd strayed. Hell, some days, Liv wasn't sure she had forgiven her yet. And there was no forgetting. Not when her baby brother had a different father than she and Ingrid and Amber. In the big scheme of things, it wasn't her business, and it had happened so long ago. Both of her parents were gone now, and it was useless to dwell on this. Stupid to blame her mother for what she had done.

Liv's infidelity wasn't her mom's fault, but dammit all that Mom was gone and she couldn't talk to her about it. She had been so hurt by what her mom had done all those years ago. So young and so in love with love and so betrayed and indignant on her dad's behalf. Now, all these years later, Liv wished she would have asked her why.

"Liv?"

She jumped when someone touched her shoulder. Turning her back to the windows, she stared at Kristen and blinked away the memories of her mom. Kristen studied her, her face twisted with concern, so Liv dug deep inside for a smile and faked a yawn.

"Hmm?"

"You okay?"

"I'm good." She nodded. Kristen narrowed her eyes at her and huffed out a frustrated sigh. Liv wondered what her friend would say if she told her. If she announced in the lounge tomorrow over coffee that she'd had a brief, scorching hot affair with Asher Crowe, what would Kristen say? Well, she would be horrified. Obviously. Liv had been married for over twenty years. Liv had children. Family was sacred to Kristen, as it should have been to Liv. Wasn't like she had taken her clothes off for Dylan, for a student—just the thought racked her body with a violent shiver—but still. She had done something wrong. And for no reason. No one would ever understand her motive. *She* didn't understand her motive.

"Wanna get a drink tonight?"

The last thing Liv wanted to do was get a drink. Right next to going home to Wade, actually. He would either hunker down in his garage all night or watch TV. Liv could hardly navigate a room with him these days, because the tension was so thick.

She was tired, but it hit her suddenly that maybe Kristen needed to unwind. Maybe Liv had been a bad friend lately, so caught up in her own world that she was blind to everyone else. One drink wouldn't hurt.

"Sure."

"Great." Kristen flashed a quick smile and then turned away. Liv watched her make her way back to the door, stopping once to talk to Bella Simon, who'd just slipped inside the room as the bell rang. Bella glanced at Liv over Kristen's shoulder, her face painted with guilt. She arched her eyebrows apologetically and then ducked into her seat in the second row as Kristen slipped out of the room.

"Tardy again, Miss Simon," Liv said quietly.

"Technically, I was in the room when the bell rang," Bella said quietly.

"Technically, a tardy is when you're not in your seat and the bell rings."

Liv folded her arms over her chest and cocked her head at the girl. If she had a dollar for every time Bella was late, she could buy herself a new Kate Spade bag.

Bella nodded, but before she could speak, Liv turned away. She didn't want to have this conversation. Didn't want to deal with tardies or absences. She didn't want Bella to serve detention. The quicker she could pack up her bag and walk out tonight, the better.

She stepped around her desk and picked up a whiteboard marker. Ignored the heaviness in her belly at the thought of going home. She had to do something. Leave. Talk. Confess. Change. *Something*. She and Wade had been living in limbo for months now. Even if he didn't suspect her infidelity, he had to know something was up.

She twisted the cap off the marker and wrote the word *final* on the white board. Amidst the groans from her class, she heard the kids getting out their iPads, shifting in their seats.

Other than the nights her sisters and their families had been over, she and Wade and the kids hadn't had dinner together in ages. They hadn't taken family bike rides or walks since last summer. While she'd spent time with both kids, whether it be shopping with Gracie or playing pitch and catch with Charlie, she avoided time with Wade.

And then seethed with frustration and hatred when he spent time in the garage.

Her hand stilled, the tip of the marker against the board. She hated finding herself alone with him. And yet, she was ridiculously angry with him for hanging out in the garage, working on his cars.

"*Gatsby*, Mrs. Girard. It's *The Great Gatsby*."

Dylan's voice traced that same shiver up her spine. Liv squeezed her eyes closed, but the memory wouldn't go away.

Asher Crowe's hips pinning hers to the bed, pumping hard and fast, his lips sliding slowly up her spine.

Liv took a deep breath and looked over her shoulder. Dylan winked at her, and Liv fought a wave of nausea. She nodded, turned back to the board to finish writing the book title, and then turned around.

"Looks like this end-of-school thing is getting to me, too," she said with a forced laugh. "What else, guys?"

"How about nothing?" Gage Miller suggested. The rest of the class snickered.

"How about cumulative from the beginning of the year?" Liv moved around to the front of her desk and perched there. She crossed her ankles, shoved the thought of them wrapped around Asher Crowe's waist from her mind, and rested her hands on the desk at her sides.

"You can't do that."

Liv looked up in surprise. Gage glanced at Dylan and then back at her.

"Why can't I?" She shrugged. "My class. I can test you on anything we studied this year."

"I didn't study anything," Gage announced with a grin.

"And your grade reflects that, Mr. Miller," she said sweetly. "Which unfortunately means you and I have the distinct possibility of hanging out and doing all of this stuff again next year."

"Burn!' Dylan Crowe laughed, dodged Gage's fist, and looked back at Liv. "Mrs. Girard, you got any aloe for Gage?"

Liv grinned, but she noticed that Gage looked pale.

"Relax, Mr. Miller. Study for the exam, and I'm sure you'll be fine."

"You don't want me back in your class?"

"No, not particularly." She stood again and paced the room. "Guys, come on. What else have we been doing in here this semester? We read *The Great Gatsby*. Is that all you remember?"

"I don't remember—"

"Can it, Gage." She shook her head without looking at him. "Does anyone remember?"

"So?" Kristen shrugged her eyebrows and her shoulders at the same time. She sank back in the booth and stared at Liv anxiously. "What do you think?"

"Mmm." Liv winced and leaned forward to rest her elbows on the table. She propped her chin in her hand and stared at Kristen. There was a swallow of beer left in the bottle, but she didn't want it. Her phone had buzzed a few minutes ago, but she hadn't wanted to interrupt Kristen to dig through her purse and look at it. Kristen had just ordered another drink, and Liv felt guilty for not wanting another. For wanting to go home. Especially knowing that once she got home, she would wish she were still out.

"What do I tell her, Liv?"

Liv pursed her lips and shook her head.

"Girls are mean, Kristen," she finally answered.

"Really? That's all you've got for me?"

"No." Liv groaned out loud and rolled her head on her neck. "No. I just…I don't know what to say. Girls are mean. Sasha's a great kid."

Kristen looked away, her eyes glassy with unshed tears.

"I took that brat last year. I took her to Disney with us."

Liv watched Kristen's chest expand on a deep breath, heard the catch in her voice.

"And now this. I can't believe she's doing this—"

"Honey, of course you can believe it." Liv shrugged. "Yes, it sucks. But yes, girls are mean. Another week and Sasha can hang with the neighbor kids. She just needs the change of scenery."

"Did Gracie have friends like that?"

"She did." Liv nodded. She sat back in the booth and reached for her beer. Kristen watched her drain it. "In grade school. She kind of found her niche in high school. Sasha will, too."

"So I'm just supposed to ignore it?" Kristen asked quietly. "Is that what you're telling me?"

Liv swallowed down the taste of guilt and warm beer. Yes, she kind of wanted Kristen to let it go, because she needed to check her phone. What if it was Wade texting her? Looking for her?

"No." Liv winced and met Kristen's eyes. "No. Of course not. It sucks. I know."

Liv often forgot that Kristen was quite a bit younger than she was, and Kristen's kids were younger, too. Sasha and Allie, ten and eight, were cute girls, if a little bit geeky (crazy about Harry Potter) a little bit lanky, and beanpole skinny (carbon copies of their mother). Sasha wore her black hair boy short, wore big black-framed glasses, and had more freckles on her face than Liv had seen on all of her students combined in all of her years of teaching. She also had an incredible laugh that made everyone around her happy, beautiful blue eyes, and a great singing voice.

And mean girl friends that were currently trying to ditch her from summer camp.

"I'm sorry." Kristen shoved her fingers back through her own short black hair—shorter even than Ingrid's, minus the ridiculous purple streak—and closed her eyes. "I'm sorry, Liv."

"For what?" Liv shook her head, even though Kristen couldn't see her. She flinched when Kristen moved her hands just enough to rub her eyes. Afraid her friend was going to gouge her eyeballs out, Liv moved again and reached over the table. "Kristen, stop." She touched Kristen's hand and arched her eyebrows when she dropped her hands and opened her eyes.

"Dumping this on you." Kristen blinked and rubbed her eyes again. She laughed softly and shrugged. "You've got your own stuff to deal with."

"It's okay," Liv said quietly. "It's hard to see your kid hurt and not be able to fix it."

"She tries to be tough, ya know?" Kristen sniffled. "What about you?"

"Tough as nails," Liv said with a wink. "Don't test me."

Kristen laughed softly. She picked up her margarita and sipped from it.

"You're not feeling this," she mumbled.

"What?"

"You should've just told me you couldn't come out tonight."

"What? Why?" Liv frowned. "I just finished my beer."

"What's going on with you, Liv?"

Her phone buzzed again. She held her breath for a second and finally glanced at her purse.

"I'm sorry." She reached for it. "I just need to check this."

Kristen nodded and waved her apology away. Liv nearly sagged in relief when she saw the texts were from Gracie and Amber. Gracie wanted her to know she was going to a movie with a couple of friends. Amber's text was harsh, naturally, asking if she planned to do anything tonight.

The house.

God, it felt like they'd been working on their parents' house for years instead of months. Liv sighed and rubbed her forehead.

"Nothing's going on, Kristen." She put her phone down without responding to Amber and turned her attention back to her friend. "It's just been a hard year."

Kristen studied her silently. Finally, she nodded. "Losing your dad."

"Losing Dad like we did. Having Ingrid come home. Amber's thing with her fiancé." Liv stretched, but the sudden ache low in her ribs was still there. Ingrid had lived a whole lifetime away from her, from the family. Liv felt another pinprick of jealousy that Amber had known Ingrid had regrets about not having children before she did. She picked up her phone and touched the home button.

"But they're okay now, right?"

"Yeah." Liv shrugged. "Amber and Nathan are happy. It's just...I don't know, Kristen. It's just a weird time right now. So much good stuff going on, but there's still a lot of...resentment...and some hard feelings, and it's like we put one fire out and then another starts and someone gets it under control and then we have another...It's—"

"Hard to get ahead?" Kristen guessed.

"Hard to know where anything stands at any given time." Liv's throat was tight, and her voice came out gruff, and she cleared her throat. "Bring Sasha in tomorrow."

"What?"

"After school. I'd love to see her."

Kristen offered Liv a little smile, but she shook her head. "She has track practice."

"I miss her."

"Liv, you've got enough on your plate with your family without adding mine to the mix."

That knife in her throat slipped a bit and cut her again. Kristen had no idea how true her words were. Afraid to try and answer her because who knew what she might say now, Liv reached for Kristen's margarita and took a healthy drink.

CHAPTER 5

*L*iv fought the urge to tiptoe into the empty kitchen. Wade was here somewhere; his truck was in the driveway. Irritated with herself for being careful, she slung her purse down on the counter and dropped her keys beside it. She'd stayed later at the bar with Kristen than she'd planned and only because Kristen had called her out on her comments about Sasha. When Kristen had asked if she was just supposed to ignore it, she'd been zapped with guilt because there was no hurt that equaled what a mother felt for her child, and Liv knew it.

So she had ordered another beer. Put the stuff with Amber and Ingrid out of her head. Tried to shove Wade and Asher Crowe to the back of her mind, though that was harder, and suggested things for Sasha. Things like instead of Sasha going to camp, she get a paper route. Rather than missing her friends, getting involved in art classes or trying a musical instrument. She asked Kristen if they planned to do a family vacation. All things Kristen had already thought of, of course, because Kristen was racking her brain for something to take Sasha's mind off the girls who were treating her badly. Liv would do the same, and she would feel the same if she were in Kristen's shoes now.

Her phone buzzed again; this time with a call instead of a text. Liv stepped out of her low-heeled sandals as she dug her phone from her purse. Not surprised to see Amber's name on the screen, she stifled a groan to answer the call.

"Are you over there?"

"Well, I was. But no one else can bother to show up."

"Amber, I had something to do."

"I don't even wanna know what you had to do," Amber snapped. "Look, I wasn't going to say this, but I think—"

"I went out for a drink with a friend, Amber." Liv pinched the bridge of her nose. No, it wasn't Amber's business, but she hated that Amber automatically assumed she had been doing something wrong. That she was still involved in a fling. Frankly, she hated that Amber knew it had happened. She hated that Amber needed to judge her, and she most definitely hated being the standard by which Amber measured romantic relationships.

"Just. I don't want to know—"

"Jesus, Amber, I teach with her. She asked me if I wanted to grab a drink. She needed to talk about something."

Liv crossed the room and yanked the refrigerator door open. Amber was so quiet, Liv wondered if the call had dropped.

"You still there?" she asked as she squatted down to look inside the fridge.

"Yeah." Amber sounded distracted. "I'm sorry. I didn't realize…"

"What? That I have friends?"

Finding nothing appealing in the fridge, Liv climbed to her feet and swung the door closed. She glanced at the window above the sink. The backyard was still lit with late evening, but shadows were falling fast. She wondered if

Wade had eaten anything when she hadn't come home earlier.

Her stomach growled, but she didn't move. Hard to decide what to fix when nothing sounded good.

"Do I know her?" Amber asked quietly.

"Kristen Richards," Liv answered. She turned, propped a hip on the counter, and crossed her free arm over her middle. "Need me to get a note from her promising I was with her?"

"Where's Ingrid?" Amber asked. Marveling at her little sister's high-road approach, Liv took a second to process what Amber had actually said.

"I don't know."

"Did we not decide the other night that we were meeting at the house to work tonight?"

Liv bit her lip, thought back to the other night, but all she'd taken away from that night was that Ingrid had sort of wanted a baby, and Amber knew, and Ingrid had never confided that to her.

"I don't know, Amber. I don't remember." She sighed and pushed off the counter as Charlie wandered into the room.

"Where's Dad?"

Liv shrugged. "The garage, probably."

"Just looked." Charlie shook his head. "When's dinner?"

"…just…I think we need to do it."

"Do what?" Liv said into the phone. "What?"

"It's disgusting," Amber said. "It's yellow. And tacky. And peeling up in the corners."

"I'm hungry."

"Okay." Liv nodded at Charlie and watched as he left the room.

"So? What do you think?"

"About what?" She stretched and covered her mouth when she yawned. Went back to the refrigerator and pulled the door open again as if she might find something new there now.

"God, do you ever listen?"

"Amber—"

Liv heard the sudden dead air and knew Amber had hung up on her, but she stared at her phone in shock. So much for Amber's newly-engaged bliss. She had gone back to being the same pain-in-the-ass girl she'd been before she and Nathan had worked things out.

Liv lowered her hand to the counter and carefully set the phone down. She still felt guilty for only being half there for Kristen tonight, and the fact that Kristen had let her off the hook because she was still dealing with grief and with her parents' estate only made the guilt worse. Now she had Amber mad at her again, because she'd listened to Charlie for a second and missed something Amber said.

And her stomach was still growling.

She should find Wade and see if he wanted something.

Still, she didn't move. She shifted her weight from foot to foot and ducked her head. Closed her eyes. Instead of the bad things, her mind led her to a random night with Wade when the kids were little. Wade and Charlie had donned goofy paper chef hats and fixed and served she and Gracie mac and cheese for dinner. Rather than cleaning up when they were finished, the four of them had built a blanket fort in the living room and huddled inside it, reading to each other. If Liv remembered correctly, the kids had been in the Dr. Seuss phase at the time. When she'd read *Hop on Pop*, both of them had attacked Wade, and Liv had laughed and then curled up beside him on the floor when the kids tuckered out and slowed down.

"Hey."

His voice was sometimes like sandpaper on her skin, rough and harsh, and she hated it, almost like she thought she hated him sometimes. Tonight, it was warm, soft, and Liv waited to see how her body reacted.

"You hungry?" Wade asked her.

She nodded without looking at him.

"Charlie is, too."

He moved slowly, but Liv felt the air shift when he stood behind her. He dropped his hands on her shoulders, making her jump and hunch them forward.

"Did you eat?" she asked him.

"No." He pressed into her and kissed the back of her head as she lifted her chin. "Waited for you."

Perfect opportunity for her to tell him where she'd been. Or for him to ask her why she was late. Liv said nothing; she only leaned a bit when he moved his hands to slide them around her waist.

"You okay?" His voice was gruff now.

"Yeah." She nodded. "Yeah, I'm fine."

"You looked upset when I came in. Who was on the phone?"

"Amber," she said quietly. "She's upset with me for not coming over to the house tonight."

"Were you supposed to?"

"Apparently." She turned her head. Kissed him back when he brushed his lips over hers in a quick kiss. When he still didn't ask, Liv took a deep breath and stepped away from him. "Kristen asked me to meet her for a drink tonight."

"You can't celebrate yet." He held up a finger as if to shame her, but the grin on his face took the sting out of his words. "You guys have a week left."

"She just needed to vent," Liv mumbled. "And Wade, that week feels impossible right now."

"You'll get there, babe," he promised her. "Just hang on a bit longer."

She swallowed at the knot in her throat.

"You look tired." He stepped close to her again. Lifted his hand and stroked his fingers over her face. She ducked her head, uncertain if she was angry for him to say she looked tired or touched that he'd noticed she was exhausted.

"I am." She turned her face into his hand and closed her eyes.

When Wade rubbed his hands down over her arms, Liv stepped closer to him and rested her head on his shoulder.

"Liv." His gravelly whisper chased a chill up her spine. She squeezed her eyes closed at the raw emotion she heard. She didn't need another person needing her for anything. Not right now.

Rather than start anything, or attempt to start anything, Wade simply closed his arms around her and held her. For a long moment, they stood silently in each other's arms, Liv's fingers linked loosely at his back.

"Are we eating or what?" Charlie's grumble preceded him into the kitchen. "I'm hungry."

Liv stiffened and lifted her head from Wade's shoulder. She sighed when Wade smoothed his hands up over her back and stepped away from him when she opened her eyes and found Charlie watching them from the doorway.

"What're we doing?" He rolled his eyes.

"What do you want?" Wade asked, and for just a moment, Liv thought he was addressing her. She swallowed hard and glanced at him, relieved to find him looking at Charlie. She didn't know what she wanted. For dinner. For ever. She didn't want to be on the spot at the moment.

"Where were you, Mom?" Charlie shoved his hands in his pants pockets. His eyes bored into her, his gaze heavy with accusation. Apparently, it was her fault he hadn't thought to find something to eat on his own.

"With Kristen, Charlie," she said quietly.

"I don't get why you always go out drinking—"

"Charlie, your mother went out with a friend for a drink. She doesn't *always* go out *anywhere*."

Liv started to protest, to argue with Wade. She wasn't sure how she felt about him sticking up for her. Charlie's sullen stare changed her mind. She shook her head, irritated again by the feeling that she was suffocating.

"Let's go out," Wade suggested. Liv held in a sigh. She was tired, and she'd just walked in. The last thing she wanted to do was go out for dinner. She looked over her shoulder at the stove and decided the *last thing* she wanted to do was actually fix dinner. At least if they went out, she could sit back and let someone else do the work.

"Sounds good." She nodded and looked at Charlie hopefully. "Where?"

"What do you want?" Wade asked him.

"Barbeque," he answered. Liv felt her stomach twist in protest, but when Wade glanced at her for her reaction, she simply nodded and shrugged.

"Sure." She reached for her purse and her phone. Charlie bounded out of the room, probably to brush his teeth and comb his hair and do whatever else teenage boys that had suddenly discovered girls did before leaving the house.

"What would happen…" Wade met her eyes and then let his gaze roam to the phone in her hand. "If you left your phone here?"

She blinked and watched without a word as Wade pried her phone from her hand with gentle fingers and put it back on the counter.

"What if Amber calls?" she asked quietly.

"What if she does?" He shrugged. "We'll be gone an hour and a half. Two, tops. She'll live."

Liv pursed her lips and studied his face.

"You don't have to be in control all the time," he reminded her. "Let Ingrid and Amber deal with it."

"With what?" She frowned and cocked her head.

"Whatever it is Amber was pissed about this time."

She laughed softly, but she recognized the pressure in her throat and turned away from him before she cried.

"I don't even know." Her voice was thick with tears. She sniffled and shook her head. "I think she told me, but Charlie was talking to me at the same time."

When she glanced at him over her shoulder, he arched his eyebrows.

"We need you at home, too, Liv."

Maybe he only meant that her family, her husband and kids, missed her and wanted to spend more time with her. What she heard was that she should have been home to fix dinner tonight. That she still had laundry to do because she hadn't finished it on Sunday. That Wade felt neglected in the bedroom and maybe the tender moment just before Charlie barged into the kitchen with his whining was just a lead in to sex.

She gave Wade a sharp nod, glanced back at her phone, and then picked up her purse. Not a big deal. She could leave her phone here if it proved something to Wade. She grabbed her purse and turned to him expectantly.

"Liv."

"What, Wade?" She sighed. "Are you ready? We need dinner, don't we?"

Jaw set, his lips in a grim line, he muttered something and walked out of the room ahead of her.

CHAPTER 6

*S*he beat Amber and Ingrid both to the house the next afternoon. Then again, maybe neither of them would show up, and it would be her night to sit here and twiddle her thumbs and be angry with them for wasting time. She pulled her Traverse farther down the driveway and parked it even with the back door. Rather than get out immediately, she pulled the keys from the ignition and stared straight ahead at the garage. They had barely touched it yet. Frankly, Liv thought that should be Ezra's job. He hadn't done much to help them with anything, and on the one hand, Liv got it. They were going through their parents' belongings. What did Ezra care about old bed linens and blankets and Mom's knickknacks and magazines? But the garage was sort of his territory, wasn't it? What did she and Amber and Ingrid want with old coffee cans full of bolts and screws and rusted old tools and extra tubes for bike tires?

Sure, Ezra was busy. He had a job. He had a wife and a new baby at home.

But Amber was busy. She had a child—a teenager, and Liv would be the first one to say teenagers were almost more trouble than infants—and a fiancé and a photography business, and Ingrid had a full-time career and a boyfriend at home. And she had a job, too. A job and kids and a husband. She and her sisters had been sacrificing their time to take care of the estate. Why the hell couldn't Ezra pull his weight?

She huffed out a sigh and rested her head on the seat. Maybe Ezra didn't feel that he needed to help them because Dad wasn't his father. She drummed her fingers on the steering wheel and let that thought fill up the car with her. She'd probably never say that to Ingrid or Amber, but alone, she was free to wonder about it. He and Dad had been close; for all practical purposes, Dad was Ezra's dad, too. But Ezra still had Mike, his biological father. What if he was out hanging out with Mike rather than helping them deal with the house?

She didn't have a clue what Ezra was doing, and it wasn't fair to think he might feel that none of this was his responsibility. Amber was closest to him, but she'd never go picking her brain for information about their brother. Amber would protect him to the death, anyway, so it would do no good.

With another small sigh, Liv got out of the car and swung the door closed. She moved slowly around the front end, trailing her fingers over the hood and imagining Wade coming unglued at her for touching the car that way. She didn't care.

They had talked some over dinner last night. Well, not about what was going on between them. They certainly couldn't do that with Charlie with them. But they talked some, and they had laughed together. Wade had shared with her a few stories about his crew on a recent job site. Liv had laughed quietly about one of the guys stepping in a bucket of drywall mud, only to fall quiet when she realized Wade was simply watching her, as if he was hungry for the sound. Charlie had been oblivious to them. Normally, Liv would get irritated with the kids for being on their phones, but last night, she hadn't cared that Charlie was texting someone. She had enjoyed the connection she and Wade had shared, so she let Charlie go.

Of course, when they got home, Wade had turned the garage light off, and Liv had gone to bed with her heart in her throat, thinking that he would come to her and hold her. Instead, after she'd washed her face and put her nightgown on, she had heard Charlie talking to him in the living room. Didn't sound like anything important—nothing about school or girls—but on the other hand, with a mother as emotionally distant as she had become, maybe any time Wade gave Charlie was important.

She had gone to sleep alone in their bed, her back to Wade's side. And Wade was already in the kitchen scrambling eggs this morning when she climbed out of bed.

Ingrid wanted to sell the house. If it had been Ingrid's decision, she'd have sold the house the day after Dad's funeral. She would have listed it as it was, washed her hands of their family, and walked away. She would have lost the opportunity to be with Luke if she'd handled it that way. Liv stared up at the house now, eyes drawn to the window she used to sneak out of when she was a kid, and wondered if Ingrid was happy that things had happened as they had. Yes, she was in love with Luke Ashley, but did she miss Chicago? Did she regret being in close quarters with the rest of them?

Liv moved around the back of the house now and wandered through the yard. The sun had been hiding all day, so there were no shadows to speak of. But Liv felt them just the same. She lowered herself to sit on the bench of the picnic table and leaned forward to rest her elbows on her knees.

She saw Asher today. During her planning period—second hour—she had gone to the restroom and then ducked into the office to check her mailbox. Asher had been at the end of the hall huddled in conversation with the athletic director. Her heart had pounded a bit harder and shot ice through her veins. He looked the same now in his creased dress slacks and button down shirt and tie. His dark hair had been combed neatly in place, though she'd had to do a double take because she'd seen it mussed and sweaty, the way it looked after she ran her fingers through it.

There was no denying he was sexy. Even now, the memory of seeing him at school hours old, Liv could feel a tiny wave of desire in her belly. As if he had eyes in the back of his head, he had turned and looked at her over his shoulder. He had eyed her coolly and then turned back to his conversation, apparently unaffected at seeing her. Liv had wobbled on into the office on shaking knees, with the memory of him kneeling on the bed behind her and driving into her painfully hard warring with the fear of him telling someone what they'd done.

Maybe he was good-looking. Sexy. But now if she had to use one word to describe him, she would say lethal.

Asher Crowe had the power to destroy her. If not her marriage, he could almost certainly destroy her career.

"Hey."

She took a deep breath and turned her head to watch Amber's slow, deliberate approach.

"Hi." She looked back at the gate at the back of the yard as Amber sat down beside her, a foot of the old bench with chipped red paint between them. Liv dragged in a ragged breath and sat up straight. "I'm sorry about last night."

"'s okay," Amber said quietly.

Liv raised her eyebrows. Had she really expected Amber to apologize?

"I wasn't going to go with Kristen." She shrugged. "But I decided I was being selfish."

"Is everything okay?"

Liv snorted and turned her head the other way. She eyed the base of the tree she and Ingrid used to climb when they were kids.

"With your friend."

Liv nodded, because eventually things would be okay for Kristen and Sasha, and even if they weren't, she wasn't going to talk with Amber about it anyway.

"Sure."

"I'm sorry." Amber's tiny words hung in the air. "I had a bad day. Yesterday. I lost some shots for a project, and I was pissed about that. I rushed out of the studio, because I didn't want you guys to be pissed at me for being late. And then…"

"We weren't here." Liv finished her sentence.

From the corner of her eye, she saw Amber shrug.

"Look, I get that you were upset, Amber." Liv glanced at her. Their eyes met, but Liv looked away quickly. "And I'm sorry I didn't get what you said on the phone last night. Charlie was talking to me, and I missed whatever you said."

Amber nodded.

"I just…" Liv shook her head. "I just…there's a lot going on at home. And there's just nothing there, too, and I'm trying to keep my head above water right now."

"Does he know?"

"I don't think so."

"Are you going to tell him?"

"I don't know." Liv looked at her again. "What I do know is that I don't want to be lectured by my little sister. Live my life before you tell me what you think, okay?"

Amber's mouth dropped open, but she closed it quickly and turned her face away.

"Sure, Liv."

"I don't get why you're still so unhappy." Liv wanted to lean into her, but she was too far away. "Are you and Nathan okay?"

"We're good."

"Then it's still Ingrid?"

"No. No." Amber shook her head. "It's fine. I'm good. Maybe being a bitch is just a bad habit."

Liv snorted and rolled her eyes.

"Runs in the family, I guess."

"You said it."

"Can I ask you something?" Liv took a deep breath. She hated the little flutter in her belly, the unease she felt with Amber. It was kind of new to her, since Ingrid had come back home. She and Amber hadn't been the kinds of sisters who read each other's minds and hung out all the time, but they'd talked enough that Liv hadn't felt timid about talking to her. Then again, Liv had never asked things of Amber. It had always been the other way around. If Amber needed something, she had come to Liv.

"What?" Amber stretched. Liv winced when she heard her back pop.

"Did Ingrid come out and tell you that?"

Amber blinked at her and finally shook her head.

"Why does that bother you so much?"

"Why did it bother you that I read her manuscript before you did?"

Amber rolled her eyes.

"You had her for thirteen years, Liv."

The words hit her in the stomach and robbed her of her breath. What the hell did that mean? She opened her mouth to ask Amber what she meant by her comment, but when she heard a car engine cut out and then the sound of a car door closing, she thought better of it.

"Where are you going?" Amber looked up and watched her walk back toward the house. "Olivia, what's going on?"

She didn't stop and wait for Ingrid to come down the driveway. Instead, she yanked the screen door so hard, she nearly fell backwards off the small stoop. Rage warred with something foreign in her belly. She pulled her keys from her pocket and shoved the house key into the lock, pinching her finger as she did so. She muttered as she turned the knob and pushed the door open, cringed when it got away from her and banged against the wall.

Might be foreign, but she knew exactly what it was.

She swept her gaze over the small mudroom and then moved on into the kitchen, eyes on the long island counter. Mom used to stand there at that counter and make dinner while she and Ingrid sat on the other side to do their homework. Liv hadn't ever paid much attention to the magic Mom worked in the kitchen, not enough to be half the cook she was, but she had loved all the baked treats and the attention she and Ingrid got in that small window of time before Dad got home from work.

Well. Before Mom decided she wasn't happy. Before she was messing around on Dad and pregnant with a new family.

Liv took a few steps forward, eyes welling with tears. She rested her hands on the counter and hung her head. She could almost hear her mom's voice. Asking her and Ingrid what they learned at school. If they wanted cookies or apples for a snack. Reminding them that they had to have their homework finished if they wanted to play outside.

The screen door opened behind her, but she didn't move. Not even when she heard Ingrid and Amber's conversation about the files Amber had lost. Ingrid was commiserating with her; Liv figured she'd lost a file or two through her writing career. Liv had certainly done it, though losing a lesson plan couldn't compare to losing a photo file for a client or a chapter or two she'd bled out at a computer.

She squeezed her eyes closed, chin still on her chest, and felt hot tears slide over her face.

"Hey."

She stiffened when one of them rested a hand on her lower back.

"What's on the agenda today?" Ingrid asked. Liv sniffled and gulped in a breath. "Liv? Are you okay?"

"I'm fine." She barely had the energy to push the words out, and she knew neither of her sisters had heard her. Because she wasn't fine, and because she didn't want to talk, she fisted her hands on the counter and slowly stood up straight.

"What's wrong?" Ingrid stroked her hand up now from her lower back and over her shoulder. Liv shook her head and stepped away from Ingrid.

"We had words," Amber mumbled.

"Why? Over what?" Ingrid asked quickly. Liv shook her head, irritated with Amber for speaking for her. It wasn't that she and Amber had had words. Liv suspected the three of them would never get over the jealousy and the spats. She couldn't imagine a time when she could look at Ingrid and Amber and not want to be part of what they were doing, feeling left out if they didn't specifically include her.

"Olivia."

She tucked her hair behind her ear. Wrong move. Now Ingrid could see her face. Liv turned away when Ingrid stepped in front of her.

"I can't do this." She shook her head. "I can't."

"Do what?" Ingrid whispered.

"Liv, I'm sorry." Amber didn't sound particularly sincere, but she spoke quietly, as if she was exhausted, maybe sad.

"Mom used to be here every day, Ingrid. Every day we came home."

"I know." Ingrid nodded. "I remember."

"And Dad used to watch the news every night, and we climbed up and down that tree all day every day." Liv covered her face with her hands. Shook her head when Ingrid curled her fingers around her wrist. "Wade and I were together the first time out back, and I told Mom that I was pregnant with Gracie right here in the kitchen, and Mom went into labor with Amber in the mudroom—"

"Liv." Ingrid's low, steady voice slid around her shoulders in a warm caress. "Liv, breathe."

"I can't do this."

"Do what?" Ingrid tugged gently at her wrists. "Do what, Liv?"

"Sell this house!" Liv wailed as she dropped her hands to her sides.

"We have to sell the house." Ingrid raised her eyebrows. "You know that. We can't let it sit here—"

"Mom and Dad are gone. My kids are leaving—"

"What? Gracie's going to school next fall." Ingrid nodded. "She'll come back home. And Charlie's—"

"If something happens with me and Wade, I'm gonna lose my kids. I'm gonna lose everything!" Liv batted Ingrid's hand away when she reached for her. "This house is all I have, Ingrid."

"What happened with Wade?" Ingrid cocked her head. "Did something else happen?"

Liv stepped away from her again. She felt Amber's eyes on her, but she refused to look at her as she paced the length of the island.

"I saw him again." She pushed her hair off her face and held it at the back of her neck. "Today. I saw him today, and it hit me that he can ruin me. I ruined my marriage, but he can ruin my life—"

"Wait, wait, wait."

Liv felt a tiny wave of satisfaction that she'd finally gotten under Ingrid's skin. Her sister had finally raised her voice. But the satisfaction was short-lived, because all the other stuff was pushing around inside her, making it hard to breathe. Not to mention she didn't like herself too much these days. Said a lot about her that she needed to grab onto everyone she could to take them all down with her, didn't it?

"What do you mean? You saw him today?" Ingrid asked, the calm restored to her voice again. "Amber. Do something."

"Are you kidding me?" Amber sounded hurt. Liv turned to look first at Ingrid and then Amber.

"Get her a beer. A shot of brandy."

Liv almost laughed at the relief on Amber's face. But the amusement quickly melted into guilt and then hardened into sorrow. How had her parents really thought they could have two separate families and that everything would be okay? What choice had they had, though? Should Mom have terminated her pregnancy with Ezra? Taken care of things so there would be no Amber at all?

Ingrid approached her cautiously. She reached out again with slow movements, almost as if she meant to disarm her. Liv supposed maybe it was a little bit like that, although her sharp tongue was her weapon of choice. Might be a little complicated to take that from her.

"You okay?" Ingrid asked her again.

Liv saw Amber glance at her over her shoulder. She stood at the refrigerator as if she was trying hard to follow Ingrid's orders but scared to miss out on something. Her mouth, her words, failed her now, and Liv could only shake her head.

"I'm sorry." The apology was too little for everything she'd said, everything she'd done in the past six months. But it was all she could manage. Ingrid, still careful, stroked her fingers up over Liv's arm.

"Liv." Ingrid stilled her hand and curled her fingers around Liv's upper arm. "C'mere." Liv rested her forehead on Ingrid's shoulder as her sister moved in closer and took her in her arms. "It hurts. I know. Sometimes it's like a knife ripping right through you."

"Says the thriller writer," Amber mumbled. "There's a beer on the counter."

Ingrid jerked around to look at Amber, still with her arms around Liv.

"I'm gonna go back to the studio," Amber continued. "Nathan and Hadley—"

"Amber." Face still buried in the crook of Ingrid's neck, Liv unwound her arm from Ingrid's waist and reached blindly for Amber. She sobbed softly when Amber slipped her hand in hers and gave her a gentle squeeze. "Don't leave. Please?"

"You guys don't need me here," Amber said quietly. She pulled her hand away from Liv's. "You've already told me you don't want my opinion on anything. We're not gonna get anything done on the house—"

"Jesus, Amber." Ingrid sighed.

Liv pushed Ingrid away with gentle but firm hands. She sniffled again and swiped at her eyes. When she looked at Amber, she found her baby sister studying the toe of her shoe rather than looking at them. She felt another stab of guilt for her thought earlier, for thinking that her parents had been mistaken to think they could blend the four of them together into one family. They were a family. Fractured, maybe, but still family. Maybe it was her job to pull them all together now.

Yet another thing she could tack onto her list of failures.

CHAPTER 7

*I*ngrid met her eyes and nodded toward the table. "Sit down."

Liv watched her sister grab the bottles on the counter and twist the tops off of them one at a time. She gave Ingrid a quick shake of her head and turned to Amber, who had given up the study of her shoe but was still fighting to avoid looking at her.

"Will you stay?" Her voice was thick and scratchy with the emotion she was trying to control. Amber tucked her hands in her pockets and shrugged.

"Sure."

Liv watched her, determined to wait her out and make eye contact. But Amber still hadn't looked at her by the time Ingrid had the three bottles open. Ingrid held two bottles out in offering. Liv took hers without looking away from Amber, but she didn't drink from it.

Amber finally huffed out a sigh, flicked her gaze over Liv's, and reached for the beer Ingrid held for her.

"Amber." Liv arched her eyebrows when Amber finally met her gaze again. "I'm sorry."

Amber nodded and shrugged Liv's apology away.

Fighting down the irritation—Liv wasn't sure why she was apologizing this time, because she wasn't sure what she'd done and it might be nice for someone to apologize to her— she snaked her arm around Amber's shoulders and pulled her in for a quick hug.

"We're always apologizing." Amber squeezed her extra hard. "But we never stop hurting each other."

Again Liv wondered why this time was her fault.

"Hey, I'd take it while you can get it," Ingrid reminded her. "Olivia Girard doesn't apologize often."

"I need your support." Liv ignored Ingrid's comment and whispered to Amber. "Not your criticism."

"I know." Amber hung on tighter. "I know, Liv."

"So what happened before I got here?" Ingrid asked after a few moments of quiet. Amber backed away from Liv. She ducked her head and wiped at her eyes, clearly with no intention of answering Ingrid.

"What do you say we put Ezra in charge of the garage?" Liv rubbed the skin under her eyes and then smoothed her fingertips over her forehead.

"That'll happen when hell freezes over," Ingrid mumbled.

"I know, right?" Liv nodded. When she realized they were both watching Amber, waiting for her to step up and defend their brother, she took a deep breath and turned her back to them. Beer still in hand, she made her way across the floor to the same table the whole family used to gather around for meals.

The three of them had dragged almost everything up from the basement in the last couple of weeks. The kitchen floor was still cluttered with boxes and the contents of the boxes, but it was slowly coming together. Liv sank into the seat at the end of the table, where Dad used to sit, and finally took a drink. She swept her eyes over the boxes on the floor and then over the tabletop. The box of old pictures was gone. Apparently, Amber had worked her way through it. Either that or she'd just chucked it all together and either taken it home or thrown it all away. Liv wasn't sure she even cared which Amber might have done.

"So." Ingrid cleared her throat. Sprawled in the kitchen chair, Liv felt her whole body tense with anticipation for whatever Ingrid was going to say. "Can I tell you something?"

A ribbon of ice slipped through her body. Liv focused on the table in front of her, where the leaf dropped into the main frame. In her head, she could hear her mom warning her and Ingrid to be careful not to pinch their fingers in that spot when they helped with the table. When it was only the four of them, they hadn't needed so much space, so they rarely used the leaf. Only for special occasions, like dinners with their grandparents.

She lifted her head now and noticed that Amber was looking at Ingrid with fierce intensity. Overcome with another wave of jealousy, she dragged her eyes away from Amber and gave Ingrid her attention.

Apparently, she wore her worry on her face.

Ingrid rolled her eyes.

"I'm fine." She sighed as she sat down at the opposite end of the table. "I'm fine. Good God. Do you guys want to go with me to my next appointment? Or do you want to start checking them yourselves?"

Amber stood at the table, still hesitant to sit with them.

"Hannah's pregnant," Ingrid continued. "She called Luke last night."

"Hannah? Luke's daughter?" Amber asked.

"Yeah." Ingrid pressed her lips together and nodded. "I haven't even met her yet, and now there's going to be an extra person in the mix."

Liv watched Ingrid closely, looking for a crack in her composure. Was she still just nervous about meeting Luke's daughter, or did it bother her that Hannah was going to have a baby?

"Stop looking at me like that." Ingrid barely breathed the words, but she kept her eyes glued to the brown bottle on the table. "Look, Liv. Yes, I wish that I'd have been lucky enough to have a baby. But I didn't. End of story. It's not a big deal. I'm not devastated. I'm not scheming ways to get my hands on Luke's grandchild. I'm not thinking about screwing around with birth control now with the hopes of getting pregnant."

Liv swallowed hard. She gave Ingrid a curt nod, but she wouldn't meet her eyes.

"Okay."

"The thing is…" Ingrid drew in a deep breath. From the corner of her eye, Liv saw her shrug. "Luke's not happy about it. Hannah's not even seeing anyone."

"Oh." Amber gave a quiet moan of commiseration. "But she's not sixteen, either."

"Exactly."

Liv heard a note of anger in Ingrid's voice.

"Did you guys fight about this?"

"No." Ingrid leaned forward and rested her elbows on the table. "We didn't fight. But we argued."

Liv shot Amber a quick look. Amber grinned and pulled a chair out.

"You fought about it," she told Ingrid as she finally dropped to sit down.

"He's angry, and okay, maybe it's not the best time for her, but she's an adult." Ingrid combed her hair from her face and then folded her fingers together behind her head. "Right? She'll handle it. Luke had her on speakerphone, and she was so excited. I could tell Luke was pissed, but he didn't say much."

"Like, how much did you argue over this?" Amber asked her.

"It wasn't bad." Ingrid shook her head. "It just frustrated me."

"This happened last night?" Amber asked Ingrid.

"Yeah. I had my keys in my hand when she called, and Luke wanted me to stick around. He puts us on speakerphone now when she calls. Poor girl. She's never even met me, and she has to talk to me all the time."

"Is she gonna stay out there?" Liv studied what appeared to be an age spot on the back of her hand, rather than look at either of her sisters. "Or come back here?"

"Why would she come back here?" Ingrid asked quietly. "She and Luke don't have...they weren't together enough when she was a kid."

Liv shrugged. Maybe that was exactly why she should come back home. Then again, Hannah moving home and having a baby and dumping that baby on Luke, or on Ingrid, wouldn't be good for anyone.

"It's not a big deal." Ingrid took a long drink of her beer. "I guess it was just our first...disagreement."

"Did you have makeup sex?" Amber lifted her feet to her chair and curled her toes around the edge. She turned her head to Ingrid and rested her cheek on her knees. Liv could still see that she was grinning.

"We had sex," Ingrid nodded, "but there wasn't a blowout fight, so I don't know if that qualifies."

"Nope." Liv reached for her bottle and shook her head. "Doesn't."

"So next time we should let it simmer a day or two and have a knock down drag out?"

"It's kind of fun." Liv almost smiled, but it hit her then that she and Wade hadn't had makeup sex in ages. They hadn't fought in ages. Was that because she didn't care anymore or had Wade decided their marriage wasn't worth it?

"Are we gonna talk about it?" Ingrid asked after a few seconds of silence.

"Makeup sex?" Liv met her eyes. "Amber would have to remind me how it goes."

"You said you saw him today."

Liv's stomach pitched at the thought of Asher Crowe in the hallway at school earlier today. The way his dark eyes had zeroed in on her and nearly pinned her in place. Uncomfortable with her thoughts and Ingrid's disapproving gaze, she squirmed in her chair and took a drink.

"Liv." Ingrid spoke her name on the tail end of a disappointed sigh. Olivia blinked at Ingrid as her sister closed her eyes and shook her head.

"No." Liv leaned forward over the table and reached as if she could stretch across the table and touch Ingrid. "No, Ingrid. Not like that."

Ingrid rested her elbow on the table, propped her chin in her hand, and opened her eyes to look at Olivia. Her gaze wasn't exactly suspicious, but she certainly looked wary.

"Then what?" she asked quietly.

"He was…" Liv saw him again in her head and gave herself a mental shake. "He was at school. I saw him in the hall."

"Did you talk to him?"

"No." Liv rubbed her fingers over her eyes and down over her face. "No. But."

"You want him?" Ingrid arched her eyebrows. "Is that it?"

"No." She dropped her hands to the table and stared at Ingrid, wide-eyed. "No. It's just…seeing him there. Seeing him in my space, in my world, is startling."

"Who is it, Liv?" Amber asked quietly.

Olivia turned her head to look at her little sister. She considered avoiding the question, but then she wondered if Amber was testing her. If Amber even knew she was testing her.

"Do you know?" Amber looked to Ingrid, assuming Liv had confided that to Ingrid.

"Asher Crowe." She whispered the name before Ingrid could answer Amber, but when Amber turned her face—eyes wide, mouth open in shock—she wished she would have kept her mouth shut and held on to that piece of information.

"Asher Crowe? Are you crazy?"

Pinned by Amber's disgust, Liv closed her eyes to hide.

"Who's Asher Crowe?" Ingrid asked, though neither of them answered her.

"Yeah. I guess I am," Liv said softly.

"Jesus Christ, Olivia," Amber groaned. "You went to bed with the devil himself."

She nodded.

"Who is he?" Ingrid tried again.

"Well, for starters, all the money in this town?" Amber's voice was sharp with disapproval. "Half of it's his."

"What's he do?"

"Women. Sex is his business."

"Amber." Liv blinked her eyes open and shook her head at Ingrid.

"He owns a trucking company," Amber told Ingrid. "He owns a few of the convenience stores in town. And he owns a bar."

"Where'd he get his money?"

Liv shrugged when she realized Ingrid was talking to her. "I don't know. Wasn't much pillow talk."

"What do you mean?" Ingrid turned her attention to Amber again. "Sex is his business?"

"He's into sex," Amber answered simply. "Rumor has it he also owns a movie studio."

"Amber." Liv sighed. "He's just a guy."

"Did you do it in front of a camera?" Ingrid asked her.

"No."

"Not that you know of." Amber arched her eyebrows.

Liv winced and ducked her head. The thought of any hidden cameras watching, recording, what she'd done with Asher Crowe made her gag.

"Take it easy," Ingrid told Amber. "It's just a rumor?"

"He's slick, Ingrid. Like, the guy's a snake."

"Has he threatened you?" Ingrid asked Liv.

"No." She shook her head. "No. It's not…it's not like that. I told him I didn't want…"

"And he was okay with that?"

Liv barked a sarcastic laugh. "Really, Amber? You think he's gonna be upset because I told him I didn't want to see him again? You said it yourself. He's got plenty of other women."

"Is he married?"

"Yes."

"And you teach his kid?" Ingrid asked her.

"Yep. And the kid is just like his dad."

"Here." Amber tapped her phone screen a few times and then slid it over the table toward Ingrid.

"That's him?" Ingrid cringed.

"Yep."

"Damn." She huffed out a quick breath.

Liv looked up when Amber pushed her chair back. The harsh squeal of the chair on the floor chased a chill up her spine.

"Where are you going?"

"Nowhere," Amber said quietly.

"Amber, this stays right here. Please promise me you won't repeat it. To anyone."

Amber nodded.

"I get it."

"Promise."

"I promise, Liv."

"He looks like mafia." Ingrid decided.

"What?" Liv glanced at her.

"Good-looking, but too slick. Scary."

Lethal.

Exactly what she had thought at school earlier when she'd seen him.

"What're you gonna do?"

"Do?" Liv echoed Ingrid. "What's there to do? You told me not to tell Wade."

"Yeah, but if you're gonna fall apart every time you see the guy, it's going to be a problem."

"I didn't fall apart—"

Ingrid made a show of looking around the kitchen and then swinging her gaze back to her. "What was this then?"

Liv laughed softly. She stood, shoved her own chair back in a loud crash, and picked up her beer. "This was me. Feeling left out with you two."

"What?" Ingrid asked, but Liv crossed the kitchen without looking back.

"Liv, wait!" Amber called after her. Emotions right back at the surface, throat tight around a steel blade of hurt and pressure, she shook her head and hurried back outside.

a gloomy sky threatened rain as Olivia pulled her Traverse into the long driveway at the side of their house. A thunderhead hung, menacing, in the western sky. Liv scrambled out of the SUV, but she hesitated at the back bumper, head turned to take it in. It startled her to realize the snow was gone, and the trees were full and green, and the grass itself looked greener today than it had yesterday.

Yes, it was late May, and yes, Grace would graduate so soon it made Liv's head spin, but she wasn't sure where the time had gone. The time since Gracie had been five and starting kindergarten, yes. But just since Dad had passed away, and Ingrid had come home, time had flown by faster than the speed of light.

Liv curled her shoulders inward, around the kernel of hurt inside. She'd let it happen. She'd looked away from her life, from her family, and she'd missed out on the smallest of details. And yet, wasn't all of life lived in the smallest of details? She'd been there when Gracie had waltzed out the door on her friend Josh's arm to go to the prom last month. Liv had stood in the same room with them, with Gracie and Josh and their friends and Wade and Charlie, and she'd taken the required pictures. She'd even remembered to print a few. Wasn't there a shot of Gracie and Josh stuck to the fridge right now with a blue letter G magnet? And what about the snapshot of Gracie, alone, in her sleek silver dress, tucked in the corner of her desk calendar at school? Liv had caught Dylan Crowe eyeing it one day, and she'd been so upset over it all day that she'd thrown up when she came home later.

Liv had been there when Ingrid moved in with Luke. She and Wade had pitched in and helped move a lot of Ingrid's stuff when they'd brought it home from her apartment. But where had she been in the beginning of that relationship? How had her sister gotten so involved with him without her knowing?

And how the hell had she blinked only to find herself in her mother's shoes as far as her marriage went? Okay, she wasn't pregnant, so there was something positive to focus on. But she was older than her mom had been when she had strayed. Shouldn't she have known better?

Liv blinked at the sound of the back door opening. Gracie pushed the screen door open and propped it on her foot.

"Mom?"

"Hmm?" Liv turned her head to look at her daughter. Feasted on the site of the beautiful, happy girl who would soon be leaving home. Liv missed her already, but she wasn't sure if it was because she knew she would be leaving, or because Liv had been emotionally absent the majority of the last year.

"Did you..." Gracie hesitated, and Liv took a deep breath and started walking again. She took one last look at the sky and then reached for the screen door to go inside. "What's wrong?"

"Nothing. Why?"

She'd done damage control before she left her dad's house. Slipped away from her sisters again and into a bathroom. Wiped carefully at her eyes, at the eyeliner her tears had smudged. She still felt like hell, but Gracie couldn't possibly know that.

"What're you looking at?" Gracie ducked around her and tried to see out the garage door. "What's out there?"

Liv smiled when her daughter stood up straight and met her eyes. Her hair was piled in a loose, messy twist on her head, and her lip gloss was worn away, and only a line of dark pink liner ringed her little heart-shaped lips.

"Looks stormy," she answered, expecting Gracie to roll her eyes. Instead, she stared at her silently and nodded.

"We should go for a walk. Before it starts raining."

Surprised by the suggestion, Liv looked around the mudroom. She would love to go for a walk with Grace, but she hadn't talked to Wade at all. She didn't know if they'd had dinner. She should probably throw some laundry in the washer. And she had left a plate on the counter this morning. She would rather take a go at all of that and save Wade the inconvenience.

"Is Dad home?"

Gracie arched her eyebrows and then laughed softly. "Mom. You just parked right by his truck."

She had, but she'd been too far inside herself when she pulled in to notice. In too much of a hurry to check out the clouds to care that Wade's truck was in the garage. She grinned now and shrugged.

"Daydreaming."

"No kidding?" Gracie rolled her eyes, but they laughed as Liv followed her into the kitchen. She set her purse and her bag on the counter. Thinking she smelled something sweet, she sniffed curiously.

"Did you guys eat?"

"Dad and Charlie had pork chops."

"What did you eat?"

"I wasn't hungry." Gracie shrugged. "Told Dad I'd wait for you."

Liv winced and nodded. She was tearing her family apart. Whether she was sneaking around with someone else or with her sisters working on Mom and Dad's stuff, she wasn't here where she was needed. She had told herself in the beginning that it was okay. She *wasn't* needed. Gracie and Charlie were old enough to take care of themselves, and Wade could pass hours in the garage, so what did it matter if she wasn't home? Now the guilt clawed through her stomach and settled under her heart. What if she was wrong? It struck her suddenly that she wanted to be wrong. Yes, her family was capable of taking care of themselves, but it would be nice if they needed Liv there simply because they wanted her around.

"Why does it smell like chocolate?"

"Charlie made brownies," Gracie answered. "You hungry?"

Liv watched her daughter's hands as she opened a cabinet to grab plates.

"Um." She wasn't. Not even kind of hungry. Not with a stomach full of emotion. Seeing Asher Crowe at school earlier had set her off, and the rest of the day had either been a dose of heartache or envy or fear and just now, guilt, and she couldn't imagine eating anything. "What if we took a walk first?"

Gracie's eager nod was another wallop right in her gut.

"Let me go change my clothes?" She arched her eyebrows hopefully and let her eyes cruise down over her daughter's athletic little body. Gracie was dressed in loose-fitting athletic shorts and a t-shirt, and Liv was more than half convinced that if she changed her clothes, she would be more comfortable. At least there would be more room for the mess of emotions in her stomach.

"Okay." Gracie nodded.

As Liv hurried through the house, she wondered where Charlie and Wade were. Sounded like music coming from Charlie's room. Still didn't tell her where Wade was, though.

She doubted he was hanging out to listen to Ed Sheeran. Probably in the other garage with his true love.

She unbuttoned her khakis as she walked into their bedroom. Slipped them down over her hips and kicked out of them. She tossed them at the bed, left them lay when they missed and hit the floor.

"Hey."

Bent over the middle drawer of their dresser searching for a pair of yoga pants, she spared Wade a quick glance when she heard him at the door.

"Hey."

"Gracie said you were home."

She closed her fingers around the knit pants and pulled them from the drawer. She didn't answer him. Only raised her eyebrows as if to drive home the point that she was, indeed, home. Wade watched her step into the black pants and ease them up over her legs.

"How was your day?" he asked her. Liv started on the buttons of her chambray blouse, but she held his gaze. Shrugged. Her day sucked, but there wasn't a minute of it she wanted to share with him. Certainly not a minute of it she *could* share with him even if she wanted to.

Face blank, he drew in a deep breath and hung his head low. Liv catalogued his arms up over his head, braced on opposite sides of the door. His faded jeans hung low on his hips, and his gray t-shirt didn't quite meet the denim. Liv eyed the slice of skin in between.

"Get anything done at your dad's?"

Well, they had hashed out some of the details of her infidelity, but she couldn't tell him that. She didn't feel like going into the part about her feeling left out with Ingrid and Amber. They had spent some time digging through one of the last boxes from the basement, but she doubted Wade was interested in a child's set of jacks or old building blocks or even the old hedge clipper they found and wondered why it wasn't in the garage.

"Got through another box," she mumbled.

He should be angry. He should rail at her because she was never home. Seemed like no matter what she did, he didn't care. Liv bit her lip, tempted to tell him the truth. She wanted to push him. To hurt him. To see what he would do. What he would say.

"Find out what Amber wanted last night?"

She shrugged her blouse off her shoulders and dropped it on the floor near her khakis. Wade dropped his hands and made his way into the bedroom to stand in front of her. Mouth dry, she tried to swallow as she watched him lift a hand and stroke his finger down her chest and between her breasts.

She jerked her eyes from his hand and looked up again.

"She thinks we need to put new flooring in the kitchen."

Again, she waited for Wade to blow up. To suggest, as Ingrid had several times already, that they needed to stop sinking money into the house and just get it on the market. And let it go. Let it be someone else's problem. He didn't. Instead, he let his eyes slide over her face and down over her breasts, her pale blue bra.

When he tugged on one of the straps, she shook her head. Before he could argue, before he could remind her how long it had been since they'd been together, she covered his hand with hers.

"Gracie's waiting for me downstairs." She stepped away from him. "We're gonna take a walk."

He groaned. Liv squeezed her eyes closed as she pulled a t-shirt from the drawer she hadn't closed yet.

"Ingrid's not happy."

"Needs to be done."

"What?" Surprised, she turned to him as she pulled the t-shirt over her head.

"The floor. It looks terrible."

"It's probably as old as I am," she reminded him as she worked her arms through the sleeves of the shirt.

"You've aged much better than the floor." He said it with a wink, the corners of his mouth tipped up in a smile.

She laughed. "Thanks?"

"You guys should probably redo the kitchen. The bathrooms. Probably wouldn't be a bad idea to rip the carpet up and refinish the hardwood."

She arched her eyebrows and nodded, still laughing. "Ingrid would kill you. Like. I don't even know. One clean shot." She aimed her fingers at him like they were a gun.

"What's her hurry?" He backed up a step and sat on the edge of the bed.

"I don't…" Liv shook her head and shrugged. "I don't know. I think it's just a big headache for her. Trying to move on with her life and having the estate hanging over…our heads."

"I would think it wouldn't matter now, since she moved back here." He stretched his arms over his head and then lowered his hands to his hair. Scrubbed the top of his head and Liv's eyes were drawn to the silver threaded through the dark blond. There was more there than the last time she had paid attention.

Remembering that Wade had said something about Ingrid, she only nodded. Surprised herself when she moved to stand in front of him. Wade grunted softly when she covered his hands with hers and leaned over to drop a kiss on the top of his head.

"I miss you, Liv," he whispered. "I know this is part of it, but God, I miss you."

His words, the thing about knowing this was part of it, zapped her. Filled her with terror and nerves, and rather than agree or ask what he meant, she lowered her mouth to his and kissed him. Hands still in his hair, she touched her lips against his and then hesitated. When he lowered his hands and settled them on her waist, she stroked him with her tongue.

"I thought Gracie was waiting for you." He dug his fingers into her waist, tugged her closer until she was straddling his lap.

"She is."

Neither of them moved, though, except closer. Wade's hands slid lower over her back to cup her butt, and Liv smoothed one hand down over the back of his head. She stroked her fingers over his neck, as he moved his tongue in a slow, hot slide against hers.

"I love you," he whispered, and because she couldn't say it back—she couldn't find the words anywhere inside—she moved her hand to frame his face, his lips, and kissed him again, deeper still. "Livvie."

"Ssshh." She shook her head and then tucked her face into his neck to breathe in his familiar scent. She sighed, longing and tears fighting to cut loose as he rubbed his hands up over her back again.

"Mom?" Gracie's voice was suddenly loud and close, but Liv didn't jump away from Wade. She lifted her head and then held her hand up without looking at Gracie, asking for just a second.

Their daughter sighed, but Liv could tell without looking that she'd walked back out of the room and left them alone.

"I fixed you a plate," Wade told her as she extracted herself from his arms and eased off his lap. She nodded as she brushed her fingers over her lips, Wade's gaze heavy and sharp enough to hurt.

"Thanks."

"I love you," he said again, and this time, she knew he needed to hear it. He had said it again because he needed her to say it back. She opened her mouth, but the words wouldn't come. Wade arched his eyebrows expectantly.

She choked on the only words she could get to move up her throat and past her lips.

"Me, too."

She ducked her chin again and turned away to grab a pair of socks from another drawer. Wade watched from the end of the bed as she squatted down in front of the closet to grab her running shoes.

CHAPTER 9

*L*iv watched the neighbors' yards slide by as she and Gracie walked through the subdivision. Maybe her neighbors thought she was craning her neck to be nosy and see into a front window or two, but she was suddenly obsessed with the passage of time and therefore, the clues that spring was old news and summer was just around the corner. Winter brown grass had become thick, luscious green, and several houses boasted landscaping with flashes of vivid color and beauty.

Her mom had liked flowers. Struck suddenly by the memory of the pictures Amber had recently shared with her and Ingrid, Liv swallowed a mouthful of sadness. A budding photographer, even when she was just a kid, Amber had snapped tons of pictures of their mom's flowers. Amber had gone on to become a brilliant photographer, and Liv loved the way her little sister captured life—the beautiful and the horrible—but those pictures of Mom's flowers would never be artwork.

But they were memories. Even Amber's amateur photos taken with a junk camera when she was a kid evoked in both her and Ingrid a mix of yearning and grief.

She glanced at Gracie when she felt her fingers brush her wrist. Head and heart still full of her mom and Ingrid and Amber—there was no relief when her sisters filled her so completely and stripped her down to the girl she used to be and then left her wide open and alone—she blinked at her daughter. When Grace realized Liv hadn't been listening, she drew in a deep breath through her nose. Liv watched her nostrils flare and wondered if that tell—the anger, God, Gracie was high on anger these days—was better or worse than the typical eye roll.

"I'm sorry," Liv said quietly, and she fought to stay in the moment with Grace, because in her head she heard Ingrid telling Amber to take Liv's apologies when offered, because she didn't extend them often. "What did you say? What were you going to ask me when you met me in the garage?"

Grace chewed on her lower lip for a moment and studied Liv closely as if trying to decide if she should forgive her for being distant. Again.

"Did you remember to order the cake? For the party?"

Liv breathed a sigh of relief. She wouldn't have wanted to lie, but she didn't have to.

"Yes, I did. It'll be ready around noon the day of your graduation."

Gracie nodded, but her brow was still furrowed, and her shoulders were stiff. Liv wondered what else she had missed.

"What's up?" she asked softly. She reached for Gracie's hand and held it for a moment.

"Annika's going to join the Peace Corps."

"What?"

Because Annika had been one of Gracie's best friends since kindergarten, Liv couldn't imagine the girls going a day without seeing each other, let alone months at a time. She had worried about how they would handle going to different colleges. She racked her brain now, but she was pretty sure she would remember if Annika had mentioned this before.

Liv hadn't been the best mother to begin with—what mother would ever claim to be good at what she did—and the past year had made her doubt her maturity, her adulthood, her sanity, but Liv had been with Gracie and Charlie both—a lot. She would definitely remember if Gracie had mentioned that her best friend had decided to join the Peace Corps.

"Her parents split up—"

Liv sucked in a sharp breath and winced when it sliced through her windpipe. She hadn't known the Hanovers were having problems. Again, she was sure if Grace had told her that she would remember.

Poor Annika. An only child, the separation was probably particularly hard on her.

Liv blinked Grace into focus again, but, like a coward, she quickly averted her gaze when she saw a flicker of fear in her daughter's eyes. No. She changed her mind. Why would it be particularly hard on an only child when his or her parents separated? Watching her parents navigate infidelity and whatever other issues there had been—because didn't there have to be an underlying issue to instigate the infidelity—had crushed her and Ingrid. They'd been younger than Annika, and so it had taken a while for them to understand the situation. Well, Liv had just waded into the same waters, and she *still* couldn't say she understood the situation. But she and Ingrid had finally realized Mom had been with someone else. Probably, neither of them got the full impact of what those words meant exactly, but they got it on a kid's level.

Obviously, Grace had noticed that their house had grown a little quiet and cold.

"She's too young to join the Peace Corps," Liv said now, desperate to escape the clinging sense of doom that clung to them like they'd walked through a spider web.

"She's eighteen," Grace reminded her.

"Where's she going?"

"I don't know. Somewhere in Africa."

"Wow." Liv arched her eyebrows. She waved automatically when Ruben Kroshinsky steered his ancient blue Cutlass by them, en route to his house a street down from theirs.

"Her dad lost his job."

"Why?"

"He got fired for embezzling money or something."

"What?" Liv shot Gracie a look of disbelief. "Are you sure?"

Grace didn't look at her, but even with the side view, Liv recognized the familiar eye roll. She almost laughed, but knowing it would only infuriate her daughter, she controlled herself.

"Annika told me." Grace stopped abruptly, and Liv was two steps past her when she realized it and turned back to her. "He might get arrested."

"Is that why?" Liv stepped back toward her, toes first, as if she had to tiptoe up to the question. She and Grace had always been close, but Liv would be the first to admit, she'd pushed—gently—Grace away this past year. She hadn't known how to be unhappy in her marriage, her life, with her daughter plastered to her side like a postage stamp. Fortunately, Grace had thrived. Taken a leap into more social activities and more school related things, including student government. She'd run for student council for the first time. Helped plan two of the dances for the student body and the teachers' appreciation luncheon.

The distance Liv had purposely put between them would serve Grace well when she left for college in the fall. And it had provided Liv with the space she'd needed to flounder. But she couldn't deny that she missed her daughter.

"What do you mean?" Grace leaned over to touch her toes. Liv looked around, wondering why her daughter had decided to lean over and stick her butt in the air precisely where she had. No cute guys her age around here.

"Why'd you stop walking?" Liv felt like she could walk to

Florida and back, maybe. Too much energy. Too much negative energy pumping through her body. Not to mention, if she kept walking, she could keep Amber and Ingrid and, yes, Asher Crowe, on the back burner.

"I'm hungry," Grace mumbled. "Can we go back home?"

"Are you kidding?" Liv sighed.

"Whatever." Grace took a step toward her, but Liv shook her head.

"It's fine." She dropped her arm around Grace's shoulders when she turned around, and they headed back to the house. She should make a point of going up to Charlie's room to say hi to him. "Charlie leave any brownies?"

Grace snorted in response.

"Is Annika leaving because her parents can't afford to send her to college?"

Still with her arm around Grace, Liv thought her daughter felt smaller and more fragile than she looked.

"Maybe." She shrugged her shoulders dramatically. Liv let her arm fall away, though she still walked close by her side. "Maybe she's embarrassed because her parents fucked everything up so bad."

"Badly," Liv corrected her. Gracie shot her a quick grin, and the two of them shared a laugh.

"You still love Dad, right?" Gracie asked. She looked the other way now, and she sounded like she was ten and not eighteen, preparing to leave home for the first time.

Liv swallowed hard. She did. She would always love Wade as her children's father. He was a good man. Honest. Hard-working. Responsible. Affectionate. She just wasn't sure she was *in love* with him now, or that she'd spend the rest of her life in love with him.

Things Gracie didn't need to know. If she left, it would all explode and make a mess of everything they all valued. If she didn't, her doubts and her fears would be her little secret.

"I do," she told Gracie. "I do."

"And you always will? Even if he fucks something up?"

Liv held her breath when Grace looked at her. Was she referring to Annika's dad? Embezzling money? Embarrassing her mother? Embarrassing Annika? Or had Grace misread the vibes between her and Wade? Did she feel the tension between them? And if she did, did she assume it was something Wade had done?

"Dad's not gonna fuck anything up," Liv promised her. "Quit with the f bomb. You have my attention."

GRACE DISAPPEARED AFTER THE TWO OF THEM SAT TOGETHER AT the bar to eat the leftover food Wade had plated for them. Liv had stayed tuned in with her while they ate. They laughed together over some of the antics the senior class had pulled through the year. Liv, the teacher, shouldn't find the pranks amusing, but Liv, the mom, did. They made plans for the summer, most involving the pool, good reading material, and sunscreen.

Liv wasn't sure what summer would bring. On the one hand, nothing should be different. Dad was gone, now, and the house would eventually belong to someone else. But she and Grace would still hang out together at the pool, and Grace would still rush home to change clothes for an evening at work at the mall or an evening out with her friends. But on the other hand, hadn't everything already changed? Liv was now an adulterer, and Amber was engaged to Nathan, and Ingrid had moved back to the area, and she shared a house now with one of Wade's closest friends. Maybe she was just being paranoid, but Liv felt an urgency where her sisters were concerned. If she waved them away and pretended nothing had changed, would they move on together, without her? If she summered like she always did, would she emerge from the sun and the lazy dog days to find that Ingrid and Amber were joined at the hip, and there wasn't room for her in their relationship?

Not for the first time, she thought about Ezra. What must it be like to be a guy? Ezra was quiet, but he was sharp, and he had to feel the current of unease and jealousy flowing among them. Did he ever feel like a third wheel? Did he ever wish he were closer to any of them? Amber claimed they were close, but Liv didn't think they spent much time together.

She finished rinsing the dishes she and Grace had used and then loaded them in the dishwasher. Grace's question—well, Grace's doubt—about the graduation cake made her doubt herself. So she stood at the refrigerator for a moment and studied her checklist. Maybe she had performed the tasks on autopilot, but she'd marked off everything on the list. Invitations had been sent weeks ago. The cake was on order. Liv had plans to pick up veggie trays when they picked up the cake. She had trays of deli sandwiches on order from Pagano's and ground beef stocked to make maid rites. She and Wade had picked out Grace's gift together: a necklace, with a fine gold chain and a delicate gold cross that would hang horizontally.

Liv laughed softly at the thought of her daughter wearing the cross and flinging the f word far and wide. Maybe Grace had been saying it for years, out of earshot of her parents. Probably she had. Liv had heard Charlie cut loose with it when he was thirteen. She didn't love to hear it from her kids' mouths, but she'd never been the mom to threaten to wash their mouths out with soap, either.

She climbed the stairs to a hard, almost metallic beat. Certainly a departure from Ed Sheeran earlier. At the landing at the top of the steps, the metallic beat mixed with something a little lo-fi and depressing, and again, she laughed, this time at the absurdity of living with two teenagers.

She had to knock twice on Charlie's door before the music paused. When she heard him tell her to come in, she opened the door and leaned in. Surprised to find her son sprawled over his bed with his nose in a book, she cocked her head and stared at him curiously.

"You're reading?" she finally asked, when it became obvious he was going to ignore her.

"Yep."

"Why?"

With less than a week left of school, Liv knew Charlie wasn't reading something for homework. Then again, she couldn't believe he was reading something by choice.

"Why not?"

She opened her mouth to argue, but she caught herself.

"How can you concentrate? With the music?"

"It's either that, or hear Grace's funeral dirge."

Liv snorted, and then feeling disloyal to her daughter, she pressed her hand to her mouth.

"Understood," she said quietly, and she and her son shared a grin. "What're you reading?"

"Aunt Ingrid's first book."

A cold flash of surprise traveled from her head down to her toes. She had managed to shove Ingrid and Amber and the whole ugly afternoon out of her head, and now it was back. And she always tended to forget that her sister, Ingrid, was I.G. Arenson, and it was wildly disconcerting to have that thrown at her like this, and even more so because it was Charlie who had said it. She used to threaten to take away his Xbox if he didn't do the required reading in school.

And now, here he was a few days from summer vacation, nose buried in *Need*. It was a good book. Graphically violent and the sex scene half way through the book had rendered Liv an oversensitive, undersexed puddle of need when she'd read it years ago. She had assumed then that her sister was living large and loving the hell out of her big city life, and she had pestered Wade for sex almost more then than she had recently. Not that he minded.

Then.

She considered telling Charlie he shouldn't read it. Figured in this day and age, both of her children could teach her a thing or two, and sighed in defeat.

"Just don't go getting any ideas," she finally told him. Arms folded over her chest, she gave him a pointed look.

Charlie rolled his eyes, but the pink in his cheeks told her he knew exactly what she was talking about. He couldn't possibly have read that scene, because he appeared to be less than a quarter of the way through the book. Liv wondered if there'd been chatter about the book, about that scene, at school. Ingrid had come in to talk to Amber's class, and she'd been invited back to speak with the rest of the English classes, too.

Liv had not invited her to come to her classroom. But Andy Silver, dean of students, had. Liv had sat in the back of the room that day, alternately fascinated by her sister's imaginary world, her brain, and her success and put off by all of the above.

"Darn, Mom." Charlie shrugged and shook his head. "I was thinking about murdering someone with one of Dad's tools tomorrow."

She laughed and then overcome with love for her baby, she stepped into his room and leaned over to hug him.

"Mo-om!" He tried to pull away from her, but she managed to drop a kiss on the back of his head.

She winked at him, amused by another eye roll as she ducked back out of his room. The metallic beat started instantly and followed her down the hall, past the funeral dirge as Charlie had called it, and to the master suite. Naturally, the room was dark and empty. She toed off her shoes and used her foot to nudge them into the closet. Pulled the comforter and top sheet back and then stripped out of the yoga pants and t-shirt. She carried her nightgown with her to the bathroom where she finished undressing and tossed her bra and panties on the floor by the whirlpool tub.

CHAPTER 10

She found Wade in his garage, though he wasn't working on his current love. Navigating the loud country music—she had a headache by now—she found him at his workbench in the back, bent over his laptop. She stood behind him for several long moments, watched him peruse Ebay, and wondered if he ever stayed out here at night, watching porn. They used to do that together, too, on occasion, and Liv was suddenly desperate to know where they'd lost it—what they'd had together—and when exactly things had started going wrong.

The Boze speakers mounted in the corners of the garage blared a George Jones song, but Liv refused to hear it, to listen to it. She blocked it, concentrated on the streaks of silver she'd seen in Wade's hair earlier. His shoulders. His waist, still smallish as it had been when he was younger. Standing behind him in nothing but her nightgown, she lifted her hand and studied her wedding ring. They had been kids when they married; older in years than Ingrid and Scott, but the couple of extra years they had on her sister and brother-in-law hadn't meant smarter or wiser, by any means.

Still. Ingrid and Scott had burned out within a year. She

and Wade had recently celebrated twenty-four years. That was a lot to throw away just because she was restless. Would he forgive her? If he knew? She wouldn't tell him. Ingrid was right. Cheating had been bad enough; confessing to him just to clear her conscious would be cruel. She could just get her shit together and be the wife he deserved.

She wasn't convinced she wanted to.

"Hey." He straightened when she moved up behind him and slid her arms around his waist. His body tensed, but Liv let her eyes roam from the side of his face to his laptop. No chat boxes open. No windows minimized where he might have been looking at porn. Just Ebay, where he was apparently looking at a framed print of a racecar driver Liv had never even heard of.

"Thanks for dinner." She kissed his cheek and then pressed her face to his. When she folded her hands together over his stomach, he covered them with his. He nodded, but he didn't say anything. Instead, they held onto each other and listened to some steel guitar.

She squeezed her eyes closed when his chest expanded as if he was taking a deep breath and gearing up to speak. But when he did, his voice was gruff and quiet.

"Is it ever gonna get better?"

Liv wondered what *it* he referred to. *It,* as in the constant clashes with her family, the constant bickering over their parents' estate? Or *it* as in the demons Liv was fighting, the ones she refused to share with him? (She couldn't name them; how could she possibly explain them to anyone else?) Or, was he simply referring to their marriage?

Because she had no answers, she smoothed her hands over his flat stomach and tugged at the tail of his Girard Drywall t-shirt. He shifted slightly on his feet as she unbuckled his belt and then twisted the button and slowly unzipped his jeans.

"Liv."

When she slid her fingers under the waistband of his shorts and cupped him in her hand, Wade hung his head and bit off a string of f words peppered with adjectives like holy and hot and sweet. She'd come down with sex in mind, though she'd assumed it would be quick. An easy fuck to get him off and ease the tension again. She hadn't let him make love to her in ages; since Asher Crowe had touched her, sex with Wade had been functional at best. Never sweet and never about anything other than the pay off.

Her knees were weak as she stroked him, and her stomach, her sex, clenched with need. She had left her panties upstairs to give him easy access. Now, rather than the quick, angry fuck she'd wanted, expected, she wanted more. She wanted his mouth on her. She wanted him to stroke her until the familiar orgasm burned through her and left her in tears. She wanted him to drive into her as she rode out the last waves of that orgasm, and she wanted to wrap her legs around his waist and squeeze him hard and make him come.

But maybe that was selfish of her.

"Livvie." He groaned when she wiggled her hand and then reached inside his jeans with her other hand. "What're you doing?"

She pushed his jeans lower and pressed her back against his. Her nipples were hard, and she wished they were naked. She needed the skin-to-skin contact.

"Olivia, don't start something you're not willing to finish."

She inched his jeans lower still and then dragged her fingertips back over his bare ass. Satisfied smile on her face when she felt him shiver, she molded her hands over his hips and then slid one hand back over his ass again.

"What're the kids doing?"

One hand still on his ass, she moved the other over his hip to his stomach and then she stroked her finger from the tip of his cock down to his balls.

"Fuck, Liv."

When he thrust forward, she took him, closed her fingers around his hard, thick shaft and stroked him. He twisted finally, determined to see her, to look at her. She let him, but when he reached for her, she shook her head and lowered herself to her knees in front of him.

"Not here," he said quietly, but his eyes were narrow and his gaze sharp when she took her nightgown off and dropped it on the floor at his feet. "You are so fucking gorgeous."

A jab of guilt hit her as she stared up at him from the floor of the garage. She fought to push Asher Crowe from her mind. Saw her husband watching her. He wanted her; he wanted her mouth on him. She could see it in the way he held still, like stone, to control himself. But in his eyes, she saw more. Wade Girard loved her. Did she deserve that kind of love, or was she just a foolish woman who had wandered and found herself in bed with a wolf who had the power to destroy her?

"Liv."

She stroked her hands up the back of her husband's legs and pressed her face to his thighs. She kissed him, simple kisses she dragged over his skin until she opened her lips and claimed him.

LIV FOUND A BOUQUET OF TULIPS ON HER DESK THE NEXT morning, and though they were beautiful and the colors were cheerful, she froze in the doorway of her classroom, heart beating in terror and her stomach filled with dread. She moved to her desk in slow motion, and several of her students crowded around her as she pulled the little white envelope from the clear plastic piece that held it. She had closed and locked her door when she left yesterday, and she opened the envelope with trembling hands, trying to puzzle out who the hell had a key to her classroom and who the hell would leave her flowers.

She had given Wade a blowjob in the garage the night before, yes. Naked, on her knees on a cement floor, she had wrung every last bit of the orgasm from him, and she had licked her lips as she climbed to her feet and then kissed him like a porn star. She had kissed him with hunger and need that she told herself she was faking, but when they heard the back door open and Grace yelling for her, and Wade had dropped his hands from her aching body, and she'd grabbed for her nightgown, she had realized she wanted to be with him, and, after hours of tossing and turning, she still wanted her husband with a passion she wasn't sure she had ever felt.

Wade might bring her flowers for something like last night. But he wouldn't send them to school like this and risk embarrassing her after what had happened in his garage. He fixed her coffee and breakfast this morning, and he held her a moment longer when he hugged her goodbye, but she knew the flowers weren't from Wade.

Her students pawed at her hands, at the card, trying to read it before even she could. She loved them, and she loved that they were so excited for her, but she was afraid the card, the flowers were a twisted gift from Asher Crowe. She knew there was nothing special about her fling with him, nothing special about her to him that he would give a damn one way or another if she wanted to see him again. In fact, Liv could probably point to ten different teachers or moms right here around school that were either fucking Asher Crowe or had done him at some point in the past. Still. Her open classroom door and the bouquet of flowers were a little too *Fatal Attraction* to her, and she braced herself, expecting to see a cryptic *A* or *Mr. C* on the card and wondering how the hell she would explain that to her kids. The card should say *Love, Wade* or *W* or *Mr. G*.

"What?" The voice belonged to Tye or Todd Wheeling; Liv

could *barely* tell them apart by looking at them. Twins, they sounded alike, too. "Why is she—"

Liv pulled her arm up and away from the kids and eyed them all with barely concealed frustration.

"Really?" she asked them. "It's an enclosure card with flowers, not a check from Publisher's Clearing House. Besides, would you want everyone hovering around you to read over your shoulder?"

Her students scattered and moved reluctantly to their desks. Most of them were whistling and catcalling, teasing her about Mr. Girard sending her flowers. The truth about what she and Mr. Girard had done last night flooded her face with heat and color, and she turned her back to them as if she simply wanted to move behind her desk. She heard one of the Wheeling twins say something about Mrs. Richards, and then she turned the card over and saw that it was indeed signed *Kristen.*

She took a deep breath and ducked her head. Stroked her fingers over the bridge of her nose and waited for the inevitable discussion. What exactly had Mrs. Girard done for Mrs. Richards that she should send her flowers? Men of all ages got a sexual thrill from thinking of women together, and though Liv didn't flatter herself—she was too old for any high school boys to crush on her—Kristen was both cute and sexy.

Not hearing the expected comments, but suspecting someone was whispering them, she looked out at her students and waited for silence. They all turned, finally, to look at her.

"Mrs. Richards and I had a drink together the other night," she told them. "She needed a friend. She was worried about a family matter."

It wasn't their business, but she thought maybe she could make an impression on them about rumors and also about being mean or bullying other students.

"What family matter?" Todd Wheeling asked her. Liv glanced at the flowers, overcome with regret that she hadn't been more sympathetic to her friend the other night.

"One of her daughters is having some issues with her friends."

"Sasha."

Liv turned toward the voice and nodded at Lily Patterson.

"Mrs. Richards was talking about that yesterday."

Liv nodded again. "It's hard. When your kids are hurting, and you can't fix it, it's hard to accept."

"Why can't you guys fix it? You're teachers."

Liv swept her gaze over the room and shrugged. "Well, yeah. But we're not Sasha's teachers. And we can't even fix it when you guys do something like that to someone else."

"What do you mean?"

"Kind of makes things worse, doesn't it? When an adult sticks his or her nose in to take care of it?"

Liv looked to her left when she heard the knock on her door. She smiled when she saw Kristen and started toward her.

"Gimme five," she told her class. "And keep it down."

"Hey." Kristen grinned at her.

"You didn't have to do that," Liv told her.

"I wanted to." Kristen sounded bubbly. Liv eyed her curiously. "I love you, Liv. And I appreciate that you took the time to go out with me. I know your life has been turned upside down lately. I feel guilty for forgetting that and dumping all of that on you."

"Oh my god." Liv rolled her eyes. She laughed softly. "Kristen, you didn't dump, and it's okay."

Kristen nodded. "Guess what?"

Liv watched her friend bounce a few times on her toes.

"I don't know. You got a check from Publisher's Clearing House?"

"What?" Kristen frowned. "No. Sasha signed up for some art classes. She'll be learning to paint—"

"That's great!" Liv's relief for Kristen nearly dissolved her bones. She wobbled on her feet.

"And," Kristen held up her hand, "she decided to try violin lessons. She's so excited."

Liv reached for Kristen and gave her a quick hug.

"I'm so happy for her," she said sincerely. "And for you."

"So maybe we can go out when school's out?" Kristen suggested. She squeezed Liv back, and when Kristen stepped away from her, Liv eyed her wearily and nodded.

"Sure. Of course."

"And we can get things squared away for you."

"What?" Liv laughed softly.

"I wanna see you happy again, Liv. It's been so long since you've been yourself."

Liv opened her mouth to say something, to argue, but what was there to say? She couldn't tell Kristen what was going on in her life. Some days, she hated that her sisters knew what she'd done.

"Sounds good." She gave in and backed a step toward her room.

"Holding you to it."

"Absolutely."

CHAPTER 11

"Who are those from?"

"Oh, wow. So pretty!"

Liv heaved a sigh of frustration as she backed out of her car and straightened up. Amber leaned around her and closed her door, but she still held Liv with that piercing gaze as if she thought the flowers were from the man she'd shared dirty sex and never conversation with. Liv glanced at Ingrid as the three of them started up the rutted grooves in the yard that had been the driveway all the years their parents lived here.

"Kristen."

Amber hefted her camera bag over her shoulder as they walked. Liv noticed the sun glint off the diamond engagement ring as Amber situated the strap on her shoulder.

"Why would Kristen send you flowers?" Amber asked, and Liv stuck there, lingered, listening for judgment in her sister's voice. At the same time, Ingrid was talking about how sweet it was that her friend had sent flowers.

Liv ran her tongue around her mouth, over her teeth, more to give herself time to think rather than sweep her teeth clean of anything green. She hadn't had green stuff for lunch anyway. She'd wolfed down a school cafeteria hotdog and applesauce and scalloped potatoes. Kind of a weird combination—the lunch ladies simply labeled the last days of school lunch as potluck—but it had hit the spot.

She was angry with Amber, but she was trying to parse out why. Was she angry that her baby sister was still holding her to higher standards and still disappointed in her for her infidelity? A little bit, yes. But, she couldn't jump down Amber's throat for assuming the flowers were from Asher Crowe, because her fear that he'd sent the bouquet just to mess with her had been very real this morning.

She suspected it was still anger, still a feeling of betrayal over yesterday. Over every day since Ingrid had come home, and Amber had started choosing time spent with Ingrid, or even time wallowing in the grief Ingrid had left her with, rather than spending time with Liv. Never before had they hung out all the time, but just watching Amber watch Ingrid, a little bit starstruck and infatuated, was like a twist of a knife in Liv's back. She would have given Amber anything she needed. Still would. But she thought Amber might die in need of something from Ingrid, before accepting anything at all from Liv.

They had left her alone for a while yesterday, after she got up and walked out of the kitchen. She'd gone upstairs to the bedroom she and Ingrid had shared when they were kids and sequestered herself in the large closet they shared. The door wide open, she had sunk to the floor and propped herself on the wall and finished her beer. She hadn't intentionally focused on anything, on any thoughts, but she had remembered tidbits of conversations between herself and Ingrid through the years. The day Ingrid had first gotten her period. The night she had lost her virginity, determined to keep it from Ingrid but spilling every awful detail the minute they were alone in their room. She remembered dressing for church and for proms and giggling together over stupid things, and it crossed her mind that she'd had the best of both worlds. A little sister to confide in, to be friends with. And then later, a baby sister to hold at a distance and withhold secrets from, though she hadn't done a lot of that when they were younger. What did a little girl care about her older sister's wedding night?

She had remembered, too, the long suffering and her mom's final breath. That she and Ingrid had been at her side, hand in hand, and they'd held each other at her deathbed and then again later at her funeral. They comforted Amber, but with the ease and familiarity of a second or third cousin, not their sister.

And in the years in between, when Ingrid was gone, Liv had been strong and stoic, and she had missed Ingrid. But she'd lived. She had been honored to be with Amber when Hadley was born, more than happy to babysit Hadley when she was little. Thrilled to catch up with Amber on the rare occasion her sister came around. They had missed Ingrid together, though when they talked about her, they rarely admitted that. They had taken their share of shots at Ingrid for walking out on their family, and they'd read her books more than once and spent hours over wine or beer discussing them. Liv wasn't sure about Amber, but initially, she had wanted to hate I.G. Arenson's books. She'd wanted to be able to rip into them and pick apart Ingrid's grammar. She had hoped to find holes in the plot, loose ends Ingrid had forgotten and left to hang. Two-dimensional characters who showed no growth through a story arc.

She had found a few typos in all of the books she'd read, same as any other author. She had fallen in love with damned near every character Ingrid created—perhaps those characters were Liv's nieces and nephews from Ingrid just as Grace and Charlie were Ingrid's—and even if she hadn't appreciated every plot twist Ingrid had used, she'd given in and admitted to herself that she was a fan.

When she had found her dad dead in the house, she'd run to him and fallen to her knees to administer CPR. But he was already gone. She'd called 911 and then Ingrid, and from the depths of her soul, she had blamed her sister. Not for Dad being gone or for Mom's death six years before.

But for leaving her.

For leaving her with the siblings she had never known as well as she'd known Ingrid.

Maybe she had a lot to apologize for. Mouth dry, Liv studied Amber's profile as they walked.

"What?" Amber sighed without looking at her.

Not ready to apologize, to accept her share of the blame for how they had grown up and for how they still treated each other as pawns if it suited them, Liv shook her head and looked away.

"I told you she was worried about Sasha," she said quietly.

"No, you didn't," Amber corrected her. "You told me nothing. As usual."

Liv bit back her reply, the reminder that Kristen Richards was none of her business. She breathed deeply and stared at the flowers she was carrying. She had decided to take them inside the house and give the place a little cheer. There hadn't been nearly enough in so long, except maybe Ingrid and Luke bouncing that bed as if they had been determined to break the box springs or jump to the moon.

"Her daughter was all excited about going to camp with her friends," Liv told them. They stopped at the door and waited for Ingrid to unlock it. "But her friends decided to freeze her out at the last minute."

"I hate mean girls," Ingrid mumbled as she pushed the door in, grabbed for the knob, and missed. They all cringed as the door crashed into the wall, and then they filed in quietly.

"I was a mean girl," Amber admitted. "I think."

"No doubt." Ingrid raised her eyebrows, but Liv saw her grin and realized she was teasing Amber.

"Shut up." Amber snorted and rolled her eyes.

"You think that dude made it to his car last night?" Ingrid put her purse on the counter and then stretched and yawned. Liv glanced at Amber to find her laughing out loud.

"I hope not. He had no business driving."

"You guys went out last night?" Liv asked quietly.

They didn't need to answer her; both of them clammed up and stared first at each other and then her, faces pale with guilt.

Liv nodded. "Thanks for the invite."

"Liv." Ingrid made a move toward her, but Liv side-stepped her.

"It was sort of spur of the moment," Amber offered. "You already left."

"Whatever, guys." Liv put the flowers on the island and took a moment arranging them in the vase to avoid looking at her sisters.

"We just grabbed a quick supper—"

Liv nodded and glanced back at Amber. "I have a cell phone."

Amber's eyes closed in slow motion. Liv swallowed hard and rubbed her face. Didn't matter. She had gone home where she needed to be. And anyway, there would always be times when they were together that Liv would feel slighted. Wasn't like she could play the poor me card all the time. Even though Amber did.

"I'm gonna go take a look at the garage," she decided, again only to avoid Ingrid and Amber. Certainly not out of any burning need to tackle anything in the rickety old garage, jam packed with junk.

"Liv." Amber reached for her as she slipped back through the kitchen, eyes on the back door, still open and resting against the wall. She tapped her back pocket and realized her phone and her purse were still in the car. She didn't care. She didn't need the damned phone anyway.

"Liv, don't." Ingrid's voice was small and quiet, and Liv closed her eyes against the mental image of a much younger Ingrid standing just inside their bedroom, asking Liv not to go out and leave her at home to be bored.

She stopped at the door, but she didn't turn to look back at either of them.

"You went home. Luke called me and said he was working late. Nathan and Hadley had already had dinner, so Amber and I went out and grabbed something."

Liv drew in a deep breath. She shrugged and nodded and reached for the handle on the screen door.

"You and I were always close," Ingrid whispered. "And you've been here with Amber all the time I was gone. Is it wrong for us to see each other? To want to spend time together?"

Walk away, she told herself. Just go outside and find something to do.

She dropped her hand to her side and then turned. She glanced at Ingrid over her shoulder, opened her mouth to say something, and changed her mind. Determined to walk away before causing another scene, she reached again for the door.

"Liv."

"We aren't, though, Ingrid," she said, facing the screen door. "We were close when we were younger. And then you moved, and we both got busy with life—"

"We talked," Ingrid reminded her. "We talked on the phone. We emailed. We—"

"Yeah." Liv twisted around finally, her knees weak, to look at her sister. Ingrid stood five or six steps behind her, Amber another few steps behind her leaning on the island counter. Liv let her eyes roam from Ingrid to Amber and then to the tulips her friend had given her. "Yeah, I guess. If that's how you define a close relationship, sure. We've always been close."

Ingrid was too sharp to miss the sarcasm in Liv's voice, in her words, so Liv assumed she simply chose to ignore her. She had chosen to ignore the feeling, the hurt Liv wanted to hide from them.

"And you've had good times with Amber." Ingrid shrugged. "It was dinner. It was an hour—"

"Yeah, Amber and I had, like, I don't know? Three good times. In all the years you were gone. And then there were the times Amber called me because she needed me for something." Liv lifted her eyes again to look at Amber. "Maybe I didn't care enough when we were younger. Maybe it was okay that you preferred Ingrid to me."

Amber flinched and covered her face with her hands.

"Fortunate for you that your favorite sister finally came back home, huh, Amber?" Liv took a step backward and reached for the door handle. "You don't need me anymore. I got it."

As she turned toward the door, she saw Ingrid start to move toward her. She catalogued Ingrid's hesitation and then Amber's sob—her face still buried behind her hands— and the way Ingrid looked from her to Amber, and she walked out. Without a glance at the door, she headed back down the drive to her car. Thankfully, she had pulled in last so she simply climbed in, started the Traverse, and backed out of the drive without another glance at the house.

Her hands shook, though she clamped her fingers tightly around the steering wheel. She hurt so deeply inside, she thought nothing would soothe the ache. Her babies couldn't touch it, not that she would want them to see her so devastated. She wanted Wade, but she needed the *old* Wade, and *she needed to be the old Liv* for that to work, and no matter that Wade didn't even understand the difference, she could *never* be the old Liv again.

She drove without purpose, without thought, but tears blurred her vision. She could see well enough to drive, but she felt exposed, cruising down Maine with tears rolling off her face. Kristen lived on the south end, and it occurred to Liv as she pulled to a stop at the curb in front of the brick bungalow that she hadn't called, and maybe she should have.

She sat for a moment. Focused on her breathing and swiped at the tears on her face, dabbed at her eyes. She couldn't ease the pressure in her chest or her throat, but she pulled her sun visor down and checked the little rectangular mirror to make sure she didn't look like a drunken raccoon with mascara and eyeliner smeared all over her face.

Kristen's car was in the drive; Mike's truck was nowhere in sight. She only hoped the girls were occupied, because she didn't want them to see her so undone. The thought almost made her change her mind. Kristen's girls might think she was crazy, and dammit all she probably was, and she might scare them. And besides, what right did she have to come here and drop this all at her friend's feet and ask her to listen? She'd been so distant with Kristen the other night, and anyway, Liv was in a mess of her own making.

The mess, the reminder of the mess she had made of her life, spurred her into action. She pulled her keys from the ignition and pushed her door open at the same time, climbed out before she could change her mind again. She aimed the key fob over her shoulder and locked the car as she headed up the front walk.

Kristen answered the door within seconds, which was probably a good thing because Liv had started second guessing herself as she walked up the porch steps.

"Hey!"

"Hey." Liv dragged in a slow, deep breath and felt her nostrils flare. Nothing else. No calming sensation. She arched her eyebrows hopefully and hated herself for coming here. "Busy?"

"Fixing dinner," Kristen answered simply. "Come in."

Liv nodded, but she hesitated. Looked over her shoulder at the Traverse at the curb and finally turned back to her friend. Kristen hung half way out the door, her arm outstretched to hold the screen open for her.

"Are the girls home?" Liv asked as she took the screen door and then followed Kristen inside.

"Nope. Playing on the neighbor's trampoline."

Though Kristen led the way to the kitchen and couldn't see her, Liv nodded anyway. She could do this. She didn't have to spill her guts. She didn't have to say a word about the way she'd wrecked her entire life with one foolish decision. She didn't have to tell Kristen she and her sisters were at odds. Again. She didn't need to worry about Ezra tonight. She could hang out here in the kitchen with Kristen and watch her cook and let the distance from her life calm her.

"That sounds like fun," she said without realizing she intended to say anything. "Ingrid and I begged for a trampoline when we were kids."

"Did you get one?" Kristen asked as she pulled the refrigerator door open. Liv was prepared to tell her no if she offered her a beer. But the pitcher of tea looked cold and inviting, so when Kristen glanced at her in askance, Liv nodded.

"Nope." She set her keys on the table and folded her arms over her chest. "No trampoline. Mom worried that we'd get hurt. Dad worried neighbor kids would get hurt, and we would get sued."

Kristen set the pitcher on the counter to take glasses from a cabinet. She shot Liv a small grin and shrugged.

"They're different now. With the netting around them and stuff."

Liv nodded and shrugged enthusiastically. She hadn't meant to lecture Kristen or warn her on the dangers.

"What're you fixing?" she asked as Kristen splashed tea in the glasses.

"Stir fry."

Liv took the glass Kristen offered her and murmured her thanks. She hitched her hip on the counter by the sink to stand near Kristen when she returned to chopping the vegetables.

"Your girls eat stir fry?"

"Yep."

"Wow. Charlie wouldn't try vegetables until he was thirteen."

"Does he eat them now?"

"Green beans." Liv laughed softly when Kristen cut her an amused look. "Loaded with bacon and salt."

"He must be eating something healthy," Kristen mumbled. "He's growing like a weed. Still."

"He likes meat," Liv answered simply. "Meat and potatoes."

Just like Wade.

She didn't say that, because the pain that ripped through her when she thought the words took her breath away. She loved him. Didn't she?

"You wanna talk about it?" Kristen asked without looking at her.

Liv pressed her lips together and looked out the window above the sink.

"Are those your flowers on the other side of the drive there?"

"No." Kristen didn't need to look to answer. "Driveway's the property line."

"They're pretty."

"Mm-hmm."

Liv swallowed hard. Thought about the flowers on the counter at her parents' house. Wondered what her sisters were saying about her right now. If they had given her a second thought. She would be inclined to say no, they hadn't, but she knew them too well. She had no doubt they were discussing her mess. Maybe Amber was filling Ingrid in on the gossip about Asher Crowe.

"How's Sasha?"

"She's good." Kristen's voice was full and firm, but she added a nod, and then she glanced at Liv and offered her a smile. "Thank you."

"Stop thanking me, Kris." Liv shook her head. "I didn't do anything."

"You had some ideas that made me think, and Sasha's feeling better." Kristen set her knife down and rinsed her hands off.

Liv took a drink of the tea and avoided her friend's eyes.

"Olivia?"

Liv shook her head quickly. "Okay if I just hang out here for a few minutes? Anything I can do to help you?"

Kristen turned sideways at the counter as she dried her hands. Liv worked hard not to look at her, not to meet her eyes, but she was drawn to Kristen's gaze.

"Hang out as long as you want."

CHAPTER 12

*S*he noticed his truck this time, but she didn't expect to find him in the kitchen. Obviously waiting for her. It wasn't late. Not by any standard. Not even five-thirty. The kitchen was lit with natural light, and she hadn't paid attention, but it was possible that the light on the automatic garage door might still be on, because she didn't think Wade could have beat her home by much.

"Where were you?"

His voice came from the far corner of the kitchen. Liv took a moment before answering him. She set her purse on the counter. Carefully put her keys there beside it. And wished she'd have just come home earlier rather than go to her parents' house. She loved her kitchen; the whole goddamned house was beautiful. But she would like that splash of color Kristen's flowers had provided right about now. She'd like that little reminder that she had a friend out there.

Was he angry?

He hadn't sounded terribly angry, but he sounded guarded, and his voice was gruff. Certainly not happy to see her.

She lifted her eyes to find him at the kitchen table on the

far side of the room. Still in his work clothes, old khaki shorts with the carpenter's pockets. Faded blue Girard t-shirt. She noticed the streak of dirt and sweat up over his left cheekbone as she made her way down the counter, stepping gingerly as if she would step on his heart or maybe even her own and add to the damage. Still in his work boots even, though the laces were untied and loosened.

He leaned forward as she approached the table. Rested his elbows on his knees and watched her with a wary, worn look. She smoothed her sweaty palms over her royal blue capris and studied him, not just his face, but the whole of him. A flash of last night hit her between the eyes, and she caught her breath, taken back by how badly she wanted him.

What would he do if she told him that?

"I was at the house, and then I went by Kristen's."

"Kristen's." He nodded and turned his head as if he couldn't bear to look at her a second longer.

She reached out and hooked her fingers around the back of a chair to pull it out.

"I got into it with Ingrid and Amber," she admitted.

"You're always into something with Ingrid and Amber."

Her throat suddenly tight with emotion, she sank into the chair and simply nodded. Wade glanced at her when she sobbed, but she pressed her fingertips to her lips to hold the rest of it in.

"What was it this time?" he asked quietly.

The knife of emotion still wedged solid in her throat, she blinked at her tears and shook her head. She wished he would move. Take her in his arms and just hold her. He wasn't aware that things had changed, and she was willing— just for now— to pretend that things were the same. But Wade didn't move, and Liv squeezed her eyes closed.

"Ingrid called me, Liv," he said quietly.

She turned a bit toward the table and propped her elbow

there. Rubbed her fingers from her lips, up over the bridge of her nose, and then her forehead.

"She was worried about you. Said you three had gotten into it, and you walked out. She called you. Texted you. And you wouldn't answer."

"It hurts, Wade," she whispered, still not looking at him. "It hurts to watch them develop a relationship."

"They're entitled to it," he reminded her.

"I know." She nodded. Tried to swallow again. "Still hurts...the way Amber begs for her attention. When I've been here. I never left."

She felt his gaze, heavy and intense, but she didn't lift her head.

"I tried to walk out before saying things I shouldn't." She rolled her lips inward and huffed out a breath. Lifted her free hand and swiped at her nose. "I need someone to get me, Wade. It hurts. Losing my family is so goddamned huge, and it hurts. I went to Kristen's."

"Liv."

She sniffled and finally raised her head to look at him.

"Do you hear yourself?"

She stared at him blankly, waiting for him to go on.

"Why didn't you call me? Do I not get you?"

She didn't know if it was what he said, his question. *Did* he get her? Hell if she knew. They used to be a team. These days, she was impossible to deal with—she hated herself most of the time, how could Wade love her?—and Wade was still back in the contentedness of their marriage, the slow dying of the passion and the adventure. Or maybe it was the tone of his voice. The hint of desperation, the hint that he wasn't as in the dark about what she'd been doing as she thought he was.

Or maybe it was the look on his face. A little bit shell-shocked. A little bit worn and sort of sad.

Afraid to answer him, no idea what to say anyway, she hung her head and covered her face.

"I'm your husband," he reminded her. "You couldn't come to me?"

"Wade." She sighed, but her voice broke, and she bit back a sob.

"What're you doin', Livvie?" he whispered. "Goddammit, Livvie, what're you doing?"

"There's nothing, Wade. Nothing inside me right now—" The dam broke, and she slumped her shoulders and cried.

"What're you doing to us?"

Their eyes met.

"What're you doin' out fuckin' around on me?" He started harsh; his voice sharp and angry, but it broke when he said *fuckin'*, like he couldn't bear the thought of her cheating. Liv flinched. Closed her eyes to hide from his pain. She leaned over and rested her head on the table.

She didn't have the breath or the energy or the guts to deny it.

"I love you so much."

He bit the words off as if it pained him to say it. She heard him move, heard him scoot the chair back to stand.

"I love you."

"Wade." She gasped when he dropped his hands on her shoulders and gave her a hard squeeze.

"When did you stop?" His whisper chilled her. She held her breath when he leaned closer to her and kissed her hair. Frozen, she listened to his boots as he crossed the kitchen. Heard the back door open and close and then she was alone in the roaring quiet.

She squeezed her eyes closed, determined to hold back the image of his face. The anguish she'd put there so carelessly. Tired of fighting it and losing the battle, anyway, she sniffled and blinked her eyes open. Still stretched out over the table, head buried in her arms, silent tears burned her face. She'd hurt him. She'd known it would destroy him, and she'd done it anyway. Even now, with Wade's quiet words sliding over her shoulders and curling up against her skin and chilling her, she couldn't go after him. She couldn't go to him and throw her arms around him, because while she felt bad for hurting him, she felt worse for herself. She pitied the cold, soulless woman she'd let herself become, and she hated that pity as she wallowed in it.

A long, low hum sounded somewhere behind her. Rather than startle her, it ignited a spark of anger inside her. Her phone. Probably one of her sisters desperate to make contact and make sure she hadn't wrapped her car around a tree on the drive home so they could go out and grab a drink when they were done talking about her at Mom and Dad's.

Why had Ingrid decided to call Wade? Why now? Why get involved? Liv didn't think for a second that Ingrid had hinted to Wade that Liv had been unfaithful. But her call had forced his hand. Or his mouth. To say what he'd apparently been thinking about for a while. If Ingrid had stayed the hell out of it, maybe she could have ridden out the rough spots, and she and Wade could have eased back into that sort-of-being-happy stage that had lasted for several years of their marriage.

She jumped when she heard the back door open. Figuring it was Wade, that either he'd come back to kick her while she was down or maybe to change clothes or pack a bag and hit the road, she stayed right where she was. Face buried in the crook of her arm. She did close her eyes again, wishing she could pretend she was sleeping.

The footsteps that approached her across the kitchen were too light to be Wade's, and for a second, Liv panicked. She couldn't face her kids like this. When it had been her secret, her own dirty little secret, she managed to box it away and talk to them like everything was fine. Now that Wade knew, now that she had stuck him with that knife and given it a little twist, everyone around would notice him bleeding, and everyone she loved would see the blood on her hands. She was guilty. She had torn her family apart. She was the bad guy, and she deserved the anger her kids would surely direct her way.

"Liv?"

Ingrid.

Still with her head buried in her arms like an ostrich with its head in the sand, Liv refused to look at her sister.

"Amber is a wreck—"

Amber. Ingrid hadn't come here to check on her. She'd come to defend their baby sister, because Liv had hurt her feelings.

"I don't really get why the three of us can't—"

Liv took a deep breath and lifted her head. She rubbed her face with slow, gentle fingers and wished the throbbing in her head would ease. Just one thing. If just one thing could go right, she'd be grateful.

"I don't really give a damn about Amber right now," she said quietly.

A glance at Ingrid as she flattened her palms on the table for leverage and pushed herself up to her feet told her Ingrid had been crying, too.

"What happened?"

When Ingrid stepped toward her, Liv stepped away, careful to keep the distance between them.

"Thank you." Liv swallowed hard. "For calling Wade."

"What—? Were you—? Where'd you go?"

"To Kristen's."

Ingrid bit her lip and then huffed out a sad sigh. "You walked away from me and Amber to go to Kristen's."

Liv shook her head and looked away. "I went to Kristen's to feel wanted."

"Olivia."

"It doesn't matter, Ingrid." Liv lifted a shoulder in a listless shrug. "I just need to be alone."

"Why?"

Liv flicked a glance at her, but she flinched when she saw Ingrid's eyebrows jump in alarm.

"He knows?" Ingrid barely uttered the words, but Liv still ducked her head and turned away from her. She stood with her back to her, hands on her hips, and concentrated on breathing. She couldn't have this conversation now. What if Wade walked back inside?

"Are you okay?" Ingrid whispered.

Liv hitched her shoulders and jerked away from Ingrid's hand on her back.

"You think—? You—? Are you kidding me?" Ingrid's voice throbbed with pain. "You think I told him?"

Liv lifted her chin when she heard the door again. This time the sound of Wade's heavy boots clomping through the mudroom was unmistakable. She waited, her body frozen, prepared for another confrontation and slumped with relief when she heard him on the steps. She turned back to Ingrid. When she saw that Ingrid was about to speak, Liv cut her off with the shake of her head.

"I need you to go."

"Livvie—"

Liv yanked her hand away when Ingrid reached for her again.

"I can't do this now." Olivia raised her eyebrows and rolled her lips inward. "I can't, Ingrid."

When her sister simply stood there, big eyes glassy with tears, Liv tossed her hands up in defeat and walked out of the room. Nowhere to go. No one to turn to. She went upstairs.

She wished she had the courage to talk to him. To explain. To make excuses. To say she was sorry.

Instead, she tiptoed down the hall to their room and stood outside the door. She watched to see if he was throwing clothes together, planning to leave her.

$\mathscr{N}$either of them spoke, but something in the way Wade turned away from the door and then sank to the side of the bed told her he knew she was there. She watched him lift his foot and tug his boot off. It fell to the floor with a muted thunk, and Liv almost opened her mouth to ask him what he was doing. His boots belonged in the mudroom, not up here. Her eyes moved over the back of his head and his hunched shoulders, and she thought he seemed smaller, a little thinner through the shoulders. She clamped her mouth shut and watched him take the other boot off and let it fall next to the first. Rather than look at him, she stared at the boots, one of them on its side, and remembered a night long ago when the kids were little and she and Wade had danced the night away in their bedroom. Smaller house. Smaller lives. Younger bodies and maybe younger, wiser hearts. If not wiser, then maybe simply kinder. Neither of them had yet acquired the careless, blasé attitude some did when marriage became mundane and even burdensome. They had laughed as he tugged her against him and wrapped his arms around her to hold on. He'd been in the process of changing clothes after work, and they danced to a stream of music on the clock radio. Liv had worn an outfit she had thought then was stylish, something she had most probably sold in a garage sale since then. Gracie had made a mess of her afternoon snack, and Liv remembered Wade licking his thumb and rubbing a smudge of applesauce from her chin. She had laughed at him, and the music had changed to something upbeat, and still Wade—in his heavy boots and cargo shorts, unbuttoned and half way unzipped—had held her close and slow danced her.

He glanced at her over his shoulder, but when he didn't say anything, Liv tried to breathe. She choked a little on the air, thick with tension, and suddenly, she felt a quiver of nerves in her right leg. Wade had just dismissed her, and she looked at her leg and noticed she was trembling, and her left knee—the one holding her weight at the moment—felt weak.

"What're you gonna do?" She found her voice, and she wondered if Ingrid was still downstairs and where the kids were. They interrupted every damned serious conversation they had tried to have in the past ten years, and they had hovered close enough to make sex a rushed, harried thing, and now when Liv desperately wished for a distraction, for that interruption, she and Wade were alone like they were the last two people on the earth.

Would she want him then? Love him? Would she know for sure, or would it be a forced choice?

She heard him breathe. A deep, harsh snort that she felt rip through her chest, slicing off a piece of her heart as it shot through her. She balled her hands into fists, wishing there was a safety bar to hold onto when your marriage was falling apart, and waited for him to speak.

He shook his head finally and then shrugged, and it was his indifference that clawed its way back inside her and grasped her heart and yanked. Did that mean she loved him? If she could hurt like that? Or was it just guilt?

And why, after being married to the man as long as she had been, couldn't she tell the difference?

"I dunno, Liv." He leaned forward and rested his elbows on his knees. Buried his face in his hands and then dragged his fingers back over his head. Liv watched his blunt-cut nails scrub through his short graying hair and tried again to breathe. Winced when she felt that sharp pain in her chest again. He shook his head, still hunched over his knees, and Liv heard him draw in a deep breath. Afraid he was going to speak, she turned to walk away.

"Liv."

Back to the doorway, to him, his voice chased a chill up her spine, and the hair on the back of her neck prickled. She stopped, but she kept her eyes trained on the plush sand-colored carpet in the hall.

He moved. She heard the swoosh of his body against the comforter and the quiet growl of the mattress as he stood. Still, she waited for him to speak. To say something. Anything.

Liv felt that same tremor down her leg, and the carpet at her feet tilted upward. She winced, heard a small sob slip from her mouth. She propped her hands on her hips and ducked her chin to her chest.

"What?" Irritated by his silence, his reluctance to say anything more, she lashed out, swinging and hoping to connect. "What, Wade? Say something."

She listened to him shuffle across the bedroom and wondered if this was their life. Would she be hearing that same shuffle when he was an old man? Too old and tired to pick up his feet as he moved from the bed to the bathroom? Had she broken them? Or would they stay together, suspended in this silence, as her punishment?

He still didn't speak, and Liv shot him a look over her shoulder. Propped in the doorway where she stood just moments before, arms folded over his chest, he stared at her, sullen and angry. It struck her again, that desire she had felt when she found him in the kitchen. Wade Girard was good-looking and a good man, and regardless of what was going on in her head, in her heart right now, she had most definitely loved him once.

"Oh, God." She turned to him. Hunched her shoulders and covered her mouth to hold in the cry. "Wade."

She wanted to speak. To talk. To say she was sorry. But the emotions—the guilt and the regret and the emptiness that might have driven her to infidelity—stuck in her throat, and she coughed and sobbed.

"Why?"

He barely moved his lips, and he spoke so softly, it was possible she imagined it.

She opened her mouth again; this time she managed to get his name out. She reached for him, shocked when he dropped his arms and stepped closer to her. The tears that streaked her face when he slid his arms around her waist were hot and sticky, and when he rubbed his chin and his familiar five-o'clock shadow against her face, she ducked her head and nuzzled her lips to his neck.

"I don't know what to say to you." He spoke quietly, his lips at her ear. Liv heard the desperation in his voice, but there was no hesitation in the way he pulled her tight against him and smoothed his hands over her back.

She slid her arms around him and linked her fingers loosely behind his. He was strong and solid, and it felt good to be there, to be in his arms. But she knew herself well enough to know how quickly that comfort, the feeling of Wade's arms around her, could go from good to suffocating, and she wanted to be ready to bolt. To hide.

He needed her to say something. She knew it. She knew how badly he needed to hear her say she loved him. But she couldn't. Her mouth couldn't form the words, and she still felt empty, and again, she wondered where the kids were. She and Wade wouldn't solve anything at the moment, with or without the kids around. And yet, part of her still wished for an interruption.

Wade shifted her in his arms. Moved his hand and cupped her chin to make her look at him. Eyes blazing with intensity, he stared, waiting for something she couldn't give him.

When he leaned in to kiss her, she closed her eyes, relieved to hide from him. He hesitated, and it struck her that she missed the way he used to do it. The way he used to take control and tease her and the way the gentle pressure of his lips would slide into slow, deep kisses that hinted at the way he would touch her, make love to her.

She missed it, and yet, she was the one who'd changed him. She'd taken away his confidence.

The house was silent around them as they stood together, their lips whispering against each other like two kids trying to find the courage to touch tongues. Like a husband and wife trying to find their way back to each other.

There hadn't been many kisses like this since she'd broken her wedding vows. Quick kisses dropped on her lips or more often, the corner of her lips, as she dashed away from him. Somehow slowing down and tasting Wade on her lips and tongue after what she'd done seemed more intimate and more of a betrayal than opening her legs to another man.

"Livvie." Wade curled the fingers of his right hand into her hip and yanked her against him, middle to middle. Lips open in invitation, a tiny sob slipped from her mouth and Wade pressed his mouth to hers and swallowed it. He stroked his tongue over hers, and Liv felt that hole inside yawn, stretch to be near him, anxious to be filled again.

"Wade," she whispered, and she smoothed her hand up over the soft t-shirt that clung to his broad shoulders, and again, she felt his desperation to hear her say something. To declare that she loved him, that she was sorry.

And again, Wade needed, and Liv couldn't give.

"I don't wanna lose you, Liv." He framed her face in his hands, and Liv was cold where he'd held her and then moved. "Tell me I'm not going to lose you."

"I can't." She drew back from him, tears blurring her vision. She shook her head and covered his hands on her face. "Wade, I don't—"

"Mom? Dad?"

Liv blinked and then moved her hands over his to wipe her eyes. Wade's hands still held her face steady, forcing her to look at him.

"When's dinner?" Gracie hollered from downstairs. "What's going on? Where is everyone?"

"We can't do this now," Liv whispered. She sniffled, and Wade kissed her again, a quick, rough peck on her lips, and then he dropped his hands, and she stepped away from him. Irrationally angry at Grace—she'd wanted that interruption two minutes ago—Liv hunched her shoulders again and folded her arms over her chest, needing the barrier between them. Wade stared at her and let her flounder in the silence that roared in the hallway now.

She took a deep breath and finally turned away from him. Her legs were weak as she padded back down the hall to the stairs.

"Where are you going?"

Voice caught in her throat again, in the mix of emotions, she only shrugged and shook her head. Chin down, she kept walking.

"Livvie."

At the top of the stairs, she turned to him. He hadn't moved.

"Are you going to him?"

Liv wondered if he knew who she'd been with. Rather than ask, she simply shook her head no. The thing with Asher had been over for a long time. Not that what they'd done had ever been about comfort or friendship or love. She wouldn't go to him now even if it hadn't ended.

"Is it over?" Wade scrubbed his hand over his head, drawing Liv's attention to the silver threaded through his hair again. He curled his fingers around the back of his neck and hung his head. "Can you at least tell me that much?"

She heard the TV downstairs. The ridiculous cartoon voices were like a million little ice picks in her skin. She shivered and rubbed her hands up and down her arms. How could Grace and Charlie be watching cartoons when maybe she and Wade were breaking too badly to be fixed?

That thought brought her back to Ingrid and Amber. Had Ingrid rushed out to tell Amber that Wade knew about Liv's affair? Were they kicked back swapping stories or opinions right now?

She tried to speak, to answer him. Her voice was so small, just a gruff whisper, and she said yes, and she saw Wade cock his head as if he couldn't hear her. As if he needed her to say it again.

"It's over," she said softly.

She held her breath, because she knew her husband well enough to know he had more questions. God yes, he would need to know more, and didn't he have the right to know? But she couldn't do this now. Not with *Spongebob* and Grace and Charlie downstairs and the worry over Ingrid and Amber pounding at the base of her skull.

He drew in a deep breath; Liv saw his nostrils flare from where she stood. She pressed her lips together, forced herself to stand up straight and take whatever he said.

But he only nodded. She watched him turn and disappear into their bedroom, and she wondered if he would sleep with her tonight.

CHAPTER 14

"*W*hat're you doing here?"

Liv jumped and smacked her head on the low, angular ceiling.

"Ouch." As she ducked her head and rubbed the tender spot, she looked back to find Ezra leaning on the rail at the top of the attic stairs. "Jesus, Ez. I thought I was alone." She moved her hand from her head to her chest and rubbed at the rapid beat of her heart.

"Sorry." He did sound sorry, and she couldn't help but compare her brother to her sisters. True, she wasn't around him often, but the lack of drama in the time she spent with him was appealing.

"You scared me to death," she moaned with a wince. Heart still pounding, she eased back from her knees and scooted around on her butt to look at him. It was late. Dark outside, and the dim yellow light cast from the plain bulbs in the ceiling threw shadows into the corners.

"What're you doing?" he asked again.

She held her breath, because she wanted to lash out at him. She wanted to be alone. She had walked out of the house, out on Wade after their—whatever that had been in the upstairs hallway—and because she assumed her sisters were back at home with their happy families, she had come to her parents' house. For silence. For comfort. She had hoped whatever ghosts were here would chase her own away, but she hadn't been here long enough to feel better yet, and she resented Ezra's company.

Rather than answer him, she looked back at the trunk she'd been looking through. She and Amber and Ingrid had gone through the majority of the attic, and there wasn't much left up here. But she needed a distraction tonight, and she had remembered there were still two smaller trunks tucked away full of her parents' things. Junk, she had discovered, but she didn't care. It beat thinking about Wade and the way he'd looked at her tonight. What he had said to her. That he didn't want to lose her.

She picked up an old plastic pitcher, faded from bright yellow to something close to beige, and held it up as if to offer it to him.

"Do you remember this?"

Ezra settled his butt on the top step and rested his elbows on his knees. He shook his head and then leaned over to plunge his fingers back through his dark hair. Liv felt a moment of concern for him, but his hands in his hair made her think of Wade, and she looked away.

"Mom always had tea in it," she mumbled. She pulled the white lid off the top and tipped the pitcher to see the tea stains. "Ingrid and I took it outside once to play with it. I mean, it's stained and gross. We figured it wasn't a big deal."

"But it was."

"Yep." Liv laughed softly. "Mom got so mad at us."

"Mom's temper never lasted more than five seconds," Ezra reminded her.

She looked up at him quickly. "Yeah, she mellowed by the time she had you and Amber. Not to mention, you were her baby boy, so you did no wrong."

"Except the time I snuck out and took the car—"

"You did what?" Liv twisted around to lean on the trunk, though she couldn't claim it was comfortable, and looked at Ezra. She rested the pitcher in her lap, fingers cradling it as if it were Waterford Crystal rather than generic plastic.

A sheepish grin crossed his face, and Liv noticed his dimple. Something he got from his father. She had been appalled, humiliated that her mother had had an affair and even worse, gotten pregnant as a result. When she was older, she had taken a closer look at Michael Seckman and decided he was attractive, and her brother certainly was good-looking with the best features of both parents. But the dimple and the reminder of the dysfunctional family she grew up in and the reminder that she had followed in her mother's footsteps for no good reason as far as she could discern made her stomach ache.

"My friends were all going to a party. And I wanted to go—"

"Don't even tell me Mom and Dad said you couldn't go." Liv rolled her eyes. "I think if you would have asked them to bring you Russia on a platter, they would have had it delivered with a sing-a-gram."

"Russia on a platter?" Ezra laughed. "What the hell is that?"

Liv was almost startled to feel the grin on her face. She shrugged and tossed her hands up helplessly.

"You know what I mean."

"I do," he admitted with another of those sheepish grins. Liv watched him fist his fingers, hands hanging loose between his knees. "But for the record, they didn't give in all the time, and they said no that night."

"Wait." She sat up and patted the old wooden beams of the attic floor.

"What're you doing?"

"Looking for a pen and a paper, so I can write that down."

"Shut up," he said without heat. "I got a D on a math test that day."

"Mmm." She nodded as she leaned back to get comfortable again. Sighed when she remembered that wasn't going to happen. "That would have done it."

Their parents had valued learning and good grades, so she wasn't surprised by what he said.

"I snuck out."

Liv grinned again.

"What?"

"Ingrid and I used to sneak out all the time," she said softly. She ignored the twinge of sadness at the thought of the bedroom she shared with Ingrid, the window they climbed out of so many nights when they were teenagers. Reminiscing about those days with Ingrid a few months ago, not long after Dad's funeral.

"You guys had a good window for that, too." He nodded.

"But we never stole the car."

"I didn't steal the car!" He put his hand up as if to stop her. "I borrowed it."

"Did you really think they wouldn't notice?"

"They might not have if I hadn't sideswiped the fence post at Tracker Farms."

"You went to Tracker Farms? Isn't that, like, an hour away?"

Ezra shrugged as if he couldn't be bothered with details like that.

"Scraped the paint down the side of the car."

"Ouch."

"You're not kidding *ouch*," he agreed, eyes wide like a child's. "Dad grounded me for two months."

Liv arched her eyebrows, impressed by the punishment. She had assumed Mom and Dad had doled out all the harsh punishments to her and Ingrid. She eyed Ezra silently as he ducked his head again and pushed his fingertips into his eye sockets. Did he miss Dad the way they did? How could she possibly ask that kind of question now when she had never taken the time to ask Ezra what he thought about his parentage before?

"What?"

She blinked and realized he had caught her staring. She shook her head and lowered her gaze, embarrassed to admit what she was thinking.

"You still haven't told me what you're doing here," he reminded her.

In response, she lifted the pitcher in offering again and half turned to look at the trunk she leaned on. She mumbled something about needing to sort through the rest of the junk, but her heart wasn't in it, and she knew when she looked back at him that he didn't believe her.

"Without Ingrid and Amber?" he asked quietly.

Unnerved by his direct gaze and his interest—concern— she drew in a deep breath and licked her lips.

"Does this hurt you, Ezra? The way it—" She stopped talking when she heard how ridiculous her question was. Ezra rubbed his hands down over his face and pulled the skin taut. He sighed and covered his mouth with his hand. He stared at Liv silently, his expression unreadable.

She squirmed on the floor and said a silent prayer that she wouldn't end up with splinters in her butt. She closed her eyes and wished with the fervent urgency of a kid that she could rewind and take back what she had just started to say. When she blinked and opened her mouth to apologize, Ezra moved just enough to speak around his hand.

"I'm sorry," she gushed as she braced herself for whatever he might say.

"Does it hurt me like it hurts you guys?" The only indication that he felt anything about her question was the slight arch of his eyebrows.

"Are you close to him?"

She flinched when he started to speak and stopped, choked with emotion. He squeezed his eyes closed and cleared his throat. The sound was harsh in the still attic.

"Of course it hurts, Liv." His voice came out sideways. "He was my dad."

She nodded and averted her gaze, uncomfortable with his grief, and guilty for not handling it well. She wasn't that close to her sisters, but if either of them were sitting here now, struggling with sorrow, she would move. She wouldn't hesitate to go to either of them and offer comfort.

"I'm sorry," she said again. "I guess I should have asked a long time ago."

"What? Which one of them I considered my dad?"

She groaned softly at his harsh tone.

"Don't mind me." She swallowed hard. "I'm fucking everything up these days."

She held the eye contact, but she wanted to run. She remembered then that she had come here to be alone, and another wave of irritation rolled through her.

"That why you're here? Alone?"

She nodded, but she didn't want to get into it.

"I come here at night sometimes," he said after a few moments of silence.

"Why?"

Ezra shrugged. "Just to look at all of it again." He raised his head and took in the exposed beams in the ceiling, the cobwebs strung from one beam to the next, the dust coating on the simple light fixtures. The dust on the bulbs themselves. "To remember."

When he glanced at her, she nodded. She could understand the need to look at, to touch, everything as if to claim it all, to memorize everything that would soon be gone.

"But why at night? Come when we're here," she urged him quietly. She had a sudden need to go to him, to put her arms around him, to know her brother as more than a kid who had grown up with the same parents, in the same house. She knew her sisters would feel the same.

"Right." He nodded and ducked his face behind his hands again. "You guys have more drama than the desperate housewives."

Liv snorted, prepared to argue, but she only shrugged and offered him a guilty smile when he looked at her.

"You might be right."

"I might be." He grinned.

"You're close to Amber, aren't you?"

He nodded. "I am. And no, I'm not sharing any gossip about her, so don't ask."

"Not asking," she promised and shook her head. She kept her mouth shut. Didn't announce that she was happy he and Amber had a good relationship, because that would sound sanctimonious and ridiculous coming from someone who couldn't even keep her own marriage in working order.

"Nathan's a good guy."

Liv nodded. "I like him."

"So's Wade."

She hoped he didn't see her flinch. Wondered how much he knew. Which of her sisters had told him.

"How's Samuel?"

Maybe she really wanted to ask how Shay was doing. She stared at her brother and remembered the lazy way he and his wife had danced around each other the other night at the house, as if they were too tired to make much of an effort at fun or flirting. She wouldn't ask. Not after she already put her foot in her mouth and asked if Ezra missed Dad.

"He's growing," he answered with a big grin. "Sleeping a little better."

"Good." She ignored the ache inside. Ezra's son was a beautiful baby, but at the moment, thinking about him made her miss that age with her babies. The tenderness Wade had shown them when they were tiny and breakable. The way he had doted on her when she was pregnant. The way he had held her and loved her through the miscarriage.

"It's a little easier for Shay." Ezra nodded.

Liv raised her eyebrows. Wondered if that was an opening to ask after her sister-in-law without seeming nosy.

"Is she doing okay?"

Maybe Ezra would think she was nosy. Liv was concerned. Shay had always been so vibrant and bubbly, and so far, motherhood had dwarfed her. She didn't want to see it, to see Samuel and his needs erase her.

Ezra sighed. Started to answer her, stopped and closed his mouth, and finally shrugged.

"She has her good days."

Liv bit her lip and told herself to stay out of it.

"Has she talked to her doctor?"

Ezra's immediate nod told her he didn't care to get into the details, so Liv turned her attention back to the trunk.

"Good." She nodded. "She'll be fine."

"Do you think so?"

She froze when she heard the tiny note of desperation in her brother's voice. Wondered if she should simply assure him that Shay was just going through postpartum depression and she would be fine. Or if he did want to talk.

"I do," she said quietly. "It's hard, Ez. Be patient with her."

"You dealt with it?"

She glanced at him and saw the hopeful arch of his eyebrows.

"Yeah." She nodded, decided there was no need to get into the miscarriage. She had experienced those baby blues when she had the kids. Maybe not to the extent that Shay did, but she certainly understood what her sister-in-law was feeling.

"I just—"

Liv licked her lips and waited for Ezra to say more.

"Is she taking anything, Ezra?" she asked quietly.

"What do you mean?"

"Did her doctor prescribe anything?"

"Shay hates medications."

Liv sighed and nodded. Of course, she did. She'd always been that way.

"I know. But it might help," Liv pressed in a softer voice.

Ezra avoided her eyes when she looked at him again.

"I'm doing what I can."

When she saw that he was looking directly at her now, seeking approval, maybe, she started to nod. Enthusiastically, at first, and then slower, and finally, she huffed out a tired sigh and studied him through a woman's eyes, through his wife's eyes, rather than her own.

"What?" On her knees now, she licked her lips and shrugged. "What do you do to help her?"

He blinked. Stared at her silently. She sensed that she had pushed too far, so she turned back to the trunk. She should go home. Didn't feel a damned bit better about any damned thing, but she needed to go home. She had to get up tomorrow. Pretend that nothing was different, even though now everything about her life was different, and go to work.

With a quiet groan, she eased her knees off the floor and sat back in a squat. After a moment, she started to stand.

"Watch your head!" Ezra warned her just in time to save her from hitting her head again.

"Thanks," she mumbled. She rubbed the sore spot from before and frowned when she felt a small bump there already. "I'm gonna go home, Ez."

"Everything," he said as she stepped backwards, shoulders hunched to avoid hitting her head until the ceiling was high enough that she could stand straight. She felt a cobweb stretch over her face, and she batted it away with a cringe. Glanced at Ezra as she rubbed her hands vigorously over her arms. "I do everything for her."

She nodded. "Good. Keep doing that. She'll come out of it."

Probably. Liv saw a little flame of hope flicker in Ezra's eyes, and as she moved closer to him, she watched it burn out. She said a silent prayer that Shay would come out of the depression, that she would find herself and remember that she loved her husband and bond with their baby. Not all women cheated, she reminded herself. Not even all the women in her family, because Ingrid and Amber were happy with their relationships, and both of them thought less of her for what she had done to Wade. Surely given enough time and understanding, Shay would be herself again.

"You sure you're okay?"

She answered with a quick nod, but Ezra moved quickly and snatched her chin in his hand to force her to look at him. The eye contact too intimate to bear, Liv closed her eyes.

"I'm fine."

"Liv."

"Come around more, Ez," she whispered. "We need you, too."

"Liv—"

She shook her head quickly when he dropped his hand. When she opened her eyes, she reached for him, rested her hands on his chest.

"I don't mean to put more pressure on you," she explained. "I just want you to know we want you to be part of everything we're doing."

The harsh lines in his face softened just a touch. Liv wondered how long it had been since anyone had loved him. She remembered she was in no position to judge Shay, because it had been a damned long time since she had loved her own husband.

"I love you," she said quietly. Ezra nodded, but her eyes flew over his face to the bob in his throat as he fought his emotions. She threw her arms around him and wondered if she had ever hugged him—other than those obligatory hugs at their parents' funerals—and decided she didn't care what he thought. Before she could move, she felt his arms slide around her waist, his face pressed close to hers.

"Love you, too, Liv." His voice was gruff. He gave her a quick squeeze and then dropped his arms as if to shoo her along. She stepped away without looking back. Made it half way down the stairs and stopped.

"Will you be okay?" Eyes on the threadbare carpet on the second floor of the house, she waited for him to answer yes before she moved.

CHAPTER 15

*L*iv's stomach fell when she turned the last corner in their subdivision and saw the lights on in the house. Of course, they were up. It was just nine; no one in their house went to bed by nine. Not since the kids had gotten older. Struck again with the memories of her babies, her throat was tight with emotion. Her cold fingers gripped the steering wheel as she tapped the brakes in front of the neighbor's house. Funny. From out here, the Girard house looked as it always had. People out here looking in would probably assume she and Wade were happily married and that Liv was simply tending to her parents' estate with a loving hand and heart all the times she left the house.

A live wire of nerves buzzed in her hand as she reached to open the garage door. She refused to look at Wade's truck, though it was there beside her car. He was home; he would be up. The question was what was he doing. She tiptoed into his workshops, uncertain about what she hoped to find. Did she want Wade to be in the house, pining away over her because she walked out earlier? Did she want to go inside and pick up where they had left off? Or did she hope to find him out here buffing out scratches in a paint job or detailing the hood or a quarter panel of his new baby? Did she want him to be indifferent to her? To what she had done to him? If he was working on his car, did it mean he didn't care? Or had his hobby, had restoring cars become a necessity for him, something he could control because the rest of his life had gone to hell? The workshop was dark and quiet, and she stood for a moment dreading the next confrontation.

Was that it now? Would every day in her marriage be nothing more than confrontations strung together with parental duties and professional responsibilities threaded in? She stood for a moment in the mudroom, eyes on Wade's boots, as she tried to puzzle it out. Did she want that life? Did she want to go on like this? The constant knot of dread in her stomach? Lashing out at everyone in her life just because she was miserable? Did she want to push through the chill in her marriage and find the love she and Wade had shared? Find more? Or did she want to walk away? What if she left, and she woke up every morning to a new life? One without the guilt. The dread. The sadness.

The thought shook her to her core. She sagged against the back door and wrapped her fingers—still cold—around the doorknob. Nevermind the fact that leaving Wade would ruin her relationships with her children. Life without him wouldn't make her happy. Just the thought made her chest hurt, like someone was squeezing the life from her.

So why did the thought of all the days she had shared with him, all the mornings yet to come when she awoke in their bed next to him—why did that not make her feel better?

She found Charlie at the kitchen counter, shoving down what appeared to be an entire package of Oreos. He flicked his eyes up from his phone and mumbled something around a mouthful. Liv nodded at him, though she had no idea what he said, and said hey and glanced at the clock. She felt a jab of guilt for not taking a minute to talk to her baby, but her mind, her heart, were both on Wade right now.

Still just nine. Tears of frustration burned up her throat, because she couldn't go to bed now. She hadn't been sleeping well. She sure as hell couldn't go to bed at nine and sleep until six. She wasn't sure what option that left, other than rambling through the house all night hoping to avoid her husband. Hoping to crash into her husband somewhere in the dark.

Her stomach a mix of dread and hunger since she hadn't eaten anything, she squared her shoulders and climbed the steps to the bedroom. Gracie's door was closed; Liv gritted her teeth against the sounds of Bastille played at concert volume. Relieved to find the lights off in the master suite, she ducked inside, dropped her purse on the end of the bed, and stepped into the bathroom, turning on the lamp at her side of the bed as she passed it.

Liv moved her eyes over the double sink she and Wade shared. She wasn't looking for things to be annoyed about the way she sometimes did. Dried toothpaste in his bowl and his comb or deodorant on the counter weren't such a big deal anymore. Not when you threw in infidelity. She just didn't want to look at the mirror. She didn't want to see her reflection, because she didn't recognize herself most days. Somewhere in the past several years, she had become hard and cold, and Liv was afraid her bitterness was starting to show in her face. Cold eyes and brittle smiles made even beautiful people ugly. What would that kind of emptiness do to her face? She kind of wanted to hide that part of herself from everyone.

Then again, that bell had been rung, and everyone she cared about knew what she'd done. Well. Not the kids. *God, please, don't let the kids find out.* She heard her own whisper, heard the catch in her voice. She hated herself for hurting Wade. For dragging Ingrid into her secrets. For disillusioning Amber. And coming between her sisters and their men, because she knew damned well they'd both told her secrets, and asking their guys to lie for Liv was wrong. Even lies of omission were wrong.

But it would kill her if her kids found out what she'd done to their father.

She slapped her palms down on the cool marble counter and lounged against it. Chin ducked to her shoulder, tears slid over her face. She wanted to break. To slide down the wall and bury her face in her arms and cry. But crying alone would hurt more right now, and she wasn't sure she wanted Wade to hold her. She wasn't sure she wanted Wade to see her like this. Over him. Over them. Drawing a deep breath, she lifted her head and finally met her eyes in the mirror. The lamplight in the bedroom spilled into the bathroom; half of her face was in darkness, the other in gray shadow. Her bloodshot eyes blinked back at her. Liv lifted her left hand and pressed it gingerly over the small knot at her hairline. She whimpered quietly. Dropped her hand to the counter again and considered Ezra. Did he know? Would Amber tell him? Or did he just recognize the walking wounded?

She wasn't, though. She couldn't be the victim here. She was the aggressor; Wade was the victim. With a long, low groan, she flipped the light switch and then leaned over the sink and splashed cold water on her face. She wasn't sure if the grit she felt was all in her head or if she still had the silken threads of a cobweb wound through her hair and over her face, but the cold water felt good. When she stood, she saw Wade's reflection in the mirror.

Startled for the second time that night, she managed to close her mouth on the yelp.

"Where were you?"

"What?"

"Where'd you go?"

Liv groped blindly for the hand towel hanging to her right. She closed her fingers around it and dabbed at the water on her face.

"I went to the house." She said the words into the towel, expecting them to be enough. Thinking that she would lift her head and find him gone as quickly as he had appeared.

"For what?"

With an irritated sigh, she slumped backwards and rested her butt on the counter.

"There's still so…" She stopped talking when she saw the mask of indifference on Wade's face. "To get away…from you." She spoke quietly, but her words were harsh and caused him to flinch. Liv ignored the little rush of energy the tiny victory brought her. Maybe ignoring it could make up for feeling it in the first place.

He nodded.

"Did you talk to Ezra?"

"What?"

"Did you?"

"How do you know Ezra was there?"

"Because I followed you."

"You—?" Anger shot up her spine like steel, and she straightened and took a step toward him. "You followed me? What the hell, Wade? What are you, like, a private eye now?"

"You're saying I should trust you?"

The trace of laughter in his voice zapped her, broke that spiteful pride in her spine. She slumped again to lean on the counter and braced her hands at her sides, the towel trapped under her right hand.

"Does he know?"

"What?"

"Does Ezra know?"

"No."

"Your sisters?"

Liv flinched and averted her gaze.

"Wade, leave them out of it."

"You dragged the whole goddamned world into this. Look at how many people you've hurt."

"What goes on between you and me is none of their business."

Wade's whole body sort of shimmied with his exaggerated shrug.

"It wasn't their place," she tried again. "To say something."

"I'm not blaming them, Liv," he said quietly.

She nodded and sniffled. Lowered her gaze to the tile floor.

"Did the kids eat?" She brought her hands together, left the towel on the counter, and picked at her thumbnail.

"We ate."

She nodded, curious but determined not to ask what they'd done for dinner.

"I put a plate in the fridge for you."

She lifted her chin and stared at him with suspicion.

"Why?'

"Because I didn't think you ate anything," he answered.

She shook her head and stepped away from the counter toward him.

"Why are you being nice to me?"

"I'm not being nice." He turned to walk out of the bathroom. Liv followed close enough to reach out and touch him if she wanted to. She didn't. Her eyes roamed over the bedroom, deceptively cozy in the glow of the lamp. The door was closed; she could see from where she stood across the room that it was locked. She swallowed a bit of unease and turned her attention back to him. Apparently she wore her uncertainty on her face, because Wade rolled his eyes and shook his head. "I put what was leftover on a plate. If you don't eat it, I will tomorrow."

She hunched her shoulders and folded her arms over her chest. On the opposite side of the bed, Wade began his nightly ritual.

"And I locked the door so I could ask you where you

were, and the kids wouldn't barge in and ask why I'm asking."

"Do they know where I went?"

He unbuttoned his cargo shorts and rolled his eyes again when she looked away.

"You had your mouth there last night, Liv." His voice was hard and cold, and Liv wanted to throw it in his face that she'd put her mouth on him, but he had been the one to react. He had taken her head in his hands, and he had bit off every curse word she'd ever heard and she knew a lot of them—she was a high school teacher, for God's sake—and he had thrust his hips forward, and he had blown his wad just as he pulled away from her. "Remember?"

She let her eyes travel from his face, down over his broad shoulders and his belly and stopped them at his zipper. She remembered. Hell yes, she remembered. Funny how she could be so...what was she? Indifferent? About what was going on? But she still wanted him.

"Do you really think I'd hurt you?" His voice was gruff as he kicked out of his shorts. Liv licked her lips and then met his eyes again.

"No." She shook her head. Wade Girard would never raise a hand to a woman or a child. He wasn't capable of inflicting physical pain on anyone.

Wade pulled the comforter back on his side of the bed and adjusted his pillow. Liv watched him, stepped back out of his way when he rounded the bed to duck back into the bathroom.

"Do they know?" she whispered.

"The kids?" he prompted her as he plucked his toothbrush from the holder on the sink. "Do the kids know you're having a fling?"

She winced when he peeked his head out the door to look at her in askance.

"Wade." She sniffled. "It's not…I'm not seeing him anymore."

"You didn't think he loved you, did you?" He pointed at her, toothbrush in hand. Liv swallowed hard and took a step backwards. She moved again and again in stutter steps until the back of her legs touched the bed. Grateful, she sank to the edge to sit down.

"No." Because she'd never entertained the idea that Asher Crowe might love her. He struck her as incapable of love.

"Guys like that don't love, Livvie. They're ruthless—"

"What did you tell the kids?"

Her small voice cut him off with the power of a shout. He stared at her for a long moment, his eyes locked on hers, and it dawned on her that he must know whom she had been with for him to say what he had. Somehow that made her indiscretion that much worse.

"Honestly, they didn't ask." He shrugged and stepped back into the bathroom. "You're gone all the time. What's another night to them?"

"I have been at the house with my sisters almost every night since—"

"I can't hear you." He raised his voice so she would hear him over the running water.

She swallowed hard, but the ache in her throat was stubborn and refused to ease. Her legs trembled beneath her as she stood and moved back to the bathroom. Wade leaned over the sink and ran water on his toothbrush.

"I've been at the house. Every night I've told you I was there, I was there." She watched his shoulders, his back, for an indication that he heard her that time.

He didn't react. Liv counted the seconds while he brushed his teeth, irritated with his ridiculous commitment to hygiene when she wanted to talk to him. She needed him to believe that she had never told him she would be at her parents' house and done something else. No matter what she had done, she hadn't lied about that.

When he rinsed his mouth out, she opened her mouth to speak again. Stifled a groan and shifted her weight from foot to foot when he made a show of rinsing his toothbrush and then wiping the counter down.

"Wade." She reached for him. Watched her hand, studied her wedding ring. Considering touching him. What it would mean. What it might lead to. Lifted her foot and hovered there in her uncertainty. Goddammit, she didn't want to lose him. But she wasn't ready to love him again, either. Not yet.

What the hell is your problem, Olivia? She squeezed her eyes closed as she brushed her fingertips over his back. His shorts hung so low on his hips that she saw the black elastic waistband of his briefs. His t-shirt had ridden up his back to expose a slice of skin when he leaned over, but she'd touched him higher. Safe spot. The soft tee a barrier between their skin.

"What?"

"I never lied about going over there."

Scared of what he would say next and pissed off at herself for her fear—did it matter what he said? Really?—she bit her lip. Her eyes devoured his every move, from the way he dried the bottom of his toothbrush before dropping it back into the holder next to hers to the lift of his shoulders and the way his chest and back expanded when he took a deep breath. She felt that dread deep inside rear its head again. No, Wade would never hurt her. He would never hit her, push her. But he had a temper, and he had lungs, and he could roar with anger, and right now, he had a reason.

Finally, he turned toward her and gave her his undivided attention.

"Does that matter, Liv?" He shrugged.

Her nose prickled with the need to cry. She pressed her lips together and waited for him to say more.

"I mean, are we gonna split hairs here and talk about just exactly when you lied versus when you were doing exactly what you said you were doing?"

She jerked her gaze from his and shook her head. He was right. What difference did it make? She had lied. Maybe not outright. Because she wasn't sure her husband had challenged her or questioned her even once on the nights she'd been with another man. She turned away from him as anger surged through her. As far as she knew, he had never noticed she wasn't around.

Still. Lies of omission were lies.

She sniffled and wiped at her eyes.

"How?" Back to him, she made her way back to the bedroom. Stopped at her side of the bed and pulled the comforter back. She glanced at his side to make sure hers was even, as if by making their bed more inviting, she could fix what was broken.

"What?"

"How did you find out?"

She stepped out of her sandals and then unzipped her capris. Too tired to undress—today might have lasted a week for all she knew—she perched on the side of the bed and looked at him.

"Tony Rice told me he saw you at a riverfront establishment."

The dread, guilt, shame shot up her throat, and Liv lowered her head and covered her mouth with her fingertips. It was one thing to hurt him. Another that her family knew what she had done to him. But for Wade to find out about her infidelity through a colleague was unforgiveable. She had humiliated him in his world.

"I'm sorry," she whispered, and though she meant them from the bottom of her heart, the words were inadequate.

"Was he talking about The Barn? Or the High Rise Inn?"

She swallowed hard, but the shame coated her throat, and

she gagged. The Barn was a bar and motel known for the sorts of encounters married people had with people they weren't married to. You could rent rooms by the hour or the night. Liv wanted to protest, to argue that she wouldn't be caught dead in a place like that. But she and Asher had fucked in the front seat of his car, his car parked right in front of her house one night because there had been nowhere else to go at the time.

"The Inn." She licked her lips.

"I would think he could have swept you off to Chicago or Manhattan."

"Wade."

"So Mr. Classy fucks just like the rest of us, huh?"

Liv turned her face away from Wade. She closed her eyes, his face, the inquisitive curve in his eyebrow, still in her mind. She groaned and shook her head, but her next thought was the way Asher had slapped her ass and driven into her from behind, and no, he didn't fuck like everyone else. Most definitely not like her husband.

"Nevermind," Wade muttered. "I don't wanna know what you're thinking."

"When did he tell you?"

"What?"

"When did Tony tell you?"

"This morning," he answered. Surprised by that, Liv looked at him again. He leaned on the door now, and she wanted to call him back, away from the door, in case the kids walked by and heard him. "I had my suspicions."

She stared at him silently. Wished he would have shared his suspicions a long time ago.

"I'm sorry," she said again. "I thought we were discreet."

Wade snorted, his eyes wide with disbelief.

"That's what you're sorry for?"

"I just…" She leaned, climbed half way over the bed, and started to stand but he shook his head. He didn't want her near him. "I just meant I'm sorry for you to find out this way."

"Yeah, it's a great day at work when a friend you've known for twenty years tells you he saw your wife getting out of a Mercedes with some stranger's hand on her ass."

She stood, but this time, she turned away from him. Pushed the capris to puddle at her feet. Shrugged her arms from her pullover top and then pulled it over her head and dropped it, too.

"Goodnight."

Her fingers closed around her nightgown behind her pillow. *Goodnight?* She lifted her chin and twisted to give him a sharp look. She heard the catch in his voice, and she knew he was raw and bleeding inside. She eyed him curiously, wondered if it made him angry for her to know how deeply she had hurt him.

"Goodnight?"

She heard the throb in her own voice and reached up to plunge her fingers through her hair. She cried out softly when she bumped the bruise on her head.

"What's wrong?"

She shook her head, but he was already moving toward her. Tears burned her face as he cupped her chin in his hand and studied the bump on her head.

"What did you do?"

"Nothing." She pressed her lips together and met his eyes.

"Livvie, did you ice that?"

"I'm fine, Wade," she mumbled.

They stared at each other for a long moment, and Liv thought again of how long the damned day had dragged on, and tomorrow was another day, and she had to play this all out again. They could never go back. Wade would never see her the way he used to.

She sobbed out loud, sickened by the thought. Sickened by her behavior. By the fact that it crushed her—took her breath away—to think he would no longer see her as his wife, the woman who loved only and forever him, and still, she wasn't certain what she wanted from him, for their marriage.

Had she inherited her selfish heart from her mother? Or was this simply who she had become?

"Goodnight," he said again, and she watched him leave the room, her vision blurred with tears and her breath stolen by the sadness, the loneliness that swelled inside her.

CHAPTER 16

*L*iv had assumed all through Gracie's senior year that she would cry at her graduation. Trouble was, she was so exhausted from everything that had taken place throughout the year, more specifically the past week, that she didn't. She was dry-eyed and distant all through the entire goddamned ceremony, and she was irrationally angry about it. She found herself inching away from Wade during the ceremony, arms crossed over her chest, shoulders rigid, as if her emotional freeze were his fault.

Maybe other parents looked at her and judged her as cold and unfeeling. Maybe the brittle smile she plastered on her face before they left the house looked more like a grimace, and maybe no one in her family gave a damn what she thought anymore.

The emptiness inside her had opened up and swallowed her, and she felt inside out. "Pomp and Circumstance" and the graduation march ripped her open, and Liv envisioned blood all over the athletic field. But there were no tears. Wade moved closer to her, no matter how many times she tried to step away, and his arm was heavy around her waist. She shot him a look once, one that others might interpret as a smile of pride or joy, but Wade had to recognize the panic inside, the way she was silently screaming for him to back off. The fact that he arched his eyebrows at her and squeezed her hip in a tight grip told her that he was thinking of the kids, and if putting on a show of togetherness was necessary, then by God, they would earn Oscars tonight. Gracie's beautiful face beamed with excitement, and Liv snapped pictures and murmured congratulations to other parents and her senior students who graduated with her daughter. But she didn't cry.

She couldn't. It figured the one time she wanted to cry, her eyes were dry.

Gracie drove her own car to the ceremony, and somewhere between the white graduation caps and gowns and the parents dotted in between and the flashes of cameras and phones and the stadium lights and the toothy smiles, they lost Charlie. Liv didn't care that he found a different, better—cooler—ride home, except it made for a long, quiet drive for her and Wade. She shifted in the front seat; the dress she had picked out a couple of months ago for the occasion tight around her middle. At least her heels—Gracie had picked them out and proclaimed them cute *for her*—were mostly comfortable. Still, she dropped her head back against the seat as Wade drove and looked forward only to getting home and changing her clothes.

The rest of the evening would drain her. The graduation party. Hard enough to have kids who were Gracie's friends as well as her former students and some future students as Gracie knew several incoming seniors, too, at her house. Wade's family would come. They had planned the party so long ago, and Liv had been thrilled then to think that Ingrid would be here for Gracie's celebration.

She had avoided Ingrid and Amber the last couple of days. In fact, she hadn't seen Ingrid since the night her world had changed when Ingrid called Wade because she was worried about her. And she hadn't seen Amber since earlier that day when she walked out of their parents' house and drove away, a bundle of raw nerves and hurt feelings.

Liv turned her head to look at Wade. Watched in silence as he navigated streets he could drive with his eyes closed. Did she wish she could go back to that day? Maybe stay longer at her parents' house? Have it out again with her sisters? Would that change anything? If she would have answered Ingrid's calls, would Wade have confronted her about what he found out? Or would he have let her go, let her spin her lies like a black widow?

Would that be better than this?

No. If Wade had kept his accusations from her, eventually, he would have made a fool of her.

The same as she had done to him.

She opened the door before he stopped the car in the garage.

"Did you get more condiments?" he asked as she scrambled out of the car and almost wobbled on her heels. She bristled at his question, because of course, she had enough condiments, and she bristled at his word choice because why the hell couldn't he just say mustard and ketchup like the rest of the world? She rolled her eyes and swung the car door shut.

"Yes."

Her legs ate up the distance between the car and the back door, but the door was locked, and she froze in her tracks. Rather than look at him as he came up behind her, she fidgeted with her wedding ring.

"That ring stays on your finger." His voice was low and tight in her ear. Liv hunched her shoulders, ice shooting through her at the suggestion that she would take it off.

"Wade." She touched his hand as he jammed the key into the doorknob, but he shrugged her off, twisted the key, and then pushed the door open. He stood back, waited for her to go inside. She glanced at the kitchen as she walked through the mudroom to the wide stairs, the polished wooden railing one of Wade's points of pride in the house. She needed to get things out for the party, but she had time to get upstairs and change her clothes first.

She wondered as she stripped out of her dress and kicked her heels off if a Sunday afternoon party would have been better than a rushed affair tonight. It was already nearing eight o'clock. Sure, they had all thought tonight would be better when they planned it, Gracie included, because nothing said *party killer* more loudly than Sunday. But she was tired, and she wanted nothing more than to put on comfy sweatpants and curl up in the recliner downstairs and stare at the TV or a book.

She jumped, yanked from her thoughts when Wade marched through the door. Her mouth went dry when he purposefully closed the door and clicked the lock.

"We don't have time—"

"We do, actually," he told her, and Liv flinched when he circled his fingers around her wrist and yanked her against him. "We have plenty of time for the kind of sex you've been giving me since you found someone else."

"Wade." She shook her head, but he ignored her. Didn't kiss her. He nipped at her neck, instead, the cords flexed as she threw her head back intending to say no.

"Do you know how gorgeous you are?" His whisper was hot on her skin, and his hands molded her sides and her back. He sank his fingers into her backside, cupping her possessively and holding her hard against his middle. "Do you know how it makes me feel knowing you let him touch you?"

"Wade." She swallowed hard. "Please."

She thought she meant to say no. To remind him this wasn't the time. Having this conversation was crucial to saving their marriage, but not with family and friends on their way to the house to celebrate their daughter. But when she heard her own whisper, when she heard the throb of need, she realized she had moved and her hands were wrestling now with his belt and the button of his trousers.

"You're mine, Olivia Girard." He ground the words out like he had a mouthful of glass, and he shoved her panties down over her hips. Liv's hands shook as she let go of his slacks and helped him with her panties. "You belong to me, and I want to kill that fucker for ever—"

Liv grunted as Wade spun her around to face the wall.

"Ever—"

"Wade." She bit her lip when he gripped her hips, steeled herself with her hands on the wall as he drove into her from behind.

"Putting his dick inside you."

She was wet, and she hated that she wanted this even though Ingrid and Amber would be waltzing in downstairs at any moment. They would let themselves in and turn the slow cookers with the maid rites on low, and Liv heard Wade's breath choppy and excited in her ear.

His hard thrusts filled her completely and then left her empty for a second and then he was back inside her. His fingers curled painfully hard over her hips. She took his anger, his aggression, and it fueled her need. She was wet and desperate for a release. Her breasts ached, her nipples stiff and sensitive in her bra.

"Do you love him?"

"No."

"Livvie, do you love Asher Crowe?"

"No." She pushed back at him, wanting to end the torture. His strong, steady strokes felt so damned good, but she needed more. She needed him to come, so he would do her. She needed his hands on her. "Wade, please?"

"Who, Liv?"

He was getting close. She knew him, his actions, well enough to know he was ready to explode inside her. She pushed back again, but he fought her. Held her hips firm as his strokes shortened and quickened.

"Who do you love, Olivia?"

She gritted her teeth, determined to wait him out. To make him come and turn to him. Ready to beg him to touch her. She loved him. Dammit, yes, she loved him. But she wasn't ready to give in. She wasn't ready to accept the happiness they should have in their marriage, because that emptiness inside her was still huge and dark and menacing.

"Olivia." He dug his fingers into the skin over her hips, and she cried out in pleasure and pain. "Who do you love? Are you in love with—"

"You, Wade." Her voice broke. "Damn you, I love *you*. I *love* you."

He let go. Liv felt his release, explosive and hot inside her. He leaned into her, trapped her between his body and his left hand propped on the wall in front of her.

"No one." He rested his forehead on her bare shoulder. "No one is ever supposed to touch you like this, but me."

She hung her head and closed her eyes.

"Wade."

He bit her shoulder. Not playfully. Not painfully. Again with the possession, she decided. Maybe he wanted to mark her as his. Maybe he did want to hurt her.

"Wade?" She reached back and smoothed her hand over his right hand, his fingers still curled around her hip. "Please?"

She tried to turn around, but he wouldn't budge.

"Wade." She threw her head back and tried to meet his eyes. "Please? Make me come?"

He didn't move at first, and Liv growled with need. Finally, he lifted his hand from her hip and drew a long, languid stroke up her side. Liv shivered as he gathered her hair in his fingers and moved closer to press an open mouthed kiss on her neck.

"We don't have time for that, Liv," he whispered as he dropped her hair and stepped away from her.

"What?" She turned around when he moved, mouth falling open when she saw him lean over to snag his trousers from the floor and toss them over the end of the bed. He padded into the bathroom in dress socks and a dress shirt, his erection gone, but his package still impressive. "Are you kidding me?"

"Ingrid and Luke are downstairs."

"You…you—? When you knew—"

"I fucked you," he said with a nod. "Is that how you like it now?"

"You son-of-a-bitch." She muttered the words, but she knew from the smug grin on his face that he heard her. He closed the bathroom door in her face, leaving her seething with anger.

Liv stayed on the go most of the evening. She wanted a shower after what had happened with Wade, and it was out of the question with guests already downstairs. She had cleaned up as best as she could and changed into something more comfortable, and then she stayed on the move. Easier to put it out of her mind if she was doing something with her hands. Easier to avoid her sisters, too, if she didn't stand still.

Thankfully, Gracie seemed to enjoy herself. That mattered more to Liv than anything else right now. These kinds of milestones only came around once in a lifetime and cheaters and failed marriages were a dime a dozen. Liv watched her daughter interact with her friends. She noticed Gracie interacting a lot with Jarret Conrad, which surprised her in part because Gracie hadn't really talked much about boys, and she hadn't talked much at all about Jarret. She stood with Wade's mom and his sister, beer in hand, and nodded along with their conversation, but she watched Gracie and Jarret, with a mix of joy for her daughter and envy for their happiness. She would never have considered herself a person to get caught up in the past, but since her dad had passed away, she couldn't seem to get her head in the present. She longed for the excitement and the adventure in Gracie's life.

She looked away when she zeroed in on Jarret's fingers framing her daughter's face and his lips grazing hers. Grace had been kissed a few times before; she'd told Liv about a couple of goodnight kisses, but that didn't mean she wanted her mom to watch it happen.

In her haste to get away, to stop seeing Jarret's mouth on Gracie's—she'd had him in class and it seemed skeevy now to watch him kiss her daughter—she excused herself, turned, and ran smack into Amber. Amber opened her mouth to say something, no doubt to remind Liv that she was the lesser of her two older sisters, but Liv simply shook her off, and hurried into the kitchen to find something to do.

With a hard heart and a stomachache, she started putting things away. Storing leftover sandwich meat in containers and putting clips on open chip bags. She wasn't sure when Ingrid had joined her, but suddenly, they were working together and whenever she glanced at the window—full dark painted it black—she felt guilty that Gracie's night was over and she hadn't enjoyed it.

Not that Grace would ever know that. Her head hurt, and Liv thought part of it might still be from where she whacked it so hard in the attic the other night, but mostly it was the tension. She and Wade had either tiptoed around each other the last two days or traded quiet, overly polite comments about the weather and the party and nothing about their marriage.

She was sore about earlier. Pissed at what he'd done, yes, but sore, too. She thought she might have a bruise on her hip, and it almost felt like he had left a mark where he bit her shoulder. And he had hit her in the pride and the heart, too. Smug and delighted to wind her up and walk away, leaving her panting and unsatisfied. The hell of it was that she deserved it. But part of her wondered how much she had to take before he decided they were even.

"Liv."

"Hmm?" She blinked the counter back into focus. Swiped at her eye and ignored the way Ingrid's eyes burned a hole in her back.

"We're done."

"Okay." She nodded. She held her breath, waited for the kitchen to feel different, for her sister to give up and leave her alone. When she finally heard the door open and close, she moved. The party guests trickled in a few at a time to thank her and offer her congratulations again. There were the expected comments about how she could laze about all summer now that the school year was over. Unwanted hugs and kisses from Wade's family.

Quiet ticked around her in the empty kitchen. Alone for the first time since Wade had used her upstairs, the sadness, the pain, rushed her and ripped her breath away. She collapsed against the counter and leaned to bury her face in her hands. A sob tore through her. She scrubbed her hands over her face and then stood up straight when she heard voices in the garage.

Ingrid and Wade. Laughing. She couldn't make out distinct words, but they were having a fun conversation while Liv was inside breaking into hundreds of little pieces that weren't going to fit back together again. She swiped her arm under her nose, grabbed another beer from the cooler, and slipped outside to the deck.

While the kitchen was clean, the deck was still dressed for a party. Granted, it was messy now at the end of the night, the way a girl after a party looked bedraggled—dress shabby and worn, makeup smudged—but it was enough to send another wave of regret through her. She had wished the night away, and now it was over, and she had felt nothing since Wade had walked out of the bedroom earlier. Nothing but rage and hurt.

Ignoring the crepe paper she and Gracie had twisted into ribbons over the tables earlier in the afternoon, Liv pulled a lounge chair to the far end of the deck and dropped into it, grateful that the charade was over. She had the entire summer to lick her wounds. The entire summer to hole up alone and remember just how to pull off a poker face.

She took a swig of beer and closed her eyes as she swallowed. Wondered if Gracie had left with Jarret. Surely, there were other parties going on right now, and Liv assumed her daughter had gone to at least one. That was a given. She wasn't thrilled about the kiss she had seen, but it could be worse. What if she'd seen Asher Crowe's son kiss Grace? What then? She gagged, her mind blurring images of herself with Asher, and herself with Wade earlier tonight, and then her innocent daughter getting caught up with someone like that.

"Are you fucking kidding me right now?"

CHAPTER 17

*L*iv sucked in a sharp breath, but she refused to look up.

"Olivia."

Ingrid groaned out loud, clearly frustrated. Liv sniffled. She would break if she tried to speak right now, if she had anything to say. She didn't, though, so she readied herself for Ingrid's tirade. After seconds, maybe minutes, when it didn't come, when there was only silence, she looked at Ingrid.

Their eyes met. They sky was the color of ink, a deep midnight blue ringed in black. The floodlight on the far end of the deck made Ingrid's eyes shine. It was either that or the tears. Tired, Liv looked away again. When Ingrid shifted her weight, she assumed she was going back inside or to the garage. Instead, she sat on the side of Liv's lounge chair, scooting sideways and nudging Liv out of the way.

"Is this about Wade?" she whispered.

Liv only stared at her. Ingrid put the bottle down on the deck and reached for Liv's hand.

"Do you really believe I would do that to you?" Her voice was a gruff mix of indignation and hurt. "Do you think I told him?"

"No," Liv said so quietly, she wondered if Ingrid heard her.

"Then what're you doing?" Ingrid squeezed Liv's hand. "You've been avoiding us since—"

Liv sat up and twisted around in her seat, suddenly sure that Amber was there with them.

"She went home, Liv," Ingrid told her. Guilt pricked her heart, and then she felt guilty for feeling more guilty than sad. Truth be told, she missed them. Both of them. But that didn't change the fact that she was hurt to be taken for granted. Just because she was the oldest sister didn't mean she was okay with being left out.

"She didn't tell me goodbye."

Ingrid's stare was heavy, and then she leaned forward, and those harsh, hungry eyes were closer, and Liv was suffocating.

"You mowed her over when she came to tell you goodbye. Blew her off and walked away without letting her get a word out."

"What? No, I didn't—"

"You did. I watched you do it."

Liv considered defending herself. Telling Ingrid she had other things on her mind, but that invited questions, and she didn't want to engage in conversation. Not with Ingrid.

"Is Gracie dating that kid? That kissed her?"

"I dunno." Liv shrugged. Was she? Had she been dating him for a while, and Liv was just too self-absorbed to notice?

"Are you comfortable with that?"

Liv blinked and looked at Ingrid with wide eyes. "What am I supposed to do? Tell her she can't date until she's twenty?"

"He had his hands all over her."

"Ingrid." Liv flinched.

"I know." Ingrid sighed. "It's hard to look at your kids, at

Hadley, and know what we were doing at their ages. And not worry."

Liv laughed softly.

"We've had the talk."

Ingrid answered with a wry grin. "What was that like?"

"Hell." Liv's grin faded as she considered what happened between her and Wade earlier. Things you didn't necessarily discuss with your daughter: how to handle it when your husband treats you like the whore you are.

"So. Here's the thing."

Liv watched Ingrid's shoulders hitch and her nostrils flare. She didn't want a grand declaration, and it seemed like Ingrid was gearing up for something along that line. She wanted to be left alone. She wanted quiet. She wanted to drink her beer. She wanted to go to sleep out here. Away from Wade.

She wanted. What? *What* did she want? If she could just figure out the answer to that question, she could stop dragging everyone else along on the Olivia Girard Misery Train, despair or bust.

She managed to hold in the frustrated itch that simmered into a sigh in her mouth.

"Ez said you've been going over to the house late at night after me and Amber are gone."

Liv ducked her head. Maybe Ingrid was trying to lead up to something nice, but what Liv heard was that she and Amber were still hanging out, with or without her.

"Liv, please don't do this." Ingrid's voice faded to a whisper again. "I came home to be with you—"

"You came home to move in with Luke—"

"I came home to be closer to you and Amber. I came home to get to know my sisters again. I came home to help you help her plan a wedding. I came home to spoil my nieces and nephew, because as you were so concerned about not so long ago, I can't have my own children. And yes, goddammit, Liv, that hurts. It hurts that I can't give him a child. I'm sick about meeting his daughter, because I want him to have a relationship with her, but I'm so envious I can't give him that. And—"

"Ingrid—"

Ingrid shook her head and held her free hand up to keep Liv from interrupting her.

"I came home because I thought you wanted me to be here. I thought I was welcome here, and now that I'm here for good, you're acting like a baby because I want to build something back with Amber, too."

Liv averted her eyes.

"Why are you doing this?" Ingrid squeezed her hand. "You know I love you. You know that. Maybe we've grown apart, but you know me. *You know me.* Amber doesn't."

"Do you know what it feels like to be used?"

"I'm using you?" Ingrid blinked and shattered the glass in her eyes. "Are you saying that—"

"There's a whole lot of everything and nothing going on with me right now, Ingrid."

"Yeah, and a week ago, you would have talked to me, to me and Amber, about it."

Liv closed her eyes.

"I was with her," she said quietly. "I was with Amber when Hadley was born."

Ingrid was watching her when she opened her eyes. She arched her eyebrows, waiting for Liv to go on.

"I'm sure she wanted you."

"I'm sure she didn't," Ingrid argued. "Not by that time."

"Only baby I've seen delivered." Liv sighed. "Sometimes I dream about that. Not Hadley…not the…birth. But the way Amber held my hand."

"So you don't think I deserve Amber's forgiveness."

"I don't think it's a situation that calls for forgiveness," Liv answered simply. "I don't think you deserve her worship."

Ingrid let go of Liv's hand and rubbed her eyes. "I never asked for it." She pushed her hair back from her face, drawing Liv's attention to the purple streak through her spiky bangs. "Ezra told Amber you asked him if he was grieving for Dad."

Liv flinched. "Unforgiveable." She nodded. "I know. The words were out of my mouth before I knew I opened it."

Ingrid pursed her lips. "Ez wasn't angry." She licked her lips. "He said it was nice that one of us finally acknowledged the elephant in the room."

"As if it wasn't a thing all through the years."

"The elephant, maybe," Ingrid said quietly. "But no one ever asked Ezra what he thought or felt about it."

"Yay for me."

"And Amber loves you, Liv," Ingrid continued. "I don't know why you have this warped thing in your head that Amber has to choose one of us. I don't know why we can't all get along—"

"Are you telling me you were one hundred percent confident and comfortable with me and Amber last January?"

"No. Of course not. I was gone a long time." Ingrid groaned. She sat up straight and started to move off the chair. Liv touched her arm, scooted sideways to give her more room, and finally drew her knees up to her chest. "But I'm willing to try to get through all of this bullshit red tape everyone keeps throwing up."

"So maybe you're the bigger person than me," Liv mumbled.

"And as far as worship goes, Amber thinks you walk on water, and that's why whatever's going on between you and Wade bothers her—"

"What's going on between me and Wade is none of her business."

"Except you made it her business."

"You did," Liv reminded her. "And nobody's perfect,

Ingrid. I'm sorry I can't be the picture perfect fucking married wife for my little sister. But to be honest with you, that's the least of my concerns right now. I don't give a damn what Amber—"

Ingrid shook her head slightly and lifted her hand, touched her finger to Liv's lips. Liv's heart fell to her lap as she waited for Wade to appear at her side.

"Don't say something about her you're gonna regret, Liv. Please? She loves you so much."

Liv held her breath for the count of three.

"My marriage is suffering, Ingrid," Liv said simply. "I know I've done this to myself. I get it. But right now, it's all I have time to feel."

Ingrid met her gaze. She waited for a moment, as if Liv might say more. When she didn't add anything, Ingrid nodded.

"If that's how you really feel…"

"Ingrid."

Liv scrambled to follow Ingrid when she stood up, but she had to climb over the lounge chair. She kicked her beer and had to stop and right the bottle. Thankfully, she had drunk enough that it didn't spill. Ahead of her, Ingrid swiped at her eyes as she crossed the deck to go back to the garage. Liv slipped inside and ducked into the half bath in the hall. She splashed cold water over her face again and then tried to hide the damage to her eyeliner.

Ingrid's face was a little splotchy when she joined them in the garage. Probably Wade and Luke knew she had cried out on the deck, but Liv knew she looked wrecked. She wondered as she moseyed up to stand by Wade—she left a foot of space between them—if Luke knew what she had done. She would never ask; she wouldn't ask Ingrid because to do so would be asking her to admit to breaking her trust to share something with the man she loved and to ask Wade would be asking him to say yes, he had been completely humiliated in front of his peers.

Luke stood with his arm around Ingrid, and Liv longed for the same sort of gesture from Wade. Instead, he offered her a smile that didn't reach his eyes and the reminder that he set her up and hurt her on purpose earlier this evening. Wade and Luke talked more about the cars in a recent movie, and then when the conversation turned to a thriller movie, Ingrid threw in her thoughts, and Liv was plagued with jealousy near hatred for her sister. Why could she stand here and speak so freely with Luke and Wade when Liv couldn't remember how to form words?

When Luke and Ingrid left, she and Wade walked them out. Wade reached for her then, but his hand was rough on her side. Her jeans had rubbed on that spot on her hip and now his fingers rode the same spot, and she wanted to smile at Ingrid, at least when they left, because the longer they let this fester, the harder it would be to scar and get on with it. But probably her face looked more like a grimace, and when they drove away, Liv wondered if Charlie was home.

She didn't want to be alone with Wade.

She was wrong before. He could hurt her. Not the bruises. Those were incidental; she knew that. But he'd set her up. He had used her, and that hurt more than anything he could do to her with his fists.

The sounds of Luke's truck engine fading in the street, she pulled away from Wade and hurried inside. It crossed her mind that she should clean the paper tablecloths and crepe paper and sagging balloons from the deck. Exhaustion won out, though, and she slipped up the steps to the bedroom. Charlie's door was open, the light off. She stepped inside, knowing he wasn't there. He had probably gone to a friend's house. She wouldn't ask Wade. She wouldn't give him the satisfaction of being the better parent tonight.

She didn't want him to see her fear, her unease, at being alone with him, either.

With a small, sad sigh, she stepped backwards out of Charlie's room and ran into Wade. Without making eye contact, she slipped by him down the hall to the master bedroom. The beer she had consumed—three, tops—burned its way back up her throat at the same time her stomach growled.

The house was so big with just she and Wade home, and yet, when he was beside her in the same room, it felt unbearably small and claustrophobic. She wished Ingrid and Luke hadn't gone, though it had to be awkward for the two of them with her and Wade's issues on display.

"Did I hurt you?"

Liv froze when she heard his voice behind her. She rubbed absently at her hip, and now she dropped her hand to her side and turned to look at him. Propped in the doorway, he looked to have aged ten years since the incident earlier.

"No." She shrugged and looked away.

"Liv."

She put her hands up to ward him off when he approached her. He held his up as if she were a wounded animal he needed to cajole in order to be rescued.

"I saw you rubbing your side a lot tonight."

"Wade." She pushed his hands away from her jeans, but he was determined and his hands were back at the button and zipper immediately. She held her breath as he parted her jeans and eased them over her hips. With gentle fingers he slid her panties down enough that they could both see the dark marks his fingers had left on her skin earlier.

"I'm sorry."

She withered under his gaze. Humiliated by the whole scene, she shook her head and planted her hand on his chest to hold him off.

"Whatever," she whispered. "It's not a big deal."

She pushed again to get him to back off and then grabbed her nightgown from the bed. Wade watched her as she walked into the bathroom. For the first time in their marriage, she closed and locked the door to keep him outside.

CHAPTER 18

*L*iv sipped her coffee as she pulled into the drive and parked just past the sidewalk. Just to be sure there was no room for either of her sisters to park her in, she got out of the car and eyed her back tires and the sidewalk and the space between her rear bumper and the street. Satisfied that she couldn't be blocked in, she reached back into the car, careful not to spill the coffee, and grabbed her purse. She eyed the house with trepidation as she swung her car door closed.

She had planned to get up early. Before dawn, really, and make coffee and come over here. There was nothing so pressing that crazy hours like that were necessary, but she wanted the solitude. She wanted sanctuary from Wade, from the ghost of Asher Crowe, although let's be honest, he cut more of a vampiric figure with his slim figure and tailor-made suits and that hungry gleam in his eye. She wanted to hide from her siblings in the attic. To remember them, rather than visit with them.

She had been awake before dawn. But the whole getting up and putting one foot in front of the other thing had been too much to process. It had been a restless night, and she had lain awake for a while, blinking at the ceiling as the dark bedroom lightened to gunmetal gray. She had dreamt about the party, about all of the disasters that can happen at parties, like running out of condiments and dropping the cake and forgetting to stock the cooler with beer. She had dreamt about Gracie's graduation. In that dream, Liv had fallen and sprained her ankle, and when she awoke, she assumed the dream bruise in her ankle related to the purple finger marks on her hip, even though that bruise wasn't really what hurt.

Wade had been asleep beside her, and she had been surprised through the night to feel his body there in their bed. He had disappeared last night when she went into the bathroom and locked the door. She had taken a long time to get ready for bed. She had even soaked in the tub, though not for relaxation. She had wanted to wash the sex away, and by extension, she had hoped to wash away the shame he had left her with. But it lingered, and when she had come out of the bathroom, gearing up for yet another argument with him, she had found the bedroom empty.

Rather than go to bed, she wandered the house, navigating by slivers of streetlight and memory, to look for him. When she had made a complete circuit and still not found him, her stomach had done a topsy–turvy spin. What if he had left? What if he had packed a bag while she was locked away in the bathroom trying to forget not the way he had manhandled her, but the cruel smile he'd thrown at her when he walked away from her?

Even the thought of him leaving for a night, for an hour, left her sick inside. What if he had driven to a tavern, and now he was bellied up to a bar, slamming shots? What if he tried to drive home? What if he found someone more appealing and more fun than Liv, and he was fucking that stranger while Liv was at home playing blind man's bluff?

She didn't believe that of him. Wade wouldn't hurt her that way. But then again, a year ago, she would have sworn she would never do something so cruel to him. Heart hammering so hard her pulse throbbed in her fingertips, she checked the garage for his truck.

And then she'd heard him. He was on the deck, and once she knew that, once she knew for certain he wasn't out somewhere looking for revenge, she wasn't sure she wanted to see him. She had hesitated in the kitchen, icy fingers on the counter where Charlie had wolfed down the Oreos the other night. Finally, she had tiptoed to the window above the sink and looked outside with reluctance that draped over her shoulders like a cape.

It had taken a moment for her eyes to adjust to the darkness, but the fact that she was slinking around in the dark helped. He was sprawled in a lawn chair, legs spread wide before him, staring at midnight. Liv's heart had hurt so badly, she'd found herself rubbing her chest.

He had cleaned the tablecloths and crepe paper up. There was no evidence of a party.

She had tiptoed back upstairs, certain he wouldn't come to bed with her, and when she turned over in the night and felt his thigh close to hers, she had been surprised. And a little bit relieved. Still, she'd been alone in bed when she woke up, and she'd reached for Wade's pillow and rested her head on it, searching for comfort.

His pillow, the sheets, smelled of his cologne and his shampoo, and Liv had closed her eyes for a few moments and tried to remember the last time they made love. When she couldn't put her finger on a specific memory, when the only things that came to mind were either her betrayals with Asher Crowe or forcing Wade to get things done quickly and holding him at a distance, unable to stand his gentle touch or his tongue in her mouth, she had finally climbed out of bed.

Since she had bathed the night before, she'd thrown on athletic shorts and a Girard Drywall t-shirt, skipped the makeup routine—too exhausted to give a damn what she looked like—and piled her hair in a messy knot on top of her head. She smelled the coffee before she got downstairs. Desperate to find *him* downstairs *with* the coffee and so afraid that he had already gone to do something, anything that did not involve her, Liv had hesitated on the steps. Her knees had gone soft, and she had eased herself down to sit right there.

She had everything in the world to lose if she lost Wade. So why couldn't she reach for him with both hands and hold on?

He found her there on the stairs. When she saw him standing at the bottom, she swiped at her eyes to brush the tears away and watched him warily, uncertain what he was thinking.

"I made coffee," he offered.

She nodded. Said nothing.

"Are you hungry? I can make—"

"No." She cut him off. She couldn't eat. Not now. And if she did decide she wanted to nibble on something, she didn't expect Wade to fix it. "Did Gracie come home last night?"

"No."

She winced.

"She texted you," Wade said quietly. "She stayed at Annika's house."

Relieved that Grace had texted, Liv took a deep breath. Wade had read her texts. Not that there was a single text on her phone that he shouldn't see. She and Asher had never texted each other. She'd never told another soul about it, other than her sisters. But it still rankled that Wade had picked up her phone and looked at her messages.

"Charlie?" When her voice came out gruff with emotion, she cleared her throat.

"He asked last night if he could go to Evan's."

She nodded. Of course Charlie had asked Wade if he could go to his friend's house. Because probably, Liv had been knee-deep in party guests she wished would leave or she had been in the kitchen wearing the scowl that seemed to be her new look.

"I've…" Wade blew a long, deep breath through his nose and ducked his head to study his boots. He was dressed for work. And he wasn't sure how to tell her he was going to be gone all day. Funny. He spent a lot of Saturdays working. Why would he think *this* Saturday would be any different? "I have a job I need to do today."

Didn't matter. She wasn't going to sit here at home anyway. Still pissed her off that he would be gone again on a weekend, but when he lifted his head and pierced her with that stare, she tried to soften the anger on her face.

"Okay." She nodded.

"What're you doing today?"

It wasn't that he asked that bothered her. It was that he asked *now*. After he found out she had been with someone else, he cared enough to ask what she had planned for the day. She thought about telling him it was too late to worry about leaving the gate open once a dog escaped.

"Going over to the house," she said quietly.

"You and Ingrid had words again. Didn't you?"

She shrugged, unwilling to admit just how badly she was handling every last thing in her life.

"Livvie."

She bristled at his gentle tone. Closed her eyes, because she felt naked and vulnerable. But she waited, arched her eyebrows, silently asking him to go on. To say something nice. Her hands shook with the need for him to say something nice. Afraid he would notice, she wrapped her arms around her middle.

"I want you to be happy."

His words were a knife in her throat, and she sniffled, but she couldn't speak. She wasted a few seconds trying to contain herself, and then she opened her eyes, afraid that he had gone. Still there. Rather than walk away, he climbed the first two steps and then hesitated, steely gaze heavy on her heart.

Suddenly shy and afraid of what he was thinking, Liv opened her mouth to chatter. She considered asking him what he and Ingrid had been laughing about in the garage last night, and she thought about asking him if he'd seen their daughter in a lip lock with Jarret. And then Wade climbed another step and knelt there in front of her.

Liv let her eyes close when he reached for her. She gasped quietly when his fingertips grazed her lips. Rather than worry about what had happened yesterday before the party started, than think about Asher Crowe's hands on her breasts, she concentrated on the sounds of Wade breathing. The feather light stroke of his fingers down her neck.

She opened her eyes when he kissed her. Surprised to find him watching her, she barely moved her lips to pucker up and kiss him back. He leaned forward and rested his hands on the step where she sat, one at each of her hips. Kissed her again. Soft, gentle pressure, his mouth warm and firm.

"I don't know how to make you happy." He said the words against her lips, and she almost laughed, because she sure as hell didn't know what she needed to be happy. She didn't, though. She didn't laugh, and then Wade trailed the tip of his tongue over her mouth, and when she parted her lips and he stroked his tongue over hers, she felt a rush in her belly and her thighs, and she tasted coffee.

When he tried to pull away, she lifted her hands to frame his face. Kissed him, wishing it would be enough. That he would just *know* she loved him, and that one day maybe she could say it again. That today would not be that day.

"Can I come by later?" he asked her.

"The house?"

He was calm, still. His skin was warm under her fingers. Liv hung her head, propped her forehead against his chin. How could he kiss her like that and not feel it? Her heart beat so hard, it hurt. Her fingers itched with energy, with the need to scrape through his hair and dig into his shoulders.

"Yeah."

Was he testing her? Or did he really want to come by? Did he want to see their progress? The lack of progress?

"Yes."

He nodded. Finally, he moved, and Liv shivered when he rested his hand on her shoulder.

"Did you tell Ingrid I think Amber's right about ripping up the flooring?"

The sarcastic laugh rolled out before she could catch it.

"No." She lifted her head to meet his eyes. "I might come home with my eyes scratched out if I suggest that now."

Wade raised his eyebrows, but he grinned.

"I hope not." He rubbed his thumb over her lips, and she knew the moment was over. She flicked her gaze to his mouth, wanting to kiss him again, but she let her hands fall away as he stood up. "Your eyes are too pretty to scratch out."

She rolled them and offered him a sad, lazy grin.

"What're you doing, Wade?" she asked when he backed down the steps. "I can't read you, and I'm scared—"

He stared at her long enough that she squirmed uncertainly. The nervous fire in her stomach raged higher into her throat. Not even the coffee sounded good now.

"I'm trying, babe."

Trying. Trying to forget? To hurt her? To keep her off guard? To forgive her?

"Wade—"

"I'll see you later, okay?"

Her eyes had filled as he turned to walk away, but she nodded and she said okay, and when she heard the door open and close and she was alone, she had climbed to her feet, and finished the stairs on weak knees and filled a travel mug with coffee.

"Are you gonna stand out here all day, or are you going inside?" Ezra's voice jolted her from her thoughts. She turned to look at him and then glanced at the street. His truck was parked in front of the neighbor's house, and she had been lost in thoughts about Wade, so no wonder she hadn't seen it.

"I don't know," she answered with a tiny shrug. "Are the wicked stepsisters in there?"

"The wicked stepsisters don't speak ill of you," he told her as they moseyed up the driveway. "And they aren't step-sisters."

"Right." She nodded. "And I'm the queen of England."

"Gracie's party was nice last night."

The party was nice, but Ezra and Shay had not stayed long, and Liv recognized the comment as his way of changing the subject. She wondered which of them was his favorite sister, but decided she wasn't going to ask. At the moment, she was batting zero on relationships and doubted she was anyone's favorite anything.

"It was." She would play nice with Ezra. And avoid her sisters. And wait for Wade to come by. Best plan she had for the day at the moment. Her phone buzzed in her purse as they neared the back door. Ezra offered her a smile as she peeled off toward the door and he went on to the garage.

"You've seen them in concert how many times?"

Liv steeled herself with a deep breath as she stepped inside. She rolled her eyes at the wonder in Amber's voice, but she pulled her phone from her purse and concentrated on it so she didn't have to look at her sisters.

"Five," Ingrid answered. "But twice, we were in seats so far away, the people on stage could have been…"

Liv looked up when Ingrid's voice trailed off. Their eyes met, but neither of them said anything. Ingrid watched her with a guarded expression, and Liv was reminded of what she said to her last night. That nothing else mattered at the moment because her marriage was on the rocks. Never mind that she'd been the one to wreck things, and relationships with siblings ranked pretty high on the give-a-damn scale, too.

Though Liv's eyes were locked with Ingrid's, she still noticed the way Ingrid's shoulders moved and her chest expanded even though she was trying hard not to show any weakness. Needing to take a deep breath was a sign of uncertainty at the very least, but Liv had no desire to dive right back into the battle. Instead, she lowered her head and looked at the text from Gracie. She wanted to know where she was, and that left Liv wondering where Grace was, if she had come home and wanted to talk about something.

Something. Liv bit her lip. *Not something.* Jarret. Jarret and a party and probably alcohol, though Liv had lectured Gracie on countless occasions about how reckless alcohol made a person and how decisions that might usually require a lot of thought might fly out the window if a person was drinking and Liv froze at the counter, struck with the question of Gracie's virginity.

Had it still…been in tact last night? Had Grace graduated from high school a virgin? Or had she slid right through that experience while Liv was riding her classmate's father in a rented bed with a time limit on the activity because she had to get back home to her family?

If she had graduated a virgin, did she go to sleep last night…this morning…still a virgin? Would she tell Liv?

"You okay?" Ingrid's voice jarred her out of her thoughts.

She nodded, typed out a quick response to Gracie that she was at the house, and then set her phone down. She took a drink of her coffee, saw that the flowers Kristen had given her, the flowers she had left here the other night when she left in a rush, sore at her sisters for going out without her, were dry and nearly colorless. She stifled a wave of sadness, ignored the way her neck prickled at Amber's stare, and swung her purse up to put it on the counter.

"Yeah. I'm fine." She prided herself on sounding fine. Wondered who Ingrid had seen in concert five times that had Amber so in awe and picked up the vase. Ingrid watched her carry it to the sink and dump the water.

"Gracie willed Hadley her lunch seat." Amber sounded reluctant, and Liv shot a quick glance at Ingrid. Expecting to catch Ingrid nudging Amber along with a nod, she was almost disappointed to find Ingrid's direct gaze staring back. "You know. That senior thing they do in the yearbook? Willing someone their jersey number or their locker—"

"I know how it works, Amber," Liv interrupted her. She flinched at her cool tone and clipped words, but she couldn't stop herself. "I'm a teacher there, remember?"

She heard Amber's voice, but she couldn't make out a word. Maybe she'd moaned out loud. Ingrid sighed impatiently. Liv tossed the flowers in the garbage can and rinsed the vase out.

"So that's it?" Amber finally asked her. "You're gonna hang over here and talk to Ingrid, but not me?"

Liv eyed the vase carefully. Save it? Pitch it? Didn't she and Wade have ten other vases in similar shapes and colors? The memory of last night flashed through her mind. The way he'd done her against the wall and left her panting for him. The grin on his face when she realized he set her up. That her sister was in the kitchen waiting for them to come downstairs.

The sweet, soft kisses this morning.

She cleared her throat and set the vase down on the counter. She didn't want it, but she'd toss it later with other things they pitched from the house.

"I'm not here to talk to Ingrid, either." She finally turned, skirted her gaze over Ingrid, and looked at Amber. "Except to tell you that Wade agrees with Amber—"

"Wow." Amber's eyebrows shot up in surprise. "Maybe I'm not the idiot little sister, after all?"

"Wade agrees with Amber on what?" Ingrid's voice was

small, no nonsense. Liv watched her inspect her fingernails rather than look at either of them.

"Ripping up the linoleum. The carpet."

Ingrid, still studying her nails, blinked and arched her eyebrows.

"So he's speaking to you?" She looked at Liv with only her eyes. "Or did he yell that to you from the other end of the hall? What, Liv? What's going on?"

"Wait."

Liv glanced at Amber. Her kid sister looked like hell. Her hair looked unwashed, stringy, pulled into a messy ponytail at the nape of her neck. The skin around her eyes was dark and pinched-looking. The rest of her face was pasty, and she had a headless horseman on her chin. Liv wondered if something had happened between her and Nathan. She dropped her gaze, relieved to see the diamond on Amber's finger.

"What's going on, Liv?" Amber tucked her hands in her pockets as if she'd noticed Liv look at her ring and didn't want the attention. The concern in her eyes, in her voice, might have been Liv's undoing. But her phone buzzed again, and Liv nearly lunged for it, grateful for an excuse to blow Amber off.

CHAPTER 19

*L*iv expected, hoped, that Gracie would say she was coming by. She wasn't sure if she wished that for selfish reasons, so Gracie could save her from her sisters, or if she just wanted to see her daughter, run her fingers over her face and down her arms and hold her hands and make sure she was okay. As if doing those things would allow Liv to know what exactly her daughter had done last night. Didn't matter, because Gracie's next text simply said she was home and she was going to bed.

Liv felt both sisters staring at her as she stared indecisively at her phone. Should she *ask* Grace if she was okay? Let it go? And trust that if Grace needed her, she would reach out to her? Or go home and check on her?

"Liv?" Ingrid's voice was closer now. Liv sighed and tucked her phone back in her pocket. She reached for her coffee, disappointed to feel that the mug was almost empty.

"Is there more coffee?" She looked past Ingrid who stood within touching distance now and winced when she saw that the coffeemaker was off, the pot on the burner empty, save for the dry brown ring around the bottom.

"I can make more," Amber offered, and Liv ignored the eager tone of her voice and nodded.

"Is everything okay?" Ingrid looked at her pointedly, and Liv wondered what she was getting at. Had Wade waltzed into the kitchen last night after fucking her and announced that Liv would be down soon, after she cleaned herself up? When Liv only narrowed her eyes at Ingrid, she sighed as if she was exasperated. "The texts?"

"Oh." Liv drank the last of the coffee Wade had made for her. A feather of warmth unfurled inside her at the thought of waking in the middle of the night to feel his body next to hers in bed. She rolled her eyes at herself—when had she turned into a lovesick teenager with warm fuzzies over finding her husband in bed with her?—and stepped around Ingrid to rinse her mug out at the sink. "Just Grace telling me she's home."

"She didn't come home last night?" Ingrid yelped.

Liv bumped the faucet and met Amber's gaze. Amber sort of rolled her eyes, but she caught herself as if she remembered she was currently Team Ingrid. Despite the reminder that she wasn't Amber's favorite sister, Liv felt her lips tip just a smidge with a smile. She wondered briefly what Ingrid would be like with a teenager. Maybe it was easy to be sancti-monious when you were backseat parenting your sisters' kids.

"She stayed over at her friend's house," Liv answered simply. She rinsed her mug out and set it in the sink. Skated her eyes over Amber as she looked over her shoulder at Ingrid. "And she did text to let us know last night."

"What's that supposed to mean?" Amber asked quietly.

"Not supposed to mean anything," Liv told her. "Just telling Mother Superior over there that it's all covered."

Liv reached for the dishtowel on the counter to dry her hands. As she tossed the towel down, she ducked her head and rubbed the back of her neck. Her head hurt suddenly, or maybe not suddenly. Maybe she'd had a headache since earlier this week, and she'd grown used to it and only noticed it now and then.

"Why wouldn't Wade be speaking to you?" Amber stepped behind her and sunk her fingers deep into her shoulders. Liv dropped her own hand, closed her eyes, and groaned out loud.

"God, that feels good."

"What's going on, Liv?"

"He knows," Olivia mumbled.

"Wade knows about—?"

"Like Ingrid didn't tell you."

"Ingrid didn't tell me." Amber huffed out a sigh and then gave Liv a final squeeze and stepped away from her. Liv looked over her shoulder at Amber and then glanced at Ingrid who was now bent over, elbows on the far end of the counter. "Why didn't you tell me?"

Ingrid shrugged. "Not my place."

"Right." Amber nodded. "Like you guys never discussed me and Nathan and my issues."

"Your abandonment issues?" Liv rested her hip against the counter as the coffeemaker started to hiss and thump its way through a cycle. "The ones about your favorite sister leaving you here with me and Ezra?"

"You are such a bitch." Ingrid rolled her eyes as she stood up straight. Liv waited for Amber to unleash her anger, but Amber only shook her head and moved in behind Liv to look out the window.

"Jesus, what the hell is he doing?"

Liv turned when she heard the sharp disbelief in Amber's voice. She leaned into Amber to look out the window, shocked to see Ezra going at the picnic table with a crowbar.

"What *is* he doing?"

"He can't do that!" Amber plopped her hands on the sink

and hoisted herself up to get closer to the window. "Ezra! Dammit!"

Liv saw that Amber intended to thump on the window to get his attention, but she needed her hands on the sink for balance. Liv thumped the window, but she only sighed and dropped her hand away.

"He's got earbuds in," she mumbled. "He's not gonna hear me."

"It's a picnic table." Ingrid sounded bored.

"Yeah, it's the picnic table where we used to have our afterschool snack when it was nice outside."

"Olivia." Ingrid shoved her fingers back through her hair. "My God, you can not be emotionally attached to every goddamned item in this house. The benches are pitted and worn, and the table has that big chunk off the end from that storm that uprooted that little tree by the alley—"

Liv stared at Ingrid silently. Ingrid sighed and threw her hands up helplessly.

"What?" she snapped. "What now? What?"

"Do you hear yourself? Ingrid, don't you care? Everything in this house means something—"

"We can't keep everything!" Ingrid argued. "We can not keep every thing that has some kind of sentimental value attached. Do you get that?"

"Do you?" Liv shrugged and shook her head. "Do you know what that means?"

"What?" Ingrid frowned. She narrowed her eyes at Liv uncertainly.

"Sentimental. Emotional attachment." Liv licked her lips. "Are you familiar with those words?"

"Sometimes?" Ingrid swallowed hard. "If it weren't for Luke? I think I'd move back to Chicago."

"Of course you would." Liv nodded. "You're good at running."

"I did not run!" Ingrid yelled. "Goddammit, Olivia! I got

married, and we left. I wasn't running. Why do you have to keep dragging this shit up?"

Liv's eyes burned. Why, indeed?

"Maybe you don't run, but you strike at everyone. You take everything out on everyone else. We get it!" Ingrid roared. "We get it loud and clear! You're not happy. Your life sucks, therefore you're gonna make us miserable and take us down with you."

Liv sniffled. "My life doesn't suck."

Ingrid raised her eyebrows and shook her head as if to argue.

"It didn't," Liv whispered.

"Then why are you so unhappy?" Ingrid swiped at her nose. "What are you so bitter about?"

"I hate that you aren't affected by what we're doing."

"That I'm not affected…" Ingrid sighed. The sudden quiet in the house was uncomfortable. Liv heaved a deep breath and considered going home. Except it wouldn't solve anything. Either the three of them—four of them if Ezra ever decided to get involved—needed to plow through this emotional baggage, or they had to agree to finish the estate and walk away.

The coffeemaker's slow, shrill beep pierced the quiet, and Ingrid moved first. She yanked a chair out from the table and sat down hard. Liv watched her lean forward and prop her elbows on her knees.

Beside her, Amber moved next, to pour coffee.

"I'm not unaffected." Ingrid sounded like a robot. "I'm just trying to be practical. This house is huge, and Mom and Dad had a ton of stuff, and we can't keep it all."

Liv took the mug Amber offered her. She moseyed over to the table and sat down at the opposite end from Ingrid.

"Ezra asked me about the picnic table," Ingrid continued. "He's not destroying the frame. He's redoing the table and the benches. So it'll look better and be sturdier, and no one will have to pick splinters out of their ass when they sit on it."

"Maybe he should be concentrating on the garage first," Liv suggested.

"Yeah, maybe so." Ingrid shrugged. She moved only her eyes to watch Amber approach hesitantly and set her mug on the table. "Then again, if you guys are gonna redo the whole house, sounds like he's got all the time in the world."

Liv pulled her feet up to her seat and curled her toes around the edge of her chair.

"I told Wade you'd probably scratch my eyes out if I said anything."

Without looking her way, Ingrid shook her head. "Too girly. I'd just hit you in the nose."

"Great." Liv sipped her coffee and cut loose a low moan of appreciation. "Thanks, Amber. I needed this."

"Is that it? Are you gonna play nice now?"

"No." Liv shrugged when Ingrid glanced at her.

"Are you okay?" Ingrid asked after a few moments of silence. Liv pressed her lips together when she remembered the rest of her life, everything outside of this room. Her daughter who might have experienced more than one rite of passage last night. Her husband who knew she had cheated, who had used her and then taunted her last evening and then said sweet things and offered her gentle kisses this morning.

"I dunno."

A sudden flash of movement reminded Liv that Amber was in the room with them. She lifted her eyes and watched Amber hoist herself up to sit on the counter. Considered a caustic remark about being a rebel, but she decided against it. And then she had to stop herself from preening over the fact that she had taken the moral high road. Once.

"How did he find out?" Amber kept her eyes on her own mug. Liv's eyes were drawn to the ring her little sister now wore. She was engaged, and that meant there would be a wedding, which meant there would be a maid of honor. Liv's chest ached at how that would go. Of course, Amber would choose Ingrid. Unless she felt guilty after how Liv had behaved lately and asked Liv, in which case they would all be miserable. Again.

"She thinks I told him."

"Did you?" Amber shot Ingrid a look of alarm.

"Wow." Ingrid laughed humorlessly. "No. I wouldn't do that to either of you. Nice to know you think so little of me."

"I don't think you told him." Liv wrapped her hands around her mug. "I never thought that."

"You were angry with me for calling him—"

"Why did you call Wade?" Amber asked Ingrid.

"The day…" Ingrid waved her hand at Liv dismissively. "The day Liv got mad and walked out. When we couldn't get a hold of her." She shrugged and finally sat up straight. She reached for her mug, but she hesitated. "I was worried about her, so I called Wade."

"What was the purpose of that call?" Liv frowned.

"I have never told your secrets," Ingrid whispered. "I kept this from Luke—"

"I know that." Liv studied the rim of her mug, the black liquid inside it. A wave of warmth slipped through her chest to her belly at Ingrid's words. She hadn't told Luke. But she felt guilty, too, for being a reason Ingrid would hide something from Luke, so she pretended to be unaffected. "I know that neither of you would say anything to Wade."

"I called because you wouldn't pick up your phone." Ingrid sounded sad. "I didn't know where you went. I knew you were pissed—"

"I wasn't pissed, Ingrid," Liv argued.

"Right."

"I was hurt."

"Liv—"

The shrill squeal of the screen door cut Amber off. Liv

watched her sister twist around to see who had come inside and thought again about how her dad would read Amber the riot act for sitting on the counter.

"Hey."

"Your dad would have a fit if he saw you sitting up there."

Wade's voice was like a drug the way it warmed her blood and took her breath away.

"So Liv keeps reminding me."

Amber's happy grin was a knife in Liv's back.

"You ladies are killing it in here." Wade appeared at the end of the counter. He threw a smile out toward Ingrid. Kept it in place when he looked at Liv, but she noticed it cool significantly. She sucked in a sharp breath and tried to smile back. "Ezra's working his ass off out there."

"First time for everything," Ingrid mumbled. She didn't crack a smile, but Liv caught her wink. If Liv had said it, Amber probably would have launched herself off the counter at her to defend Ezra. But Amber only laughed at Ingrid.

"More coffee?" Wade asked Liv in disbelief. He leaned on the end of the counter, and Liv felt a wave of jealousy that he chose to stay there by her sister instead of coming over to be near her. Aware of how ridiculous it was to feel that way, she opened her mouth to offer him some, but Amber beat her to it.

"Thanks," he said with a slight shake of his head, "but, no."

"Luke and I watched that movie last night when we got home," Ingrid told him. Liv watched the two of them talking, again struck with jealousy. Why could her sisters talk to him when she was sitting here struggling over every word she might say? She drank her coffee, told herself to be happy that he'd come by as he said he would. He seemed happy. Like the old Wade. It was only when he looked at her that she could see the lines around his eyes and the sadness, the disappointment she had drawn on his skin this past week.

"Gracie's home," he told Liv when the movie conversation wound down. Liv nodded.

"She texted me."

"Said she was gonna go to bed. They were up all night."

Liv wondered who *they* were, and she wondered why Gracie had fed Wade more details than she had Liv, and she was keenly aware of both Ingrid and Amber watching them with sharp eyes.

"I'm glad she had fun," she said quietly, hoping like hell that Grace had had fun. What if she hadn't? What if she'd told Wade it had been a horrible, long night and she and Annika had argued? Or what if Jarret had been there and pushed—

"Those were the days," he said with an ornery grin, and Liv wondered if he was referring to the things they used to do when her parents were at home pretending to believe they weren't doing bad things or if he was just saying in general how youth is more fun in retrospect.

"So you really think we need to pull the linoleum up in here?" Ingrid asked him. Liv watched her climb to her feet and snatch her coffee from the table and wander into the corner tamping down the curling edge of the very same linoleum she was defending.

Wade grinned back at Ingrid when she glanced at him sheepishly.

"It's bad, guys." He shrugged. "I mean, you haven't even considered the appraisal. Buyers are gonna want a termite inspection done. When's the last time anyone saw the flooring under the linoleum?"

"I think Liv was, like, three?" Ingrid closed one eye as if it would help her think. Liv laughed with her, but her heart wasn't in it. It hadn't even been a week, and already this game with Wade was wearing her out. He couldn't just forget it. Not yet. Too soon. Too easy. She would be suspicious if he did. But it hurt to watch him stand here with her sisters and carry on as if their marriage wasn't hanging by a thread.

"Mom wanted something new," Amber mumbled.

"What?" Liv moved so quickly to look at Amber that she splashed coffee over the rim of her mug.

"She wanted tile." Amber sighed. "Dad said no."

"When?"

"Mmm." Amber pursed her lips to consider. "I was fourteen or fifteen the first time she mentioned it."

"Why would Dad say no?" Ingrid asked her.

"Same reason he never poured a cement driveway. Same reason the garage looks like it's gonna collapse?"

Ingrid looked at Liv.

"You saying Dad was tight?"

Liv snorted and rolled her eyes.

"I'm just saying I think it's worth considering." Wade propped his hand on his hip, his fingers looped in the tool belt he still wore. Liv let her eyes slide down over his cargo shorts, over the zipper, down his legs, and then over his boots. Cheeks warm because she knew one of them was watching her, she took another drink and looked at the spot in the corner that Ingrid was trying to stomp down into place.

"We can vote on it," Amber suggested.

"Yeah, and Liv's gonna kiss your ass now, and we're gonna pour our life savings into fixing the house up just so we can sell it."

"Ezra gets a vote," Amber reminded her.

"Why would you say that?" Liv asked Ingrid. "We finally have a civil conversation, and you have to start this all over again?"

"You think for one minute I'm stupid enough to think you're over it?" Ingrid looked at her like she was nuts. "We still haven't gotten to the heart of why you stormed out of here the other day."

CHAPTER 20

"Walk me out, Liv?" Wade's quiet words were a lifeline. For a second. As soon as she crossed the kitchen to lead him out of the house, she decided she'd grabbed a shark in the water to keep from drowning. She'd carried her coffee with her, and when they stopped at Wade's truck—parked right behind her, his tailgate in the street—she wished she would have left it inside. Not that she wanted to touch him.

Well, she did. She wanted to throw her arms around him and hang on, but she wasn't sure he would welcome the intimate touch, and so she crossed her free arm over her middle. Rather than look at him, she eyed his truck, so close to her Traverse, the bumpers were almost kissing.

"I didn't hit your car," he promised her. She started to argue, to tell him of course he didn't hit her car, because they paid bills together and who the hell wanted to deal with scratches and dents and insurance claims. But she stopped herself and then again found herself nearly preening for keeping her mouth shut. She was behaving ridiculously.

"I know." She nodded.

For a moment, the way his truck was pulled in so tight

behind her car made her think of the way he'd taken her last night. It still galled her that he had turned her on like that. Rough hands. Hard, fast moves. If she would have known he intended to humiliate her as he had, she would have taken care of herself.

"You doin' okay?"

She dragged her eyes from the grill of his truck to look at him.

"Sure, Wade. Doin' great."

"Things were a little tense in there."

Her eyes fluttered closed when he linked his fingers at the back of her neck and rested his arms on her shoulders.

"Aren't they always?" she mumbled.

"Are they?"

She blinked when he pulled her just close enough to rub his chin against her forehead.

"What?"

"You know what?"

Liv drew away from him and shook her head, wondering what he was getting at.

"The only times I've seen you truly happy lately is with your sisters."

"Wade—" She started to deny it, but the words caught in her throat. Shouldn't she say that he made her happy? Surely there were times in the past few months that Wade had made her happy, weren't there?

"They make you laugh." His voice was gruff. Liv pressed her lips together as he cupped her chin in his hand. "They make me remember the woman I fell in love with."

"I don't know where that woman is anymore, Wade."

"I see her." He stroked his thumb over her lower lip. "Now and then, I see her."

She huffed out a breath and winced at the sharp pain in her chest.

"She's gonna ask Ingrid to be her maid of honor." She

frowned at the catch her in voice. "Why was I good enough and now I'm not?"

"Livvie." Wade shook his head. "Hon, you were with her when her baby was born. That's huge. Do you think Ingrid feels bad for missing that?"

"But Ingrid was gone," she whispered. "I'm here. I've always been right here."

"Why am I not enough for you?"

Liv squeezed her eyes closed and tried to tug her face from his grasp. But Wade wouldn't let her go. She blinked again, this time her eyelashes wet with tears.

"I have loved you to the fucking moon and back." He raised his eyebrows and shrugged. "And you're still out there looking for something better."

"It wasn't like that, Wade," she argued. Their eyes met, and a flash of pain ripped through her at the hurt in his eyes. "It wasn't like that."

A car rambled down the street out front. The loud blare of a horn made Liv jump. Wade dropped his hands away from her. Both of them glanced toward the street. Their gazes followed a purple Dodge Shadow as it crawled by. Liv wondered if the driver was cursing Wade's truck, though there was plenty of room to get by. She figured Wade was more concerned with and horrified by the dull purple paint job on the Shadow that appeared to be the product of plain paintbrushes.

She turned her attention to the coffee in her hand and considered tossing it. But she had asked for it, and Amber made it, and her head still hurt.

"Are you gonna leave me?" she whispered, afraid to look at him.

"Is that what you want?"

She flicked her eyes up to meet his gaze and shook her head. "No. No. I don't know what I want, Wade."

"Dammit, Liv," he groaned, obviously angry and hurt and

sad and a million other things she didn't have time to consider at the moment.

"But I don't want you to leave." Her voice was low, but steady. She took a step toward him and reached out as if to touch him. He stared at her hand for a long moment, finally took it in his and squeezed.

"I'm so fucking mad at you right now."

She nodded and ducked her head to dab at her eyes.

"I know."

"But I sure as hell don't wanna throw us away, Liv."

Eyes downcast, she saw his boots move closer to her and looked up quickly. She didn't necessarily want or expect the same gentle kisses he'd given her earlier.

"I gotta get back to work," he said softly.

"Okay."

He kissed her head, the scruff on his jaw brushing her forehead again.

"Livvie?"

She lifted her face to look at him as he stepped away from her toward his truck.

"Hmm?"

"Fix this," he whispered and jutted his chin toward the front of the house. "Figure it out."

She watched him climb into the truck and start it. Stepped back when he backed out of the drive and drove away without another glance at her. She hadn't wanted a kiss. But she had wanted his arms around her.

She stood for a long moment after he was gone and the street was quiet again. Tears slid over her face, and she wondered if the neighbors ever watched the drama at the Williams' house. Ezra whaled away on the picnic table, but Liv left him to it and went back inside. She would go back at the attic. Didn't matter that they had gotten almost everything. Almost wasn't good enough. Besides, the attic would be far away from her sisters, and no matter what Wade had said, she wanted to be far, far away from them.

They were crowded into the corner when she stepped inside. The corner where Ingrid had stood a few minutes ago trying to wedge the linoleum back into place to convince Wade and Amber that they didn't need to worry about replacing it. Except now they were laughing, and Liv spared them a glance. Squatting together, Ingrid noticed her first. Her eyes watered, but she dashed at them frantically, as if to hide that she was laughing.

"What?" Amber asked quickly. She twisted around to look at Liv, obviously as entertained as Ingrid was at whatever they were talking about. She was still laughing softly, even as she wiped at her eyes and smeared eyeliner over her face. "Hey."

Liv watched Ingrid roll her eyes and yank Amber back to look at her. She smoothed the pad of her thumb over Amber's face—thank God she'd forgone the lick of the thumb that a mom would employ before doing the rub over the face—and Liv swallowed glass. The gesture was so motherly that her first thought was of their mom. The way she used to pull her and Ingrid's hair into pigtails for church and the way she'd hoist them up on the bathroom counter to wash their faces after they ate chocolate.

And then she remembered the way Ingrid had packed Amber around on her hip when she was a baby. Liv had done her share for Amber, but Ingrid had treated their baby sister as if she were her own.

Liv took a slow, deep breath and looked down at her hand, remembering the murderous grip Amber had when she was in active labor, pushing to deliver Hadley.

"Did Wade leave?" Ingrid stood up. She was no longer laughing, but she was still smiling and loose and happy, and Liv looked from her to Amber. Without a word, she turned and headed down the hallway. She would go up the front steps, just to get away from them.

"Liv?"

She stopped in the entry hall and hunched her shoulders.

"Did he leave?"

Her throat was so tight with emotion, she knew she couldn't speak. Instead, she turned back to them and lifted her hands as if to say what do you think?

"Liv?" Ingrid moved in closer, too close, and took her hand. Amber reached for her other hand and took the cup from her. Liv started to argue, but the coffee left in it would be cold by now, anyway. "Are you okay?"

"No. Ingrid, I'm not. I'm not okay." She shrugged. "Okay? Satisfied? I'm not okay."

"What did he say? Was he angry?" Amber curled her fingers around her elbow, but she leaned away to set the mug on the first landing of the stairs. Liv swallowed a small cry and wondered what the hell Amber meant. Was he angry? Now? When he found out? When he questioned her?

"He seemed okay," Amber told her, and Liv bit her tongue. Of course, he seemed okay, she wanted to say. Did they really think Wade would come unglued right there in front of them?

"Sit down," Ingrid said quietly.

Smothered now with their concern, Liv shook her head violently. But Ingrid took a step toward her, and she was already too close, and Liv had to back up. Two more steps and Ingrid boxed her into the window seat. Behind her, Amber put her arms around her and eased her back to sit down, as if she were an invalid, and a wave of rage flooded her.

She sat sideways with Amber curled around her back and Ingrid at her feet.

"I really just want to be alone," Liv said softly. "Please."

"Luke and I made out here once," Ingrid mumbled as she

looked around the small room. Unimpressed, Liv only stared at her. But Amber's snort drew her attention, and she twisted around to look at her. "You know what's perfect?" Ingrid continued.

Amber arched her eyebrows urging Ingrid to go on.

"When a guy's so into you he gets you off and expects nothing in return."

"So." Amber cocked her head at Ingrid. "Translation, you had an earth-shattering orgasm right here where we're sitting."

"Wasn't earth-shattering," Ingrid hedged. "I mean, didn't even crack the window. But…"

"Did you return the favor?" Amber asked her.

"I did, but not in this particular spot or at that time."

"Hmm." Amber nodded. "Nathan and I had post-breakup sex on the floor there one night."

"Really?" Ingrid looked over her shoulder to study the spot Amber indicated. "The floor? I'm too old for that."

Amber laughed softly.

"Not kidding. The last time Luke and I were together, I felt like I pulled something. And we were in bed."

"I had some bruises," Amber mumbled pensively. "Bruised my pride, but I'd do it again." She grinned when she looked back at Ingrid. Her eyes skated over to Liv's. "Not the breakup part, but the rest of it."

Liv sniffled and closed her eyes.

"He loves you," Ingrid said softly. "Twenty-four years, Liv."

"Ingrid."

"I love you," Ingrid reminded her. "And I love him, and I am begging you to fix this. Fix your marriage."

Liv tugged her hands away from Ingrid's, shrugged Amber's arms off her, and climbed to her feet. Her sisters watched her climb the stairs. Liv's head rang with the words *fix it.*

CHAPTER 21

Since graduation was on Friday night, Liv didn't truly feel that she was on summer vacation until Monday rolled around. She pretended to be sleeping when Wade hit the button on the alarm clock and rolled out of bed. Watched him through slitted eyes as he slipped through the shadowy bedroom to the bathroom to dress for work. He kissed her goodbye. Just a brush of his lips over her cheek because she was still pretending to be sleeping. But the touch of his lips was too hard to ignore, and she blinked at him there in the semi-darkness.

The weekend had been all stops and starts, sweet whispers, and angry stares. She knew she owed it to him, the anger and the possessiveness and the moodiness. He was entitled to what he felt, and she reminded herself to be patient. She stretched in their bed when he was gone, rolled over to his side and buried her face in his pillow and reminded herself she needed to consider what she had done and why she had done it. She had been the one to cheat, and she had to take responsibility for it. But there was a reason it had happened, and she needed to dig deep enough to find that reason before anything could change.

Not one to stay in bed long once she was awake, not when she was alone anyway, she slipped into the bathroom and showered not long after Wade left. She dressed again in athletic shorts and one of Wade's old t-shirts, and it crossed her mind as she went downstairs that she was clinging to his possessions because he still wouldn't give himself to her. It was one thing for him to kiss her now and then, quite another for him to put his arms around her and hold her.

Charlie slammed a glass of orange juice, flashed her a smile, and headed out before she could ask where he was going. She made coffee and then stood in the open pantry doorway for the duration of the coffeemaker's cycle trying to decide if she was hungry. She wasn't. But she couldn't remember when she had last eaten anything other than a cookie here or an apple there.

The coffeemaker beeped, and her mind back in the kitchen Saturday when Amber had made coffee just because Liv had asked if there was any made, she sauntered back over to pour herself a mug. Gracie was still sleeping. Liv had ducked her head into her room to check on the way from her bedroom. On her stomach, arms up under her pillow, her daughter slept peacefully. Grace had been in and out all weekend, and Liv had snatched what bits of conversation she could from her, and she'd seen the rosiness in her cheeks and decided whatever might have happened Friday night, Gracie seemed okay.

She would still ask, given the first opportunity.

Maybe. Maybe not. Maybe it wasn't normal for a mom to ask about that stuff. Her mom hadn't, but then her mom had been of a different generation. And besides, she had Ingrid to talk to about stuff like that. And just like that, Liv was sad again.

She had stayed up in the attic until afternoon on Saturday. When she came down, she found Ingrid in the family room boxing Mom's knick-knacks from family vacations taken through the years. Amber was in the kitchen, pulling old cookware from the cabinets Mom hadn't used as often as those next to the stove. Liv had carted down a few more trash bags filled to bursting from the attic, and she had left the house with a sense of accomplishment and a bone-deep weariness of her sisters, but without further conversation with either of them.

Wade's words had echoed in her head the rest of the evening. All day yesterday. Liv laughed with her sisters. True enough. They did make her laugh; they were great, when things were great. But their relationships were volatile and dangerous, and Liv just needed to do one thing at a time.

But she couldn't do one thing at a time, because when she thought about Wade now, she thought about how he said when he watched her with her sisters, he saw the woman he had fallen in love with. Trouble was, Liv wasn't sure she could be that woman again, and if she couldn't be that young, naïve woman again, maybe Wade couldn't love her.

She sipped her coffee, still trying to get excited about eating something. She went so far as to take a box of cereal from the shelf in the pantry, but nothing about wholesome and grain and no transfats tempted her to eat, and she set the box back on the shelf as she heard the back door of the house open.

She glanced over her shoulder, curious as to which of her guys had forgotten something. Most likely not Wade, as he'd been gone longer. She deflated and leaned against the pantry door when she heard Ingrid and Amber's voices. Liv caught words like hairpiece and jackass and then Amber threw in something about the park and a barn, and Ingrid's sarcastic laugh abraded her skin like sandpaper.

The two of them were deep in conversation when they rounded the corner and stepped into Liv's kitchen. She stood sideways, twisted around with her head resting on the pantry door. Amber still talking, Ingrid's face lit up with a smile when she realized Liv was looking at her.

Liv felt the rush of love, of happiness, that Ingrid's friendship brought her. Amber finally realized Liv was standing there, and her eyes jumped from Ingrid to Liv and back to Ingrid.

"Hey." Ingrid was the first to speak, and Liv realized it had been that way over the weekend, and she wondered now if it was always that way when the three of them were together.

"Hi." She wanted to ask them what they were doing. Remind them that they both had jobs, even if she was off for the summer. But the rude questions would be a dead give away that she didn't want them around. She heard Wade again in her head, and so she swallowed the words down and simply watched them.

"We brought breakfast." Ingrid held up a wax bag from the bakery café Liv favored and Ingrid didn't. Her stomach almost growled, and then she almost growled at Ingrid for sucking up and hitting her coffee place instead of Java Infusion. When neither Ingrid nor Amber moved further into the room, obviously waiting for Liv to invite them and ask them to sit down, Liv finally sighed in defeat and stepped away from the pantry.

On the verge of asking why they weren't at work, Liv bit her tongue and moseyed to the island counter and leaned against it. Looking at either of them made her feel raw, so she kept her eyes on the bag as Ingrid's nimble fingers opened it. Liv studied Ingrid's hands and considered that they were worth a fortune to her sister. Sure, she could use a speech-to-text software if she had to, but Ingrid's hands spent countless hours over a keyboard. Liv's gaze touched on the ridiculous oversized silver ring Ingrid wore, and she wondered if Luke would ever ask her to marry him.

"So." Ingrid pulled a couple of muffins from the bag, flicked her gaze up to meet Liv's, and looked back at the baked goodies. "I was up at four today, and I've already put in several hours, and my head hurts, so I took a break."

"Why does your head hurt?" Liv asked quietly.

"Gee, I don't know," Ingrid mumbled. "Maybe because I'm a little stressed."

"Stressed about what?" Liv realized they'd brought breakfast, but neither of them was carrying coffee, so she turned away to get mugs from the cabinet.

"You're funny." Ingrid's voice was soft and light, and Liv took a deep breath to hold her frustration at bay.

"Maybe you have a headache because you got up at four," Amber suggested.

"Well, after tossing and turning for at least an hour and thinking about Truman and Harlowe, my back was killing me, so I got up."

"You were awake at three?" Liv cringed. She poured them both coffee. "Do you ever take anything?"

"Who're Truman and Harlowe?" Amber asked.

"Characters." Ingrid's answer was clipped and short, as if she wanted to shut down any conversation about her books or her writing habits. Liv met her eyes when she handed a mug of coffee to each of them.

"And no. I don't take anything," Ingrid said with a small shake of her head to dismiss the thought.

"Why not?"

"I don't wanna get addicted to anything." Ingrid shrugged. "Besides, I do my best plotting in the small hours."

"Do you sleep through the day?"

"Why are we—?" Ingrid sighed. "I didn't come over here to talk about my insomnia."

"Wonder if Mom had problems sleeping?"

"It's menopause, isn't it?" Ingrid mumbled. She took a sip of her coffee and cringed. "Jesus, Olivia, that's so damned strong, it might kill me."

"It's not menopause." Liv rolled her eyes. "You're in your early forties."

"Okay, so perimenopause." Ingrid looked over Liv's shoulder. "Is there shade out there? On the deck?"

"Yeah." Liv nodded. She grabbed a few napkins and what appeared to be a cranberry orange muffin and followed Ingrid to the French door that led to the deck. "Do you have night sweats?"

"Sometimes," Ingrid admitted. They chose seats around the table; Liv decided it was nice out here, and she was hungry, so maybe it was okay that they were here.

"Painful sex?"

Ingrid had her mouth open to take a bite of her own muffin, but she snorted and then coughed and rubbed her chest. "Ouch. I think I just snorted blueberry muffin, Liv."

Liv thought of the mark Wade had left on her hip the other night.

"The only time I've had painful sex lately was about a week ago when Luke and I got carried away in his truck. Ever been nearly bent in half backwards over a steering wheel?"

"Aren't you kind of old for that?" Liv asked. She blinked at Ingrid, trying to imagine how that worked, and then when she remembered being on her knees on the concrete garage floor the other night, she blushed and looked away.

"Where…" Amber cleared her throat and tried again. "Where was his truck?"

"In the garage," Ingrid said simply. "Couldn't wait to get inside."

"Seriously, Ingrid." Liv sat back in her chair and pinched off a bite of her muffin. "How long can you function on such little sleep?"

"Been doing it for about twenty years, so I think I'll live," Ingrid answered.

"It's the curse of the creative mind—"

"I didn't come over here to talk about me—"

"Why don't you, though? Why won't you talk about your writing with us?" Liv pushed her. The muffin was delicious, but now Liv wished she had eggs or bacon to go with it. She was still hungry. When had she last eaten a good meal?

"Because you're not interested," Ingrid said with a frown. "It's fine. It makes me feel like a freak sometimes. Amber and I talked to—"

"What makes you feel like a freak sometimes?" Amber shoved the last of her breakfast in her mouth and chewed slowly, eyes zeroed in on Ingrid.

"The writing?" Liv asked. "Your books?"

Ingrid sighed. "Talking about it. You guys make me feel weird about it, so I'd rather not talk about it."

"Why do we make you feel weird?" Amber cocked her head and blinked at Ingrid.

"Do you talk about writing with Julie and Rafe?"

Ingrid yanked her eyes away from Amber and looked at Liv.

"I used to." She nodded. "I don't talk to them as much these days."

"So you bounced ideas off Julie? But Liv and I make you feel weird about it."

Ingrid took a deep breath. She finished her muffin, wiped her hands and mouth on a napkin, and then took a drink.

"Amber and I—"

"You asked me about what I do," Amber reminded her.

"What?"

"You asked me about my processes. You hang out at the studio sometimes." Amber glanced at Liv. When guilt washed over her face, Liv restrained an eye roll. "You've gone with me on shoots."

Rather than answer immediately, Ingrid looked at Liv, too. It was bad enough to know that the two of them had been spending so much time together. The fact that both of them watched her now, after spilling the beans about it, as if she might come unglued, embarrassed her.

It hurt, too, but damned if she wanted to admit it.

"Why?" Liv coughed to cover the squeak in her voice. "Why did you guys come by?"

"I thought that when Ingrid moved home, we would do more of this stuff." Amber sounded sad. "See more of each other."

"Yeah, well, you and I have both lived here forever, and we didn't do this stuff when Ingrid was gone."

"What's going on with you and Wade?" Ingrid's firm voice made Liv think of their mother. She even felt a chill climb her spine as if her mom had delivered the question as the opening line of a lecture.

Liv sucked in a quick breath and squinted her eyes.

"Not going there," she said softly.

"I told you about having a lump removed from my breast. I told you that Rafe and I…had a moment…I told you—"

"And you told Amber that you wanted kids," Liv reminded her. She sipped from her mug. "And you didn't tell me about your surgery or about what happened with Rafe until well after the fact. And Amber never told either one of us much about Nathan. If I remember correctly, we found out that he proposed the first time because Hadley told us. We just found out who our fourteen-year-old niece's father is. And—"

"Hadley's going out of town this weekend with Kyle and his family."

"Do what?" Liv's chest seized with fear. Hands ice cold now, even wrapped around her mug, she turned to look at Amber. "How can you just…let her go? I mean—"

"How do I not let her go, Liv?" Amber whispered. "I started this—"

"Amber, she was pushing you to know who her father was," Ingrid argued in Amber's defense.

"I know. And once I talked to him and told her about it, she asked me if I had done it to punish her. If I was going to send her away to live with him."

Liv winced. She set her mug on the table and reached out to stroke her hand over Amber's arm.

"She doesn't believe that—"

"No, I know." Amber shook her head and leaned forward to put her mug on the table, too. "I know. We talked. She's… we're okay. Things are better, and Nathan's so good for her. But in the meantime, I started this ball rolling, and she's been spending a lot of time with Kyle and his family."

"Family?" Liv raised her eyebrows.

"Hadley has two half-brothers."

Liv winced at Amber's sharp tone. Of course, Amber had told her Kyle had two sons, and if she remembered correctly, they were into soccer. But did family mean more than that? His parents, maybe? Did Hadley have grandparents around? Other aunts and uncles?

"Aren't you scared?"

"Yeah." Amber nodded and shrugged. "Of course I am. But—"

"Of what? What are you afraid of?" Ingrid asked her.

"Losing her."

"That's ridiculous, Amber. She loves you."

"Yeah, but she's lived her life without a dad. Now she's got that. And she's got siblings. Kyle's wife is nice, and Hadley and I fight so much. What if she decides she likes her better than me? What if it's more fun living there?"

"People don't just stop loving people and switch teams like that—"

"Don't they?"

Liv hadn't realized she spoke out loud, until Amber and Ingrid both turned to look at her.

"You really don't love him anymore?" Amber whispered.

"Why does my having a relationship with Amber threaten you so much?"

"It's not a threat." Liv shrugged. "It just feels like the few times Amber and I were together were fake. I feel like she used me. Just until you got back to save her."

"Olivia." Amber groaned.

"Everyone….in my life…takes me for granted." Liv licked her lips. "Everyone." She stood up and crossed the deck to the rail, arms folded over her chest.

"Liv."

She turned back to them slowly, met first Amber's gaze and then Ingrid's.

"That hurts." She sniffled and looked away.

"Maybe we both just feel…felt…" Ingrid corrected herself and raised her eyebrows. "Maybe we both felt comfortable….solid…with you. Enough to lean while we tried to find our way back to each other."

"Well, surprise." Still with her arms folded over her chest, Liv shrugged. Ingrid's intense stare pinned her in place, but Liv finally broke the eye contact and lowered her gaze to the deck. She stared at her red toenails—she and Gracie had gone together for pedicures just a couple of days before graduation —and remembered for a moment the way the arches of her feet had molded perfectly over Asher Crowe's calves.

"Surprise what?" Amber asked quietly.

"I have feelings, guys," Liv mumbled.

Had she enjoyed it? The dirty stuff with Asher? The first time had been a thrill, sure. The thought that after twenty plus years of marriage to the same man, after a few pounds here and a few pounds there and lines around her eyes or lips, another man found her attractive had been a turn on. The sneaking around had added to the thrill, of course. Hadn't the sneaking around with Wade when they were younger been half the thrill of making out with him? Or sex, when they had taken it to the next level? And yes, she had come a few times when she had been with Asher.

But had she enjoyed it? Had Asher Crowe gone out of his way to give her pleasure? The way her husband did? The first orgasm with him had blown her mind, but then she was lonely and she missed her husband, and she missed him again when it was over, because rather than hold her and whisper to her the way Wade did, Asher Crowe had eased her off his lap, adjusted his dick and tucked it away behind the zipper of his trousers.

"Good God, Liv, it was a quick supper—"

"And Ingrid hanging out at your studio. Shadowing you on shoots. It was all about you showing Ingrid what you do. How you do it. Letting her take the wheel, so to speak."

Amber licked her lips and opened her mouth to argue, but Liv shook her head.

"Why're you here? I have stuff I need to do."

CHAPTER 22

*I*ngrid stared at her, apparently stunned silent by what she just said. The air thick with hard feelings and resentment, none of them moved for a moment. Finally, Ingrid sucked in a deep breath, and Liv felt life, time, move again. She watched Ingrid gathering their napkins. She balled them into one fist and reached to pick up her own mug.

"Amber and I talked to Ezra about the house," she started, and Liv's tiny, selfish victory over hurting her vanished in anger over what Ingrid just said.

"You what?" Liv sighed. She moved hesitantly, joined them at the table again and sat down. "What do you mean you talked to Ezra about the house? This is what I'm talking about, Ingrid. There are four of us."

Ingrid stopped moving, full hands over the tabletop, and stared at Liv. Her eyes were bloodshot, and today, rather than making her eyes pop, her makeup made her look wan. Instead of owning the guilt, Liv bit down on her lip to make something else hurt.

"We asked him when he could meet with all of us, so we could talk about…the house and make the decisions together." Ingrid's gaze was full of disappointment. Liv dragged her eyes away, feeling chastised, as if Ingrid were the oldest and wisest sister.

"What did he say?" Liv's voice was gruff, and she thought maybe that was because she swallowed back the apology she knew she owed to Ingrid.

"He said he doesn't care what we do."

Liv rolled her eyes and then let them close. They burned with emotion when she heard Ingrid stand up.

"Sit down."

"I have some errands I need to run—"

"I'm sorry." Liv huffed out a jagged sigh. Sprawled in her chair, she rubbed her knuckles over her chest, her heart, and sniffled. "I'm sorry."

"Are you?" Ingrid asked quickly.

"Yeah." Liv nodded, surprised to realize she meant it. "I am."

She opened her eyes to find both of her sisters watching her.

"I know you moved back to be with Luke, and I'm happy for you." She swallowed hard, caressed her neck with her fingertips, and forced herself to keep going. "I just hoped there would be more between us."

Amber sighed, but Liv shook her head before she could speak. "All of us, Amber."

"I don't understand why we can't all have the same relationship." Ingrid stared at her with doe eyes, shrugged her eyebrows when she saw that she had Liv's attention.

"It's okay," Liv mumbled. "You guys are younger. You both have flexible—"

"Don't do that. Olivia, you and I grew up together. You can't—"

"Wade said..." Liv reached to push her hair off her face. "He said he wants...the marriage...our marriage..." Tears welled in her eyes and slid over her face, and Liv felt Ingrid's and Amber's stares like flames. "I'm afraid he'll decide he can't forgive me." She laughed, but it was hollow and bitter. Feeling exposed under their stares, Liv leaned forward in her chair and rested her elbows on her knees. "I'm afraid he'll leave…and I still can't…"

From the corner of her eye, she saw Ingrid put the napkins down and then gently, so as not to make a noise and break the moment, she set her mug down again and waited.

"Can't what?" Amber coaxed her.

"I can't say the words. I can't just tell him I love him."

"Do you? Love him?" Ingrid asked.

Liv answered with a grudging nod. "I do. But…"

"But what?" Amber skimmed her fingers up over her arm.

"I don't know. I don't know, and there's something, isn't there?" Liv sobbed. "Normal, happy women who are in love with their husbands don't just go looking for something else."

"Liv," Amber whispered. "Maybe you're being too hard on yourself."

Liv shook her head. "You wouldn't say that if you saw the way he looked at me when he told me he knew."

"But you love him," Ingrid reminded her.

"But—"

"No, I get it." Ingrid nodded. "I do. You gotta figure out what made you…"

"Cheat." Liv's voice hardened on the word. "I cheated, Ingrid. Say it."

"Okay. But you have to figure out the why." Ingrid arched her eyebrows at Liv, as if she were talking a child through the reasons why she had to brush her teeth or make her bed in the mornings. "To save what you have."

After a short hesitation, Liv answered with a curt nod.

"But you do love him," Ingrid reminded her. "And you do want to save your marriage."

"He'll never look at me the same way again."

Liv looked up when Amber stood.

"Where are you going?"

"More coffee," her sister told her. Liv, feeling childish, looked away to hide her relief that she hadn't chased Amber off. "You want more, Ingrid?"

"I don't know, because I think I'm having chest palpitations already." Ingrid took a deep breath and shot a frown at Liv.

Amber snickered. "I'll make some."

Liv watched her cross the deck and step inside.

"I know you don't believe this, but she thinks you walk on water."

"I don't believe it, and I don't walk on water, and none of us should think that of anyone, because no one's perfect." Liv shrugged off Ingrid's words irritably. "I'm just me, Ingrid. I don't want to be anyone's example on how to live."

"How's Gracie?" Ingrid asked. Liv watched her rub her hand over her stomach. "What? I'm still hungry."

"Me too." Liv chuckled. "I don't remember the last time I ate."

"Maybe she'll bring the other muffins out." Ingrid eyed the door hopefully.

"Muffins, hell. I could do a plate of bacon and eggs."

Ingrid grinned. "Have any?"

"Yeah, but I'm not fixing anything."

"Want me to?"

"No." Liv shook her head. The last thing she wanted was for her sisters to think they had to take care of her. "Gracie's fine, I guess. I didn't see much of her this weekend."

Ingrid rested against the back of her chair and folded her arms behind her head.

"I don't know how you do it."

"Do what?"

"Parent. How did you sleep Friday night knowing what she might have been doing?"

Liv opened her mouth to answer her, but when her thoughts turned to what happened earlier that night with

Wade, she changed her mind and closed her mouth so tight, her teeth clicked.

"Would you ever know? If she did…"

Liv shrugged.

"Did you tell Mom when you lost your virginity?"

"No." Ingrid laughed sadly. "I told you."

"And I told you." Liv grinned. "I don't think Gracie's been with a boy, but I could be wrong."

"But does she talk to you?" Ingrid cocked her head and stared at Liv with narrowed eyes.

"Is this research?"

Shocked, Ingrid took her turn at flapping her mouth and not making a sound.

"I'm just asking, Ingrid, because I know next to nothing about your professional life. I don't care if you're poking for that reason—"

"Well, I asked because I admire both of you for being moms, and as we've established, I wish I could have had that blessing. I'm curious," she admitted with an exaggerated shrug, "and I'm concerned. I think it would make me crazy wondering about my child's secrets. Especially knowing the things I kept from Mom and Dad."

Liv ran her tongue around her teeth and winced when her stomach growled.

"It does make you a little crazy," she said softly. "But not always. Gracie's a good girl, and I trust her. And there's always all the other stuff. To think about. And I think that's part of being a parent."

"What is?"

"Balancing everything. Observing what they're doing and being open to whatever they need to talk about, but giving them room to make their own decisions. Sometimes the mistakes we make are the best teachers we could ask for."

Ingrid pursed her lips and skirted her gaze away from Liv.

"And besides," Liv shook her head, "I don't know that I would want her to save herself."

"Her virginity?" Ingrid asked with a frown. Amber stepped outside again, a plate with the remaining muffins in hand. "Is that what you mean? Save herself for marriage?"

"Yeah." Liv looked up at Amber with a smile. "Did you fry any bacon and eggs in there?"

"Was I gone that long?" Amber's gaze jumped from Liv to Ingrid as she set the plate on the table. "What did I miss?"

"No, I'm hungry," Liv answered.

Amber perched on the edge of her chair. "I made more coffee. Liv, yours was a solid chunk in the bottom of the pot."

"Exaggerate much?" Liv rolled her eyes.

"Do you think Hadley's a virgin?" Ingrid asked her.

"God, I hope so." Amber bit her lip.

"But would you want her to save herself for her wedding night?" Liv turned to Amber, sincerely interested in her answer.

"Why?" Amber eyed her suspiciously. "Did Hadley tell you something—"

"No," Ingrid answered when Amber glanced at her. "No. I just...I was just telling Liv that from where I sit, I think it would be harder than hell to be you guys. To be moms. To know how to handle this stuff."

"And I'm honestly interested in what you think."

"And you're gonna ding me when I tell you, and you're gonna judge me, because you both do all the time. I'm not a good mom—"

"Amber." Liv sighed.

"You are, Amber," Ingrid told her. "You're good with Hadley."

Amber snorted. "No. I wouldn't want Hadley to save her virginity for her wedding night." She spoke in a monotone, eyes on the plate of muffins. "Not very Catholic of me, but I haven't seen the inside of a church in years, if you don't count

Dad's funeral." She turned her face to Liv as if inviting her
to argue.

"I agree," Liv admitted.

Amber blinked at her and then looked to Ingrid.

"Really?"

"So you want her to get the wild stuff out now? Is that
what you're saying?" Ingrid asked Liv.

"No." Liv let a wave of sadness roll over her before she
continued. "Not really. I just think girls are either expected to
wait for marriage, or they're labeled promiscuous. And I
don't think that's fair."

"Test drive the car?" Ingrid suggested.

"I guess. But maybe it's as much about getting to know
what kind of driver you are as well as finding the right car."

"I agree," Amber said with a slow, deliberate nod.

"I don't want Grace to hook up with just anyone. I want
her to feel respected, maybe loved. But I think it's important
for her to take some time to herself, too."

Amber nodded again.

"What happened Friday night?"

The abrupt change of subject startled Liv. She lifted her
eyes only to look at Ingrid, a knife of hurt slicing through her
at the memory of Wade and what happened in the bedroom.

"With Grace?" she hedged. "I don't know. I've hardly
seen her."

Ingrid shook her head. "With you."

Liv wanted to play dumb, but Ingrid didn't give her a
chance.

"And Wade."

"What do you mean?" Her words came out in a harsh
whisper, because Ingrid's question and Wade's stunt left her
breathless and sore.

"Something happened between the ceremony and the
party." Ingrid's tiny shrug almost got by Liv. "You were a
mess that night."

Liv groaned and ducked her face to her hands.

"Not so anyone else noticed," Ingrid continued, "but Amber and I did."

Liv pressed her lips together and swallowed hard.

"I hurt him." She licked her lips. "I guess I have to sit back and take it."

"What did he do to you?"

"Ingrid."

"You're not gonna tell us?"

"Do you really want to know?" Liv gave her a pointed look.

"Sex?"

Liv shrugged, flustered by Ingrid's questions.

"He's using sex against you?"

"Don't I deserve anything he dishes out?" Liv countered.

"Do you?" Ingrid shrugged. "Is he cheating? For revenge?"

"No."

"Would you allow that?"

Liv started to say no, but she caught herself. "Ingrid, it doesn't matter if I would or would not allow it. Wade wouldn't do that. I made the mistake. I was wrong."

"So what's he doing to you to pay you back?"

Liv sniffled and reached for her mug. When she found it empty, she simply stared into it, as if she might find answers there.

"I'll be right back," Ingrid told her as she stood up.

Liv watched her cross the deck, aware of Amber watching her at the same time.

"She hates to see you hurting."

Liv glanced at Amber, but she said nothing.

"Remember the night Nathan and I left your house, and you guys were all here playing cards?"

"I do," Liv said softly. "And I wish you guys would have stayed longer."

Amber started to say something, but she stopped herself and flashed Liv such a sweet smile, it took her breath away.

"We went home, and we…"

Liv grinned and nodded. "Yeah, I was there the next morning when you were changing the sheets."

Amber nodded, but she wasn't smiling anymore. "Yeah. We were all over each other that night. He left me the next morning."

"Amber." Liv reached for Amber's hand, but Amber shook her head just slightly. She wasn't suggesting something was wrong in her relationship. She was offering to Liv that Nathan had hurt her in a similar way and still loved her.

Liv rolled her lips inward and nodded as she looked away. "Something like that, yeah."

"Liv?" Amber sounded uncertain now.

"Hmm?"

"I don't love her more than you." Her voice was gruff. "But I knew her better."

Liv turned to look at Amber.

"That's all. And I still feel like the unwanted little sister when you guys are together."

Liv saw the way Amber's hand shook as she reached to dab at her eyes. When their eyes met again, Liv swallowed hard and nodded.

"Okay."

"And I don't blame you for what's going on with Wade." Amber shook her head so violently, Liv jumped backwards. "No. I mean…please don't think I'm judging you. I'm not judging you or Wade. I just….yours was always the marriage that proved to me it could work. It breaks my heart that you aren't happy."

"Amber." Liv sighed. "Oh, kid, it's not Wade. It's not Wade that makes me unhappy."

"Then what is it?" Amber whispered.

"I don't know, but it's all in me," Liv admitted. "I don't

know what's going on inside me that's making me so mean. I just know I can't change it right now."

"Talk to someone," Amber urged her.

"What?" Liv eyed her curiously. "Like a marriage counselor?"

Amber shrugged. "Or a friend. Does Kristen know what's going on?"

"No." Liv waved the question away. "I wouldn't burden her with this."

"Liv, sometimes it helps just to get it all out there."

"Wasn't it just Ingrid preaching that to you?"

"She was right."

"Holy truth serum," Ingrid sang as she walked outside with the coffee pot in hand. "I heard that. Amber Williams just admitted that I was right about something."

"Once, Ingrid. Don't get too excited."

"Oh, I'm gonna revel in my rightness for a few minutes, thank you very much."

Liv laughed softly as Ingrid filled each of their cups. When Ingrid rested her free hand on her shoulder, Liv reached up to cover it with her own.

CHAPTER 23

*E*xhausted, Liv stretched and twisted around to pop her back. Her neck and shoulders hurt like someone had stuck a knife in them, and she winced when she rolled her head on her shoulders to stretch. The photo album was heavy in her lap. She scooted back just enough to lean against the couch and rested her head on a seat cushion. Eyes closed, she smoothed her fingers over the page protectors, the faces of her childhood safe beneath the plastic.

The room was dark, other than the circle of yellow lamp-light that shone on her and the album like a spotlight. She wondered what time it was, but she didn't care enough to look. She'd left her phone in the kitchen, and the thought of getting up to find it made the rest of her body hurt. Charlie had asked her earlier if he could go with his friends to another friend's camp for a bonfire. She said yes, but she had asked him very quietly to be careful, and she must have looked pathetic because he not only promised he would, he had crouched down beside her, given her a one armed hug, and dropped a kiss on her cheek.

She didn't know where Grace had gone, only that she was with friends. They had hung out over lunch after her sisters left. Liv had hung on the edge of asking about the weekend, and she had spent so much time studying her daughter and pretending not to that Grace had finally asked her what she was looking at. Liv had only smiled and shrugged. Let Grace chalk it up to her already getting emotional over Gracie leaving. Had to be better than digging in and asking Gracie something she would consider too personal.

"What're you doing?"

Wade's voice chased goose bumps up her arms. Liv didn't move, except to take a deep breath.

"Nothing."

"Kids home?"

"No."

She could ask him what he had been doing. Where he had been. Odds were he had been out in his garage working. He hadn't told her at dinner what his plans were, and he had disappeared when his plate was clean. She reminded herself that he was trying; she had hurt him, and she had to give him time.

Still, the fact that his disappearing act was part of what had driven her to cheat made it hard for her to wait patiently.

She opened her eyes and found him propped in the archway to the living room. His t-shirt pulled taut over his shoulders, and his arms folded over his chest, he was just distant enough to be cool and sexy. A flutter of nerves slid through her belly and up into her chest when he pushed off the archway. He dropped his arms, and for a moment, Liv thought he was going to walk away. He turned toward her as she said his name.

He sat beside her on the floor, though he left a good foot of carpet between them. Afraid to meet his gaze, Liv let her eyes roam down over his bare legs stretched out on the floor in front of him. She looped her finger in a hole near the waistband of his shorts, but when he didn't say anything, she moved and hunched back into herself.

"Is it really over?" he finally asked her. She almost laughed, but she caught herself. He sounded uncertain, as if he really believed she might be sleeping with someone else even now.

"Yes."

"When?"

Her gaze flew up to meet his, startled by his question.

"What?"

"When was the last time?"

She huffed out a shaky breath and raised her eyebrows. "Just before Christmas."

Apparently, she had been stupid enough to think that would reassure him, because when the pained look flashed over his face, she felt the sting of disappointment.

He nodded. "The first time?"

She leaned forward and studied her hands on the album. Smoothed her thumb over her fingertips and then twisted her wedding ring.

"I don't know." She shrugged and shook her head. She did know. She knew the exact date and time when she first betrayed her husband. But sharing the details of her infidelity was humiliating.

"Liv."

"The last week of October."

"Jesus." He flinched. Turned his head away from her.

"Wade." She reached for him. Touched his arm, the skin over his hard bicep warm. She missed the safety of his arms around her. He jerked away from her touch. Liv licked her lips and nodded, reminded herself she was to blame.

"Two months." He cleared his throat. "You were seeing someone for two goddamned months—"

"No." She shook her head.

"No?"

She didn't look up, but she knew when he turned to look at her.

"It wasn't like that."

"What does that mean?"

"I was with him…" She swallowed down the rush of vomit and took a deep breath. "Maybe five times? It wasn't like we…were together…all the time."

"If it were me?"

She saw him shrug.

"Would it hurt you?"

Her hands blurred when her eyes filled with tears. She nodded. Smoothed the first tear that fell over the back of her hand.

"Yes."

He was quiet, but he didn't move, and Liv wondered what that meant. She pushed the album away and drew her knees up to her chest.

"Did you think I wouldn't find out?"

She squeezed her eyes closed and dropped her forehead to rest on her knees. The tears slid over her face silently. Had she really thought he wouldn't find out? Of course not. She hadn't cared. She couldn't sit here and tell Wade that the thing with Asher Crowe was completely set apart from the way she felt about Wade. Because what she had done with another man was every damned thing to do with her husband.

"I'm sorry," she whispered.

"Every time I close my eyes, I see you with him."

There was nothing she could say except I'm sorry, and those words were so empty, so inadequate after what she'd done to him. She lifted her head, but covered her eyes with her hand.

The silence that pressed in on them was heavy enough to suffocate her. She needed to hide from him, but if she did, if she left the room now, he would disappear and go back to his damned garage.

"Asher Crowe."

She turned her face away from him, but she answered with a curt nod.

"Why him?"

"Does it matter?" she sobbed.

When he didn't answer, she turned back toward him, still hiding her eyes behind her hand.

"Yeah." He nodded and shrugged his eyebrows. "It does to me."

"He was there."

"So you were so desperate to cheat, anyone would have done?"

"No."

"Then it was him."

"No." She wiped at her eyes.

"One or the other, Liv." He turned sideways and leaned on the couch.

"I didn't go looking to cheat," she said quietly. She shook her head and finally lowered her hand to look at him.

"So then Asher Crowe swept you off your feet."

"No." She reached for him. Stroked her fingers over his cheek. "No, he didn't sweep my off my feet. It just happened."

Her heart dropped when she saw him shut down, his eyes blank and cool.

"Don't lie to me now, Olivia. There's no point."

Liv took a deep breath, the use of her full name so unlike Wade she suddenly felt chilled. She turned sideways and scooted a bit closer to him. Pretended not to notice when he edged backwards.

"I was leaving school." She licked her lips. "It had been a bad day. I wasn't even paying attention to where I was. He was in the parking lot."

"After school?"

She shook her head. "It was evening. I was there for an English Club meeting."

"So you chose to fuck a man like Asher Crowe? In the backseat? Of his Mercedes, maybe? On school property?'

Uncomfortable with how close to the truth Wade was, Liv squirmed a bit and lowered her gaze.

"He put his window down. Greeted me. I..."

"You what?"

"I didn't want to stand around and talk. To anyone. I was in a hurry to get home."

"Why?"

She shook her head. "I don't know. I was tired."

"What changed your mind?"

"He asked me how my day was."

Wade stared at her, obviously waiting for more.

"And?"

She licked her lips and lowered her gaze again.

"That's it? That's all it took to get in your pants?"

"He asked me how my day was," she repeated.

"What happened that day?"

"Nothing," she whispered. "Whole lot of nothing going on then, Wade."

He lifted his hand and reached toward her. Tucked a strand of hair behind her ear.

"So it's my fault."

"I was lonely," she whispered. "But it's my fault."

Wade scooted closer to her, but not so close that their bodies touched. Liv moved her hand, stretched it over the space between them, and skimmed her fingers over the back of his hand.

"Do you wanna leave, Liv?"

She looked up at him quickly, startled by his question. Twisted to her knees and moved closer to him. Wade cupped her face in his hands and rubbed his thumb over her lips.

"No."

"You're not happy." His voice was tight with emotion.

"You said you don't want to lose us, this," she reminded him. "Wade? Didn't you say that?"

Tears streaked her face again. When he moved one hand down her side and around her waist, she slid her leg over his lap to straddle him.

"I don't." He shook his head. "But you're not happy. With me. You haven't been for a long time."

"It's not you," she whispered.

"Livvie, don't lie to me. You were with someone else—"

"But, it's not you," she said again. "It's me. It's me, Wade. I know that sounds cliché, but it's true."

"Did you come? With him?"

"Wade." She avoided his eyes and stroked her fingers back through his close-cropped hair. "I don't want to leave."

She kissed him. Her body shook with fear—the whole thing in the bedroom last Friday still in her mind—but she pressed her lips against his and silently begged him to kiss her back. She heard a small hum of pleasure when he did and realized it had come from somewhere deep inside. He let her lead, but when she slid her tongue inside his mouth, he moved his own over hers, hungry to taste her.

"I don't want to leave," she whispered when she broke the kiss to trail soft kisses over his chin and his neck. She tugged at the tail of his shirt, rubbed against his erection and thrilled to the knowledge that he wanted her. His skin was warm and soft, and she molded her hands up over his back and then around to his chest, his t-shirt soft on the back of her arms. She sighed with pleasure when he pressed a kiss to her neck, tugged at her earlobe with his teeth.

"Liv."

He cupped her butt in his hands and then smoothed them over her hips. She moaned out loud when he slipped his fingers inside the front of her shorts.

"Wade." She sobbed when he stopped there.

"Did you come with him?"

"Yes. But—"

He shook his head. Pulled his hand from her shorts.

"Goddammit, Wade, please? Please touch me."

"I can't, Livvie. Not now."

The sweet kiss he dropped on her cheek should have taken the sting out of his words, his rejection. But she was stunned and hurt when he lifted her from his lap and stood up. She watched him walk out, silent tears burning her face.

CHAPTER 24

*O*livia learned quickly to appreciate the quiet, uneventful days. Wade wouldn't give in; whether one of them picked a fight and they ended up screaming at each other up and down the steps (unfortunately both kids witnessed more than one such episode) or they skirted each other in the house and treated each other as polite strangers, whether they crashed together in anger and the kisses taken were rough and teeth-clashing or they found a moment of peace and maybe love in each other's arms and the kisses were sweet and giving, Wade walked away before things got out of hand. As a result, Liv waded through her first few weeks of summer vacation tied in knots, missing her husband a little more each day, and saddened by the possibility that things would not get much better.

Would she leave? No. No matter what she had been thinking that first time she'd taken Asher Crowe into her body, no matter what she had thought each subsequent time, she didn't want to lose her marriage, her husband. But she knew better than to assume that Wade would stay, that he would eventually forgive her and they would move on.

Gracie spent a lot of time with her friends, and though Liv

wished for some of her attention, she wouldn't have it any other way. At eighteen, Gracie's free time should be spent with friends, kicked back enjoying the lazy days of summer. Besides, whenever Grace did throw Liv a few moments, she either watched Liv with such curiosity and suspicion or she flat out asked what was going on with Liv and Wade, and Liv wasn't prepared to answer those questions. She never would be, and she prayed every night she went to bed that Wade would never tell the kids the truth about what had gone wrong.

"Hey." She looked up when she heard the screen door squeal. The house was hot, and her glasses had slipped to the tip of her nose, and she eyed Ezra as she pushed them up. "Did you bring me one?"

Ezra looked at the apple he was munching on and then shrugged and offered it to her. She laughed and turned her attention back to the papers spread out on the counter in front of her.

"What's all that?" He stopped at the end of the counter and wedged in close to her. Physically tired from working in the garage and mentally tired from dealing with the mess she had made of her own life and still trudging through the mess that was her parents' estate and the way she and her siblings were handling it, Liv leaned into him and rested her head on his shoulder. Her brother's body was lean and hard; she wondered absently if he worked out or if his physique was natural. Their dad had been in pretty good shape, or so they had all thought. Michael Seckman hadn't appeared all that different, at least not to Liv, but then she hadn't seen the man in years, either.

"Things we've talked about doing with the house."

Ezra crunched another bite of his apple and leaned an elbow on the counter. Liv watched his eyes move over the papers.

"New carpet." He arched his eyebrows. "In every room?"

"No." She shrugged.

"Ah. Hardwood in the dining room and the den and tile in the kitchen and bathrooms." He shot her a cautious look. "This is gonna be expensive. You know that, right?"

She sighed and nodded as she stood up straight. "I do. We haven't decided on anything yet."

"House has been sitting vacant now since January."

"Yeah, except we're always over here," she reminded him. "What does it hurt if we do the upkeep outside?"

"Neighbors might think the world stopped turning if we did any upkeep," he mumbled.

She laughed quietly and shook her head. "Dad took care of the yard."

"We could maybe put a new basketball hoop up."

Liv winced when he crunched another bite. "You put a hoop on that garage out there? The whole damned building's gonna come down. With everything in it. Might as well have a bonfire and roast some marshmallows."

Ezra stepped around her and moved to stand at the window over the sink. He polished off the rest of the apple with a giant bite and then glanced at her with a frown as he tried to chew. She rolled her eyes, but she had to laugh.

"We could put a pole up."

"There's no driveway anyway," she reminded him. "Isn't it hard to dribble in grass?"

He laughed and pulled the cabinet door under the sink open to toss the apple core.

"We did it," he answered with a shrug.

"Who did?"

"Me and the guys." He washed his hands. "So pour a cement pad. Or better yet, a driveway."

Liv crossed her arms over her chest and wandered around the counter to the first barstool. She scooted back to sit and considered his suggestion.

"So. For weeks we've been trying to get you to come and

talk to us about the house. Weeks during which you've avoided us and said do whatever we want, and now your ideas on the house are pouring a driveway and putting in a basketball hoop?"

"Where are they?" He turned to face Liv and rested his butt on the counter. "Ingrid and Amber?"

Liv's sigh turned into a yawn. She ducked her head and covered her mouth. When her eyes started watering, she rubbed them and then dropped her hands to the counter and stared at Ezra.

"Um. Amber and Nathan are doing the bridal registry thing." She laughed softly when Ezra cringed. "What? What's that about?"

"I hated that."

"But you needed stuff." Liv shrugged. "Right? You register so your guests give you things that you can use."

"First?" Ezra arched an eyebrow at her. His sheepish grin told her he knew she was amused, but undeterred, he continued. "No. We didn't need stuff. Shay and I both lived on our own for years, so we had stuff. We had sheets and towels and dishes. Just like Amber and Nathan do. And second?"

"Hmm?" She lifted her chin.

"Why is it your job to make sure I have pots and pans? Silverware? A mixing bowl?"

"It's just the way it works, Ez. Guests bring gifts. You register so you don't get seven of the same salad bowl."

"It just so happens that Shay and I got four cheese graters and three crockpots, and no, guests shouldn't be required to bring gifts."

Liv eyed him suspiciously.

"What? You don't want to spring for something for Amber? Is that it?"

He laughed and shook his head. "No. I just don't like the process. I'd rather give Amber and Nathan cash. Maybe they have something special they would use it for."

"What would you use it for?"

"Me?"

"You and Shay?"

Liv waited anxiously for his answer. When he opened his mouth to speak but then closed it again, she fell forward over the counter.

"Ezra?"

"Where's Ingrid?"

He turned to look out the window again, and Liv stared at his back in disbelief.

"She's working."

"Edits."

"No, actually. She's writing. Started a new book."

"Hmm."

"Do you ever read her books?"

"Yep." Ezra nodded. He folded his hands into his pockets. "She's good."

Liv watched her brother study the view through the window. She almost asked him where Shay was, but she didn't. It was Saturday; maybe she was with her family. Maybe she was at home doing laundry. Liv missed her, and she wanted to see Samuel, but she sensed it was better not to bring her sister-in-law up again.

"So what do you think?"

"I told you she's good," he answered. "Kind of weird to look at my sister and think she writes that kind of violence, but—"

Liv nodded when he looked at her over his shoulder.

"Yeah, but I meant with the house." She rubbed her forehead and then her eyes and then stared at her brother. "What do you think? Make the investment? Or get out now and sell it as it is?"

Ezra pursed his lips.

"Does it matter what I think?"

"Would I ask if it didn't?"

"You three have already decided—"

"We three haven't, actually," Liv argued. "C'mon Ezra. What do you think?"

Ezra's gaze climbed the walls and roamed over the ceiling. He looked sad, a little bit wistful when he turned his attention back to her.

"It's a money pit, Liv." He tossed his hands up.

She nodded, not sure how she felt about his response. She was torn over the whole thing. A month ago, she would have hung onto the house with both hands just to hold on to the shared past they all had. Now she wasn't sure. It *was* a money pit. Renovations were going to cost them an arm and a leg. A lot of time. Strangers in and out of the house, because if they decided to do this, she was going to push to hire professionals to do the work. Not to mention, she had enough on her plate right now at home. If they cut the house loose and moved on, she would be at home more often.

The thought stole her breath away. Because right now, she wasn't sure if being home more would be a good thing. The kids were busy. Sure, they might like to have the laundry cycle completed sooner, and they might like more home-cooked meals and treats. But they didn't miss her, not the way they would have when they were younger. But what about Wade? What would he do if she were home more? Would they fight that much more often? Or would he close himself off in his garage to work and leave her to wander the empty house, looking for something to do?

"Can you imagine it, though?"

Ezra's words, the childlike wonder in his voice pulled her from her thoughts. For a moment, she thought Ezra wanted to know if she could imagine something with Wade. Either the two of them living separately in the same house, again, or the two of them working together to love each other and save their marriage. But when she blinked and focused on Ezra's face, she saw that he had gone back to checking out the house. His head tilted back, his eyes roamed the high ceiling again.

"This house? Fully restored? It's gorgeous." He spoke in a hushed tone, a hint of reverence in his words.

"You…" Liv frowned and cocked her head to look at him closer. "You wanna do it. You wanna dig in and do it."

Ezra blew out a long, ragged sigh and puffed his cheeks up. He shrugged and nodded.

"I'd love to do it, but I don't have a lot of cash to toss into the coffers," he said simply. "Therefore, I don't think my vote counts."

"You're a Williams, Ezra," she said quietly. "Your vote counts."

THE GARAGE WAS ALMOST EMPTY, BUT THAT WASN'T SAYING MUCH since the contents were scattered all over the yard and makeshift drive. Liv stood with her hands on her hips, breathing hard after helping Ingrid drag an old window air conditioner out of the furthest corner. Together, they managed to lift it enough to slide it onto a big piece of cardboard and then they had pushed and tugged together until they nearly collapsed near the row of bushes that lined the garage. It wasn't really an occasion to celebrate, because at the moment, the place looked like a flea market, and the neighbors would put up with this for exactly five seconds.

Liv eyed Ingrid, whose pose nearly mirrored her own, except that her chin rested on her chest as she sucked in deep breath after deep breath. Nathan held a ladder against the yard side of the garage, wedged between the yews planted there. Liv decided the bushes needed to be trimmed, and then she studied Nathan and the ladder closer because she thought the ladder they'd pulled out of the garage had two rungs broken in the middle. She almost warned him not to use it, to just toss it in the burn pile, but she happened to look up and she noticed Amber on the roof of the garage.

"Is she nuts?" she mumbled, and though she hadn't meant for anyone to hear her, she heard her sister-in-law chuckle behind her. Liv turned and swung her gaze to Shay, who had accompanied Ezra today, dressed to work with them on the garage and whatever else they got to before the day was over.

"She is, yes," Shay said with a firm nod. "Certifiable."

"What's she doing?" Liv hollered at Nathan. And then rather than wait for Nathan to answer her, Liv cocked her head and held her hand up to shield her eyes from the sun and sought Amber out again. "What're you doing?"

Amber held up the camera around her neck as if that explained everything.

"Get down before you fall and break an arm," Ingrid called to her. Liv was glad it was Ingrid who had issued the warning, although she was thinking it, too.

"You're thinking of Ezra," Amber answered as she crept along the roof.

Shay giggled, and Ezra sputtered an argument, and Liv and Ingrid exchanged a look. Liv looked away, turned again to look behind her at the house when she heard the squeal of the screen door. Wade, dressed much the same as he would be if he were working for hire rather than cleaning up at his in-laws' estate, carried a rolled section of what looked like linoleum over his arms, stretched out in front of him. He tossed it awkwardly to the ground, dusted his hands off, and lifted his eyes to look around.

Even out here, surrounded by her family and by any neighbors who might currently be watching the Williams' show out their windows, Liv felt naked in his eyes. Not attractive. Just exposed. He held her gaze when their eyes met, wiped his hands off on the seat of his cargo shorts, and then lifted the tail of his shirt to swipe at the sweat on his face. Heat of a different kind rushed her when she saw the smooth expanse of his stomach.

They hadn't made love since the night of Gracie's graduation. Well, she wouldn't count that. Not because he'd left her hanging, but because the whole thing had been cold and angry and over in less than five minutes, and so really, she didn't know when they last *made love*. He wanted her. They had made out like kids on several occasions, and Wade never tried to hide his erection. But when things heated up, he put the brakes on and walked away.

Liv assumed he was punishing her. But she wondered how long this could last.

Finally, he broke the eye contact. But Liv watched him saunter down the driveway toward Luke. She watched the two of them as they assessed the window unit she and Ingrid had dragged out. Liv barely remembered the thing from the front family room, and she figured if it had been in the garage that damned long, it was dead and could not be resuscitated. Luke took his ball cap off and wiped his forehead with the sleeve of his t-shirt before tugging it back on.

The middle of June had come, and like clockwork, the humidity had sky-rocketed, and it was miserably hot outside and almost unbearable in the house. Ingrid had called an HVAC guy over to check the central air unit. All of them had taken the news of the dead compressor badly. If they were going through with the renovations—at this point, Liv likened it to a resurrection because it didn't seem possible that it could happen—the first order of business was either a new compressor, which would not come cheap or a new central air and furnace unit, which was going to cost roughly a third of Gracie's tuition and room and board next year.

She wondered if Luke knew. Ingrid said she'd kept it from him, but what about Wade? Did he talk to his friends about personal stuff? Liv never thought about it before. Now the possibility burned through her like acid. What if everyone here knew what she'd done to her husband?

"Did we—?"

Liv swung her gaze to Ingrid as she approached her. Her shirt collar was ringed in sweat. Beads of sweat clung to the ends of her spiky hair.

"What?" Ingrid stared at Liv with big eyes. She ran her fingers through her hair and then wiped them on the butt of her athletic shorts. "Why are you looking at me like that?"

"Just wondering if your purple streak runs when you sweat."

Ingrid laughed softly and rolled her eyes. Liv marveled at the change. A few short months ago, a smartass comment about Ingrid's hair would have brought out the claws.

"You should do blue," Ingrid suggested. "Some blue extensions down your back."

"Right." Liv nodded. "I'm gonna call the salon and get right on that."

Ingrid grinned and looked away. She glanced at Luke and Wade and then looked back toward the house.

"Did we decide? I don't remember deciding to do this for sure."

Liv blinked at Ingrid and then reached to dab at her eye when she felt the burn of sweat.

"We talked about it last night," Liv reminded Ingrid.

"Right. We talked about it, and I don't remember making a final decision, and now Bob the Builder there just ripped part of the kitchen floor up, and we're fucked."

"Bob the Builder must've been tired of the indecision."

"You're defending him?"

Liv drew back as if Ingrid had slapped her. "Um. Yeah. Because I'm already in the doghouse, Ingrid. Next step is the curb."

Ingrid whooshed out a quick breath and shook her head.

"Wade Girard!" she bellowed.

Liv stared at her with big eyes. Wade and Luke both turned to look at Ingrid. Liv wanted to grab her and slap her hand over her mouth to make sure she didn't say something stupid. Now wasn't the time for her sister to make some grand gesture in her defense.

"What?"

"What gives? You just tore half the kitchen floor out of the house."

Liv turned her wide-eyed stare to Wade.

"Not quite half," he corrected her. "The good news is the subflooring looks good."

Liv looked from Wade back to Ingrid and shrugged.

"I don't remember agreeing on this—"

"That's because Luke had his tongue crammed down your throat and his hands in your shirt when I announced I'd be here with bells on today to start ripping the linoleum out."

"You were watching them?" Liv asked in disbelief.

"They were at the kitchen table," Wade reminded her. "And I wouldn't have to watch if I was getting some at home."

Liv's mouth dropped open at his spiteful words. Her cheeks were on fire when he turned and walked back to the air conditioner carcass. She saw Ingrid open her mouth to question her, but she shook her head. Met her sister's eyes and silently pleaded with her not to say anything.

CHAPTER 25

*H*er back hurt, and the tension in her muscles all day made it worse, and Liv lingered in the shower. They were supposed to meet back at Luke and Ingrid's house, and maybe early this morning, it had seemed like a good plan. But she was furious with Wade for what he said, what he had implied, and she was mortified that Ingrid heard him. Knowing damned good and well that the first chance she got, Ingrid would launch an interrogation, and feeling that sharp throb of pain when she moved just so, and exhausted and thinking that the rest of her summer was going to involve the house and the rest of her life might involve fighting with a man who claimed he wanted to forgive her but couldn't take the first step away from what she had done, she wanted to stay home.

She didn't care if Wade chose to spend the evening at Ingrid's. At the moment, the hot water needling her shoulders and the steam in the room working to ease the stiffness in her muscles was far more appealing than the thought of seeing any of them. She didn't care if Wade found a replacement so he could get off, as long as he left her the hell alone. Might be safer for all of them if Liv stayed home.

There was a loud knock on the door, and then the lock popped. Liv propped a hand on the shower wall and hung her head.

"Are you coming?"

He could see her, the outline of her nude body behind the frosted glass of the shower wall. She didn't care. Didn't struggle to hide herself. She wouldn't give him the satisfaction.

"No." She laughed without humor. "Not if you have any say in it."

"Luke just called and asked us to pick up another bag of ice."

"So go pick up another bag of ice, Wade." She turned the faucet off and reached for her towel. Afraid the room would get cold fast now that he had the door open, Liv scrubbed the towel over her head and her face and then met his eyes. "I'll bring my car out."

"No."

"Why not?"

"We can ride together."

"Then you're gonna have to wait a few minutes," she mumbled. Assuming he would leave her alone, she began drying off again, head bent over her body as she rubbed the towel over her wet skin. "What?" she snapped when he didn't step out of the room. She glanced at him as she stepped out of the shower and tossed her towel on the counter.

"What's the matter with you?"

"Nothing." She reached for her body lotion and eyed Wade expectantly. "Can you at least shut the door?"

He took another step into the room and then pushed the door closed. Leaned on it and watched her with hooded eyes.

"Why aren't you talking to me?"

Liv ignored him as she smoothed her lotion over her legs.

"Liv."

"I'm talking to you, Wade. I told you to go ahead and go if

you were in a hurry, and then I said if you want to ride together, you'll have to wait."

"You avoided me at the house."

She had promised herself she wouldn't let him get to her. At the very least, she wouldn't let him know it if he did get to her. Already, that promise was circling the drain. She squeezed more lotion into the palm of her hand, angry when she got too much. With a dramatic sigh, she slammed the bottle down on the counter.

"Are you kidding me?"

"No." He shook his head. His eyes held her gaze for several long seconds, but finally, he let them slide. Took in the heated flush in her cheeks—they were on fire with anger, not embarrassment or arousal—and then lowered over her shoulders and her breasts.

She wanted to turn her back to him. She wanted to ask him to leave, but she didn't. Instead, she rubbed the lotion over her hands—annoyed again because she had too much— and then started sliding her hands up over her arms and her shoulders.

Eyes smoldering—Liv figured he was consumed with anger rather than desire—Wade stepped toward her. She stilled her hands when he touched her, covered them with his.

"What're you doing?" she whispered. He pulled her hands away from her body and rubbed them with his, as if trying to take some of the excess lotion. Their eyes met, and though she wanted to look away, she was powerless to do it. His fingers trailed feathery touches up over her forearms, her biceps, and finally her shoulders.

"Tell me what you're thinking."

"Please leave me alone. I'll be down in about ten minutes."

"At the house. What were you thinking?"

"Ingrid was pissed that you started tearing the floor up."

"We talked about it—"

"But we didn't all…vote. We didn't decide."

"Hell might freeze over before you guys agree on anything to do with the estate." The little flick of his eyebrows took her breath away.

"Why did you say what you did?" She was still angry, but her voice came out too small, too timid to show it.

"When was the last time we were together?" He moved in to stand closer to her and curled his fingers around the back of her neck. Liv swallowed hard when he moved them, teased her with a barely there caress of his thumb on one side of her neck and his fingers on the other.

"The night you shoved me against the wall if I remember correctly."

Her answer, delivered in a cool, clipped tone, caught him off guard.

"Before that."

She shrugged. "I don't know."

"When it was good."

She laughed softly, but in the still of the room, in the tense silence, it sounded like a sob. Knowing her voice wouldn't work, she offered him a smaller shrug and shook her head.

"You're the one who keeps walking away," she reminded him.

He leaned in so close she could feel his breath on her lips. Eyes locked on his, she flinched and let hers close when he traced his right hand over her collarbone and stroked the tip of his index finger over her nipple.

"It's really hard to want you," his voice was low and cold, "when I think about him. Inside you."

Swallowing was difficult with the crushed glass in her throat, but she managed. Opened her mouth quickly just to breathe again, but that hurt, too. Eyes glassy, she refused to look at him. Instead, she simply waited him out. When he moved, finally, she went through the rest of her post-shower routine. Dressed in comfortable but stylish denim capris and a white Oxford. Slapped just enough makeup on to change her look from bludgeoned and haggard to sore and tired. She ignored the shake in her hands as she dried and styled her hair. Ready not to take on the world, or even just Wade, but simply to get the rest of the night over with, she finally pulled the door open and hovered there in the doorway. She scanned the bedroom, though she knew immediately he wasn't there waiting for her. As she stepped into sandals and then added a pair of silver studs to top off the outfit, she heard the TV on downstairs. Baseball scores.

How could he say things like that and then go downstairs and check in with the MLB? How could he care what team was in the lead in the Central Division when he just unloaded on her? Did he really feel that way? Would he never want her again because she had been unfaithful? Or was this just part of the process? Petty revenge in the form of sharp words? He had sliced her open with that last line, like a cold, smooth knife sliding through skin and tissue.

Liv drew up short after one last look in the mirror on the dresser. She had pulled herself together enough for a night with her sisters—though that didn't matter after Ingrid heard what Wade said anyway—but she could also double as a corpse if the need arose.

"Liv?"

She jumped when Wade's voice echoed up the stairs.

"We gotta go."

She had hated him just then. In the bathroom. He had the right to hold a grudge. He had the right not to forgive her. He could end the marriage if he wanted to. But it wasn't fair of him to cry to her and say he didn't want to lose her and then to hit her with such vitriol just a few days later.

She sniffled, because she was tired of crying, and the last damned thing she needed to do right now was smear her makeup. Her hands were like ice, and they shook with the memory of Wade's hateful comment. She rubbed them roughly over the sides of her capris and then opened the top middle drawer of their dresser where she kept most of her jewelry. Her eyes moved over the wedding ring on her finger as she reached to pick up a necklace.

"Olivia."

"Just a second, Wade," she mumbled as she hooked the silver chain around her neck. She pushed the drawer closed and eyed the finishing touch in the mirror, satisfied that the small silver heart might get his attention. He had given it to her the first time they made love back when they were two horny kids, playing together at adulthood and relationships.

It saddened her to wonder now if they had changed all that much.

The TV was off when she went downstairs. Wade leaned on the counter, legs crossed at his ankles, arms folded over his chest. His face was unforgiving as he watched her rush in to grab her purse and her phone from the counter. Liv slid the straps of the bag over her shoulder and spared him a glance as she turned to waltz out of the room.

"Do you still need to get ice?" She was proud of herself for sounding normal. Her heart was banging on her rib cage, and electricity raced through her arms and legs and hummed in her fingertips. Her throat was tight with a million words she wanted to say but wouldn't try. She led the way to the garage and climbed up into his truck without a backward glance.

"No." He didn't look at her as he settled into the driver's seat and started the truck. He kept his gaze on the rearview mirror, an expression of boredom on his face as he watched the garage door lumber up behind them. "Nathan texted and said they would get it."

She wanted to move. She needed to move; her heart was still pounding, and she was fidgety, but she took a deep breath and folded her hands in her lap. She stared out the windshield, but as Wade threw his right arm up over the back of the seats and twisted around to back out of the garage, she was tempted to look at him. Instead, she turned her face away and watched out the passenger window as he eased the truck back.

Had Luke sent out a group text, she wondered? Did guys do that? She didn't know how often her husband texted people. She and Wade often communicated through text messages throughout a workday. Simple things like *do we need milk? Or would you stop and pick up a loaf of bread on the way home?* But did Wade text with friends?

When Wade moved his arm from the seats, closed the garage door, and then put the truck in drive, she chanced a quick peek at him. He had showered, though he hadn't bothered to shave. The light-colored scruff on his face looked gray, and then Liv decided it probably was gray. It looked good, and she had to remind herself he didn't want her, so she clasped her hands tighter together and looked away.

The thought of Wade talking to or texting with friends made Liv feel uncomfortable. Did they all know? Had Tony Rice said something to Wade in private about the day he had seen her getting out of the car with Asher Crowe? Or, God forbid, had he mentioned it in front of an entire construction crew? Her heart plunged at the thought, both for herself and Wade, but mostly Wade. How emasculating would that be?

She forgot that she was trying not to move, and she lifted her right hand to smooth her fingers over her chest. It hurt her to feel how badly she had hurt him. And she wondered again if Luke and Nathan knew what she had done.

Luke wouldn't forgive her. He and Wade had been friends for a long time; if things went south and shook out with her on one side of a fence and Wade on the other, Luke would be there for Wade. He should be there for Wade; she wanted someone to support him, but the thought of losing Luke as a friend, the thought of what that might do to her sister's relationship and the strain it might put on her relationship with Ingrid, hit her square in the gut and took her breath away.

"You okay?" he asked without looking at her.

She sniffled and nodded and then determined to sit still, she slid her hands under her thighs and stared straight ahead.

"What're you thinking about?"

"Amber," she said quietly, because even though she was really thinking about Wade and how she had messed up so badly, she was thinking about her sisters and that she loved being with them even when they still had a hard time getting along and that Amber was dreading tonight. Because Hadley was staying over with her father and his family.

"Amber?" Wade's voice gave away his surprise. He did look at her then; she felt his heavy gaze on her, but she refused to look at him.

"Mmm." She nodded. "Hadley is staying at Kyle's tonight." She was tired now and rethinking the decision to go to Ingrid and Luke's. Liv knew she wasn't warm and cozy on a good day, but lately she was acerbic and impossible to get along with. Walking into tonight in the mood she was already in was a recipe for disaster. "Amber's scared."

Wade grunted something in response, but Liv couldn't guess what it was. She didn't want to, because he was probably arguing that Kyle had the right to know his daughter. Liv agreed, but that didn't mean she couldn't understand Amber's fear. Liv's kids should love their father; Liv wanted both of them to have a great relationship with Wade. But she was still afraid of what he would say to them if push came to shove and they split up.

The rest of the drive was quiet. In fact, Wade apparently thought it was too quiet, because he turned the radio on. Liv suffered through a few songs without complaint, but she wasn't in the mood for music.

Wade and Nathan had pulled the remainder of the linoleum from the kitchen and mudroom earlier. The guys—

Luke and Ezra included—had decided the subflooring did look okay, but Liv had suggested they go ahead and have someone from a pest control agency come over and take a look. No sense in moving ahead if there was any chance something could go wrong further down the line. They were all in now, might as well do it right.

The guys had moved on to the bathroom, but Liv and her sisters had lingered in the kitchen. It had amazed Liv that the room looked so foreign to her now after seeing it for forty plus years with that same floor covering. Part of her was lost as she wandered through the room, fingers trailing over the counters and table that were still all familiar. And part of her wished they had done this before her mom passed away if this is what she wanted.

Amber's car was pulled close to the sprawling cabin Luke had built and then offered to her sister Ingrid as a dream place to live. Shay's car was pulled in behind Amber's, and Liv wondered as her fingers absently worked the seatbelt if they had brought Samuel. She hoped so; she wanted to hold someone who loved her and wouldn't push her away. Okay, maybe Samuel didn't know what love was just yet, but he would hardly push her away.

Then again, maybe it would be good for Ezra and Shay to have a night off. Her brother had never been one for the clubbing scene, but Liv knew he and Shay used to go out with their friends and enjoy themselves. She also knew they stopped all that fun stuff when Shay reached the middle of her pregnancy. Liv understood. Wasn't much fun about feeling big and unattractive and watching your husband—still trim and sexy and appealing to other women—flirt and carry on without you. Postpartum depression wasn't fun, either, and Liv understood that, too. But eventually, Shay needed to climb out of that hole before the sides collapsed in on her, and she smothered.

"Livvie."

She stopped short as she pushed the door closed. Wade had rounded the front of the truck to stand before her. Her lesson burned into her brain, her heart, she stepped back and crossed her arms over her middle to hug herself. To create a barrier between them.

Once upon a time, this man had been her everything. And she had gambled everything, and now here they were, Wade a victim and Liv the loser. She swallowed hard and steeled herself to whatever scathing comment he would make this time. Looked at him with dry eyes and waited.

"What?"

"I'm sorry." He reached for her, froze with his hands over her shoulders when she took another step back, and then dropped them to his sides. "I'm not trying to hurt you."

She took a deep breath through her nose and lifted her chin in defiance. Ignoring the ache that opened up inside her, she arched her eyebrows.

"Aren't you?"

"I love you."

She blinked and looked away, because she was not going to cry again, and she definitely wasn't going to cry here for damned sure. The hope in Wade's voice hung between them in the early summer evening.

Liv shook her head sadly and glanced at him. Licked her lips to find them dry. Maybe she was cried out.

"But you can't forgive me."

"I want to—"

"Hey!" Ingrid's voice carried to them over the front yard. "What kind of seasoning do you guys want on your chicken?"

No intention of answering Ingrid, Liv blinked at Wade. She took a steadying breath and raised her eyebrows.

"But you can't." She shrugged. "If you can't forgive me, we have nowhere to go, Wade."

"Livvie."

She stepped around him and saw her sisters standing on the front porch. Cold now, after the words she and Wade had just exchanged, Liv hunched her shoulders, tucked her hands in her hip pockets, and made her way up the drive to the porch.

"Great timing, Ingrid." She flashed a quick look at Ingrid, let her eyes slide over Amber, and went past them into the house. She might have meant it, the great timing comment. Because Ingrid had interrupted Wade, and what if he was going to say something like he wanted to forgive her but couldn't? What if he was going to suggest a trial separation? Or what if he was just going to announce that he was leaving?

But what if he wasn't? What if he would have said he wanted to forgive her, but it still hurt to think about her with someone else?

She swallowed, her throat tight with emotion, and made her way through the house to the big, modern kitchen. Luke, apron on over a fresh shirt and shorts, looked up from the plate of raw chicken on the counter. He grinned at her, but since she had expected him to be cold, it took her a moment to return the smile.

"Beer?" he offered. He picked up the plate and nodded to the fridge to invite her to help herself. Before she could move, someone approached her from behind and dropped a hand on her shoulder. Too small to be Wade, she only ducked her head.

"I'm just gonna do half and half," Luke said, and Liv knew it was Ingrid behind her, and he was talking to her.

"Sure."

When he had gone out the back door to the deck, Liv glanced to her left. She hadn't realized she was holding her breath until she saw only her sisters in the room with her, and she gasped for air.

"Wade went around outside," Ingrid said quietly.

Liv nodded.

"I'm sorry. I didn't mean to interrupt—"

"I know." Liv waved Ingrid's comment away. Amber slipped by them. Liv glanced at her and remembered, too late, that she probably wasn't in the best of moods, either, with Hadley being gone for the night. She watched her little sister retrieve three bottles from the refrigerator. Decided she should say something about it now, but she was uncertain how to bring it up.

"You okay?" Amber handed her one of the bottles. Chagrined by Amber's concern, when she'd shown none for her, Liv nodded and twisted the top off her bottle. She took a long drink and then rubbed her fingertips over her lips.

"How about you?" Her voice came out in a gruff whisper. "You okay?"

Amber shrugged as she moved to the island and pulled a stool out to sit down.

"Have to be, don't I?"

Liv studied her closely. Amber was pale. Sure, it was early summer, but Amber was too pale. Her lips looked blue.

"No." She frowned. She reached for her, took Amber's hand, and tugged her off the stool. "You don't. You don't have to be okay. Not with me."

Amber avoided Liv's eyes.

"I'm fine."

"You don't ever have to lie to me, Amber," Liv said quietly. "If you can't tell me and Ingrid when you're upset, who can you tell?"

Ingrid made a small noise, possibly a murmur of agreement. Or shock, Liv decided when she looked at her, now standing on the other side of the counter.

"You take some Prozac or something?" Ingrid asked as she squatted to get a serving bowl from a cabinet.

"Shut up," Liv answered, but her words were soft and cool. She linked her fingers through Amber's and led her over to the high four-top table in the corner. Amber still avoided her eyes as she climbed up to sit down.

"What time did she go?" Ingrid asked Amber. "Why'd you move over there? It's easier to talk to you when you're by me."

"So I can lean," Liv answered as she sat back on her own stool. "I did something to my back."

Amber finally met her eyes. Liv shook her head at the ornery smirk.

"Something I did at the house today."

"Are you and Wade really not having sex? At all?" Ingrid stood at the end of the counter.

"Get done with what you're doing so you can sit down with us."

Ingrid stared at Liv suspiciously for a moment and then turned back to the lettuce and peppers she'd put on the counter.

"Kyle picked her up around three."

"You weren't even home?"

Amber glanced back over her shoulder at Ingrid. With a sigh of frustration, she hopped off her stool, twisted it around so she was sideways to the table and didn't have her back to Ingrid.

"Why didn't you say something?" Rather than look at Amber now, Liv kept her eyes on her bottle. She picked at the corner of the label. "You should've just gone home to be with her."

"She didn't want me there," Amber admitted. "She was nervous, but she said it would only make it worse if I was around."

"Ouch." Liv winced.

"Have you heard from her?" Ingrid took a long swig from her bottle. Liv felt Amber watching her as she watched Ingrid put the bottle down and reach for her knife. By Ingrid's own admission, she didn't do much in the kitchen. Or she hadn't when she lived alone. Judging from how her sister's hands moved quickly as she cut the romaine hearts into smaller, edible pieces, she was getting more practice.

"She texted me around four." Amber dragged her fingers through her hair. "And said she was okay, but it was weird."

"What's weird?" Liv asked.

Amber raised her eyebrows and shrugged. "I dunno."

"You didn't ask?"

"I don't wanna bother her. I can't nag her when she's with him." Amber blinked and lifted only her eyes to look at Liv. "Right? Shouldn't I back off?"

"Standby," Liv agreed. "Sucks, babe."

"Wait." Ingrid tossed the romaine into the big salad bowl. "You can't just text and say what's weird?"

"No." Amber sounded sad. "Because she might answer me."

"And you don't want her to spend her time with them texting you." Ingrid frowned, but she nodded. "Okay, I guess that makes sense."

"No." Amber took a drink. "Because I don't wanna know what's weird. I can't know now. If she's miserable, and she tells me, I'm gonna get in my car and go get her and bring her home. And I can't. I can't do that."

"Amber." Liv reached over the table, palm up. Amber looked startled. She stared at her for a moment and then inched her hand up from her lap and placed it in Liv's open palm. "Whoever told you that you're a bad parent is so wrong." Liv squeezed her sister's fingers. "You're doing it. You're loving her just the way a mother should love her baby."

CHAPTER 26

*T*he stunned look on Amber's face hit Liv in the chest and the stomach like a baseball bat. It was gone instantly, and Amber's slow slide to tears pulled Liv to her feet. She moved around the table and gathered Amber in her arms. She wanted to apologize. She needed to apologize. Where the hell had she been in her sister's life that her comment could touch her as it had? But it wasn't the time. Amber needed comfort, and to apologize now to assuage her own guilt for being emotionally absent would only be more of the same behavior she was suddenly ashamed of.

"What if she hates them?" Amber whispered. "What if she wants to come home?"

"She's fine, Amber. She did okay when she went out of town with them." Liv smoothed her hand up over Amber's back. "She's okay. He's not gonna hurt her. Nothing that happened is her fault."

"But what if she's scared, Liv? This is an overnight thing." Amber pushed her back a step. She propped her elbow on the table at her side and rubbed her eyes with her hand. "You know that feeling. Like when you go to camp, and you look around, and you're surrounded by strangers, and your stomach hurts—"

"It's all part of growing up," Liv whispered. She bent her knees to dip low enough to meet Amber's eyes; Amber peeked out at her from behind her fingers. "Right? We all go through that. Just like the first day of kindergarten. You walk 'em in, and you turn 'em over to a stranger, and you leave. And when you leave?" Liv cupped Amber's chin in her hand and gently forced her to look up. "When you leave? You leave a piece of your heart there, right? And you can't function all damned day because your heart is somewhere outside of you."

Amber nodded.

"But you have to do it. Even if they cry." Liv shrugged. "Sometimes you have to push 'em. And you have to be strong when all you wanna do is cry."

"She's only spent a few hours at a time with them." Amber jerked her chin away from Liv and looked away. "Even when they went out of town, it was only, like, an eight hour thing."

"But this is the next step," Liv said quietly. "And…and, Amber?" She touched Amber's arm. "She's a phone call away. If it gets that bad, she'll call you. Because she knows you love her."

"I know." Amber took a deep breath. She nodded and dabbed at her eyes again. "I know, and I know she deserves to know him. They both deserve the chance to get to know each other."

"Yeah." Liv agreed. "They do."

"And one day soon, she'll choose to be over there with them. Instead of at home with me and Nathan."

Liv bit her lip when Amber met her gaze.

"I don't think you can look at it like that, Amber. I know how much that scares you. But wouldn't that be incredible for

Hadley? If she were that comfortable with her father and his family?"

Amber pressed her lips together and answered Liv with a tiny shrug.

"Did I show you a picture of his wife? She's gorgeous. Amber's gonna love her."

"Oh, sweetie, don't do that." Liv shook her head. "Don't ever do that to yourself. She is so lucky to have you for a mom." Liv reached for Amber's hand and drew it away from her face. "You ever look in a mirror? You're beautiful. Little bit mean sometimes, but you're so beautiful."

Amber laughed softly. "I get that from you."

"You can't get your mean streak from a sibling." Liv shook her head.

"No. I meant that being beautiful part."

"You can't get that from me, either," Liv argued. She felt a smile tug at her lips and ignored that gaping hole inside and focused on Amber.

Gazes locked, they were quiet for a moment.

"Thank you, Liv." Amber arched her eyebrows.

"You just needed a reminder." Liv leaned in and kissed Amber's cheek. "I'm sorry. I've been horrible to you, and I'm so sorry."

Amber nodded. She broke the eye contact and slid off the stool.

"Excuse me for a second," she mumbled as she slipped past Liv and hurried out of the room. Liv watched her go, oblivious to Ingrid watching her from the counter.

"I shouldn't have come tonight," she said when she finally moved.

"Why not?" Ingrid turned back to the bell peppers on the cutting board.

"I'm exhausted."

Ingrid shot her a deadpan look and turned back to slice the first of the peppers.

"We're all exhausted. Feels like we've been dealing with the house for two years."

Liv snagged her bottle from the table and wandered over to stand at the counter with Ingrid.

"Is it you? Or him?"

Liv watched her sister guide the ceramic knife through the peppers. When Ingrid moved only her eyes to look at her, Liv took a drink.

"You're not gonna tell me?"

Liv dragged her teeth over her lower lip and then whooshed out a harsh breath and leaned over the counter. Her chest was painfully tight, and her throat ached. But damned if she would stand here and cry about Wade when he might walk in at any moment.

"Too much to say, Ingrid." Fingertips over her lips, she spoke into her hands. Ingrid blinked at her muffled words.

"Have you not been together? Since—"

"We have, but—"

"Tell me, Liv." Ingrid sighed as she tossed the knife down on the cutting board. "Let me listen."

When she only stared at her, Ingrid shook her head and muttered something about trust. Liv watched her pick up the knife again. She moved before she knew she was going to. She reached and touched the back of Ingrid's left hand.

"I do. Trust you." Liv shrugged. "But this isn't the time."

Ingrid dropped her head back and narrowed her eyes at Liv. "But it's never the time."

"I'm not putting you off."

Ingrid's stare was cool and accusing. Liv lifted her eyes to look over Ingrid's shoulder. She couldn't see any of the guys through the window, but that meant nothing. Any of them could walk in at any minute.

"We haven't made love since before…" She swallowed hard and forced herself to finish her sentence. "Before I cheated."

"Are you —?" Ingrid's mouth dropped open. "Are you kidding me? Liv, that's—"

Liv held her hand up to stop her. "We've had sex." She lowered her gaze, embarrassed to admit to her sister the bare bones of her and Wade's sex life. "There's a difference."

"I know that." Ingrid licked her lips.

"Do you think she's okay?" Liv looked over her shoulder, curious about where Amber had gone.

Ingrid simply nodded. "Yeah. That was…" She hitched her right shoulder in a grudging shrug. "The nicest thing I've ever heard you say to her…to either one of us."

Liv deflated and rolled her eyes. "Are you friggin' kidding me?"

"What?"

"You're gonna play the jealous card now?"

"What? Are you still hogging it?" Ingrid shook her head and tossed her hands up in irritation.

"Look." Liv sniffled and arched an eyebrow, her eyes on the knife again. "I love you. Both of you. I don't say it much, and I'm sorry I'm not that person. But you don't, either, Ingrid. None of us is all that demonstrative—"

"All I said was that it was nice," Ingrid mumbled. "Okay? I couldn't have done that. I never dropped a kid off for a first day of kindergarten, and I don't know what it's like to live and love someone so completely dependent on me. And I couldn't have calmed her down like you did, and it was nice."

Liv licked her lips. Nodded when Ingrid shot her a look of irritation.

"Well, all I'm saying is I do. Love you." Liv threw the words out in an angry huff. "I think I'm about to lose everything good in my life, and I'm sorry I can't play nice, but I'm scared. I'm so goddamned scared of what's gonna happen…"

She picked up her bottle, but when she saw that it was

empty, she set it down again. Intending to go outside, to the front porch, she turned away from Ingrid.

"Liv."

She ignored her, but when the knife cluttered to the counter, and Ingrid grabbed her arm and spun her around to face her, she reached for Ingrid.

"God, what I have to do just to get a hug from you," Ingrid mumbled as she slid her arms around Liv's middle.

"I just told you twice that I love you, and you keep looking at me like you want to slice and dice me with that knife."

Ingrid laughed softly, but she hung on.

"Thank you."

"Thank you?" Liv repeated. "Ingrid—"

"For what you said to Amber."

"Don't thank me. God, Ingrid, I know how she feels. I want to help."

"Still."

Ingrid took a step back, but they still stood toe-to-toe.

"Oh." Liv nodded. She drew in a sharp breath and winced at the slice of pain through her chest. "I get it."

"Get what?"

"You're thanking me for saying something nice to Amber because you're protecting her. Because you're—"

"I just told you I'm thanking you because I couldn't have done what you did there," Ingrid said softly. "And yes, I'm fucking thrilled that you gave her your attention for a few minutes, because you kinda ripped her heart out that day you went off on her about…"

"About favoring you."

Ingrid rolled her eyes, but she looked miserable, like she was ready to break.

"Why can't we get past this?"

"We were," Liv reminded her. "I meant what I said to Amber. I'm sorry. I'm sorry that I got my feelings hurt—"

"Jesus—"

"And I'm sorry I reacted badly, and I do think she's doing just exactly what she should be doing with Hadley, and I do love you, and I need you both, Ingrid. I need you both right now, and I'm sorry I keep circling back to me, but I'm afraid he's gonna leave me."

"It wasn't too long ago you told me you wanted a divorce."

"I don't." Liv shrugged. "I don't want that. I don't want to lose him. I don't want to rip our lives apart. I don't want to be divorced parents to Gracie and Charlie—"

Liv looked up when the back door opened. She met Wade's eyes and held her breath when he hesitated in the doorway. Had he heard her?

"Luke needs a clean plate," he said to Ingrid. He kept his eyes on Liv, but she couldn't read him. They'd left things tense and unsaid outside, so he could still be upset about that or about what had happened or what had been said before they left the house.

Ingrid cut her gaze to Wade and then looked back at Liv.

"Where're Ezra and Shay?" Liv asked Ingrid.

"Outside," Ingrid answered as she moved to get a plate for Luke. She handed it to Wade; Liv felt an irrational flare of jealousy as her husband took the plate and grinned at her sister.

"Did they bring—"

"No."

Liv raised her eyebrows and nodded. When Wade slipped back out to give Luke the plate, Ingrid went back to the salad. Uncomfortable now with Ingrid for reasons she didn't understand, Liv considered going to hide on the front porch. She couldn't, though. If she and Wade had any hope of working things out, she had to stay present with him. She had to show him that she wanted to be with him, and apparently, she needed to show the rest of her family the same.

Shay and Ezra were standing at the rail of the deck. Facing the yard, Shay appeared to be hanging on Ezra's every word as he talked and pointed at something. Now and then, Shay nodded, and then when Liv pulled the door closed behind her, Shay turned to look at her. Her smile warmed Liv to her toes, and she felt a quick flash of happiness for her brother and his wife. She'd seen more life in her sister-in-law today than she had since Samuel was born.

Luke, Nathan, and Wade were gathered by the grill. Luke stood in front of it, a beer in one hand and tongs in the other. Nathan sprawled in a lawn chair. Wade sat at the table. He watched Liv as she approached him, eyes hungry for her every move, but still a little cold. She held her breath as she perched on a chair beside him.

She should have grabbed another beer. She could go back inside to grab one, but with Wade's less than enthusiastic reaction to her coming out to the deck, she was afraid she would chicken out and stay in the kitchen. She was keenly aware that Ingrid had not returned her sentimental words earlier, and she decided from Ingrid's tone when she questioned her about Wade and wanting a divorce that Ingrid would defend him. If it came to choosing sides, Ingrid would support Wade.

Her mouth tasted bitter. She wished again for another beer.

"Is Amber okay?" Nathan nudged Liv's leg with the toe of his tennis shoe. She gave herself a mental shake and shrugged.

"It's a hard night," she said quietly. "She'll get through it."

"She's a livewire tonight," Nathan mumbled. Wade snorted and said something under his breath about family traits.

Liv dragged her eyes from Nathan to look at Wade. When he reached to take her hand, she let him, but she felt nothing.

No energy, no desperation to hang on tight. If she did, she figured he would shake her off and walk away.

"So." Ingrid opened the door and stepped outside, Amber on her heels. Liv felt a stick of paranoia; had they been inside just now talking about her? About how she was stupid to cheat on Wade and stupid now to expect forgiveness? "I guess we're all in. On the house."

She crossed the deck to sit down. Offered Liv a beer as she did.

"Thanks." Liv took the bottle and drank from it. She drew her hand away from Wade's, surprised to feel grateful that they were all going to sit here and talk about the house. Might end up in a knock-down-drag-out, but that beat the feeling of dread she had when she thought about her personal situation.

CHAPTER 27

*B*ecause she needed a break from the togetherness—
it was almost hard to breathe—Liv stacked the
plates and carried them inside. She didn't ask for help, didn't
look anyone in the eye as she made her way inside. Dinner
had been nice. Relaxed and easy, and that surprised her. She'd
offered her opinion on flooring and whether or not they
should demolish the garage—she was shocked that was even
a question—but she had kept quiet when conversation turned
away from the house. She had no interest in talking about
sports or movies, and though she listened to Amber and
Nathan talk about Hadley and she laughed at stories about
Samuel, she didn't contribute. She'd told them the kids were
out with friends when asked, and when they were all kicked
back after they'd finished eating, she'd been thrilled for the
excuse to escape.

She allowed her mind to wander as she filled the sink with
hot, soapy water. Luke and Ingrid had a dishwasher, but
washing the dishes by hand was therapeutic. Not to mention
time consuming. She was counting the minutes until they
could leave and get home, and she and Wade could go their
separate ways.

"Hey."

She looked to her left when the door opened and Amber walked in carrying the tongs and the serving plate in one hand and the salad bowl in the other.

"Hey." Liv was happy she had calmed down. She wasn't fooled. Amber would walk on eggshells until tomorrow when Hadley was back at home. Or maybe, forever was more accurate, because you just did when you were a mom. Nothing mattered but your child's happiness.

Stunned by the realization that she'd lived that way, Liv looked away from Amber and picked up the first plate to wash it. She'd always put Grace and Charlie first, and last year, she had snapped. She'd been restless and angry, and she made a huge mistake. Rather than approach Wade and rock the boat, rather than blow her resentment sky high and pick a fight with him, she had turned outside her marriage to relieve that tension. The boredom. The heartache.

Maybe she had told herself she hadn't wanted to fight with him because fighting would hurt the kids. Now look at the mess she had created. Look at how badly she had hurt the kids, whether they ever knew the truth or not.

"Need some help?" Amber offered.

Liv started to say no. She would rather be alone, and Amber didn't need to hide out in here. No one outside hated her. No one out there was angry with her or disappointed in her.

"Sure."

"She texted me," Amber said quietly as she picked up the dishtowel from the counter.

"Yeah? She okay?" Liv cocked her head and waited anxiously to hear how Hadley was doing.

"They had pizza delivered," Amber told Liv. "And they're watching a movie."

Liv nodded, but she didn't move. "But is she okay?"

"I think so."

Liv leaned in and bumped Amber's arm with hers. "You okay?"

Amber laughed, but Liv heard the sadness.

"You gonna lean on me when Gracie leaves for college?"

"Oh, God." Liv groaned. "Don't remind me." She laughed, but the thought of Gracie leaving in the fall stole her breath away. "Yeah, I am. That okay?"

"Absolutely," Amber said with a sweet smile. "Liv?"

"Hmm?"

"Thanks—"

"Amber, don't—"

"For taking my side with the house. The floors and stuff."

Liv pursed her lips. "It's not about sides. I'm sure all of us would love to see everything completely redone top to bottom in that house. If it weren't for the money, I'm sure we'd all be gung ho."

"Still. Whenever I mentioned it…" Amber shrugged. Liv watched her hesitate, choose her words carefully. Making sure she didn't slam Ingrid, Liv figured. "I got shot down. I appreciate your support."

"Well, if you're gonna get technical and grateful about it, it was Wade who supported you."

Amber stretched and leaned into Liv to see out the window better. She grinned and looked at Liv.

"Do you kiss that spot?" she asked. "On his lip?"

Liv opened her mouth to answer, but Amber's question and the ornery grin on her face caught her off guard.

"What?" She laughed softly.

"The scar," Amber prompted her.

"He fell on concrete steps when he was ten," Liv said softly. "And of course I kiss his scar. It's on his lip."

"I would, too."

"What?" Liv rested her hands on the edge of the sink and stared at Amber in disbelief.

"Oh, come on." Amber rolled her eyes. "He's so frigging

hot, Liv. What the hell did you think you were gonna find with someone else? That Wade wasn't delivering?"

Liv moved her mouth to answer her, but she couldn't. Her husband was easy on the eyes, always had been. The only thing she could have hoped to gain from cheating was attention. A show of affection. Then again, hard to make that argument when she had cheated with Asher Crowe. Not a man given to emotional displays of any sort. Not a man who cherished his own wife. Surely she hadn't thought he would shower her with attention.

Maybe she had wanted Wade's attention.

"Are you telling me you have a thing for Wade?"

"No." Amber shook her head. "I got my own, thanks. I'm just saying, he's gorgeous. And if I ever got my hands on him, I'd suck that scar into my mouth—"

Olivia laughed. She reached into the water and then reached for Amber. The back door opened as the two of them wrestled at the sink; Amber squealed in protest and Liv finally managed to smear soapsuds over her mouth.

"What are you doing?" Wade asked.

Both of them laughing, Liv glanced at Wade and then looked back at Amber. "Don't. Just don't even think it. Ever."

Amber snorted and covered her mouth.

"I'm not kidding, Amber." Liv tried to brush the hair from her face, but her hands were still wet. Amber saved her, brushed her hair back, and looked at Wade.

"C'mere." Amber arched her eyebrows.

"What?" Wade grinned, but he looked at her sister suspiciously.

"C'mere," Amber repeated.

"What are you doing?" Liv grabbed for Amber's hand, but she missed. Amber threw her arms around him when he got close enough.

"Well." Wade laughed. He glanced at Liv as he closed his

arms around her baby sister. "If you're giving out hugs, I'll take one."

"I really wanna kiss this," Amber said as she drew back from him. Liv's mouth dropped open when Amber stroked her thumb over the scar on Wade's lip. "I hope Liv plays there, because that is so sexy."

"Um." Wade cleared his throat and laughed again. "Thank you?"

Amber stood on her tiptoes and kissed his cheek.

"Love you," she said quietly, and then she patted his shoulders and backed away from him. Wade moved his eyes from Amber to Liv. Her stomach dropped as he turned and walked out of the room.

"You're fired," Liv announced when Amber picked the towel up again.

"You can't fire me. I volunteered."

"You just kissed my husband."

"I kissed his cheek." Amber waved Liv's words away.

"You really think he's sexy?"

"I do. Had a massive crush on him when I was about thirteen."

"Even though he's married to me."

"I was thirteen," Amber said again.

"Well, if you're not sure about Nathan, Wade might be a free agent soon."

"That's not funny."

"No, Amber, it's not." Liv attacked the next plate. "But it's possible."

EZRA AND SHAY LEFT BEFORE DARK. LIV HATED TO SEE THEM GO, but they were holding hands when they left, so she hoped that meant they were going home to something better than what she had to look forward to. Liv was ready to go, too, but she knew she'd start at least three fights if she said so. Wade wouldn't be happy with her, and neither would either of her sisters.

When the guys started talking about work, Liv went inside. Claimed she was going after a beer, but she had no intention of going back out. Ingrid and Amber followed her in after a few minutes. Once the three of them had a beer, Ingrid led the way through the front of the house to the porch. Liv and Amber went on out, but Ingrid lingered in the living room for a moment at the entertainment center. Within seconds, music surrounded them on the porch.

"Of course," Liv mumbled. Sitting on the top step, she threw her head back to look at Ingrid when she did come outside. "Got a strobe light, too? Or a disco ball?"

"We don't need a disco ball," Ingrid announced as she sat down on the beautiful wooden swing that Liv had no doubt Luke had built. "Disco balls go with making out in the dark corners in skating rinks."

"Wow." Amber blinked as she sat down beside Ingrid. "You did that?"

Ingrid shrugged and nodded. "Well, yeah. It's what we did when we were kids."

"Says you." Liv sighed. "I didn't get to go skating much."

"Not my fault you were always in trouble."

"I wasn't in trouble," Liv told Amber. "I broke my arm skating. Mom wouldn't let me go back after that."

Ingrid snickered. "Guess she didn't care about me so much."

"Think if you broke your arm now." Amber yawned.

"I wrote my third book with a cast on."

"You broke your arm?"

"Wrist." Ingrid nodded. "Bike crash."

"Motorcycle?" Liv asked quickly.

"No. Bike. Rafe and I used to ride a lot."

"Ouch." Liv turned sideways and leaned on the end of the porch rail. "Your sister confessed to me earlier that she's hot for Wade."

"Can't blame her," Ingrid said with a shrug. "Have you looked at him lately?"

Liv had a flash of memory. The garage. On her knees in front of him.

"Yeah. I have." She smacked her lips together.

"I always thought he had bedroom eyes," Ingrid confessed.

"What?" Liv choked on a drink of beer. "Good grief. Is this true confessions?"

"He's good-looking. You got an eyeful of Luke's bare ass, and it took you a while to walk away. You said so."

"Mmm." Liv nodded and smirked. "So true."

Ingrid looked at her suspiciously.

"What?"

"You didn't…see anything else, right? I mean, he and I were…but did you—"

"Wrong angle," Liv assured her. "Or right angle, I guess."

"I'm sure Wade—"

"Stop!" Liv laughed, but her eyes burned with emotion. "Don't do that. God, I'm going crazy as it is."

"What do you mean?" Amber turned sideways on the swing. Liv marveled at how big and solid it was.

"Do you guys do it there? In the swing?"

Amber cringed, but she laughed.

"We've tried, but it's really uncomfortable."

"I bet." Liv nodded. She turned her attention to the bottle in her hands, but she felt both of them watching her. "He won't touch me."

"He won't—"

Liv lifted only her eyes to look at Ingrid. Shook her head and looked away.

"So you haven't been together at all since he found out?"

Liv cleared her throat. "Once. And it was hard and rough and took two minutes, and when he was done, he told me you were waiting downstairs."

Ingrid winced. "I'm sorry, Liv."

"He's punishing me," she mumbled.

"So why did he say what he did at the house?"

"Fucking with me," Liv said simply. "He's so angry, and I get that. But then he's so soft and so giving. I never know what to expect."

"So seduce him," Amber suggested.

"Tried that," Liv admitted. "He picked me up and moved me off his lap and told me no."

"But have you talked?"

Liv shrugged. "Some. It's the same. We talk for a minute, and then it's like he remembers and that's that."

"Give it time. Liv, please?"

"I'm not going anywhere." Liv shrugged. "But I miss him."

"Do you tell him that?"

"No. Because I'm still…"

"Still what?"

Liv licked her lips. She swept her gaze out over the yard and fixed it on Wade's truck.

"I'm angry. This is my fault. I'm in the wrong. But things haven't been great for a long time."

"You have to work—"

"If I kiss him, he turns away. If I talk to him, if I ask him to forgive me, he gets angry."

Ingrid shrugged. "Let him. Let him do what he has to do. Say what he has to say. Isn't it worth it?"

"So you're saying I need to take the beating and get on with it?"

Ingrid sighed and combed her fingers through her hair. "Maybe."

Liv's shoulders hurt with the weight of Ingrid's stare. Maybe Amber, too, but Liv thought Amber was too caught up in her worry over Hadley to care too much about Liv's marriage. Then again, Amber had made a big deal over reminding Liv how wonderful Wade is and telling Wade she loved him.

"Hannah changed her mind," Ingrid announced suddenly.

A chill rippled up Liv's spine and her heart jumped at Ingrid's tone. Still lost in thought about Wade, still breathless with fear and afraid to move and force Wade's hand, Liv stifled a frustrated sigh and swung her gaze back to her sister.

"About what?" When her voice came out gruff, Liv cleared her throat. "Having the baby?"

"No." Ingrid shook her head and shrugged as if it weren't a big deal that Hannah had changed her mind about something. But Liv saw through the indifference she wore over her face. "She's not coming back now to visit Luke."

"Why not?" Amber sounded distracted, too. Liv tilted her head and studied Ingrid's face. She knew what her sister was thinking, but she waited to see if Ingrid said anything else. When she didn't, when she only moved her shoulders in a deep, exaggerated shrug, Liv stretched and climbed to her feet. She snagged her bottle as she moved to the swing. One hand on the back of the seat, she nudged Ingrid with her leg to scoot her over a bit.

"Maybe she just isn't feeling great, Ingrid," Liv suggested.

"Sure." Ingrid nodded.

"Maybe she's struggling with the idea of having a baby," Amber offered.

Ingrid, eyes fixed on something far in the distance straight ahead, nodded again. Shrugged as if it didn't matter. It did, though. Liv could see how much it mattered to Ingrid that Hannah had changed her mind about coming home. Sure,

Ingrid would be upset for Luke, because she wanted him to be with his daughter more. But Ingrid was worried that Hannah had changed her mind because coming home would mean meeting her. Maybe Hannah didn't want to meet the new woman in her dad's life.

"Who wouldn't want I.G. Arenson as a stepmom?" Liv slid her arm around Ingrid's shoulders. "Seriously. That's like the coolest—"

"Don't." Ingrid shook her head. "First of all, we're not married. We're not getting married. I would never assume anything—"

"You should assume one hundred percent everything with that guy in there, Ingrid. He is crazy about you." Liv squeezed Ingrid in close to her and kissed her cheek. She closed her eyes, her cheek pressed to Ingrid's forehead. "And Hannah will be, too, whenever you meet her."

"I feel like she'd come home to see him if I wasn't around," Ingrid mumbled. "And I feel guilty for keeping them apart."

"Did you tell him that?"

"Yeah."

"And what does he say?"

"He says he loves me, and he's not letting me go anywhere whether Hannah comes home or not."

"Didn't you say you've talked to her on the phone?"

"Yes." Ingrid nodded.

"And things are cool when you talk on the phone?"

"Sure." Ingrid licked her lips. "But that's different. Anyone can pretend everything's okay, but coming face-to-face with reality can be harsh."

"We borrow trouble," Amber said softly. She moved her legs and twisted around to face forward. Leaned into Ingrid and rested her head on her shoulder. "You know it? All of us. We go looking for it."

"You're telling me you wouldn't be scared?" Ingrid

rubbed her hand over Amber's thigh, curled her fingers around Amber's hand when she touched her.

"Nope. I'm saying we're all scared." Amber lifted her head enough to lean around Ingrid and look at Liv. "But there's strength in numbers."

CHAPTER 28

*L*iv stretched and set her book on the deck beside her chair. She had stopped reading a while ago when the light bled out of the sky and evening crept in. Charlie and his friend were inside, most likely playing video games, although to be fair, she'd been out here for a long time and they might have moved on by now. She and Gracie had talked while she fixed dinner. Grace regaled her with stories about hanging out with her friends at the pool. Liv listened, laughed in the right places, and watched her daughter's eyes. Gracie was happy. She supposed that was all that she needed to know.

Summer nights used to be about ice cream trips and water gun fights, back when the kids were little. Curling up with Wade outside on a lounge chair and watching the stars light up the sky. He used to kiss her until her lips were swollen; she wished now that she would have paid more attention to those nights, to the way he kissed her. Maybe if she had known then that passion can bleed out of a marriage the way daylight did the sky—so slowly and so unremarkably that you didn't notice until it was gone—maybe she would have cherished what they had.

They had dinner together. Liv had gone all out with home-made spaghetti sauce, a salad, and warm garlic bread. She had poured herself a glass of wine, and she put a glass out for Wade. He had opted for a beer, skipped the salad, and after wolfing down a plate and a half of spaghetti, he and Charlie had wandered away from the table together to the garage workshop.

Ingrid had suggested she slice herself open and bleed for him, but when he ignored the smallest of gestures she offered, the thought of begging for his forgiveness took her breath away. No, that wasn't entirely true. The thought of begging for his forgiveness and Wade's cool eyes watching her with indifference took her breath away.

Before they had left Ingrid and Luke's house that night, two weeks ago now, Liv had been in the kitchen, and Ingrid had gone back outside to offer seconds of dessert to the guys. Nathan had come inside to use the bathroom, and Liv—rinsing empty beer bottles at the sink—had looked out the window in time to see her husband hunched over in her sister's arms. She wasn't sure—still wasn't sure—what had hurt her more. That Wade had taken a swipe at his face as if he were crying or that Ingrid had held him fiercely, as if by letting go, she would be guilty of letting him fall apart.

Liv had covered her mouth, not sure if she was going to cry or vomit, and she had turned to move from the window, the kitchen, and smacked into Amber. Amber, who had seen the same thing she had, but couldn't possibly have felt the same knife of betrayal. Liv had tried to push past her, but Amber had gathered her in her arms and held her for a moment while she cried. Her sister had said nothing, and Liv had been grateful then and still was, for the comfort.

Two weeks, and nothing had changed. Except the house had passed a termite inspection. The HVAC guy had come in and replaced the furnace and central air unit, and Liv had written a check from their dad's account to cover it. Her signature on the line meant she was in charge of everything; none of them had discussed the fact that Liv was the executor of the will. She didn't want the title or the power and responsibility that came with it. The fact that her last name, that writing Olivia *Girard* on the check made her feel funny was lost on the rest of them.

They weren't fighting. They were roommates. Sleeping side by side, night after night with a simple goodnight now and then. Liv missed him. Never once did she think of Asher. She didn't want anyone's hands on her; she wasn't craving the physical act of sex. She wanted her husband's love and his attention, and she hated herself when she crooned like a puppy when Wade tossed her a sliver now and then.

Amber texted her earlier, just before dinner. Hadley had done okay at Kyle's, and Kyle had invited her to come back again. Liv understood that even though Amber had been okay, because Hadley been okay, Amber was going to need reassurance every time her baby girl left to spend time with her father. The wedding planning helped somewhat, keeping Amber busy, but then again, planning a wedding certainly wasn't relaxing and sometimes Amber vibrated with anxiety. Liv had taken to doling out hugs whenever she was with her. It was more than possible that she hugged Amber to fulfill her need for physical comfort, but she decided there was nothing wrong that, either.

Liv talked to Ingrid earlier in the morning. They'd grabbed coffee and taken a stroll through the house. The HVAC guy had made such a racket, they had gone outside and perched on the finished picnic table—the one Liv wanted to suggest Ezra take since he did the work on it—and soaked up some sun and some togetherness. Liv had invited Amber, but she had begged off because she was behind in the studio.

She had nowhere to be right now, and the evening air was a bit cool, but it was soft on her skin, and she was so tired, she considered passing the night out here on the deck. Grace might come home and find her out here. Then again, why would Gracie be looking out on the deck if she got home after midnight?

No idea what time it was—she left her phone on the counter when she came out with her book and a glass of wine —she didn't move when she heard the door open. Assuming it was Wade since Gracie had left earlier with friends and Charlie and his friend were too old to come outside and ask for cookies or ice cream, she didn't flinch when he appeared at her side.

"What're you doing?"

Fighting the rush of exasperation in her throat, she shook her head and shrugged. She sucked in a deep steadying breath, and rolled her head on the chair to look at him. He stood with his hands on his hips, head hung low and his piercing gaze pinned to her face.

"Nothing."

"You been by the house?" He stood up straight, but rather than walk away, he moved closer to the chair. She moved when he touched her foot. Pulled her legs up to give him room to sit down.

"Yeah." She nodded.

"What's wrong?" He sat on the end of the chair, the material of his cargo shorts pressed up against her toes. She moved again, because she didn't want to touch him. Bent her knees this time and flattened her feet on the chair.

He pinned her in place again with his eyes.

"This is what you wanted, isn't it?" he pressed. "Redoing the house?"

"Yeah. It is." She wanted the house restored. Like she told Amber, if money weren't an issue, she would love to see the house completely restored. But now that it was happening, she hated it. She wanted to blow a whistle and call time out. Get the workers out of the kitchen, the basement. Soon enough, they would sell it, and she would have to go about her every day life with strangers living in that house with her heart. She hated that they'd invited strangers inside now. Too soon.

"Liv?"

"It'll be nice." She kept her answer simple, because talking about it made her throat feel like sandpaper.

"It's not the same now." He arched an eyebrow. "It's not the house where you grew up."

She flinched. Let her eyes close. Because it was that, too. And dammit all, why could Wade look at her and know that?

"Is that it?"

She gave him a curt nod when he pressed for an answer. Refused to talk about it, because she didn't want to lose control again.

"Can I ask you something?"

She figured he was going to ask about the house, so she nodded again. But she turned her face just slightly away from him. Kind of hurt to see him there, legs bent, elbows resting on them. Hands folded.

"Are you thinkin' about him?"

"No."

"When you're alone like this, do you miss him?"

"No."

"You sure?"

She pressed her lips together and looked at him from the corner of her eye.

"I don't think about him," she told him.

"You did."

She closed her eyes.

"When you were still with him, you wouldn't let me close to you."

"I was…" She sniffled. Breathed for a moment. "Ashamed. Of what I'd done." She cleared her throat. "And I didn't want to…drag you into that. In my head."

Wade puffed his cheeks up and held his breath for a moment.

"Amber likes my scar," he said with a quick grin.

Liv laughed softly, but her eyes burned with tears. "Yeah. How about that? When you divorce me, you'll still have my family on your side."

"I never said I wanted a divorce." He turned a bit on the chair so that he was facing her.

"No, but we can't live like this, Wade. You deserve more than this."

"You don't?"

She shrugged.

"Livvie, I just need time to process—"

"I get that," she said quickly. She lifted her hand to rub her eyes. "But the more time you need, the further apart we drift."

"Meaning you'll find someone else?"

She winced and turned her face away. She wanted to lash out, to suggest that if he'd been more attentive in the beginning, maybe things would be different. But she only took a deep breath. Shook her head.

"No." She cleared her throat. "But the more distance between us, the harder it'll be to figure things out."

"So." Wade lifted his left hand and scrubbed his fingers back over his head. Liv's eyes followed the movement, grateful to see that he was wearing his ring. "You get that I need time, but on the other hand, hurry up and get over it."

Without turning her head, she moved only her eyes to look at him. He had moved on from talking to trying to bait her, hoping to start an argument.

"I just miss you," she whispered.

"You want sex."

She shook her head sadly. Remembered Ingrid encouraging her to put herself out there for him. "I want you. I want things to be the way they used to be. I want you to love me."

Her heart hammered in her throat. What would he say? Would he push harder for a fight? Or would he show her a little tenderness? If he would just take her hand, it would be something, wouldn't it? If only he would say that he did. Love her.

"Was he ever here?"

Her heart dropped back into place, and Liv coughed hard at the flutter in her throat.

"What?"

"Did you have him in our bed?"

"No."

She prayed he wouldn't ask again, that he wouldn't rephrase the question yet again. Yes, she'd been with Asher here at this address. But it had been a three-minute affair in Asher's car in front of the house. An ugly midnight kind of thing. She would never have invited him into the house, let alone Wade's bed. But something told her that wouldn't matter to Wade.

"Was it better with him?"

"Wade," she cried quietly. "Don't do this."

"So it was? Bigger dick? Better moves?"

Liv covered her face with her hands. She rubbed her forehead and then pushed her hair back from her face.

"No. It wasn't better. It was cold. And empty—"

"But he made you come."

"No—"

"Don't lie to me." He shook his head; the warning delivered in a cold, tight voice.

"Yes," she whispered. "But, it wasn't because he…cared."

"That's…fucking great." Wade bit the words off in anger. He rested his forearms on his knees and let his hands dangle between his legs.

Her eyes filled as she stared at him. The mix of pain and rage on his face made him a stranger. She squeezed her eyes closed to hide from his hatred, but her imagination was worse. She saw herself writhing under Asher Crowe; the way he held her gaze as he moved inside her, held her through an orgasm that exploded heat and stars inside her and left her in tears.

"I'm sorry, Wade," she whispered. She turned her face away and waited for him to move.

"What if sorry isn't enough?"

She shook her head, but when his weight shifted on the chair, she turned to look at him again. He had scooted down a bit to sit closer to her.

"I don't know what else to say." The knife was back. The one she'd been carrying in her throat for months.

"Do you love me?"

"Yes."

"You don't say that, you don't tell me that unless I ask you. You say it if I ask you to say it."

She lifted her hand and rubbed her thumb over his wrist.

"I do love you, and I used to tell you all the time," she reminded him. "And you stopped listening."

"What does that mean?"

"It doesn't mean anything, Wade. It just is. It's just the truth."

He touched her leg. Stroked his fingertips over her ankle and down over the top of her bare foot.

"What would you do?" He paid extra attention to her little toe. Kept his eyes trained on her foot. "If we divorced, what would you do?"

The knife was in Wade's hand now, and he plunged it deep in her chest. The soft howl of pain escaped her lips as all of her hard edges broke, and she shattered there in front of him.

"Lose." She pressed her knuckles to her lips and shook her head. "I would lose, Wade."

CHAPTER 29

"*I* can't believe you've pulled all of this together already," Ingrid mumbled. "Even my wedding took a while to plan."

Arms crossed over her chest, Amber ignored Ingrid and studied the dress hanging from her open closet door.

"Where'd you get this dress again?" Liv asked as Amber backed up a few steps. "I mean, seriously, what bridal shop just loans out dresses for people to study?"

Ingrid laughed softly. She leaned against the headboard of Amber's bed, head turned toward Amber, but she glanced at Liv with a grin.

"I don't think I like it," Amber finally announced. She knelt down to look at it from that angle.

"What are you doing?" Liv leaned forward to see Amber better. She had dragged a wingback chair from the living room to the bedroom. Now she was seated on the other side of the bed, her legs drawn up under her as she leaned to the left side of the chair.

"Looking at it from all angles." Amber shook her head as if to tell Liv that was a stupid question.

"Because someone's gonna be on the floor looking at up you?"

"These are for you guys." Amber finally turned her full attention to them. She stood up and dropped her arms to her sides. "Remember? I'm the bride? I wear white."

Ingrid snorted softly.

"Theoretically speaking, the bride wears white." Amber leveled a look at Ingrid that told her to behave.

"I'm not wearing that," Liv announced.

"What?" Amber looked back at the dress and then turned to Liv.

"I'm not wearing it."

"Why not?"

"Hello? It's strapless—"

"And? You have good shoulders. You have the boobs to hold it up—"

"I'm too old for it," Liv argued. "I'm not wearing something strapless."

"Try it on," Amber suggested.

"Nope."

"Why does it matter?" Ingrid asked. "If you don't like it anyway?"

"It…it matters," Amber sputtered, "because I'm the bride. You guys have to do this for me."

"But you don't like it. You just said you don't like it."

"Liv. Really?" Amber sighed and threw her arms out to her sides, exasperated already. "You're gonna be a pain about this?"

"First of all, no," Liv argued. "I'm not trying to be a pain. Why can't you work with us on this? And second, why are we dress shopping like this? I mean, why not find a bridal website with a download wedding. We'll get a fancy 3D printer."

"Don't be a bitch." Amber rolled her eyes.

"I do it well, and seriously, Amber. Half the fun of planning a wedding is going with your bridesmaids or matrons or has-beens or whatever and trying dresses on."

"Oh yeah, that sounds like a thrill," Ingrid mumbled. "Maybe we could take boxing gloves just for fun."

Liv snorted and then laughed out loud.

"I don't like the dress," Amber admitted. She dropped to sit on the edge of the bed and looked at the dress again. "The cut's all wrong."

"Yeah, they cut the top of it off."

"You're not a has-been," Ingrid told her.

"You're right," Liv agreed. "I'm a fuck up. Still don't wanna wear a strapless gown."

"Wasn't your wedding dress strapless?" Amber narrowed her eyes at Liv.

"Yeah, and it was a long time ago, and I had a body to show off." Liv shrugged. "Now I have sunspots. And I have stretch marks."

"On your shoulders?" Amber snickered.

"No, my boobs—"

"No one wants to see your boobs," Ingrid told her. "You wear the elastic over them."

"No kidding no one wants to see them," Liv mumbled. "Can we please just keep looking?"

"Okay." Amber nodded. "If you try this on."

"Why?" Liv snapped. "What? You think I'm gonna put it on and change my mind? I don't like it."

"No, but this is part of the process. Right? Trying on dresses? Having fun?"

"So much fun," Ingrid agreed. She flashed them both a sarcastic grin.

"Why are we doing this here?" Liv asked again. "Seriously. Why don't we go out of town? Do a weekend trip?"

"Fuck that." Ingrid shook her head. "You're not working. Amber's her own boss, and I can pack my laptop anywhere. We could go whenever."

Liv looked from Ingrid to Amber.

"I have a friend at a bridal shop. This dress is brand new, and she told me to bring it home and see if you guys like it."

"Okay. We don't." Liv batted her eyelashes at Amber. "Next."

"Try it on."

"No."

"Good grief." Ingrid scooted away from the headboard and off the side of the bed. "I'll try the damned thing on. Okay? Then? Then can we move on?"

"Yes." Amber nodded. "How about a drink?"

"Yes. A shot of whisky would be good right about now." Liv twisted around and stretched her legs out to rest on the bed.

"Be right back."

Liv watched Ingrid look the dress over.

"Do you like it?" she asked, surprised to realize she had her fingers crossed in hopes that Ingrid didn't like it.

"Nope."

"Good." She sighed with relief.

"Where's Hadley?" Liv asked when Amber reappeared, three bottles of beer in hand.

"Stayed at her friend Tiffany's last night."

"You sure about that?" Ingrid asked as she unzipped her shorts.

Amber handed Liv a beer and then put Ingrid's on the nightstand.

"You know, she's been better…" Amber pursed her lips. "Since…."

"Since what?" Ingrid asked as she kicked her shorts off.

"Is that a tattoo?" Liv asked when she saw a purple line on the back of Ingrid's thigh.

"No." Ingrid rolled her eyes. "I have a purple streak in my hair. What do I need with a tattoo?"

Liv wagged her eyebrows in response. "Then what is it?"

"I dunno. A bruise? A vein, maybe?"

Liv narrowed her eyes. Ingrid laughed as she reached for the dress.

"Stop staring at me," she groaned. "What size is this?"

"She's been better since she's been hanging out at Kyle's."

Ingrid and Liv both snapped their attention to Amber.

"I mean…I think…maybe she's just happy? Maybe something feels different for her now?"

"You think she was acting out because she needed her father in her life?" Ingrid frowned.

"I dunno." Amber shrugged.

"So no more Kesh?"

"She sees him now and then. But he's not allowed over here if she's alone."

"And they follow that rule?" Ingrid asked. She whipped her shirt off over her head and tossed it to the bed.

"I think so."

"Here." Liv stood up and made her way around the end of the bed. She slipped the dress off the hanger as Ingrid turned to her.

"Strapless," Liv reminded her. "Bra's gotta go."

Ingrid sighed.

"Yeah, remember not long ago you guys paraded me around in a thong?" Amber took a long drink of her beer. "Fun, isn't it?"

"Not so much," Ingrid answered.

"We never did take Liv to Skinny's." Amber's voice was soft and wistful.

Ingrid laughed as she slipped the bra straps off her arms and then reached back to unhook it.

"We should do that."

"Why do I wanna go look at girls on poles?" Liv held the dress out to Ingrid and then waited while Ingrid stepped into it.

"It's fun," Ingrid answered. Liv zipped the dress and then

stepped back to admire it. Because she had to. She hated the dress, but damn, if her sister wasn't smoking hot in it.

"Fun?" she repeated.

"Yeah. Kinda like telling the guys it's not their thing. We can do whatever they do."

"Except we can't," Liv reminded Amber. "There are certain anatomical things we can't do."

"Seriously?" Ingrid looked at Liv over her shoulder. "I don't think Amber was being scientific. I think she just meant that it's not a big deal for women if their guys are at a strip club."

Amber nodded when Liv glanced at her.

"Personally, I think women are beautiful," Ingrid announced. "Well, most of them. And it's kind of a turn on."

"Watching a woman grind a pole turns you on?"

"It makes me want someone to want me," Ingrid said quietly. "It makes me want to be touched and…"

"Ogled?" Liv suggested.

Ingrid grinned.

"I don't need to want to be touched or ogled, and I don't need to be turned on. There are times I feel like I'm gonna explode if he doesn't touch me. I can't take much more of that."

"Still?" Ingrid asked quietly.

"Yeah." Liv gulped. "Still. He asked me the other night what I would do if we divorced."

"Livvie." Ingrid flinched. "Oh, God. No. Please don't let that happen."

"It's hardly my choice, Ingrid." Liv shrugged. Her beer was on the other side of the bed, so she snagged Ingrid's and took a drink. "I'm bending over backwards to do things for him. To make him need me. But he doesn't have to forgive me to need me."

"You look incredible, Ingrid," Amber said quietly.

Ingrid dragged her eyes away from Liv to look at Amber.

She swept her hand over the shimmery silver sheath and looked back at Liv.

"You do," Liv agreed. "I mean, smokin' hot."

"Right." Ingrid rolled her eyes.

"What?" Liv gave herself a mental shake. "C'mere." She dragged Ingrid to stand in front of Amber's dresser and made her look at her reflection in the mirror. "You're gorgeous. You should wear this."

"No—"

"So?" Amber cocked her head and frowned. "Now you like it?"

"No." Liv shook her head. "Ingrid makes the dress. I would look ridiculous in it."

"But—"

"Is it just me and Liv?" Ingrid met Amber's eyes in the mirror. Liv swallowed a tiny wish that it was just Ingrid. Hard to want to celebrate her sister's future marriage when hers was falling apart.

"Shay and Gretchen and Hadley."

"Then you should ask them," Liv told her. "And leave me out of it."

"You guys are the most important. I want your opinion first." Amber shrugged. "I'm not gonna leave you out of the decision. Or the wedding."

Liv bit her lip and nodded. To think that not long ago, she was sad that she assumed Amber would choose Ingrid as her maid of honor. Now Liv thought she might be okay with not even being in the wedding.

"Um." Amber arched her eyebrows. "Maybe now's a good time to tell you guys."

Ingrid turned slowly to look at her. Liv felt her heart whoosh a little faster.

Amber laughed softly. "God, you'd think I was sixteen and pregnant again."

"Are you pregnant?"

"No." Amber shook her head impatiently. "I want you both to be there. To be with me. And I want you both to stand for me—"

"Amber, it's fine," Liv argued. "Ingrid's—"

"But I'm going to ask Hadley…to be…to be my maid of honor." Amber licked her lips.

"That's perfect," Ingrid said softly.

"Absolutely," Liv agreed.

"You're sure? I don't want—"

"We're sure," they said in unison.

Amber sighed, obviously relieved they had taken the news so well.

"But I'm not wearing that dress."

"I do kind of…" Ingrid shrugged and looked over her shoulder to the mirror. Liv watched her eyes sweep low over her back. "Like it."

"What if you guys wear the same color but a different style?" Amber suggested.

"It's your wedding," Liv told her.

"Except for this dress."

"Well, yeah." Liv laughed.

"Help me out of it." Ingrid turned her back to Liv so she could unzip the dress for her. Liv obliged and stepped back when Ingrid let it slide from her chest and stepped out of it. She took the dress from Ingrid, but she froze when she noticed the shiny puckered scar on the curve of Ingrid's breast.

"What?" Ingrid asked when Liv forced herself back into action. She put the dress on the hanger and shook her head. "What?"

"Nothing."

"I think you should at least try it," Ingrid told her. Liv put the dress back on the closet door and told herself to be calm. But when she turned back to Ingrid, her eyes automatically searched for the scar again.

"Oh." Ingrid reached for her bra.

"Does it hurt?"

"No."

"Did it?"

"Of course it did." Ingrid rolled her eyes. "You don't think it's gonna hurt to have a scalpel slice through your skin?"

"How many stitches?"

Ingrid shook her head. "I don't…"

"Have you found a doctor?" Liv asked quietly. She lifted a hand, though she had no idea what the hell she was doing.

"Don't touch me there." Ingrid laughed and pushed Liv's hand away. "I haven't. I called my doctor back home."

"Home," Amber repeated.

"My old doctor." Ingrid put her bra on and then quickly yanked her shirt over her head. "I made an appointment."

"So you're gonna take the train up to your ob-gyn appointment?"

"Luke's going with me. We're going to take a few days. See Rafe and Jules. Talk to my doctor—"

Amber shot off the bed like something goosed her.

"Ingrid?"

"You and Luke. You're going to see your doctor together?" Liv frowned. "For a checkup? Is that it?"

"Yes." Ingrid nodded. "I promise. I thought we could talk and get a recommendation."

"You have mine and Amber's. You're putting it off."

Ingrid shrugged.

"By the time you get around to it, it could be too late—"

"It's not gonna be too late," Ingrid insisted. "There's nothing going on. Yes, I'm dragging my feet on the appointment. Who the hell gets excited about finding a new ob-gyn? Does that mean something's wrong? No. I check twice a month. There's nothing there."

"You're sure?" Amber sounded like she was five, rather than thirty.

"I swear to God, if I find something again, I will tell you. I wouldn't keep it from Luke, and I won't keep it from you."

Liv took a deep breath and let the relief flow through her.

"We should, like…pinky swear."

"We never did pinky swears when we were kids." Ingrid rolled her eyes. "I'm giving you my word. I don't wanna go through something like that again without you guys."

"You swear, Amber?" Liv asked quietly.

"Sure, but I'm an open book."

Ingrid snorted and then looked at Liv.

"Do you?"

"Promise."

They fell into a group hug, but Ingrid was quick to push them away.

"I would just feel more comfortable right now if I had pants on," she told them. She grinned as she stepped into her shorts and pulled them up.

"Can I just say one thing?" Amber frowned, looking pensive.

"Go for it," Liv told her.

"Okay." She nodded and looked from Liv to Ingrid. "I hope my boobs look that good when I'm your age."

CHAPTER 30

"What're you doing?"

Liv looked up as Gracie draped herself over the counter. She felt a pang of sadness but shoved it aside. There wasn't time for sadness or regret, not where Gracie was concerned. Liv wanted to focus on the present and enjoy the moments they had together, rather than look at her eighteen-year-old and see her at five, knees on a kitchen chair, elbows on the table, hogging freshly baked cookies.

"Trying to decide what to make," Liv announced. She stood up straight and groaned when her back popped.

"Why are you baking so much this summer?"

Liv swallowed hard and hoped she didn't wince at the bitter taste of guilt. She hoped her shrug looked casual, rather than practiced, and reached for her glass of tea.

"Why not? I'm bored."

"Why aren't you working at Grandpa's house?"

"There are some guys working there now." Liv drummed her fingers on the counter. "They're supposed to finish the tile in the kitchen today, but then they start ripping up carpet and stuff. So they'll be awhile."

"Have you seen it?"

"I was there with Aunt Amber and Aunt Ingrid yesterday."

"And?" Gracie shook her head.

"Looks good, but it's…" She faltered. She didn't want to sound unhappy or bitter, but the fact was that no matter how good the house would look, it was now forever changed and it hurt to look at it.

"Too crowded." Gracie read her wrong, but thankful for the out, Liv nodded enthusiastically. "Probably hard to get a feel for something when there's equipment in the way."

"True." Liv looked at her cookbook again.

"Make chocolate cupcakes," Gracie said with a grin.

"I think those are your favorite, not Dad's."

"Can I ask you something?"

"Sure." Liv's stomach felt a little funny, but she nodded anyway. "If I get to ask you something."

"Okay, but can I go first?"

"Yeah."

Liv could make a pie for Wade. But he liked pumpkin, and since it was the beginning of July, she didn't have any pumpkin pie mix on hand. She supposed she could do peanut butter cookies. She'd made them a few weeks ago, but they'd been gone in two days. They were Wade's favorite.

"What's going on with you and Daddy?"

"What's going on with you and Jarret?"

"What?" Gracie's blond eyebrows jumped, and she blinked at Liv in surprise.

"Are you dating him?"

"Me?" Gracie shook her head. "Dating Jarret?"

"Are you?"

"No. Why would you ask me that?"

Liv flipped through her cookbook until she found the page with the peanut butter cookie recipe Wade favored.

"You were kissing him in front of everyone."

"It was just a kiss."

"Pretty heavy kiss for public viewing," Liv said quietly. "Kind of makes me wonder what goes on when you're alone."

When Gracie didn't say anything, Liv peeked at her. The guilt written on Gracie's face ripped her in two.

"Mom."

Liv shook her head and held her hand up. "Were you careful?"

From the corner of her eye, she saw Gracie nod.

"You're okay?"

"Mmm."

"But you're not dating?"

"Just friends."

"Mm-kay." Liv turned her back to her daughter to gather what she would need to make the cookies. When she nearly dropped the carton of eggs, she stopped and set it on the counter close to the refrigerator and watched her hands shake.

"Mom?"

"What, hon?"

"Does it get better?"

"Yes."

"Okay."

Liv waited for more, took a deep breath, and then carried her ingredients back by Gracie.

"What about Daddy?"

Liv looked up quickly, past the awkwardness the past few seconds had created, and raised her eyebrows in question.

"What about Daddy?"

"You guys are being weird."

"What do you mean?" Liv hedged.

"You're both so stiff. So uptight. And you fight all the time now."

"Nothing's going on," Liv answered feeling the truth of those words down to her toes.

"You were fighting, though."

"But it's okay now." Liv hated lying. Because what if Gracie believed her, and Wade asked her for a divorce tomorrow? Would that lie told as reassurance end up scarring Grace?

"Mom, it's just—"

"Was it you last night? That waltzed into the living room and interrupted a hot and heavy make out session? Or was that my other daughter?"

"That wasn't a hot and heavy make out session." Gracie rolled her eyes. "Gross, but not hot and heavy."

Liv avoided Gracie's eyes as she measured the butter for the cookies. Felt hot and heavy to her, but then it had been so long since she and Wade had touched each other, sometimes bumping into him in the hallway turned her on. After that night, the night he brought up the D word, things had settled again. Liv tried to remind herself the ups and downs right now were natural. They spent a couple of evenings together since then. Watched a movie together one night, although Liv was on the couch and Wade was in the recliner. He joined her on the deck the next night, and they talked quietly about when they used to stay out all night as kids. Neither of them dared to talk about the things they did alone in the back of his car or the living room when her parents had gone to bed. Because they had talked about the old days, she had taken to wearing the necklace every day, the one he gave her when they were kids. The one she had worn the night they'd gone to Ingrid and Luke's house, and both of her sisters went true confessions on her and told her they thought her husband was hot. She supposed Ingrid had a free shot since she'd seen her and Luke together, but Amber's announcement that she would love to kiss Wade's scar had come from out of left field and shocked her.

She had the necklace on last night when Wade had come looking for her. TV on, she looked at him from her spot on the couch and then turned her attention back to the sappy romance movie. He joined her, and rather than talk, she pushed up to rest on her forearms and handed him the remote. Wade would have no desire to watch the movie, and she would rather suffer through a western or a boxing match or anything, if it meant he would stay in the room with her.

"I didn't know you still had that necklace."

Several minutes of them not talking and the actors in a different movie—Wade had, indeed, changed the channel—yelling and cutting up had passed when he spoke, so it took her a moment to realize that he was talking to her and to process what he said.

Heart in her throat, she had propped herself up to rest on her forearms again and looked at him with shock.

"Why wouldn't I have this necklace?"

He shrugged. "You haven't worn it for years."

"You gave me the one with the kids' initials on it," she reminded him. "I wear that all the time."

"Where are the kids?"

"I think they're both in bed," she had answered, though she really had no idea. It was after midnight, and she was tired. Tired didn't mean sleepy, though, so she hadn't even entertained the idea of going up to bed.

"Remember this movie?" he asked her. Still on her forearms, she looked back at the TV and shook her head.

"No."

He focused his attention on the TV; she stared at him. It felt like hours, but only minutes later, he moved. Climbed up from the recliner. Liv had tucked her chin to her chest and her head to the couch to stifle a groan. She waited for him to say goodnight, but he moved toward her instead of away from her.

"You're so pretty." He squatted by the couch, but he kept his hands to himself.

She hadn't known what to say. Maybe thank you would have been appropriate, but she didn't feel pretty. Hadn't for a long time. She had simply stared at him, too wary to be cool or sarcastic.

"When I see that necklace." He had reached for her then, and Liv had gasped out loud when he touched her, his calloused fingertips heaven on her neck. "I picture you wearing it and nothing else. In my bed."

He had been her first, and up until this past year, her only lover. Embarrassed about the first time they were together, bleeding some and yelping softly in pain, she had closed her eyes.

"I wanna see that again," he had told her. Her heart lurched. No other word for it. It had lurched—she had been nervous-sick to her stomach—and she called on every ounce of self-control she had to keep from offering herself to him. Her heart and her body were always a second away from throwing herself at him, but her brain was learning that most likely he was gearing up to hurt her again.

"But Livvie," he had whispered, and she opened her eyes at the throb of pain in his voice, "when I think about you like that, with your legs open and ready for me, I see—"

Her brain had cussed her heart and her belly and all the parts that desperately needed his attention. She had squeezed her eyes closed and moved enough to cover his lips with her fingertips.

"Please don't, Wade," she half-whispered and cried. "Please don't think of me that way."

He parted his lips and licked her fingertips. Liv had felt the stroke of his tongue deep inside and low in her belly. When he closed his lips around her index finger and sucked on it and then swirled the tip of his tongue over the pad of her finger, she had moaned out loud.

"I miss you so much." The words had come out on a whisper. Wade had eased closer, dropped to his knees, and then opened his mouth and licked each of her fingers. Tickled the palm of her hand with his tongue.

"I don't want a divorce," he had told her, and parts of her had thrilled and melted at his words, but his lips moving over her inner wrist had been so distracting. The scruff on his face had scratched softly, and Liv had held her breath, reveling in the feel of his warm breath and his hot, wet tongue on her skin, afraid to move, even to speak in case he would change his mind. "Livvie."

"I don't, either, Wade," she whispered when he prompted her. He lingered at her wrist, and her heart raced with arousal and need and pleasure. How did it feel so good just to be kissed there on that skin? When he cupped her chin in his hand, she moved. Slowly at first, afraid he would back away. And then when he finally pressed his warm, firm lips to hers, she had reached for him. Scooted closer, framed his face with her right hand and closed her left hand over his, still holding her chin.

He kissed her like a slow, southern afternoon. Hot and languid and deep, and she had let him lead. The beer he had taken with him to the garage lingered on his tongue, and kissing him made her hungry and thirsty for more. She moaned in protest when he moved to drop soft kisses over her cheek to her neck. Sighed and then whispered something like please and yes when he dragged those calloused fingers down her neck and plunged them into the neckline of her shirt.

He had plucked her left breast from her bra and rolled her nipple with his fingertips—Liv had forgotten the drag of his rough skin on her nipples and her body had clenched for him, desperate for the sensation everywhere.

When he brought his lips back to hers, she had been ready for him, and she had taken his tongue with greed, and then

Gracie's voice had rung out clear as a bell, and Liv had cried out in frustration.

"Let me just say your timing sucked," Liv announced. When Gracie cut loose a yelp followed by *ewww* only seven syllables long, she looked up and winked.

"Don't say that stuff—"

"You were worried that we're fighting," Liv reminded her. "I'm saying don't worry about it."

"You're saying I interrupted make up sex."

"What do you know about make up sex?" Liv's hands stilled on the jar of peanut butter. She tilted her head to study Gracie's face.

"I don't personally." Gracie shook her head. "I know about…hook up sex. That's it."

Liv winced. She opened the peanut butter jar. Reminded herself she had just told Amber and Ingrid she didn't want Gracie to save herself for marriage, that she wanted her daughter to learn about herself and her likes and dislikes as a woman before she allowed herself to fall for someone else. Still. Gracie *having* a sex life was different in theory than reality.

"More than—?"

"Just with Jarret," Gracie said on a soft sigh. "We're good friends, Mom."

"Yeah?" Liv lifted only her eyes to look at her daughter. "He didn't hurt you?"

Gracie opened her mouth to answer, but she hesitated. "I'm not sure how I'm supposed to answer that."

"I meant…like…respect and stuff? You're still friends. He didn't tell anyone?"

"It's all good."

"'kay." Liv sighed. "Do…do we need to see an ob-gyn?"

"Are you asking if I'm pregnant? Is that possible?"

"You bet your ass it's possible if you aren't careful. First time or hundredth time. Use protection."

"We did."

Liv sighed. Her eyes fluttered over the cookie recipe and the bowl of butter and now the jar of peanut butter. Realizing she forgot to preheat the oven, she did it now. Wondered if this was something she should keep from Wade. Wouldn't it kill him to know his baby girl was messing around with boys? But if he found out and not from Liv, would he be angry with her for not telling him?

"I'm asking if you want..." Liv stopped and shook her head. "No. I'm not. I'm telling you I think you should be on the pill."

"Condoms don't work?"

"If I were you, I'd be more comfortable being the one in control of that particular thing. And yes, use condoms, too, because you don't want any STDs."

"I can't believe we're having this conversation." Grace covered her face with her hands, but Liv saw the furious red blush on her face.

"I can't, either." Liv shook her head. "Believe me, I don't like it anymore than you do."

"Sex?"

"Talking about sex with my daughter."

"It gets better, though? Because..."

"Sweetheart." Liv huffed out a sigh and tucked her chin to her chest. She rubbed her forehead as she searched for the right words. "The first time sucks."

"But—"

"Please don't give me anymore details." Liv shook her head. "It takes a while...to figure things out. And I know you're gonna roll your eyes at me, but I have to say it."

"What?" Gracie frowned, still hiding behind her hands.

"It's so much better when you're with the right person."

"So you're saying I should have waited until I was married."

"Not necessarily," Liv said quietly. "I'm just telling you

the more you care about the person you're with, the more… satisfying it is."

"Okay." Gracie's voice was tiny. "Can I have a cookie?"

Liv laughed out loud. "I haven't even mixed the dough yet."

CHAPTER 31

*L*iv needed a drink. To hell with that. She deserved a drink. A bottomless drink. Of something strong. Something that would burn going down. She needed the drink, the time out with her sisters enough that she let them talk her into going to Skinny's, but she regretted her decision the second they stepped inside. The music was fine; something loud with what she supposed was a hypnotic beat, all the better for the dancing girls. The clientele was a bit sad, but then again, it was an early Thursday evening. She had no desire to see who might show up on a weekend. Whether the girls from Skinny's drew the dregs of society or the upper echelon, Liv didn't care to know.

Thankfully, Ingrid led them to a round high top table far from the stage and the door. It was quieter, at least, and Liv was good with not having to see the smorgasbord of breasts swinging on stage. Their waitress was covered, though it looked like she had borrowed someone's doll clothes. A thin band of spandex covered her nipples, smooshed her breasts so that half hung out from below and the other spilled over the top. She was friendly, and she brought them a bucket of cold beer and left them alone, so that was another point for her. But when Liv glanced at her as she walked away to check on another table, the display of butt cheek falling out the bottom of her tiny denim shorts almost made her change her mind.

"You look horrified," Amber said with a giggle when the three of them were alone.

"I am…" Liv looked around the bar—she would begrudgingly admit it appeared clean, the floor shined with fresh polish, and the exposed wooden beams in the ceilings and walls were actually gorgeous—and floundered for a word to describe her present state of mind. "Stunned this place exists. And I'm a little bit sorry for these girls here, and I'm a little bit undersexed these days, so yeah, I'm absolutely horrified."

"Still undersexed?" Ingrid tipped a bottle up and took a drink.

Liv only puffed her cheeks up and then sighed as exhaustion and defeat yawned inside her. Wade had told her he didn't want a divorce, but they were a long way from happy. She would take it; if this was the rest of her married life, she would take it because she loved him. Funny that she could see it now so clearly; she loved him, and if they were going to live as friends, she would live as his friend. But regret would be a third body in their bed.

"Is that why we're out drinking?" Amber nudged her with her elbow.

"What?" Liv rubbed her eyes.

"Things are still bad with Wade?"

Liv shrugged. "That's not why I needed a drink, no."

Ingrid lowered her beer to the table with exaggerated hesitation and studied her with a cool stare.

"What's going on?"

Liv squirmed under Ingrid's accusing stare. What was that about? She tilted her head and looked at her sister through narrowed eyes.

"Why are you looking at me like that?"

"Like what?"

"Like I did something wrong? What'd I do?"

"Why do you need a drink?" Ingrid's simple head shake and shrug seemed to suggest she had meant nothing by the look, that Liv was imagining it. But Liv knew better. Wired, anxious, and drained all at the same time, Liv pulled in a calming breath even as she hooked the small heel of her boot on the rung of her stool and bounced her leg.

She had been right. This wasn't a good idea. Even if the floor looked clean enough to eat off of, even if there were only a handful of guys close to the stage nursing beers and watching the girls on stage work the pole, the whole place screamed sex, and right now, she was torn between disgust at the whole scene and awareness of what was around her and the desire for what was missing in her life.

So full of emotion, even her throat was tight with the yearning for Wade and the—grief? disappointment in, for?— Gracie, she didn't know where to start. What to say. What if she opened her mouth to speak, and there were no words? What if the overload of emotion choked her, and if she opened her mouth, the last of her breath would be gone? Or what if she opened her mouth to confide in her sisters, and everything just gushed out and it was messy and neither of them could follow her, and she never stopped talking? And crying. Because she needed a good cry. Not the quiet tears she tried to hide since they buried their dad. But a real, painful, ugly cry.

Who wanted to do anything ugly in a place where girls who looked the same age as her daughter flaunted their sweet, beautiful bodies? Liv started to speak and then lost her courage or her energy or something, again, and instead, she took a drink. She made the mistake of looking around as she swallowed and choked when she saw a woman—older than Gracie, but certainly not the same age as Liv—walk by with tattooed breasts and pierced nipples.

"Are you okay?" Amber lunged toward her, as she set the bottle down and thumped her hand over her heart while she coughed. She snorted with laughter, and then her eyes burned with tears, and she remembered she needed this, too. More laughter. Even if it did lead the way right into the painful, ugly cry.

"I'm fine." She nodded and patted Amber's hand where it rested on her forearm. She still coughed, and she shook a little bit with laughter. Still, Ingrid watched her as she dabbed at her eyes, amused, maybe, but still suspicious.

"Can't you act like an adult?" Ingrid asked with a smirk. "Live a little, Olivia. There are places where people like nudity—"

"Spare me the lecture." She rolled her eyes. "I'm fine. I was just thinking…" She gave herself a mental shake.

"Thinking what?" Amber coaxed her. Liv felt Amber squeeze her arm before moving her hand away.

Liv cleared her throat. "First of all? Ingrid. I didn't know this place existed, but I'm not naïve." She arched her eyebrows, but the flash of memory involving Asher Crowe's hands on her breasts probably made the look more pathetic than menacing. "And…I was just…" Liv licked her lips. She averted her gaze. Studied the metal bucket full of ice and four more bottles of beer. "There's so much in my head right now, and I…it leaves me breathless, ya know? Like I can't talk, because…it hurts. And I'm afraid if I do start talking, I'm gonna cry."

"Liv." Amber reached over and rubbed her arm again. Ingrid stared at her silently.

"I mean, I've been crying for months now. Sniveling. Stupid." She shuddered. Noticed a tiny grin play at Ingrid's mouth. "But it's not enough. I need a big, ugly cry. I need—"

"You need an earth-shattering orgasm," Ingrid mumbled as she picked up her beer. Liv started to protest, but she only laughed. Nodded her agreement.

"I can't even tell you how long it's been," she said quietly.

"Since you've had—?" Ingrid raised her eyebrows.

"Yeah." Liv shrugged and looked away.

"You can take care of that," Amber reminded her.

Liv rolled her eyes. "I know. But it's not the same."

"Kind of like the little tears." Ingrid glanced at Amber. "Little hiccups. She needs full throttle."

Liv shook her head, but she laughed with them.

"Anyway, I was thinking how I don't want to ugly cry here with all of these beautiful girls strutting their stuff, and then the tattooed chick walked by. The timing was perfect."

"Can you even imagine how much that would hurt?" Ingrid shivered.

"I went with Kristen when she got a tattoo. Just a tiny little butterfly on her ankle. No way. And I can't imagine piercing my nipples, either."

"Yeah." Ingrid shook her head. "Had to disappoint Luke. Told him hell would freeze over before I did that."

Amber laughed and shook her head.

"You ever notice she gets all flaky when we talk about this?" Ingrid studied Amber curiously and then turned her attention to Liv. "I think she has her nipples pierced."

"I do not!" Amber yelped. "You saw it all that day you dressed me like a doll, remember?"

"Then I think you and Nathan have talked about it."

Amber shook her head and rolled her eyes.

"I read an article." Ingrid cleared her throat and made such a big deal of not looking at Liv and Amber, it made Liv's stomach a little jumpy. "About a woman who had breast cancer." She flicked her gaze up to Liv and then Amber and looked away again. "Well. I've read a lot about cancer… since…" She shrugged and rolled her hand in a circle. "Anyway, this woman is a survivor. But she had a double mastectomy. She had her chest tattooed because…she felt…Well, the scarring bothered her, and it made her feel…beautiful…"

"That's different." Liv propped her chin in her hand and shook her head. Her stomach felt twitchy now, the way it did any time the subject of breast cancer came up. She trusted Ingrid, at least eighty percent trust, to tell them if something was going on. But that other twenty percent of uncertainty scared the hell out of her. She couldn't lose Ingrid now. Not when the three of them were scaling walls. Scaling walls to shoot each other down, sometimes, sure, but maybe that was to be expected when you took three grown women and tried to sandwich them back together into familiar roles too much, too soon.

"It's not, though." Ingrid looked at Liv and then glanced toward the stage. "If the girl here needs tattoos to feel beautiful, who are we to disagree?"

Liv groaned. "Don't bring political correctness into this, Ingrid. My life is complicated enough as it is. I need to be safe to say whatever I want with you and Amber and not worry about offending someone."

"I'm not trying to be politically correct." Ingrid held her hand up to stop Liv. "I just…Women fight so hard to get what they want. To be happy. And it's exhausting, and yes, I am speaking in general terms, because I am happy with my life. But why should I judge these girls?"

"I'm not judging anyone," Liv answered, "I just said it's not for me. It looks like it would hurt like hell."

"Did he call you again?"

Liv, eyes on a brunette on stage—more specifically on the girl's very large breasts—blinked and looked back at Ingrid.

"What?" Ingrid asked when Liv frowned and then gave herself yet another mental shake.

"I don't know…I guess I'm thinking in stereotypes, but I feel like girls in places like this usually have pancake tits, and the girl on stage is huge."

"Pancake—? Really?" Amber snorted.

Liv shrugged. "You know what I mean."

"Yeah, well, what I would have to say is that other than mine, Ingrid's got the best rack of anyone in here."

Ingrid frowned and closed her eyes. She shook her head and then let out a soft bark of laughter.

"Thank you? I think?"

"What about mine?" Liv laughed, but she stared at Amber with an indignant frown.

"Haven't had the experience of seeing you parade around topless." Amber grinned. "Nor do I want to, so please don't feel obligated."

"Just another reason why I won't wear a strapless dress." Liv pointed at Amber and winked. She picked up her beer.

"Did he?" Ingrid asked, and this time, her question was intense.

"No." Liv sighed and frowned. She took a drink and let her eyes meet Ingrid's. "No. Why would you think that?"

"You're acting weird. You said yourself there's a ton going on—"

"I haven't seen him…well, I haven't been with him since before Dad died. And I don't want to. And you don't know Asher Crowe. He's not one to beg."

"You said he called you once. After…it was over."

Liv felt her eyebrows slide up in surprise. She had forgotten that. She'd forgotten that phone call and that she had admitted to Ingrid that it had happened.

"Liv, are you lying? Are you still seeing him?" Ingrid set her beer down a little hard and cringed at the crashing sound. She cocked her head and leaned forward. "You're gonna kill him. You are gonna kill him if you're still seeing someone else."

Liv stared at Ingrid silently. Overcome with emotion yet again, this time a mix of loneliness and fury and jealousy and the most volatile right now—regret—she swallowed hard and shook her head.

"Remember how we did that pinky swear? At Amber's the other night?"

"It wasn't a pinky swear, and we're not kids. And if you're still fucking around on Wade, I can't do it. I can't listen anymore—"

"I'm not lying," Liv insisted. "I didn't even have what I would call a fling. An affair. I had sex with Asher Crowe a handful of times…between the end of October and the end of December. I am *not* lying. And I'm very well aware that if I was still lying to Wade, he would never forgive me, and I'm also very well aware that your loyalties, if questioned, are with my husband."

"What does that mean?"

"Here we go," Amber mumbled. Liv glanced at her, but she was quick to look back at Ingrid.

"Well, you both made it pretty clear the other night that you'd side with the guy with bedroom eyes and a sexy scar—"

"I did not!" Amber snatched Liv's hand in hers. "I didn't. I didn't mean that. I just…Liv, I don't want you to throw—"

"What?" Ingrid apparently found her voice. Her eyebrows drawn deep in an angry frown, her gaze could freeze hell. "Are you kidding me? *Are you fucking kidding me?* Me saying that Wade has bedroom eyes means that I'd…what? I'd kick your ass to the curb if you guys divorced? Jesus, Liv, maybe I just want to remind you that he's a good guy. He's good-looking. He's sexy. He's fun. He's great with Gracie and Charlie—"

Liv ducked her head at the mention of her daughter. Ingrid stopped talking, and though some kind of techno beat surrounded them, their table was silent.

"He's not?" Ingrid finally ventured. "Is this where you tell us he's—"

"Ingrid, no," Liv whispered. "No. Stop. Stop attacking

me." She lowered her hands to the table and stared at her sister. "I know—"

Ingrid reached for her purse and pulled her phone from the outer pocket.

"What're you doing?"

Ingrid held up her index finger as she put the phone to her ear.

"Hey."

Irritated that Ingrid felt it necessary to take a call in the middle of what Liv thought was an important conversation, she sighed and reached for the brown bottle in front of her. Rather than drink from it, she picked at the label. When the corner didn't peel off clean and the paper ripped through the center of the label, she picked it up and drained it. Ingrid was talking to Luke, from the sounds of it, and Liv wondered when was the last time she and Wade had spoken on the phone that way, like they cared about where the other one was.

"He did?" Ingrid's voice jumped up in question, and she pointed at Liv and then at Liv's purse. "We didn't hear it…" She laughed and blushed. "You know it, babe. We are…oh. Okay. Hang on."

Liv pulled her phone out of her purse. She had missed a call from Wade. Naturally. She turned the phone sideways to look and saw that she had it on silent. But unlike Ingrid, she didn't feel her phone vibrate, so she missed the call.

"Wade wants to talk to you." Ingrid passed the phone to her. Liv felt an irrational surge of fear, and she moved her fingers just so in order to avoid touching Ingrid's.

"Wade?" She pressed the phone to her ear. Felt a pang in her chest when she heard his voice.

"Where are you?"

He was angry or suspicious or maybe both, and though a ripple of resentment slid up her arms and over her shoulders and made her flinch, she knew he had a right to both emotions. After what she did, didn't he have the right to question her any time she left the house?

"I'm at Skinny's," she answered quietly. Amber stared straight ahead, but Liv assumed she was lost in thought and not mesmerized by the sway of the dancing brunette's hips and the swing of her breasts. Ingrid's eyes were heavy and intense as she watched her unabashedly.

"You're what?" Kind of sounded like he laughed, but she wasn't sure, and Liv squirmed on her stool, embarrassed to be singled out and given the tenth degree with her sister watching.

"I'm with Ingrid and Amber," she told him. "Having a drink."

When Ingrid still watched her, Liv rested her forehead on her free hand and tucked her chin to her chest. Not like being alone, but she could at least hide her eyes from Ingrid. Wade was quiet on the other end of the call, and Liv wondered if he was just surprised she was at the strip club or if he doubted her.

"You're having a drink at a strip club?" he finally asked.

"Yes."

She cringed as she waited for the inevitable question. Why were they at Skinny's when there were at least fifteen other bars in town they could have gone to?

"Are you meeting someone there? Is that why—?"

Her eyelids heavy with defeat, she let them close as she shook her head.

"No. Wade, we're having a beer. Me and the girls. I promise that's it."

She pressed her lips together when she heard him breathe deeply.

"Why didn't you answer your phone?"

"Didn't hear it. Didn't feel it vibrate."

"When are you coming home?"

She rubbed her fingertips under her eyes, relieved to see

in her peripheral vision that Ingrid was studying her hands now. Then again, both of them were listening to every word she said.

"When—" She started to tell him she would come home when they finished the bucket of beer. Because regardless of the fact that they had just been sitting here arguing yet again, she needed to be here. She needed the time with her sisters. Maybe she needed to talk about Wade, and apparently she still had some fancy talking to do because even Ingrid didn't believe her, but mostly she wanted to talk about Gracie. About how damned hard it was to hand over the reins to her and how even though she said she wanted Gracie to be her own woman and that she wanted her to learn about sex before making any life-long commitments (maybe she hadn't said those exact words, but they all knew exactly what she meant that day) that it was still huge and unsettling and sad and weird to know that her daughter had taken that first step toward independence.

Couldn't talk about that with Wade, could she?

On the other hand, if he asked her to come home now, she would. She would swallow the unease and the worry—she had done it for years; in fact, she was pretty sure it was the first line in a mother's job description: your feelings don't matter, keep them to yourself—and go home to him and pretend she was fine, that she had simply gone out for a fun night.

"Whenever you want me to," she whispered, and she realized as much as she needed to be here, there was still a part of her that wished he would say *now*.

No wonder the man couldn't win. She wanted everything at once, and life just didn't work that way.

"Just…" He groaned. "Will you be late?"

"No."

"Just be careful, Livvie. Please?"

"I will."

If he had said he loved her, she would have said it back. The words were right there, on the tip of her tongue. Even knowing that saying it over the phone would take away from how much she meant it, she tasted the words and she almost let them out, but the line went dead.

He hadn't told her he loved her. She knew he did. Even during the long nights when he chose to hang out with his classic cars, she had always known he loved her. But those words in his voice right at this moment would have gone a long way toward soothing her restlessness.

She sniffled as she handed the phone back across the table to Ingrid. Thankfully, Ingrid said nothing as she dropped the phone back in her purse.

CHAPTER 32

"*I* think that would hurt." Amber's words were delivered in an almost reverent tone.

"I'm not attacking you," Ingrid whispered. "I don't mean to attack you, Liv. I'm just worried—"

Liv blinked at Ingrid. She needed to hear this, to concentrate on Ingrid's apology, if she was going to offer one. There were so many rough edges and sharp corners in her relationships with her sisters that she wanted to pay attention when the nicer things were said. But Amber's comment niggled at her like a pointer finger poking her in the back of the neck.

"What?" She swung her gaze to Amber and saw that her sister was still looking toward the stage, although she was engaged now, watching the girl work the pole.

"Don't you think?" Amber frowned. She dragged her teeth over her lower lip and took a slow, deep breath.

"The pole?" Ingrid finally looked away from Liv. She glanced at the stage and then looked to Amber. "What? Like pole burn? Maybe they use—"

Amber snorted and rolled her eyes. "No. Dancing around with your boobs just free-falling. That would hurt. Especially if they're big."

"I would guess dancing around with your boobs free-falling means nice tips. Especially if they're big."

Ingrid reached for a fresh bottle and tilted it at Liv. "Yes. I'm thinking the same thing."

"I know, but." Amber shuddered. "I mean, it hurts to jog down steps. Even with a bra on."

"It does," Liv agreed.

"Does he want you to leave?" Ingrid asked after another painfully awkward quiet moment passed.

"No." Liv shrugged.

"Because we can go—"

"It's fine." Liv held a hand up to stop Ingrid. "It's...pretty humiliating to have him call and check up on me when I'm out with you guys."

Ingrid arched her eyebrows. Liv bristled, knowing Ingrid was wondering what she expected.

"Okay, so." Ingrid took a swig from her bottle and then smoothed her lips with her fingers. "Obviously something is bothering you, and apparently it's not Wade, and you need to talk about it. But I need to wrap my head around this thing with Wade."

"What do you mean?"

Amber dragged her eyes from the stage and turned reluctantly to look at Ingrid.

"Yeah. What do you mean?"

"I just." Ingrid shrugged and threw her hands up dramatically, careful not to spill her beer. "I don't get it. I don't—"

"I was bored." Liv nearly launched herself over the table. "I was...Wade spends most of his free time with his cars. I missed him. I missed just talking to him. Being around him. I missed...making love with him. Maybe for some people once a week is great. Maybe it's nice knowing you have that time with someone. But it got...old...stale. I mean, we spend all week doing our own thing, and then Saturday night, we hang out for dinner, and the kids go out, and we go to the bedroom and have sex."

Ingrid nodded, but she kept her eyes on the table in front of her.

"The same damned sex every week. Nothing changed. We were like…robots. And then…"

"What?" Ingrid lifted her eyes to look at her when she hesitated.

"I just…I was the parent in the house. I was dealing with the kids, and no, I'm not suggesting that Wade's not a good dad, because I'm not cruel, and he's the best. But I was the one to listen to every single complaint about dinner. The one to hear all the bad shit they dealt with at school. To listen to them bicker. I do their laundry. I pick up their stuff and put it away. I'm a teacher, so naturally, the homework questions and the speech practices, it was all on me. It's still on me. I can't get five minutes to myself without someone needing something, and the hell of it is, they don't need me. Personally. None of them need me—"

"Wade does," Ingrid reminded her.

"So I got restless. And I got angry. I got tired of being the parent, when Wade was outside with his hobby. I got tired of doing stuff for Wade and watching him touch his cars with more interest than he showed me."

"I get that." Ingrid's voice was gruff. "No, I don't have kids, but I understand what you're saying."

"I didn't walk out of my house the morning the first time it happened thinking I would fuck someone else and fuck Wade over all in one. I was never attracted to Asher Crowe. I had a long day, and I was tired, and I was frustrated, and I walked out of school after a meeting, and he was there."

"And what?" Ingrid shrugged. "What did he say? How did it happen? That's what I don't get."

"You write about this stuff."

"Yeah, and I write about gutting someone with a bowie

knife, and I write about rape, and I write about guns, but I don't do any of those things. I don't own a gun."

"Have you fired a gun?" Amber asked her.

Ingrid looked at her like she had spoken in a foreign language, but she gave her a distracted nod.

"He was in his car, and he spoke to me. I said hi. And he asked me how my day was." Liv licked her lips. "First person to ask me something like that in weeks."

"And you caved?"

"I think I just shut down. I remember just…wanting to lie down and cry myself to sleep. It was dark. He reached out the window and stroked the back of my hand." Liv sighed. "And that touch reminded me of all the ways Wade didn't touch me anymore. I looked at him. He looked at me. And that was that."

"So." Ingrid rubbed her forehead like she had a headache. "You did it in his car."

"Yes."

"In the school parking lot?"

Liv shrugged when Ingrid raised her eyebrows in disgust.

"No one was around. It was dark. We didn't undress and linger over each other. He flipped my skirt up and unzipped his pants."

"Did you like it?"

"No." She shook her head. "Not really. Wasn't like it used to be with Wade. But it was something."

"Dangerous."

Liv shrugged off Amber's suggestion.

"No. I mean it was something…physical. It was a man's body under mine, moving inside me." She swallowed hard. "I didn't think it would happen again. I didn't think about him. I wasn't in love. Didn't expect anything. And yes, it happened again. It happened at the house in his car. We went to a hotel once. And yes, we were naked, and we were all over each other, and it was good. It was…" She licked her lips again, remembering Wade asking her intimate questions. "I had orgasms with him. Sometimes full throttle, Ingrid. But when we were done, we got up and we washed off, and we went back to our lives. It was very clinical."

"So, by that time you wanted him to love you?"

"No." Liv tried to smile, but it felt like a grimace. "By that time, I missed Wade so much, I was sick inside."

"So you need love to enjoy sex?"

"It's better," Liv whispered. "For me, anyway."

"If it were as cold and physical as you say—"

"What?"

Ingrid waved away her poorly chosen words. "You told me that one day at the house that he called you again."

"He did."

"Asher Crowe called you? For sex?"

Liv hung her head. She laughed sarcastically as she pushed her bangs up from her forehead. "Thanks, Amber."

"That's not what I meant." Amber nudged her with her elbow. Liv sat up straight again and rolled her eyes as Amber.

"What is this guy? I mean, I'm having visions of a mob boss or something."

"Something like that, maybe?" Liv shrugged at Ingrid. "Minus the violence. Maybe?"

"Really?" Ingrid drew back in surprise.

"Yeah. And he called to invite me to a…cocktail party…" Liv shrugged her eyebrows. "A very…elitist sort of cocktail party." Liv looked at Amber. "So apparently, I'm good enough in bed, thank you. Wade wasn't invited. I don't even know…who…would have been there. I told him no, thanks. I told him I wasn't interested in…"

"Fucking him," Amber offered with wide eyes.

"Yeah. I didn't get emotional or weepy with him. Just told him I was done."

"That's incredible." Ingrid stared at Liv with wonder.

"What is?"

"That my sister got caught up in some kind of sexcapade like this."

"It's not incredible. It was stupid." Liv grabbed a fresh beer. "And I have never regretted anything so much in my life."

"Have you told Wade that?"

"I tell him everything," Liv whispered, "when he's listening. I tell him I'm sorry. He said the other night he doesn't want a divorce, but we're still…struggling. He sees me with Asher, and he can't get past that."

"He will," Ingrid told her. "Just be patient."

"Not one of my virtues," Liv mumbled.

"No shit." Ingrid snorted.

"Not a Williams trait." Amber hid a yawn behind her hand. "We're all acerbic and blunt and a little bit aloof. Not sure I've ever heard anyone describe any of us as patient."

"Is that our legacy then?" Ingrid grinned. "We're bitches? By nature?"

"I think we're all liars," Liv announced. "We all lie, and we all do it well."

"Funny you say that after swearing this whole thing with Crowe went down the way it did and that it's over." Ingrid took a drink.

"What do you want me to do? Sacrifice my first born to prove I'm not lying? Cut off my ring finger?"

"How about your middle finger, so you can't flip me off anymore?"

"I have two of them," Liv answered, unaffected.

"I know you're not lying," Ingrid assured her.

"How? How do you know that?"

"Because lying is exhausting. Trying to remember what lie you told to cover the lie before it. And the lie before it."

"Gracie hooked up with that kid the night of graduation," Liv announced. Ingrid and Amber both paused in the act of drinking and stared at her in stunned silence. Liv arched her eyebrows and squeezed her eyes closed.

"Did you just...ask her?"

"Yep. Right after she asked me what was going on with me and Wade."

CHAPTER 33

"Why Skinny's?"

Liv felt like she had been holding her breath since last night when Wade called her and she missed the call so she had to talk to him on Ingrid's phone. They had finished the bottles in the bucket. They talked about Gracie and Jarret, though Liv wouldn't tell anyone that. Gracie might be horrified if she knew her mom and her aunts had discussed that kind of thing. Liv said again that yes, she wanted Gracie to experience life and sex and a little bit of adulthood before she ever settled into marriage—Amber had nailed her then, asked her if Wade had been her first, and she simply nodded and kept talking even though it made her feel a little Catholic school girl—but still, knowing now that Gracie had given her virginity away a few weekends ago was startling.

She confided to her sisters that now that she knew it had happened, it wasn't enough. She wanted to know if Gracie was okay, if it had hurt, if she'd been embarrassed, if she enjoyed it. If she had told anyone else. If she had been with Jarret again. Or God forbid, anyone else. If she planned to be active now. If leaving for college was the gateway to a whole new world. And she also admitted she was terrified of the answers, and even more afraid that if she asked, Gracie wouldn't tell her. After all, Liv was her mother, and it was none of her business.

Ingrid had been a little disheartened, though she had admitted she had done the same when she was younger. That she had been younger than Grace. She was sad, though, to know that her niece had passed an ancient rite of woman-hood, and therefore, she was sympathetic to Liv's own rest-lessness. Amber had been a little out of sorts over it, too, but she had also sunk into a tailspin of worry over Hadley and her friend, Kesh. Ingrid had only rolled her eyes when Amber wondered out loud if Hadley had been with him.

Liv exhaled, and to her, it felt like she gasped for a breath the way a swimmer might as she came up for air and did the flip at the wall to turn and go back the other way. Wade didn't lunge for her, though, to administer CPR. He didn't even flinch, so Liv assumed he didn't noticed that she might be dying. Instead, he worked the cork out of a bottle of dry red, the muscles in his forearms flexing, and his eyes locked on hers as he waited for an answer.

"Wine?" She lifted her eyebrows, pleasantly surprised, but hesitant to get carried away and hope for something special for the evening.

"Liv?"

"I don't know?" She shrugged. She sat at the counter as he splashed the rich red liquid in the long stem glasses he had taken from the cabinet. "I guess Ingrid and Luke go there now and then? And when she first mentioned it, Amber said she'd gone there. I never had." She took the glass he pushed toward her, pressed her thumb over the base, and stared at the wine rather than look at him.

"Ingrid and Luke go to Skinny's? Together?" He looked confused.

"Ingrid likes strip clubs," she said quietly. "I think part of it is research. She's always…noticing things. Watching people."

"Lots of good people watching at a strip club," Wade mumbled.

"Yeah." Liv nodded. She flicked a shy glance at him and looked away.

"I thought…" Wade pushed the bottle to the side and met her eyes. "I thought when you didn't answer me…you were with him."

"Wade." She puffed her cheeks up and shook her head in a tiny movement. "I promise you I'm not…seeing him."

He leaned over to rest his elbows on the counter. Liv's heart swelled with hope and excitement when his eyes slid over her face and the column of her neck and down her blouse.

"So you guys were just out having a drink?"

Liv nodded. "Talking."

"About us."

She hedged a bit. Pressed her lips together and finally nodded. "Some."

"What else?"

She lifted her glass. Touched the rim, eyes on his. Hers filled as she took a sip.

"You talk about him? With them?"

"Gracie," she whispered, praying Grace would forgive her if she ever knew she'd shared this secret with him.

"What about Gracie?"

"Something she told me," she said quietly. "I'll tell you, but I'm not sure you want to know."

"She hooked up with that kid, didn't she?"

"Yeah."

Wade's lip curled in disgust, but he shrugged helplessly.

"We were kids, too," he reminded her. "We did that stuff."

"I know." She blinked and knuckled the corner of her eye.

"So." He almost touched her. Almost stroked the back of

her hand, but he stopped and splayed his fingers over the base of his glass. "What did you think of Skinny's?"

She laughed softly, but she felt her belly slide with disappointment. She wanted to talk about them, about personal things. Things they could do to fix what was broken.

"It was interesting." She offered him a smile. Watched him as he moved away from her and crossed the room to the refrigerator.

"The girl with the melons still working the pole?"

"Yep." She nodded, saddened by the fact that he was at least somewhat familiar with the club. He took a tray from the refrigerator and carried it back to the counter. She eyed the chocolate covered strawberries. Her mouth watered, but not because she loved the treat he placed in front of her. Because they were talking about strippers and nudity, and they were drinking wine, and once, Wade had fed chocolate covered strawberries to her after they made love.

His lopsided grin tugged at her heart.

"She works at the paint store by day," he told her. "Her name's Amy. She has a two-year-old at home."

Overcome with jealousy that Wade knew details about a woman who took her clothes off for money, that Wade had talked to the woman after ogling her naked breasts, Liv swallowed hard and lifted her chin a fraction of an inch.

"Do you go there a lot?"

"Not a lot." He shook his head. "I have seen the girl with the devil horns tattooed around her nipples."

"I'm not sure what's worse," Liv mumbled. "The tattoos or the piercings." Or talking to her husband about another woman's body.

"She has them pierced now?" Wade cringed.

"Yep."

"Would you go back there?"

She sipped her wine. Shrugged and nodded at the same time. "I guess. Not a big deal."

"Did you see any lap dances?"

She hadn't. Not that she had been on the lookout for any. She had been too consumed with her conversation with her sisters to care about anything else.

She shook her head and swallowed before she spoke, but her voice still came out small and tight.

"Are you telling me you paid her for a lap dance?"

"No." He shook his head. "Haven't done anything like that since I was probably barely legal."

Liv set her glass on the counter. She tucked a piece of hair behind her ear and met his eyes.

"Sucks, doesn't it?" His voice was gruff. "Thinking about me with another woman? Looking at another woman."

"Yes. It does."

He stepped around the end of the counter and stopped just shy of touching her.

"Can I ask you something?"

Liv drew in a quick breath and nodded. She turned sideways on the bar stool to face him.

"Do I satisfy you? When we make love?"

Her eyelids slid closed, and tears caught in her lashes. She blinked and nodded.

"Yes, Wade, you do."

"So it wasn't about sex? Looking for something better?"

She shook her head as he stroked his fingertips under her chin.

"No."

"I miss the way you breathe when I'm inside you."

Afraid to break the spell, she touched him with her eyes. She swept her eyes over his face, lingering at his parted lips and the scruff over the skin of his cheeks. She longed to touch him, to feel the warmth of his skin under her hands and press her face into his neck. She missed the smell of his aftershave laundered into his clothes after so many times through the laundry cycle.

He rubbed his thumb over her throat, down to the hollow at the base of her neck.

"I wanna see you." His voice was low and heated. "You think a girl at a strip club could turn me on when I have you?"

The rough pads of his fingers on her skin made her feel fluttery and lightheaded.

"I wanna see you wearing this." He pressed on the heart pendant that rested against her chest. When he hedged closer, and his fingers fumbled with the buttons on her blouse, she sat up straight.

"Where are the kids?"

She didn't care. She didn't care if Wade stripped her down to nothing and took her on the counter and Charlie or Gracie waltzed in. She needed his touch. His love. Still. Seemed like she was supposed to worry, so she asked him and sent up a silent prayer that he would keep working the buttons of her blouse to undress her.

"Charlie is at work," he told her. "And Gracie is with Ingrid."

With a twist of the last button, her blouse fell open. Wade's heated gaze lingered on her bare belly. She gasped in surprise when he flattened his palm over her stomach and then turned his hand and rubbed the backs of his knuckles up between her breasts.

The can lights over the back counter were on, though they were turned down low. Evening sunlight lit the kitchen in lazy streaks, but Liv felt cozy at the island counter with Wade's warm fist pressed over her chest.

He stepped closer, still, and Liv shifted on the barstool. Opened her knees for him to stand between them. Her heart fluttered in her chest like the wings of a hummingbird, but she wouldn't hurry him. She wouldn't remind him that she'd done something wrong, and he was angry with her.

His eyes held hers as he brushed her hair from her face

with his other hand. Slid his fingers from her chest and over her neck. The silence in the room was punctuated only with the sounds of the soft, ragged breaths they drew. Liv might have wanted music at any other time. Right now, Wade filled her senses.

Scared that this would end, that he would stop, she parted her lips and let her eyes roam over his face as he leaned in to kiss her. There and gone, his lips were soft and warm, and she licked hers when he drew back from her.

"I wanna make you forget." He rubbed her chin with his thumb. "Make you forget—"

She couldn't bear to hear Wade say another man's name, so she shook her head violently fast and reached out to hook her fingers in the waistband of his jeans. She tugged him closer and sat up as tall as she could and pressed her open mouth to the corner of his lips.

"Make me come, Wade," she whispered. Tears streaked her face, but she let them fall. Cupped his face in her free hand and then drew back to look at him. "Make me come. Please? I just want you inside me."

His eyes searched hers. His erection was rock hard pressed against her hand and forearm. She flicked her tongue over the scar on his lip, the one her sister had asked about. A million different images flashed through her mind, including the night Amber had kissed Wade's cheek and Ingrid had held him and the mostly nude girls gyrating on the stage. But not Asher. She didn't even have to work to push him out. Her body shook with desire for the man in front of her.

He took her hand in his and kissed her palm. The stroke of his tongue over her skin plucked a chord low in her belly, and she purred softly.

"My way," he told her.

Anticipation with a dash of fear crept like chills over her skin. She caught her breath as he pushed her blouse off her shoulder. Shrugged it off when he touched the other shoulder.

"Never again, Livvie." His gruff voice dragged over her skin and chased another chill up her spine. "You belong to me."

She nodded, tried to say *I know*, but her voice broke. She added *I'm sorry*, but her throat ached. Her blouse slid from the barstool to the floor with a sexy swish sound, but Liv was suddenly overwhelmed by the scratch of Wade's fingers over the straps of her bra.

"Wade." She sobbed when he moved. Reached both hands up to cup his face and then his warm hands splayed over her back, and he twisted her bra and she felt it give. With short, uneven breaths, she watched his face as he gently tugged the scrap of silk away and let it fall to the floor.

"Beautiful."

He flicked his eyes up to meet hers, but that quickly, he looked back at her bare breasts. Liv caught her breath when he took her hands and placed them over her breasts.

"Look at how beautiful you are."

It was a command, and Liv listened. Her eyes moved over her own hands cupped around herself and her nipples, hard and straining for his touch, and she thought of the girls at Skinny's. She would never be able to take her clothes off and shake her ass for money, but suddenly she understood what Ingrid had said. She would do anything right now to feel beautiful for Wade.

"Wade." She licked her lips when he lifted his eyes to look at her. "Please touch me."

He didn't. Instead, he cupped her chin again and kissed her. His lips were firm against hers, and she cried out softly when he nudged her fingers up to make her stroke herself.

"Wade—" she gasped and moaned when he stroked his tongue inside her mouth.

He swept his mouth over her cheek, his tongue warm and

wet on her skin. She scooted to the edge of her seat and slid her arms around his waist.

"Oh, God, please." She dropped her head back to look at him when he finally smoothed his hand over her shoulder to cup her breast. Their silence was broken, but Liv didn't care. She focused on him, dismissed what she thought was a door opening. Wade filled his hands with her skin, her breasts, his thumbs rubbing tight circles over her areolas and finally he pinched her nipples and made her cry out.

He stepped back as she scooted forward to stand. Liv sighed with relief when he closed his arms around her and pulled her tight against his body. He kissed her again, but the gentle sweep of his tongue quickly heated to a desperate, hungry plunge.

When he reached for the button of her jeans, she put up a token fight. Not because she didn't want more, but because she wanted him to spend more time at her breasts. Before she could fight him, though, her jeans were unbuttoned and Wade's sure hands slid them over her hips. When he lifted her, her eyes popped open in surprise.

"What're you doing?" Her whisper sounded frantic. She swept her eyes around the kitchen, remembering that she might have heard the door open. But as he set her on the counter and stood staring at her with unadulterated lust in his eyes, she heard only their ragged breathing.

"I'm gonna touch you." He smoothed his hands over her thighs. She felt that nervous flutter in belly again, even as her chest rose and fell with the deep, spotty breathing. Desire. She didn't give a damn if someone was in the house; she wanted his hands on her.

"Here?" She stroked her fingers back through his hair.

"I'm gonna make you come," he reminded her. Mouth dry, she swallowed hard. He leaned closer and flicked first one and then the other nipple with the tip of his tongue.

"Wade." She breathed his name when he hooked his

fingers in her panties and gave them a gentle tug. When their eyes met, she lifted her hips and watched him ease the purple silk over her thighs.

She whimpered when he grabbed her inner thighs and parted her legs. Mindful of the wine and the chocolate covered strawberries, she propped her hands behind her and leaned back.

"Do you want this?"

She arched her eyebrows. "Yes."

"My mouth?"

"I want everything, Wade," she whispered. "I want your mouth. I want your fingers. I want you inside—" She gasped with pleasure when he rubbed his thumb over her center.

"Did he do this?"

"Please don't stop."

He stroked a finger inside her and added another when she shifted on the counter.

"Livvie, did he put his mouth on you?"

"No." She lifted her hips at the thrill of Wade's tongue on her sensitive skin. "No. He didn't do this."

"Did you want him to?"

"No." She sighed again as a feather of warmth unfurled low in her belly. "You're the only man who's ever touched me this way."

"I hate that he made you come."

"Please forgive me?" she whispered. "Please?"

She reached for him, smoothed her hand over his hair, and cupped the back of his head as he closed his lips over her core.

CHAPTER 34

*T*hey slept until nine, though they hadn't closed their eyes until well after two in the morning. Wade had been relentless in his need to please her, and Olivia had been a quivering mess after the first orgasm on the kitchen counter. She had cried at some point, after they'd moved to the bedroom. In the moonlit room, with Wade moving over her with slow, deep thrusts and his tongue claiming her mouth with the same soft and deep strokes, Liv had cried and whispered that she was sorry.

She had been afraid when he left their bed after collapsing over her and both of them lying together in silence, holding on while they came down to earth and their breathing slowed to normal, that he was done and the wall would go back up. He had stepped into his jeans, left them low on his hips, and promised he would be right back. Heart still fluttery and her body still tingling in all the right places, Liv had hugged her arms around his pillow and waited for him to return.

He wasn't gone ten minutes, and when he did come back, he carried the wine and the glasses. Liv had laughed softly and sat up in their bed, when she realized he had a strawberry in his mouth. When he put the wine and glasses down, he leaned over her so she could take the strawberry from his lips. She had licked the chocolate, nibbled the strawberry, and reached for him when he planted a knee on the mattress.

The house was quiet this morning. Charlie had come home at some point, and while Liv made coffee and Wade made omelets, she prayed it was after they had moved their party up to the bedroom. Last night, she had been so desperate for what was happening, she hadn't cared if the whole world would have walked in to see what they were doing. This morning, though she cherished the night she and Wade had spent, she prayed that no one had seen anything; that she was hearing things when Wade kissed her.

They stood together in the kitchen as they waited for the coffee and Wade watched the omelets. Liv wrapped her arms around his middle and rested her cheek on his bare shoulder. When their breakfast was ready, they carried their plates and mugs to the deck. It hit Liv after her first drink that even though she had come home last night, even though Wade had touched her with confidence and love and desire, even though she'd said she was sorry and asked him for forgiveness, she hadn't told him that she loved him.

She had started to. When he'd come back to bed with the wine and the strawberry in his mouth, and he had given her the strawberry and put his lips on her again, she had started to say she loved him. She had closed her mouth and swallowed the words, because she didn't want him to accuse her of mistaking sex and pleasure for love. Maybe he wouldn't have, but she wasn't naïve enough to think that one night of remembered passion, of the intimacy that had been missing from their marriage for a long time would heal everything.

Her heart tugged in her chest as she watched him fork a bite of his omelet.

"Wade." She held her mug in front of her, but she kept her eyes on him. He lifted the bite to his mouth and chewed, but he slowed to a stop and blinked at her when she spoke.

"Livvie?"

"Look, I know last night—"

"I thought it was perfect." He punctuated his interruption with a jab in the air with his fork.

"I did, too," she assured him. "I know…" She blew out a shaky breath and arched her eyebrows.

"You're making me nervous." He tossed his fork down and leaned back in his chair, eyes suddenly heavy and unhappy.

She shook her head.

"No, it's just…" She set her mug down and reached over the table. She wanted to touch him, but he kept his arms on the chair and watched her with a steely gaze. "I know I have to earn your trust. I get that. I just want to say I love you."

Wade rounded his shoulders as he slumped forward in his seat. He sighed and groaned and rubbed his eyes and then dragged his hands back over his head.

"I love you," she whispered. "I'm so sorry for hurting you."

Elbows on his knees, he covered his mouth with his fingertips and stared at her with bloodshot eyes.

"I love you, too, Olivia Girard." He huffed out another deep, choppy breath. "I love you, too. I don't ever want to lose you, but I can't…deal with…"

She flinched, afraid of what he was going to say. He couldn't deal with what she had done? Had last night been about forgiveness and finding each other again? Or had it been a goodbye?

"What?" Her whisper gruff, she cleared her throat.

"Please. Just be mine. I can't handle thinking about you with anyone else."

"I know." She nodded. And she did. The thought of Wade being with anyone else, doing the things he did to her body last night to any other woman made her stomach hurt. "I thought I was being strong. Just…keeping everything inside. I realize now how wrong I was. I should've talked to you. We should have fought and yelled and cried before. I know I was wrong."

"You should have talked to me," he said softly. Shrugged and pursed his lips. "I should have asked. It was easier for both of us to hang on to the status quo."

She nodded. Her hand shook as she reached for her mug again. Their issues weren't his fault; after all, she had been the one to cheat. But maybe they had both contributed to the mutual complacency, and Wade owning up to his part in their current situation made her feel good.

"So, when we're done here, you wanna head over to the house with me?"

"Sure." She nodded. "What're we doing? Checking progress? I was just there—"

"No. I rented a bulldozer," he informed her. She watched him wolf down the last of the omelet. Raised her eyes to his as he swallowed.

"You did what?"

"The garage has to come down, Liv."

She flinched. Drew back in her chair. He was right. One big sneeze would take the old building down. She still hated to see it go.

"I know." She nodded. "You're right."

"You okay? With the house? And stuff?"

He knew her well enough to know she hated it. And that made her warm inside.

"Can't change it back now," she whispered.

"It's for the best," he reminded her. "For selling it."

"I know."

"You okay with your sisters?"

She laughed softly. "At the moment, we're good."

"Then let's get moving." He grabbed his mug and plate and stood up. "The quicker we deal with whatever happens today at the house, the sooner we get back home."

She leaned into him when he stopped to stand at her chair. "Thank you."

"Don't thank me, Liv." His voice was low in warning. "I'm still angry. And it still hurts, but I want—"

"For breakfast," she interrupted him.

"You know I would make you breakfast everyday—"

She shook her head as she scooted her chair back and stood. "Not making me breakfast, Wade. For sitting out here. With me."

Wade sighed and nodded. Hands still full, he leaned over to kiss her forehead.

"We gotta do better, Livvie," he told her. "You and me gotta do better. Life's too short."

LIV AND INGRID WANDERED AIMLESSLY THROUGH THE HOUSE. THE kitchen floor was done, and Liv figured anyone else would love it. She hated it. She hated the tap of her sandals on the tile after forty years of the muted squeak or thud of shoes on linoleum. Part of her brain looked at the kitchen and thought hey, that fancy new tile just begs for new cabinets and countertops. And part of her thought the old cabinetry was perfect. She wondered how Ingrid felt about it, but she didn't ask. Maybe she would later. Right now, it seemed almost disrespectful to speak out loud in the halls.

The floors in other rooms were all in various states of dishevel. Liv decided it was stupid to be replacing the carpets and floors when they had painted. Sure, a new owner could paint, but wouldn't it be better to do it before the new carpet was laid? She noticed Ingrid smooth her fingertips over the wall in the family room and wondered if she felt the same way.

"Can I tell you something?"

Liv jumped when Ingrid spoke. The only sound for the

past half hour had been the rumble of the bulldozer as Wade worked in the backyard. Liv had been perched on the picnic table watching, her chest tight with dread when Ingrid had appeared from around the house. Rather than watch as the garage, which had been a steady in their lives just the same as an elderly relative, was demolished, they had come inside. They called it checking the progress rather than running away. But Liv had seen the regret on Ingrid's face; she felt the same way.

"Yeah, of course," Liv said now. "What's up?"

Ingrid leaned on the archway to the family room and folded her arms over her chest. She rested her head back and sighed and then groaned out loud.

"Ingrid?"

"More than one? Something?"

"Yeah, but do you wanna wait until Amber's around?"

"No, I don't," Ingrid said quietly. "Did you get her text?"

"About dress shopping?" Liv nodded as she asked. "Yeah. Sounds like fun."

Ingrid nodded absently. "So. I started that new book."

"Yeah." Liv shrugged. She wanted to sit down, but the guys had drug the furniture from the family room when they pulled the carpet up. She looked at the floor, had a flash of memory of the day they'd taken the tree down and she dropped and broke an ornament. When Luke had shown up. Walked into her sister's life and swept her off her feet. Thank God she had hired him.

"What?"

"What, what?" Liv shook her head.

"You have this little smirk." Ingrid lifted her hand and waved at her mouth.

"I was just..." Liv arched her eyebrows and then took a deep breath and shook her head. "Never mind."

"You're happy."

"Yeah." Liv nodded.

"Gracie and I came by the house last night." Ingrid cocked her head and wagged her eyebrows at Liv.

"You what?"

Ingrid snorted. "Relax. I walked into the kitchen and saw the wine and strawberries and skin and turned right around. She didn't see anything."

"Skin?" Liv squeezed her eyes closed. "Like?"

"He was kissing you," Ingrid said simply. Liv ducked her head as a blush exploded up her neck. "No. No, not whatever you're thinking. Like your blouse was on the floor, and his hands were on your back, and I knew where it was going."

"Wow." Liv nodded. "Okay."

"So?"

"Yeah."

"Full throttle intimate love making and not just a quick thing in the kitchen?" Ingrid asked hopefully.

"Everything," Liv whispered.

"And you're okay? You and Wade?"

"We're gonna be fine." Liv nodded. She couldn't help the smile or the way it grew into a big grin. "But that's not what I was…"

"Smirking about?"

"Yeah."

"Share with the class."

"You're not a teacher."

"Olivia—"

"I was just thinking it's a good thing I hired Luke to do some handiwork here. If it weren't for me, you wouldn't have met him."

Ingrid chuckled.

"It is a good thing," Ingrid agreed.

"You happy with this, Ingrid?" Liv looked around the family room. Hoped Ingrid knew she was referring to the house and not Luke.

"No." Ingrid shook her head. "Nope. It sucks."'

"It's gonna be beautiful." Liv tried out Ezra's point of view. "And according to Amber, this is what Mom wanted."

"Yeah. It'll be great." Ingrid stood up and wandered to the entrance hall. Liv followed her. Joined her on the front porch. They sat on the top step and stared sullenly at the street.

"Just won't be home."

"Home's where the heart is, right?" Ingrid reached for her hand and linked their fingers. "We're home. The Williams family. Not the house."

"Sure." Liv nodded. "We'll go with that."

"Amber's reading the book," Ingrid gushed.

"Okay?" Liv eyed her curiously, noted that she was white as a sheet.

"Well. I didn't...I mean, if you wanna read it, I'll email you what's written so far. But I...Amber asked me a couple of weeks ago. And..."

Liv's eyebrows shot up when she realized Ingrid was worried Liv would be angry. Jealous. Seemed a little ridiculous to Liv that the three of them were adults and all three of them tended to give into their inner children far too often.

"Okay." She nodded.

Ingrid eyed her warily.

"I'd love to read it, Ingrid." No, she wasn't jealous, but she did want to read her sister's book, and she felt a little bit special that she would get a sneak peek before Ingrid's adoring fans. "I'd read your grocery lists if you shared them."

"No, you wouldn't. Luke and I write dirty notes to each other on our grocery lists."

Liv snorted. "What? Like whipped cream for oral sex?"

"Oh, hell no." Ingrid frowned. "I mean dirty things. Detailed things."

"What if you lost your list at the store?"

"Well, either some uptight person would have a heart attack in produce or someone else in town would go home with some fun ideas for dinner."

Liv mouthed the word *wow*. She shook her head and looked back at the street.

"I'm sorry," she said softly.

"For—?" Ingrid shrugged; Liv noticed from the corner of her eye. "An offense already committed? Or are you pre-apologizing?"

"Can I do that?" Liv leaned into her. "Seriously? Because you and I both know I'm gonna say something to piss you off again. Probably today."

"Probably," Ingrid agreed.

"What else?"

"Hmm?"

"You had more than one something. That you wanted to tell me."

"Oh." Ingrid nodded and pursed her lips. "Right."

"Well?"

Ingrid bit her lip and then huffed a sigh and a groan. "Hannah showed up last night."

"Oh."

"Luke and Grace and I were shooting baskets."

"My Grace?"

"No. My niece, Grace." Ingrid rolled her eyes. "Pay attention."

"Sorry."

Ingrid laughed.

"So." She shrugged. "I met Hannah."

"And?"

"It was pretty anticlimactic." Ingrid stretched her legs out in front of her. "She's a beautiful girl. She shot some hoops with us."

"And she's pregnant?"

"Not even showing yet."

"Hmm." Liv nodded her head back and forth and finally looked at Ingrid again. "So no fireworks?"

"Those came later," Ingrid told her, "and we were very

quiet, so your sweet kid didn't hear anything."

"That sweet kid knows the secrets now." Liv felt a touch of sadness.

"No, she doesn't." Ingrid shook her head. "No woman knows the secrets after her first time. Takes a while to get it right. I'm still figuring things out, Olivia."

Liv nodded. "I know. You're right."

"So. Um." Ingrid still sounded uncertain, which made Liv's stomach hurt.

"When do you guys go to Chicago?"

"What?"

"You're hedging about whatever's on your mind." Liv, sitting forward, glanced at Ingrid and shrugged nonchalantly.

"When are you going to stop thinking everything's about that?"

"Probably never," Liv admitted. "Because...it would kill me to lose you now."

"Liv." Ingrid squeezed her eyes closed and shook her head. "It's not that. I'm gonna drag your ass along with me when we go. You can talk to my ob-gyn."

"I'll pass."

Ingrid shrugged as if to tell Liv to suit herself.

"So what the hell, Ingrid? Leave me hanging. What's wrong?"

"Luke asked me last night if I want to get married."

Liv's mouth dropped open, but the surprise was quickly replaced with excitement.

"I am so happy for you—wait." Liv cocked her head. "What's—? You don't seem happy. Did you tell him no? Why? You keep telling Amber you would marry him. What's —why—what did you say?"

"I said yes."

"Well, that explains the look of sheer happiness." Liv rolled her eyes. "What gives, Ingrid?"

"I can't marry him right now, Olivia," Ingrid said with a

sigh. "Can you imagine what Amber would say if I suddenly announced that I'm getting married again while she's planning her wedding?"

Liv eyed Ingrid silently for a few seconds. Finally, she turned sideways on the porch to look at her.

"I think she'd be thrilled for you, Ingrid," Liv said softly.

"Right. Because I'm the selfish bitch who left the family and was gone for a lifetime. Now I can finally move on and be the selfish bitch that rained on her wedding."

Liv glanced at the street as a car pulled up. Ingrid sighed when Amber pulled into the driveway.

"Guess we'll find out," Liv whispered.

"I'm not telling her."

"You are telling her," Liv corrected her. "If you don't, I will."

"Hey!" Amber climbed from the car and waved as she ducked back in to grab something. "What's going on?"

"She's gonna hate me." Ingrid leaned into Liv. "Liv, she'll hate me."

"You planning to do it tomorrow? Marry him?"

"No. But we don't want a big wedding."

"Okay, then it shouldn't matter at all."

"Okay, guys." Amber made her way through the yard, two small gift bags in hand. "I have a surprise for you. I was gonna wait and make a big deal of it. And I have Ezra's in the car, but I can't stand it. I have to show you now."

"Ingrid's got a surprise for you, too," Liv announced.

"Thanks." Ingrid turned her head to rest it on Liv's shoulder.

"What's up?" Amber directed a grin at Ingrid.

"Luke asked me to marry him."

Amber nearly dropped the bags. She scrambled the last few steps to get to Ingrid, set the bags down carefully, and threw her arms around Ingrid.

"That." Amber nodded. "That's so exciting. I'm so happy for you."

"You are?" Ingrid whispered.

"Of course I am." Amber kissed Ingrid's cheek.

"What's the surprise?" Liv asked.

"Now if I thought my other big sister could be happy—"

"Hey, they're good." Ingrid made a circle of her thumb and index finger and then poked her right index finger in and out. She winked at Amber.

"Wow. I feel like I'm sixteen again." Liv rolled her eyes. Amber raised her eyebrows. Liv smiled, and then, because even though the house behind them wasn't home anymore, her sisters would always be her sisters and she and Wade were going to stay together, she laughed. She almost didn't recognize the deep, throaty laughter as her own.

"Full throttle?"

Liv dropped her head back and hooted with laughter. "Overdrive, kid. Maximum overdrive."

"I think I'm jealous." Amber tilted her head and narrowed her eyes at Liv.

"What's the surprise?" Ingrid asked this time.

Amber smacked her hands away from the bags when she reached for them.

"Um." Amber faltered. "I um...I don't know if you'll like them...but...I wanted to save a little piece of home for all of us. I mean..."

Liv reached for her hand when Amber faltered.

"The house is gonna be gorgeous," Amber said quietly. She shrugged and shook her head. "But the minute Wade pulled the linoleum up, it stopped being home. That's my fault. I'm sorry."

"It's nobody's fault," Ingrid argued. "It's for the best. For selling it. And we have to sell it. We can't hang on to a house just for the memories."

Liv rubbed her face and then pushed her hair from her

eyes. "Yeah. Memories would just haunt the house if we let it stand."

"So?" The grin on Ingrid's face made her look like she was five.

"Um." Amber took the bags and handed one to each of them. "I've been over here a lot. By myself. And I …"

Liv pulled a small photo album from the bag and watched as Ingrid did the same.

"Oh, Amber." Liv covered her mouth and held her breath when her throat hurt too much to talk.

"They're some of the ugly pictures I took," Amber mumbled. "But I saved all of these for us."

Liv flipped slowly through the pages of photos of the dings and the scars and the junk in the house. Tears streaked her face.

"Amber, these are beautiful." Ingrid's voice sounded funny.

"They're not, though. Maybe this will be a reminder of why we did the new flooring."

"This is home," Liv whispered. "That's a house." She nodded to the house behind them and then smoothed her fingertips over the book on her lap. "This is home."

ABOUT THE AUTHOR

As an only child, Tracy Broemmer grew up with a wild imagination. An avid reader from a young age, she spent a lot of time with her nose buried in books and a lot of time making up her own stories. She penned her first book in grade school and hasn't stopped writing since.

Tracy is the author of the Lorelei Bluffs women's fiction series, the women's fiction series the Williams Legacy, and several stand-alone women's fiction novels. She has recently dabbled in contemporary romance as well.

Wedding Day Shenanigans

Holiday Fling

Indian Summer, A Novella

Dear Jaclyn Perris, A Novella

The Kiss-Off

Something Like Love

Love, Nashville, The Mississippi Queen Trilogy, Book 1